FOR PEACE AND PURPOSE

THE TUCKER CLAN SAGA
BOOK TWO

ETHAN WARRENER

For James and Marie Brazil

First edition

ISBN: 979-8-9855309-2-6

Cover art by Erin Parrot and Marcus Siebert

Contents

Characters

The Hollands

Mr. Phil Holland- Gunsmith

Mrs. Leah Holland- Phil's second wife, blood mother of Clive and
   Margaret

Ella Holland- The gunsmith's daughter, a couple years past marrying age
   with a shy disposition to account for it

Clive and Margaret Holland- Ella's younger half-siblings

Bill Puckett- The Powderman

The Taylor Boys

Amos Taylor- The clan's golden boy, a promising young man, Phil's
   apprentice guncrank

Harvey Taylor- The eldest of the boys, apprenticing at his father's
   smithy

Dale Taylor- The youngest of the boys, still shy of apprenticing age

The Drifter- Omar Walking

Mr. Elvin McDaniel- The Watchman

Ralph McDaniel- The Watchman's son and apprentice, a bookish kid

Mr. Sam Chambers- The clan Schoolmaster and Middlespeaker

The Brodys

Old Man Brody- The clan patriarch, few call him by his given name, "Salvador"

Mr. Job Brody- Local farmer and crack shot

Ricky Brody- Job's eldest son

Mr. Arnold Brody- The clan butcher

Mrs. Charlotte Brody- Arnold's wife

Becky Brody- Arnold and Charlotte's eldest daughter

Reverend Oliver Brody- The spiritual leader of the clan

The Fillmores

Mr. Rick Fillmore- Hunter and trapper

Victor Fillmore- Rick's son, of the same profession

Mrs. Sophie Fillmore- Victor's new bride, daughter to Bill Puckett and close friend to Ella and Becky

Dr. Jacob Bernhard- The clan physician

Mrs. Helen Bernhard- The doctor's wife and the clan nurse

Mr. Shane Bunton- The carpenter

Nigel Bunton- Shane's son

Mr. Alfred Bunton- Shane's brother

Bert Daly- The town good-for-nothing, a real ornery cuss

Melissa Daly- A young woman with an unsavory reputation before her marriage to Bert

The Grierson Settlement

Johnny Grierson- Head of the settlement, a mean, one-eyed son-of-a-gun

Edward Grierson- Johnny's cousin

The Coles- One of the prominent settlement families

ETHAN WARRENER

Families tending the outlying farms
The Newells- To the south
The Hadleys- To the south-west
The Job Brodys- To the north
The Craines- To the west

Other Clansmen of Note
Deek Evans
Clyde McDaniel
Joe Garmen
The Finches

Prominent Junkers
Cora Compton- The Junker Middlespeaker
Mayce Salazar- The Archivist
Jody Perkins- The archival apprentice

The Americans
Colonel Selina Armstrong- Commander of the American garrison at New Ashburn
Captain Royce Carlson- Leader of the protection force sent to watch over the Tucker clan
Lieutenant William Chitman- Leader of scouting expeditions
Lieutenant Harlow- Overseer of conscripted labor
Jarvis- Role unknown

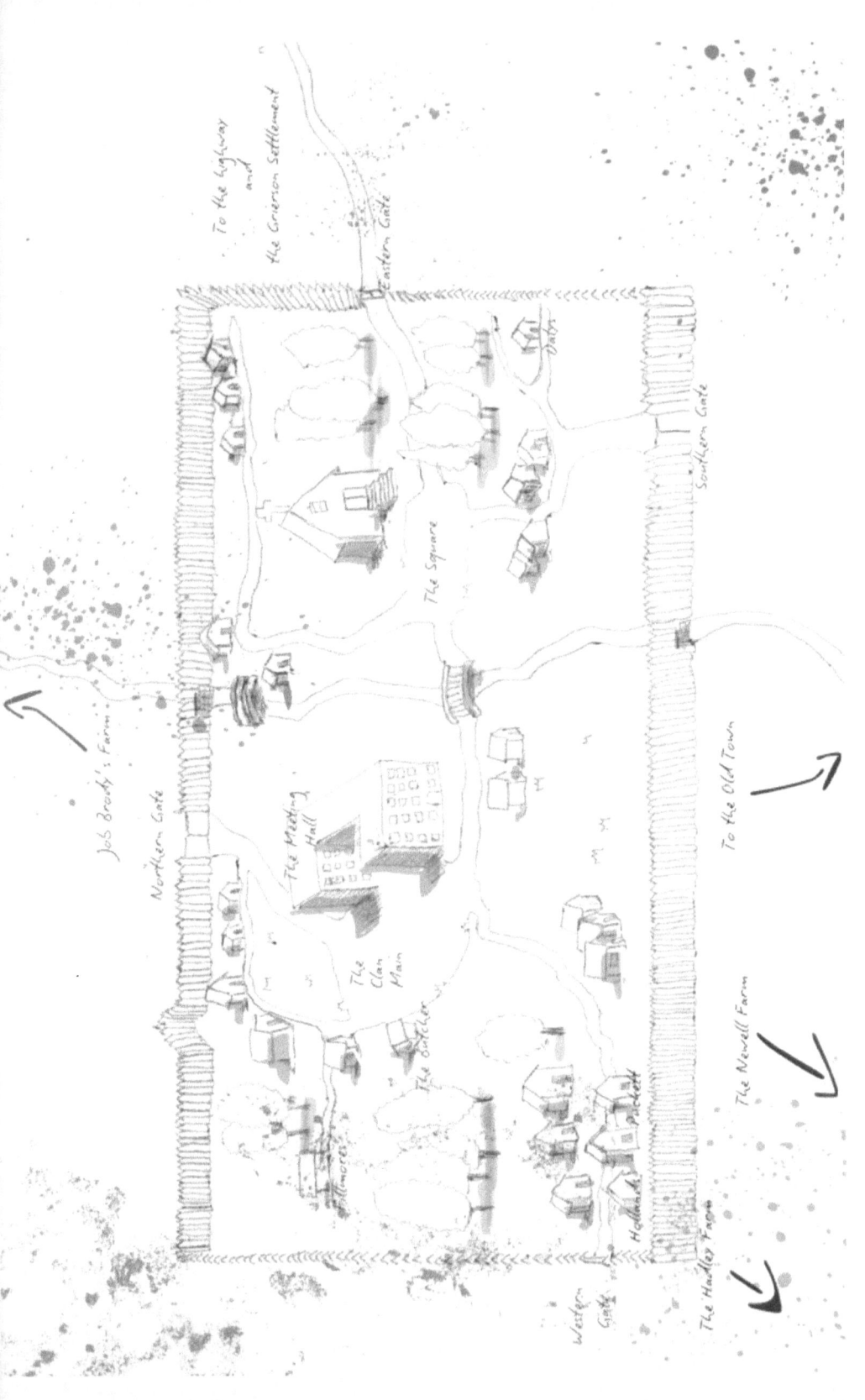

To the highway and
the Grierson Settlement

Eastern Gate

Dairy

Southern Gate

Job Brody's Farm

Northern Gate

To the Old Town

The Square

The Meeting
Hall

The Clan
Plain

The Butcher

Fillmore's

Holman's

Pickett

Western
Gate

The Hadley Farm

The Newell Farm

Chapter 1

In Which an Old Acquaintance Returns

T he ongoing chirps of insects and birds simmered in the summer
heat to make a lively stew in this stretch of wilderness. A seasoned
woodsman could sample the stew, pick out the flavors of bird species,
note the lack of alarm cries, and deem safe the open span cutting a line
through the middle of the old-growth forest. Or at least as safe as any
woods out here could be.

In the open span, a skeletal steel spire rose from a thicket of newer
growth: an old cell tower, its lower girders both supported and laden by
wooden boards and crosswise-nailed scantlings forming a long-disused
lookout point or highway guard-post. Despite such long disuse, the cell
tower still stood in remarkably good condition.

The road next to it did not. Flood debris had long since blocked what used to be a sizable concrete culvert under the highway, and the stream under the road had followed its next path of least resistance: over the road. Now, some fifty years after people stopped maintaining luxuries like paved byways and culverts, a deep gash severed the road next to the cell tower. Now the track, cracked and overgrown, was scarcely better for tread than the hilly wilderness it looped over and around like so much useless embroidery.

A score of bedraggled travelers came out of the woods from the south, up to the juncture of dry streambed and abandoned road, checking the nooks and crannies for dangerous occupants, either human or merely part-human. The untroubled bird calls may have given some surety, but a wary woodsman made an old woodsman.

The culvert made for a tidy hideout, the cell tower a nearby lookout. Together, they made for a perfect outpost, and scarcely three miles south of the enemy. The point man of the group sat down inside the relative cool of the culvert, swept the forest-green nylon rain poncho from his head, and wiped the sheen of sweat from his face. "We'll try to keep this outpost manned as long as we're able. Reach us when you can chance it, and if we ain't here, leave your message in the dirt yonder," the young man said.

Another young man, tall, lean, and dark-haired, stood at the mouth of the culvert, nodding without answering.

"I don't want to tell you how to do your job, but if I were you, I'd knife that powdermaker in his sleep, blow his stores to hell, and light a shuck."

"Will that get you what you really want?" the dark-haired young man said.

"It'll likely keep me from losing more clansmen. We was just gettin' used to the idea of you come back from the dead last winter. It don't sit right with me, chucking you back into that pigman dell."

"Ain't just about the clansmen we still have. It's about the ones we've lost." The dark-haired young man traded his breech-loading gun with

2

the more-accurate but slower-firing muzzle-loader of the Tuckers. "You lost a friend out in that killin' field. It was my cousin they raped and murdered."

"Then why didn't you go in for a straight attack right away?"

"Because it's stupid as hell. Right now, with that nitrogel powder, the Tuckers can beat us in any straight fight. I'm gonna hurt them more than a brawl ever could, 'cause half the Tuckers thought of me as one of their own by the time I left, this one gal overstandingly. I can use her to shaft the whole clan without any of 'em being the wiser. Just so long's I don't let nothin' slip."

The sitting man folded his arms. "How long, Omar?"

"As long as it takes." The young man turned away, surveying the woods beyond like a farmer about to plow a fallow field.

"For the good of the clan," his friend said.

"For the good of the clan," Omar said.

Today was going to be a good day. Ella knew it. She knew it by the squeal of her younger half-siblings playing in the garden, by her stepmother's insistent rejoinder out the kitchen window to stay away from the tomatoes, by the familiar *tink-tink* of the bicycle-tire flywheel spinning at the end of a treadle-powered lathe in her father's gunsmithy.

Life was good, even if life so often raised a contrary fist against the view. The good Lord had proclaimed it so at creation, and so it was. He'd made mankind in His image, and even if mankind had done their darnedest to muddy the picture, they had yet to scrub away the artist's brushstroke. She'd been called a fool for sticking to such a notion. Indeed, knowing the extent to which the image of God had been profaned in her own flesh gave even her pause these recent weeks. The same cursed breedmongery that had wrought the unbreds had wrought her as well, and her ancestors had been proud enough of that black mark to harrow the clean humans to extinction.

What a thing to be proud of.

Worse still, she alone among her kin knew the truth about her breeding. She was caught up in a lie meant to spare her fellow clansmen from the guilt of evil knowledge, the burden of a genocidal heritage.

Sometimes, her knowledge of goodness ebbed until it merely clung to the head-bound level, a place where the promises of Christ sat in the same useless place as her knowledge of Jupiter's moons: a fact gleaned from an ancient, otherworldly tome: known, but not felt. The absence of the feeling led some clansfolk to despise it, thinking tenderness and joy weaknesses, while others despaired when the world chewed any notion of goodness to a sticky pulp.

But Ella knew life was good, even when it didn't seem so. Especially when it didn't seem so. Joy was like the town walls, or Bill Puckett's new powder shop: it wasn't something that simply sprung up out of nature, but rather had to be built up and maintained through toil, discipline, and planning.

So, Ella had stoked the coals of joy through the lonely winters after her bereavement, had kept the embers alive when her fellow clansmen perished in a feud with the Greenbriers, and had even fanned the tender flame in the face of a brutal lie laid bare for her. She'd trusted that the vigilant joyful would find their comfort someday, in some way.

If you were stubborn enough to cling to joy through times like these, then something as simple as the bustle of powder-making apprentices beyond the closed door of Bill Puckett's new shop would be enough to tease out a smile. And, listening to the habitually shuttered powderman wrangling the largest staff he'd ever had the misfortune to inherit, she did smile.

Ella waited for a minute or two, her head resting against the door as the warm crackle of familiarity cast a golden light that seeped under the door. It was a thing nearly tangible; it pooled around her ankles and twined its way up into her gut—the smell of sawdust, the smooth roughness of calloused hands clasped in Sunday prayer, the sound of a fiddle and the murmur of folks at the end of a lively threshing bee. It was everything held in the word *clan*, everything that let you forgive the worst a body could manage.

When she at last entered, Puckett was quick to pass the most unpleasant duty on to her. "Ella, I'm gonna need you to tend to the folks waitin' outside. You can sell this to the first in line"—he handed her a box of powderized nitrogel charges, wiping sweat from his rapidly retreating hairline—"but you'll have to tell the rest I'm sold out."

"Aw, Bill, I'd rather stay in the shop or haul manure—"

"I got the carpenter's boy fetchin' manure, and I gotta watch these green learners here, lest someone blow up the shop. Mrs. Daly, you done strawed the fresh niter beds yet?" He turned to the young widow as she stepped in the back door.

"For last month, yeah," Melissa Daly said. She stretched her back to prove her point, and Ella noticed Bill avert his eyes from Melissa's more buxom attributes. He'd confided to Ella more than once in the space of the last few weeks that Bert Daly's widow brought nothing but her empty-headed looks and empty-headed scandals to his shop, but he'd refrained, at Ella's insistence, from airing his misgivings in front of their new ward.

"I need all the beds done. I gotta quadruple my nitrates," Bill said, raising as many fingers to drive the point home. "That means four times, and until I do, I'm gonna have to buy it retail from the nomads."

"It'd be easier if I didn't have to warden over little Earnest outside—"

"I ain't gonna have little ones a-runnin' around the shop. He stays outside," Bill grunted, then turned back to Ella. "Go on. Somebody knocked out front some minutes ago, and I can't imagine them's none too keen on waitin' longer."

5

"Did we double-check the powder weight on these charges?" Ella raised the box of cartridges.

"*Goooo.*" Bill pointed to the front door.

Ella sighed. She reminded herself to keep her gaze low, to close her slack jaw lest her buck teeth show, to cheer up and get it over with, that it was not enough to spoil the day. She stepped out and stared face to face with one-eyed Johnny Grierson. *Not enough to spoil the day*, she reminded herself.

"What's this I hear about Bill takin' in the town whore?" the grouchy half-breed asked without a greeting.

Ella screwed up her face. "I—she ain't..." She stammered as she tried and failed to muster a stern tone in the face of the eternally churlish Johnny Grierson.

Rather than chastened, Johnny looked amused. "Bill ain't the kind of jasper with a heart for half-breeds or widders. Which makes me wonder what kind of work he's got her here for."

Ella swallowed. "Did you come all this way to check in on Mrs. Daly?"

His sneer turned sour when the prospect of milling rumors vanished. But Johnny Grierson, not the kind of man to admit to such orneriness, supplied a business reason for coming all the way down from the mining settlement. "I got plenty of reason to come down here. Got business with Doc Bernhard. And I heard tell Bill's short on nitrates."

"He's short on everwhat you care to name. The nomads can sell us most of it."

"Saltpeter's a special order. It would take months for him to get a tolerable shipment of it in. I've leached enough out of the bat guano up at the mine to keep him stocked real nice."

"How much you askin' for it?"

"Supply and demand, hon. Two jaws per pound."

Ella had no wish to haggle even with decent folk making honest offers. She merely said, "I'll pass it along to him."

She sold off the nitrogel to the next customer in line, admonishing him to not to fiddle with the charges. "We got these charges down to the finger-pinchin' bits, both for the primer and for the propellant, down to the milligram. Don't let out near open flames, and mind your sparks. Black powder can hurt, but this much nitrogel will take your arm plumb off."

To the rest of the gathered clansmen, she said, "That's it, folks. Sold out for today."

Ella didn't stay long enough to see if the line dispersed, but she wasn't fast enough to avoid Sam Chambers darting in at the last second to tap her shoulder in that earnest, breathless way of his. "Miss Holland?" the schoolteacher said, wiping his brow and catching his breath. "I need to speak to your boss, if that's all right."

Ella faltered. "He ain't really... he's tied up right now.... What is it you need him for?"

"It's the water tower. With the spell of still air we've had, the windmill hasn't recharged our reservoir, and we're down to about a quarter capacity. Bill's been using far and away the most water recently, so it's only fair he does some time on the pumphouse treadmill. Not the news he'd like to hear, I'm sure," Sam raised his hands in a helpless shrug. "But everyone puts in to help the clan, just as everyone takes out."

"I'll make sure he hears about it, and if he can't get around to it, I'll get it done myself. Have a good day, Mr. Chambers."

The door finally safely closed behind her, and she walked back into the shop to answer Bill's beckoning. "Johnny came down," she said. "He wants to sell you some nitrates in exchange for your firstborn. Also, Mr. Chambers needs you to pay back your water debt with some foot-pumpin'."

Bill didn't look up from the measure-marked beaker he was reading. "That one-eyed cuss wouldn't make a fair trade with his own mother. He'd be a rich man if he wanted to keep me stocked, but he's gotta feel like he's breaking my fingers 'fore he can spit his shaking-hand. What was that about my water debt?"

Another pounding knock at the door made both Bill and Ella sigh as one. She turned to shoo the customer away at the front door, while Bill beat a discreet withdrawal out the back.

"I'm sorry, we're all sold—" She stopped short, her mouth open as wide as her eyes.

Elvin McDaniel had knocked, but it wasn't the sight of the sun-leathered, hatchet-faced town watchman who pulled Ella up short, nor his woebegone son behind him. It was the scraggly, dark-haired young man following them both who caught her moon-eyed stare. "Omar! You're back!" She blinked as if seeing long-lost kin come back from the grave.

There he stood, his smudged, hollow-cheeked face darkened by a thickening layer of stubble, his drooping form slouching with the total lack of fanfare Ella would have expected from a drifter like him, if she had been expecting him at all. He cracked a warm, tired smile. "Hey, Ella."

She still bated any answer, struck dumb.

"Mind if I come in?"

"Sure."

The moment Omar stepped inside, though, the scent he carried with him brought Ella back to herself. She recoiled as if he'd punched her in the nose. "Whew, you stink!"

"Been a while since I've had me a scrubbin'."

As he came inside, Mr. Puckett said, "Ella, have you got rid of them—"

"Look who's back, Bill." Ella stared at Omar as if she were looking at a balance scale that wouldn't hold true, no matter how much she tinkered with it.

Bill jumped at the sight—and smell—himself. "What the—Omar! What are you doing here again?"

8

The clan watchman behind Omar shook the mess of pigman jaws strung together on a wire. "One hundred jaws exactly. He weren't supposed to pull it off, but dogged if I ain't impressed. I reckoned I'd drop him off here before I had a word with the schoolteacher. No, Ralph, it's clan business only. You ain't stayin' today," he snapped his hardscrabble face to the side to bark at his son before the bookish kid could ask the favor. His business here concluded, the watchman walked off without the drifter and without any further explanation.

Bill scratched his cheek to fill the stunned silence. "If you're looking for a place to stay, I can kick one of the new apprentices out of your old room, but you'll have to work for your keep, same as always. I need them manure beds turned today, and I reckon after that—"

Ella cut him off. "Oh, nonsense, Bill. Omar won't be any use until he's had a bath, a wholesome meal, and some rest. Come here, Omar; let me take your things. Where's your horse?"

"The watchman's son already put it up in their stable for now. He and his pa were the ones I done wandered into."

"Thank goodness he didn't take a potshot at you. I'll see if I can get Amos to go fetch your horse for you so as we can keep it in our stable. I'll rustle you up a mess to eat."

Ella bolted from the room and stoked the coals smoldering at the bottom of the Hollands' pot-bellied stove. Once she'd stirred up enough heat to warm some beans, she ran out to her father's garage gunsmithy, where handsome young Amos Taylor stood back away from her father's lathe with his arms crossed and brow furrowed in concentration.

"Hey, Pa, Amos—"

"Hang on, Ella," her pa said before returning to his lesson. "Now, if you stick this dial onto the lead screw, it'll start turning, see? That's how you know when to punch in your cutting tool: pick a number on 'ere, and every time it comes around on that little dot, you'll hit your thread bang-on every time. Just mind your gauges and shave off a few thou every time, easy-like."

"Hey, Pa?" Ella tried again, and this time Amos spoke over her.

"Are you sure this will be worth the hassle?" the apprentice asked his master.

Phil Holland stroked his long beard with one hand as he picked up the short, thick metal pipe and peered through the .55 caliber hole running through the central axis. "Before Bill's nitrogel, maybe not. Now 'at we can hit targets from way on out, this'll likely deaden the sound so as we can take shots without the ones we're shootin' at hearin' us."

"Hey Pa?"

"Good golly, what is it, Ella?"

"Omar's back. Bill wondered if Amos could put up his horse."

"The drifter, huh? I suppose that's some good news. Yeah, go on ahead, Amos."

Ella left the shop and returned to the kitchen, but rather than tend to the beans, she ran up the stairs to her room and scrubbed a layer of dust from a cracked mirror leaned up against the wall. She loathed the face that looked back at her: a long face and horse-like large front teeth. She shook her head and picked up a plastic comb. She had neither Sophie Fillmore's sleek, straight hair, nor Becky Brody's luxurious curls. She sighed and ran the comb through her mop like she was ginning cotton.

Ten minutes later, Ella set a mess of beans and not-quite-stale corn-bread in front of Omar at the Hollands' own table. She cleared her throat and stepped away, smoothing her flax skirt before folding her hands behind her back. "There it is. Dig on in."

Omar did—and promptly pulled a couple long, pale brown hairs from his dinner. But he kept on eating—he was a drifter, after all—without mentioning it, which probably balanced out the fact that he had failed to notice Ella had done up her hair.

She left him to it, a skip in her step and a beam on her face. She knew today would be a good day.

Chapter 2

'Tis the Wind and Nothing More

G listening with sweat under the naked glow of an LED light, a young man waited for a fate worse than death. The stainless-steel shackles around his hands and feet kept him rooted to the surgical chair that comprised the sole furnishment in the tiled, windowless room.

When the door latch snapped open, the young man jerked against his restraints hard enough to draw blood from his wrists. The door swung open on silent hinges to reveal a man in fatigues too clean to have ever seen any action abroad—a colonel, perhaps, but without any insignia.

"Salvador Brody," the officer said, as if he were a doctor confirming a patient's identity before administering treatment. The young man didn't give an answer, and the officer didn't press for one. Everything at this point amounted to mere formalities.

A thick silence passed between them before the military man exhaled through his nose. "The crucible for silver, and the furnace for gold, Mr. Brody. No other way around it. You've got the same odds as everyone else. My own nephew went just yesterday."

Young Mr. Brody looked at the colonel with baleful eyes.

"You're about to become part of something far greater than you or me," the officer said. "You are about to render a great service to your country."

"I've already served my country," the sacrificial lamb said with an accent that marked him as an odd transplant from what was a mostly unmodified, backwards community.

"Any grunt can do what you've done so far. This..." The colonel leaned in, putting a reassuring hand on Brody's shoulder. "This is what you were *made* for. It's your destiny."

"I didn't get any say in what I was made for."

"None of us did. Our fates were written in petri dishes and grown in labs. But our creators knew what they were doing. Trust the plan."

"From the looks of the news, it don't look like the plan's working out too well."

The lines around the colonel's eyes deepened in a grimace that looked sincere. "A lot of people have died. People higher than my pay grade knew that going in. And I'll tell you right now, a lot more people are going to die before this is over. But you—*you* are special. You've been granted something like immortality. Progress marches on, Mr. Brody, and the next age will be an age of gods. But time and circumstances are not on our side, and it's my job to make sure the first gods of the next age will be red-blooded Americans."

A moan in the darkness rose to become a wail and woke Old Man Brody from a fitful slumber. His hand went to his raw throat, and he realized the howl had been his own. *Another nightmare.* He lay back down, waiting for the relief of reality to calm his heart.

But that relief never came. A fresh rivulet of sweat ran down his temple, and he realized he had not woken from a nightmare; he'd woken into one. Something wicked had pulled him back from oblivion. Something that was still in the room with him.

Eyes straining in the dark, Old Man Brody pulled the matchet from his bedside sheath with a palsied hand and tried to murmur, "Who's there?" He couldn't seem to get the words out—not that it mattered either way. This darkness would give him no answer.

He struck a whetstone against his matchet in a shivering swipe and lit the wick of his bedside lantern on the fifth try. Wavering orange light bloomed in the narrow confines of his bedchamber. In the aged wallpaper of the wall opposite him, words were etched: *I require sacrifice.*

Old Man Brody forced himself to blink and look away, to think of loved ones long gone—either of his two wives, smiling in the light of morning. Images of their pale, lifeless faces flashed before him, and he lost the tenuous control over himself. "Goddamn you, you won't have me or any one of mine!" he hollered. "Not a one!"

The darkness outside his room gave no answer but for the skittering of retreating claws on worn-out planks.

Elvin McDaniel was still putting on his boots, well before the early morning twilight, when a pounding knock on his door set him jumping. Even his-good-for-nothing son Ralph snapped from his dreary half-asleep trance to full alertness. "Open up, sonny. It's Brody," a scratchy voice outside said.

Elvin sat his machete back on the oaken table and opened the battered plywood front door to see what could be bugging the old man at this hour.

"Gather yourself up a posse, watchman. Work your way out from the farms until you find yourself an unbred. I reckon we got us a passel of 'em near."

"Got yourself one of your feelings again?" Elvin asked without a hint of mockery. The clan had long since learned to trust the old man's intuitions.

Brody didn't answer Elvin's question. He went ahead with his own. "Heard anything from the night patrol? Anything go in or out?"

"I ain't heard nothin'."

"We need to go house to house. Make sure no one's hurt or... missing."

Elvin frowned. "Something's really got up in your britches."

"I'd rather we hurry up and get on with things."

"Okay, Mr. Brody. Okay. I'll let you do your bloodhound thing. Lead the way. Ralph, ring the alarm bell."

The early-morning alarm had woken Ella Holland and the rest of her family, but none of them had a clue what it was all about. Her father had tried to get the story out of a courier blazing by, but the rider had known nothing beyond his orders to get the Hadleys and Newells and Finches on standby, and that the townfolk were to shelter in place.

Ella had waited in her parents' upstairs bedroom while she listened to the rumble of her father and Bill Puckett murmuring in the hallway. The apprentices staying under their roofs—Omar and Ricky Brody—had moved out to man the palisade. Amos wasn't available at the moment, having opted last night to help his father at the smithy for today.

Soon the two masters dispersed to their patrols as well, leaving Ella, her stepmother, and Clive and Margaret in the master bedroom to wait with a sawed-off shotgun and matchet between them.

They waited for what felt like hours with no word. She craned her neck out the upstairs window to watch her pa head for the town square, likely to see what the situation was.

"It's probably a miswarning. They'll clear us out in another half-hour," Ella's stepmother said in the lengthy silence following Phil's departure, more for the sake of Clive and Margaret than for anyone. Clive looked relieved at the news, but Margaret moaned with disappointment. The young girl had taken some adventurous notions into her head lately, and no stern talk would cure her of them.

Ella shifted from foot to foot, half-bored, half-nervous. A burst of commotion outside in the distance swelled like a pot boiling over. First it was the low, horn-bellow of a massive unbred, then a sprinkling of human shouts, then the sporadic crack of firearms and a far-off but powerful *whump* of a thunderous impact.

Ella and her stepmother were at the bedroom window in an instant, looking out to see a couple of the west-side McDaniels charging off toward the western gate, shouting something about a bullhusker trying to ram a breach. While Ella was still taking in this new information, the floorboards creaked out in the hall, followed by a voice Ella thought was her father's.

"Org alkin' fay. Threch ill keer."

Huh? Did he say "all clear?" How'd he get back so soon? Why wasn't he headed for the gate with the rest of the folkward?

"Kord blitten."

Ella got up and moved across the room. "Wait," Leah gasped in a sudden, terrified whisper.

Ella froze with her hand on the doorknob as the same gut-wrenching understanding coursed through her a split-second after her stepmother:

That wasn't her father on the other side of the door. It sounded like him, but it wasn't him.

On the other side of the door, something touched the doorknob. "Eye blime?"

Ella slowly, carefully wedged her foot into the crack between the floor and the door as her grasp on the doorknob tightened into a death grip. The catch was worn. It wouldn't take much to pull the latch bolt free from the striking plate. She placed a free hand over her mouth and shut her eyes with the slow deliberateness of a chandler in a powdershop.

"Help." It sounded so matter-of-fact. Plain English. "Help. Help. Help. Help?" it said with increasing rapidity.

Behind Ella, Clive reached for his mother, but she pushed him away. "Mama?" he said aloud.

"Ssssshh!" his mother hissed, too late.

A sudden, insistent pressure surged at the door, straining against Ella's foot.

"Help help help help?!!!?" The voice rose in pitch from that of a man, to a woman, until it sounded like a child screaming. Multiple limbs thundered on the door, rattling Ella's teeth inside her head. *"Help help help help help HELLP HEEEEEEEEEEELLLLLLLLP!!!!"*

Then it wasn't only something on the other side of the door, but also something thumping on the rooftop above them. The children screamed. "Two of them," Ella breathed.

"HEEEEEEEEEEEEEELLLLLLLLLLLLLLLLLLP!!!!!" The scream lost whatever human quality it had and became an otherworldly screech, warbling like a teakettle reaching an unsteady boil.

Leah Holland rushed to the window, threw open the shutters, and screamed to the now empty streets, "SCREEVLERS!"

A massive segmented body blacked out the window from above and grabbed at her shirt. Leah jerked away before it could get purchase, stumbled back against the bed, and leveled the shotgun at the six-legged creature already crawling into the room. "Cover your ears, kids!" she said a half-second before she blasted a limb off the screevler.

The force of the blast knocked the unbred back out the window—mostly. Its chitinous claws scrabbled at the sill, leaving jagged marks in the wood.

Behind Ella, the door pushed in against her with a groan as Leah leaped across the room to slam the shutters closed. She wedged her own forearm into the shutters' barn-door-style latch to keep the screevler out. But she couldn't keep out the grasping, spider-black arms.

Ella was losing the battle against her unbred, as well. Again something pushed opposite the door, and the groaning in the wood became a splintering crack as the bolt pulled free from the housing. Her foot scooted an inch across the floor. She wasn't strong enough to hold it at bay.

Clive and Margaret's screams never ceased.

Sweat coursed down Ella's face as she fought back against the monster. A crack and a wail brought her gaze back toward the window, where her stepmother reeled backward, her arm bleeding, the left shutter askew on a broken hinge, a screevler leaping over her. But instead of savaging Leah Holland, it skittered right over to Clive and Margaret. "No!" Ella screamed, reaching out impotently with one arm.

Her weight shifted a hair, and suddenly, the door swept her aside, knocking her into the wall and onto the floor, the matchet in her hand clattering next to her. Clive and Margaret sailed over her head, carried out the now-open bedroom door by the partially maimed screevler like two sacks of potatoes.

"Margaret! Clive!" Ella cried as she scrambled to her feet, seized the fallen matchet, and chased her half-sister, half-brother, and the two fleeing screevlers out into the hall and down the stairs.

A thud and the scattering of crockery across the kitchen floor signaled a scuffle down the stairs, out of sight. Someone was down there. Ella alighted the stairs to see a dark-haired young man facing off against both screevlers. "Omar!" she cried. "Don't let them get away!"

Omar stood in the doorway at the back of the house, keeping the wounded screevler from escaping. The unburdened one sought to catch his flank, but the kitchen offered little room to maneuver, and though the young man had a distinct disadvantage in appendages, the ones he had grasped a short spear and long, wicked bowie knife to ward off any attacks before they came.

The screevler still tried to risk it, knocking Omar's spear-point aside and forcing him back a step. In response, Omar moved behind the kitchen table and kicked it over towards the two unbreds, tripping them both up. Clive, the smaller of the two little ones, slipped from the screevler's grasp and landed behind it with an "Oomph!"

"Get out of here, kid!" Omar shouted when Clive didn't immediately run for it. Before the screevlers could grab for their prey again, Omar struck first at the un-wounded screevler, then at the one carrying Margaret. Clive ran off in the confusion, and when the first screevler turned to give chase to him, Ella launched herself down the stairs and caught its rearmost appendage in a wild swing with her matchet.

It wasn't enough to chop all the way through the chitin, but it was enough for both unbreds to withdraw down the hallway toward the front door rather than waste time trying to fight past Omar. At the last moment, Omar lunged over the table and buried his knife in the wounded screevler's shoulder, right between the chitin plates, before falling to the floor next to Ella.

The creature should have dropped Margaret then and there. It had a serious wound. If it had any chance of surviving, it should drop its burden and escape to find easier prey.

But it didn't. With Omar out of position, the way to the back door lay open again. It hitched Margaret into a better hold, pivoted back around, and bolted out the back door for the palisade, screaming along with Margaret the whole way.

Ella was back up an instant, seizing a butcher knife from the counter with one hand and helping Omar up with the other before following the screevler out through the garden and Bill Puckett's covered manure pits. She'd made it halfway to the palisade before Omar overtook her at a sprint, catching up with the screevler as it was climbing up.

And then the screevler was over the palings, hauling Margaret over the edge. Just before she disappeared, though, Omar seized her foot. Then Ella was there, too, both of them pulling Margaret back from her doom. The screevler's grip, however, did not falter. "Don't let me go!" Margaret pleaded. "Don't let me go!"

"I can get at it with the spear if you can hold her," Omar said, sweat pouring down his face.

"I... can't!"

The pull on the forest side of the palisade shifted, and a screevler claw reached over the wall to slash at them. It made a glancing connection at Omar's forearm, loosening his grip enough to wrest Margaret away from them. Margaret's feet flipped over the side of the palisade, and the screevler thumped to the ground in the forest. Margaret's screams faded as it dragged her into the wilderness.

Gone.

Ella met Omar's eyes and saw the flicker of impotent rage and despair. Her own heart seized. Omar swore, leaped from the palisade into a rolling landing, and charged off into the woods, chasing the screams. Ella climbed down to follow, her breath hitching in the small squeaks of a young woman losing a fight against terrified girlhood.

Chapter 3

The Unbred Shepherd

P hil Holland bolted back home, away from the meetinghouse as folks poured out of their homes on either side of the street. The news of a bullhusker at the gates and a screevler in town carried across the clan with gale-force speed. The clamor had come from Phil's neck of the woods, back where his family'd holed up. His feet flew faster than the renewed alarm sweeping the streets.

He rounded the corner nearly at a full sprint, then kicked it up to full when he saw none of his kin out in the street. When Phil neared the other Tuckers enough for them to work out his trajectory, the clan carpenter made to stop him. "We're all headed for the gate, Phil. If we don't brace it good—"

"We killed the screevler yet?"

"How the hell should I know? There was a shot somewhere around here. I just know our orders—Phil, wait! That bullhusker ain't waiting, and we ain't got any clansmen around for a breach-and-clear!"

Phil ignored Shane Bunton's warning and streaked into the front door of his home, shifting his musket to his left hand and drawing his matchet. He didn't even bother to see if Shane had followed him or gone on to defend the gate.

Inside, Phil paused for a moment and held back his ragged gasps to listen. It was silent. He wrapped his matchet's wrist strap around his hand, lest a surprise knock his sword away. He cleared the front hallway to the kitchen, then bounded up the stairs in four huge strides, the floorboards groaning and popping under his stomping feet.

The door to his bedroom, where he'd left his entire family, hung open. A thin trail of blood ran from the door down the hallway back the way he'd come. He rushed to the door and stormed inside. The room was empty, except for his dazed wife, who struggled unsuccessfully to her feet, bleeding from the side of her head. "M'okay," Leah slurred, "but the kids... I think they took the—"

Phil was already out the door and headed down the stairs. A child screamed just out the back door. Clive or Margaret, he couldn't tell.

Phil Holland bolted for the back door straight into the screevler ambush waiting outside.

Even after being blindsided by a screevler he should have known was coming, even as his musket discharged uselessly into the wall, even as he brought the keen edge of his matchet to bear, Phil still looked for his children.

A sharp, piercing pain in his side brought him fully to the problem at hand. The creature had pinioned Phil's left arm and was wrestling for his right, all the while leaning in to get at his throat with its mandibles. He could see past the insect-like mouthparts to the fleshy sound-making organs deeper inside.

21

Phil had been badly hit. He knew it. He could feel it. But he also had his sword arm free for a moment. Pushing back with the musket in his left hand, he twisted his sword into a low-guard disengage, right underneath the screevler's uppermost arm to the vulnerable underbelly.

The sharpened tip of the matchet caught on a chink in the unbred's carapace. He stabbed upward with all his strength as his insides screamed. He lifted the shrieking screevler a few inches off the ground before dropping it and stabbing it again. It fell away, but he grabbed it by upper right arm and jerked it back into a hacking chop to the neck. Two more strokes stopped its infernal caterwaul by removing the head from the body.

Phil stumbled backwards away from the twitching corpse and collapsed. "Help me," he murmured to the emptiness.

His stomach hurt. He looked down and winced. His shirt was ripped open, along with his belly underneath and the fat and muscle underneath that, and two feet of his own intestines looped down his side like a gruesome watch chain.

"Help—help me."

Clive waited a few seconds in the kitchen cupboard before daring to poke his head out. After he'd wrestled free of the screevler carrying both him and his sister, he'd heard the sounds of struggle in the backyard, then the sound of footsteps coming in through the front, running upstairs and down, and then more struggle in the backyard, ending with cries of human and animal pain. Now, there was only a low moan outside, punctuated now and then with a "Help me."

His hand went to his arm, where blood trickled down to his elbow. It didn't hurt at all.

Part of him knew he couldn't stay in the cupboard forever, that there was probably still a screevler running around, and it could smell a little boy from a mile away. He had to get back to Mama. She'd know what to do.

Someone moaned again outside the kitchen. Ma'd always told him never to follow human sounds if there were screevlers about. But what if someone needed help?

Clive decided. He tiptoed out of the kitchen, carrying a knife with him just in case.

His eyes didn't immediately fill with tears as he rounded the corner and saw what lay outside, but he felt something so heavy in his stomach it hurt. "Papa?"

Papa sat leaning crookedly against the back door frame, holding his belly where his guts lay outside him in a bloody pile. From the chest up, it was still his papa, but from the chest down, it was Mr. Brody's butcher shop. "Papa?" Clive's voice quavered this time.

Papa winced, groaning as he turned to see Clive. *Still alive.* Now Clive's eyes filled with tears.

"Ahhhh," Papa said with visible effort. "Are you okay, Clive? How's your arm?"

"I'm—I'm okay."

"Good. Good." Papa let out a shuddering sigh. His eyes stared up past Clive with the silent terror of a wounded animal.

"Papa? Are you okay?"

"M'okay, Clive. Looks worse than it is. Hurts like the dickens. I'll probably be grouchy once Dr. Bernhard sews me up."

"Papa, we gotta put your insides back in." He couldn't keep the despair from creeping into his voice. This would be the last time he talked to his pa. He knew it.

"Don't want to put 'em in yet. We'll let Doctor Bernhard give me a look over first. Then he'll get some clansman to give me some blood, and I'll be shinier than fresh-blacked boots in a couple weeks."

"You promise?"

"Can't make you a promise like that, Clive. Listen. I—"

"Land's sakes! Mr. Holland!" It was Ricky Brody, coming up with a couple of the McDaniels in tow, armed for melee combat. "Somebody go get Dr. Bernhard, quick!"

"Ricky, you'd best go in and fetch a wet towel from inside," the miller said, shaking his head. "Cover up this mess on Phil's middle here. And take Clive with you. Don't need to be seeing this."

"I don't want to leave Pa," Clive said.

"Now listen, fella—"

"Let him stay, McDaniel," Papa said. "My boy's a tough 'un. Ain't you, Clive?"

Clive nodded. "Uh-huh."

Papa winced again. "Listen, Clive. You're gettin' old enough... to know how things go. If I gotta... if I gotta go to heaven, you'll have to be big and strong for me, okay?"

He sniffed. "Okay."

"Don't cry too much. Take care of Ma and Ella and Margaret, okay? 'Cause that's what the man of the house does."

"I'll try, Papa."

"Good, good. Let's shake on it." Pa extended a trembling, blood-soaked hand, which Clive grasped as firmly as he was able.

They shook, but Pa didn't let go—just held on. Pa had tears on his own face now. "Remember, Clive: this is just in case. Bernhard's a good doctor. Fix me up real fine."

"It's got to drop her soon. It's got to," Ella said, panting alongside Omar as they plunged deeper and deeper into the woods. Branches and leaves slapped at them as if trying to slow their headlong pursuit of the quarry. Ella's heart lurched with each squalling cry from the child out in the woods, each cry acting as their lodestone in the wilderness, dragging them onward. *Don't worry, Margaret. We're coming; we'll get you.*

Then Omar halted in his tracks behind her. "Stop. More unbreds up ahead. Pigmen. Maybe another screevler."

Ella spun, hissing, *"But Margaret!"*

Omar grimaced. He spat, tossing his spear to Ella as he unslung his rifle. "Keep that matchet of your'n handy."

A few strides later, everything ahead of them went quiet. They picked up their pace. They were in the old town now—the spread-out jumble of homes, stores, and crumbled roads that had at one time marked the commercial center of a small town, but now barely distinguished itself from the surrounding hills and forest by its gravelike stillness.

"Margaret!" Ella called out. She received no answer.

The remnants of a worn-out gas station sagged up ahead of them. The screevler couldn't have gotten far ahead, but with the sudden quiet and still air, they'd have to clear the buildings one by one.

Omar primed his rifle as Ella ran up to the shattered glass door, dragging it open against the granules of glass littering the concrete. She brought her spear point up and around, looking for a pigman or screevler that might try to pounce on them from the roof. Together, they posted up on either side of the entrance, their breath still catching up to them.

A girl wept inside, and somewhere behind a barn further up the slope, leaves and brush rustled. Omar cocked his rifle. "Don't hit Margaret," Ella said.

"Ready?"

She nodded, and Omar rolled into the entrance, leveling his gun. She braced herself for the boom of the rifle, but there was none. Omar instead crept into the doorway. She followed.

In the middle of the patchwork of bare, damp earth and high weeds, framed by the shafts of sunlight filtering through gaps in the roof above, little Margaret sat alone on her knees, her head buried in both hands, her shoulders shaking.

"Margaret!"

She jumped at the sound of Ella's voice, darted forward, and wrapped herself around her older half-sister. "Get me outta here!" she said.

"Ssh, ssh. You're okay. We've got you. What happened to the screevler?"

Margaret pointed over to a dark corner of the building, where a form lay, barely moving. Ella handed her spear to Omar, who walked over to examine the fallen creature. "Let's get out of here, Omar. There's likely more about." Ella reached down to pull Margaret up.

"They're moving away. Not sure why, but they're leaving. Just let me finish this one off."

Omar placed one foot on the screevler beneath him and raised the spear to the creature's throat. It pulled ragged breaths through the socketed nostrils in its skull-like face, utterly spent. Just before he rammed the spear point home, however, the screevler's eyes flashed wide, and its mandibles opened to expose the vibrating web of flesh within. "I can no longer feel hunger. But nevertheless, I will feed," it said in the voice of a man.

Omar leaped backwards, then stabbed the wretched thing right in the throat, cutting the screevler off at the word "feed." The screevler gurgled as its eyes widened in its death stare.

Margaret was inconsolable. "We have to get away. Get away. Get me away from the man!"

Omar pulled his spear free from the screevler's corpse, not bothering for a minute with the screevler's valuable claws. "Ready to go."

"There's a man! There's a bad man!" Margaret pointed into the woods outside the back of the building, where a span of the wall had fallen in.

Omar snatched up his rifle and moved toward the opening.

"There was a man there! I think he wanted to do something bad to me!"

"Omar," Ella said, holding a shaking Margaret, "I think we should—"

"Hang on," he said, now more outside than inside. "I... I think I see 'im." He raised the rifle to his shoulder and stilled to line up a shot. But he never pulled the trigger.

"Omar?"

He didn't answer. He didn't move.

Margaret, however, had had enough. She pulled herself free of Ella's arms, jerking both Ella and Omar back to themselves, and dashed for the front door, breaking outside and toward town as if being chased by a monster. Ella had to run to keep up. "Wait! Margaret! Are you okay? Margaret! What happened?"

Ella and Omar caught up with Margaret at the bottom of the hill. Ella grabbed her by the arm and stopped her. She was still crying. "Margaret, you're safe. Listen to me. You're okay." Ella pulled her sister into a hug. "You're okay."

"The pigmen were carrying him!"

Ella glanced at Omar. His face had gone the color of fresh milk, his eyes wide and staring.

"Did you see him? Why didn't you shoot?"

When Omar didn't answer, Margaret kept on. "The screevler held me down, then the man got up and walked over to me. He ran off just before you came."

"I... I saw him," Omar said, looking off behind them.

"He smiled at me. But he had no eyes, Ella! Oh, he had no eyes!"

Chapter 4

Healing and Festering

Phil's guts were in too much of a mess to carry him over to Doctor Bernhard's, so Doctor Bernhard and his wife came to him while Phil's clansmen held him down on his own kitchen table. In the brief span it took to move Phil and get the dead screevler heaved out the back door, Phil's grim calm had wavered to a low moan. The doctor, on arriving, swept a keen gaze over the gunsmith's balled fists, his rent-open stomach, and the beads of sweat standing out on his pain-twisted face.

"What do you think, Doc?" the miller asked with a sideways glance. "Think he's saveable?"

"Dunno. Stir up that fire, get some water boilin'. Get this kid out of here."

"I don't want to leave Pa!" Clive protested.

Phil Holland's moan took on a harsher, guttural tone.

"Go on now, git!" the doctor ordered. "Got us too many cooks in the kitchen here. You can see him when I'm done."

"So you can operate, then?" Ricky Brody asked, his face white.

Phil squirmed on the table, his coiled intestines quivering like jelly. "If you can't do it, kill me quick," he muttered through gritted teeth.

"Hon, get me the laudanum."

His wife reached into his canvas bag and handed him a tincture marked with a strip of tape and grease pencil. Doctor Bernhard measured out a small amount of the precious liquid extracted from his own poppy garden and supplemented with furtive shipments from the Grierson settlement. "Toss this back; it'll take away the pain."

Phil obeyed with a grimace. "How long?"

"'Bout as long as it'll take me to get your saline prepped. I'll give you some more to knock you out for the stitchin'."

"Give it to me now."

"Wait for this dose to kick in. Ricky, get that onion over yonder and dice it up for me." Doctor Bernhard reached into his bag and pulled out some plastic tubing, needles, scalpels, and various tools. He tossed them into the pot of water set to boil on the stove. Phil ate some of the raw onions, though it took him longer and longer to get it down as the pain worsened.

By the time the pot had reached its boil, Phil was screaming, tears streaming down either side of his face, his arms and legs rigid as Ricky Brody and Clyde McDaniel held him down.

"Give 'im some more, Doc, please," Ricky begged, his gaze determinedly away from Phil's ravaged belly.

"Don't want to kill him. Give it a few more minutes."

The minutes dragged by like hours, but the screams gave way to moans, and gradually the moans gave way to exhausted sighs. He finally relaxed, and Mr. McDaniel and Ricky Brody took the pot off the stove and helped Doctor Bernhard fish his sterilized tools out of the hot water with tongs. The doctor's wife salted the water and, once the water had cooled somewhat, gave it a taste as if she were cooking soup.

"Saline's good," she said.

Doctor Bernhard measured out another, smaller dose of laudanum and gave it to Phil, who quaffed it like a man dying from thirst.

It was at that moment that another scream erupted from the back door to the kitchen. Ella stood there with a hand to her gaping mouth, Margaret coming in close behind her, and Omar pulling the girl back before she could catch a glimpse of her father splayed out on the wooden table.

"Is he..." Ella gasped.

"Not yet," Doctor Bernhard answered. "No family around 'till I'm done. Go."

Omar stayed, taking Ricky's place at Phil's side. When the pot had cooled, Doctor Bernhard checked his patient's slow breathing. Phil did not stir when the doctor brushed his closed eyelashes. Mr. McDaniel and Omar helped douse Phil's entire gaping insides while the doctor sniffed for the smell of onion all along the guts and the mess of tissue piled on the table. Rick sat nearby with blood running from a hollow needle and tube in his arm to the blissfully unconscious gunsmith—a strange quirk of the Pandemic had favored universal donors. The doctor's wife held up the yellowed notes of a long-dead medical student for him to reference while he worked, and nearby a copper wire lay next to an open lantern flame for cauterizing.

Doctor Bernhard sighed. He'd taken a small dose of laudanum himself before he'd come over, to steady his nerve. "Here goes nothin'."

Folks paced around out behind the Holland home, while others came in and out of the nearby western gate on their to-and-fro runabouts. Elvin McDaniel simply stood, resting his chin on one hand and his other hand on his hip. He didn't move when Arnold Brody and Shane Bunton rode in. Arnold gave his report to the watchman before he'd fully dismounted from his dun horse. "Whoever it was, he's a slippery little jack-racker," Arnold said, scratching behind his ears. "Looks like the bullhusker going for the gate was just a distraction. It cleared full out of here as soon as the screevlers did. As for that stranger, the Fillmores are givin' us a one-in-three chance of trackin' him more than a mile or two. This spell of still weather we've had ain't helping with the sniffers." He tapped his thin nose. Though he served as clan butcher, he was a slight man with a mild disposition.

Shane Bunton was Arnold's opposite in every regard, a man of strong arms and stronger opinions. "I'd bet my right hand this is some kind of Greenbrier nonsense," he said as he alighted his own mount. "You want to bag that son-of-a-gun, head south."

Elvin said nothing. He stared at the recently de-clawed screevler corpse lying next to Puckett's and the Hollands' garden, stroking his chin.

The butcher continued. "I sent word to the Hadleys and Newells to be on the lookout for some blind drifter type what might wander onto their crofts."

"A drifter who's tamed him a pack of unbreds?" Elvin said. "I never heard of such a thing. Mr. Brody, sir, have you ever heard of such a thing?"

Old Man Brody had agreed to go out to the old town with the rest of the posse and "do his bloodhound thing," as the watchman called it. He'd been silent during and since the brief excursion. Even now, his answer was a shrug and a curt "Never in all my days."

"Don't know what any of this is about?" Elvin asked the old man.

"I'm as dumbstruck as you are," he said, but his brooding, grim silence laid the lie bare.

Elvin frowned at Old Man Brody. "Mr. Brody, I understand if you ain't too keen on recalling the old days. But I'm about protecting the clan in the here and now. Do you got any up-sight on how to help me do that?"

"Kill that drifter first chance you get. Maybe he'll come back. Maybe we scared him off." Old Man Brody walked off back home as if that scrap of advice was more than enough for the watchman. Perhaps it was.

Elvin shook his head, turning back to the screevler. "Don't make a lick of sense. It's a lot of trouble to go to for one little kid."

"You can never tell with drifters, Elvin," the butcher said. "There's some real nasty cases out there."

"Yeah. And what kind of case you think this Omar Walking character is?"

Arnold stammered, "Uh, gee, Elvin, I didn't think... with him helping rescue the Holland girl, seems like most of the elders are swinging to Sam's way of seein' things. Folks are talking about getting Mr. Walking initiated and inked right away. Johnny Grierson'll probably throw a fit, but—"

"I know which way Johnny and Sam will go already. I'm asking what *you* think about him."

Arnold sighed. "I... think we mighta been a little too hasty banishin' him back in April. A feller don't give up a hundred jaws to get back into the graces of a clan he don't want to belong to."

"Yeah, but how does a feller come up with a hundred pigman jaws in a couple months? Ain't no way he cut them himself."

"You think he played the highwayman? Killed some folks for the cash?"

"That's what I'm wondering, yeah."

Arnold shrugged. "If he did, it weren't ours. Times we're in, a guy like Mr. Walking might be handy to have around."

"Might be," Elvin said, pacing around the screevler's corpse. "Never can tell," he murmured to himself.

He dismissed the butcher and opened the back door of the Holland home where the drifter himself paced in front of Miss Ella Holland and her little half-sister, Margaret. Margaret was still sniffling, falling into and out of a fuss, while Ella sat quiet as ever, staring with eyes as wide as ever, unkempt hair hanging ignored around a long face used to tragedy—a face torn between the relief of one tragedy dodged and the agony of one impending.

Elvin went to check in on the impending tragedy and stepped in through the back door to the Holland's kitchen. Less blood smeared the floor than he'd expected, though an awful mess befouled the hallway at the base of the stairs. It looked like Phil Holland was awake, though his head still rested back on a pillow placed on the table. Phil's wife stood at his side with a hand on his shoulder. Doctor Bernhard sighed as he tossed another blood-soaked rag into a pot of boiling water.

The doctor dipped his hands in a nearby basin of soapy water and scrubbed. "That's all I can do for now, Mr. Holland. Keep eating up that garlic and drink them herb teas, but mostly, it'll be the good 'ole immune system doing the work. I'll be over tomorrow to help change the bandages and check those horse-hair sutures."

Phil Holland sighed. "It still hurts, doc. Can I get drunk?" His speech came out slow and thick, like molasses. Whatever the doctor had given him hadn't worn off yet.

"Only what I gave you to drink. Beyond that, stick to the willow bark tea to take the edge off. Let me know when you start farting again; that's important."

"Ugh." Phil threw his head back into the pillow. "I wish I'd died."

Doctor Bernhard flicked the water from his hands back into the basin. "You got plenty of chance to do that yet. You get an infection runnin' away with you, that'll be it. You pull through, you'll be the luckiest son-of-a-gun I ever did see."

Phil snorted. "I feel *real* lucky."

Elvin stepped forward. "Mind if I have a word with the gunsmith, Doc?"

Doctor Bernhard turned. "No disrespect, watchman," he said, "but if it ain't a 'Get well soon,' you'd best be on back on outside."

Elvin ignored the doctor and turned to Phil. "Any idea why two screevlers would've hit your place in particular?"

Phil groaned and raised a hand in an indefinite movement. The doctor moved between Elvin and the patient, making shooing motions Elvin's way.

The back door creaked open again, and a small voice passed through behind Elvin. "Hey, Pa!"

"Heeeey," Phil said, brightening somewhat as his son Clive entered the room.

"I wanted to come in earlier, but Ma wouldn't let me."

"Good for her."

"Are you all fixed up? That took forever." Clive took another step closer to Phil's bedside, but without coming up all the way.

"Gettin' there. If I die now, it'll likely be from a fever like civilized folks."

"Got all your guts back inside?" To Elvin, it sounded like Clive was doing his best to sound halfway disinterested, the way grown-ups seemed to talk about their cows. The concern came through anyway—the worry of a child for his pa. Elvin looked away, uncomfortable in a way he couldn't quite put his finger on. It was his boots pinching, likely. He'd stuff them with soaked corn to loosen them up again.

"Looks like it," Phil Holland said. "I told you it weren't as bad as it looked."

"Good. Let's not make a habit out of it, though."

"H-h-hhhh!" Phil wheezed. "Dadgummit, Clive! It hurts to laugh!"

Even given the late summer nights, the dim glow on the western horizon had long since given way to pale moonlight. A keen watcher every so often might have spotted one of the half-dozen clansmen on the night-watch as they stirred along the palisade.

But Omar, pacing around Puckett's and Holland's shared garden, wasn't on the night-watch. He stopped to stare up at the sky and heave a weary sigh from his lungs. He should return to his straw tick, but he knew it would be more tossing and turning, chasing ever-skittish sleep. He'd blame it on the summer heat.

The back kitchen door of the Holland home creaked open a stone's throw away, and a little voice squeaked from within, a mortal enemy he'd saved from an awful fate. "Mister Walking, is that you?"

Margaret. "Yeah. What're you doing up?"

"I can't stop thinking about the man with no eyes."

He turned away from her. "Yeah, yeah. Me neither."

"I don't want to go to bed."

"You'll catch hell if your ma finds you sneakin' out when you should be sleepin'."

"Can I stay up with you? Please?"

He paced a little further, past the rows of potato plants just about ready to harvest. "You gonna be a nuisance?"

"Uh-uh."

"The moment you are, I'm hauling you back inside."

"Okay."

The two of them paced around the garden in silence for another lap or two, the lamb with the wolf dressed up as its kin. Omar cleared his throat. "You do bedtime stories?"

"Yeah."

"I guess we can read some bedtime stories if you can get me a lantern."

Once he'd got the lantern lit with one of the live coals banked in the Hollands' stove, Omar followed Margaret into their little living room. She pulled an old book of fairy tales off the corner shelf and curled up next to him on the family's patchwork quilted sofa.

He hadn't gotten through the first story before his clipped, tense speech softened to the low-but-expressive rumble of a proper bedtime story. As he read, squinting in the feeble lantern-light, Margaret drew closer to hear the story—something about a giant deciding whether to let children play in his garden.

By the time he'd finished the story, Margaret's heartbeat was slowing next to him, a gentle drumming through his threadbare shirt. He flipped to the next page.

From behind them came a voice. "Is it okay if I join you'ns?" Ella asked in the long, silent space between words.

Both Margaret and Omar jumped. "Oh, Ella, it's just you." Margaret waved her on down the stairs. "Sure, you can sit with us. Can't she, Omar?"

"Little extra company couldn't hurt."

Ella nestled down beside Margaret. "Can't sleep either?" Margaret asked.

Ella shook her head. "Bad dreams."

"We just finished this story. Got any ones you want to hear?"

"I'm fine, Margie. You pick."

Margaret did, and Ella and Omar took turns reading fairy tales, keeping their voices low so as not to wake the rest of the house. Deep in the gloom of their home, Mr. Holland groaned in slow-burning pain, but the steady, low light of the lantern and the easy rhythm of Ella's breathing did their work, and a couple more stories into the dark of night sent Margaret snoring softly on Ella's shoulder.

"Ready to head back to bed?" Ella said to Omar when they'd finished the fairy tale.

"You can. I'm not ready for bed yet."

"Hmm. Me neither, I reckon."

"Hmm."

They sat in silence with Margaret between them. The night crickets ticked the minutes by. The room would likely turn from black to gray in a few hours as dawn broke.

"You look tired," Ella said.

"I am. Mighty tired."

"You want to talk about it?"

Omar said nothing for a minute. He had no business saying what kept him up, let alone to a Tucker girl. But if it helped him sleep, what the hell? "Sure."

When Omar didn't immediately continue, Ella looked at him. "You... looked a little wild back there when it looked like it was getting away with Margaret."

"I... had a sister. Back when I had a clan. She was about a year younger than me. I was eleven, doing my morning chores one day, feeding the animals and whatnot. It was right around harvest time, so I was going to bed late and getting up early. I was tired that morning, wasn't thinking straight.

"It was..." Omar leaned his head back as if casually recalling some triviality. "The most god-awful scream I've ever heard. I come running down as fast as I could, down by the pond, and from there on, it was all like a bad dream.

"A pigman was out near the reeds, hunched over, chewing at something it had caught. My sister was screaming, but I didn't put the two together. Not until I saw my sister's arms flailing around underneath it. Some pigman got past all the traps, all the bells and alarms, all the stakes and fences, and run clear across open fields without no one noticing it. And it didn't go for the cows or horses or chickens or goats—it went for

Chandra. And she was screaming and hollering and taking on something fierce, but the pigman was just grunting and feeding away, eating her alive right there.

"I ran right up to the pigman, and I slapped it as hard as I could with my pitchfork. Don't know why I didn't stab it; just scared and dumb, I guess. It snapped at me long enough to get me off its back. Then it got right back to work on her. I could swear it had the devil's eyes.

"Don't know how long I wrestled that thing, but by the time I'd pinned the sucker to the ground with the pitchfork, my sister was just a mess on the grass."

"Oh, Omar, I'm so sorry."

"But she was still alive somehow. I picked her up and carried her as best I could back towards the house. I think I remember her guts trailing along behind me, but I'm not sure. Could have been her dress. Blood all over the place. I couldn't recognize her face anymore. She was making weird..." Omar sighed and took a breath. "Whimpering noises, and I knowed pretty soon she wouldn't live. I made it back to the barn before I was too tired to carry her anymore.

"I knowed what I had to do. She asked me to do it. I grabbed a corn knife from the barn to put her out of her misery. But I couldn't do it. Not to Chandra. So, I sat down beside her and let her suffer until my pa came running back from the field. He finished her for me."

The room went silent except for the three people breathing there.

"Did you dream about it tonight?" Ella asked.

"Never slept."

"And I guess that's why you became a drifter."

Omar didn't answer. If she spun a nice little fiction for herself, he wouldn't contradict it. Not if it served his purposes.

When Omar didn't respond, she continued. "Last time I had a run-in with a screevler, I lost my brother."

"When was that?"

"Going on three years now."

38

"That's still fresh."

"Yeah," Ella said. "Sometimes it is."

"Did you... see it happen?"

"No, not quite. We heard this screevler get caught in a trap on up the hill from us while I was visiting him on a roundswalk. Except the trap wasn't a Tucker trap. He had me stay behind while he checked it out. I never saw the Greenbrier arrow that killed him. When I finally got up enough nerve to go up to him, he was already turning cold. I was too scared to go out to him, and he died alone because of my fear."

"Did you ever catch the Greenbriers what did it?"

"Elvin sent out a posse, but they couldn't hardly find a trace."

"Hmm. I'm sorry."

"Thanks."

Omar tried to find the next words to say. It took longer than he expected. "Right after it happened, how did it feel?"

"Like having the wind knocked out of me."

"Or like... taking a big ole knock to the head?"

Ella nodded, looking up and out the window. "Jim... wasn't the first I'd lost. But he was the first I'd lost... like that."

"Did you think, 'The worst of the hurting is still ahead of me?' Like getting out of bed the next morning would be like climbing a mountain?" Omar looked over at Ella.

Ella looked back. "Yeah. That's how I felt." She wiped her eyes. "What was she like? Your sister?"

"Smart. But not smart the way you'd think it. It was a long time ago, and she never got old enough for it to really show. Seemed like she was just born with a head on her shoulders. Even when she was small, everything made sense to her, even when it didn't seem like it was supposed to. She didn't think, because she didn't need to. She always knowed. How about your brother?" Omar asked, hesitating a moment before he did.

Ella had a rueful smile. "He was a goofball. He liked being outdoors, outside the clan walls, out huntin', out fishin', anything but working in the shop. He might have settled down in a few more years; I don't know. He was thinking of courtin' Becky, but she was still a mite young for him, and he was too shy yet. I don't think Becky ever knew. But I think one day, she would have jumped at the chance, even if only so she could call me a sister."

Omar was hardly past twenty years old, but his shoulders sagged under an unseen weight. "It's enough to make a body tired."

"Sure is," Ella whispered almost to herself. "You believe in heaven?"

"I... think I might be too tired to."

"I believe in heaven."

"Think you'll see your brother again?"

"Maybe. I mean, sure, and my Ma too, but that's not why I believe. That's too small a reason to believe in something like that."

"You've got a better reason?"

"Yeah."

"You gonna tell me?"

"I ain't so keen talkin' about it. You said how your sister just kinda knew things?"

"It's like that?"

Ella nodded.

"That ain't too convincing. Can your thinkin' explain all the bad stuff out there?"

Ella shrugged. "I don't know. Can your thinkin' explain why there's anything good?"

"I didn't say if I thought one way or the other. Just said I was tired."

Ella gave Omar a look of good-humored disbelief. This time, he shrugged. "Maybe good and bad aren't real. Maybe it's just what we think about it. Whatever the clan elders say goes, and anything else beyond that is only nature doing what nature does."

"Maybe," Ella said, though Omar didn't think he'd convinced her, and he might have preferred it if he hadn't. "Listen, I gotta take Margaret back up to bed." She stood up. "But first, I got to tell you somethin'."

Ella stopped Omar with an outstretched arm as he stood up. "I know the real reason the clan banished you. It was easier for them to spin a yarn about you bein' a terrible ubermensch than risk you letting slip the truth about what we Tuckers are. I ain't supposed to tell anyone what I've learned, but you deserve to know what happened. It was wrong what they did to you, whatever they say about it. I knew it was wrong even before I learned I'd been lied to. Right and wrong ain't whatever the elders say."

Omar nodded. "I... appreciate—"

"I ain't done." Without further warning, she reached in and hugged Omar tight. "I knew you were a good man, even before you saved my sister." She smiled, her eyes glistening in the moonlight streaming through the window. "I knew it."

She left him there as she carried her sister upstairs. He watched her go. Of course, the girl knew nothing. He'd suspected it before, but this sealed it—three years ago, in the woods south of town, he'd killed Ella's brother.

Chapter 5

In Which Young Mr. Taylor Considers a Change in Profession

A couple days later, Omar stumbled into Bill's shop, bleary-eyed in the light of an early summer dawn. He looked at the splash of sulfuric acid clinging to the bottom of the last flask in the corner and marched himself outside to the wood pile. Earnest Daly was already toddling around with a stick, which meant his widowed mother must not be too far away.

After setting up some wood for a fire under Bill's roasting kiln, Omar followed the sound of clinking cookware in Bill's kitchen to find Melissa

Daly vigorously burning some eggs. "Need to borrow a flame." He gestured to the firebox under the sheet-metal stovetop.

Melissa nodded, wiping sweat from her forehead with one hand while shoveling the mess of eggs onto a plate with the other. "I'll be startin' a fire out yonder," Omar said, jerking his thumb over his shoulder. "Earnest gonna be okay out there?"

"There's a fire in here, there's a fire out there, there's fire everywhere." Melissa sighed, chucking a dish rag at the washwater basin nearby. "He'll be okay s'long's he don't get in your way, and if he does, give 'im a shove. He'll get the idear."

Omar opened his mouth to say something, then thought better of it. He had turned to go back outside when Bill clomped into the kitchen, pulling his suspenders up over his shoulders. "Well, now, somethin' smells pretty good. You didn't have to do that, Mrs. Daly," Bill said, a sight more friendly-sounding than he usually did when talking to his apprentices.

"I figgered if I was gonna make breakfast for me and Earnest, I might as well crack an egg for you, too."

Bill took the proffered plate of eggs and moved to sit at the narrow kitchen table. "You et yet, Omar?"

"I was a-fixin' to stir up a fire out in the kiln."

"Eh." Bill waved the notion away. He snagged his beaten-up corduroy ball cap and covered up his receding hairline to make himself look like he was closer to thirty than forty. The action seemed to have a fortifying effect on him as he considered the day's tasks. "We can wait till Ricky gets in. I want to re-seal the ductwork coming off the kiln—we can get Melissa or Ricky to gather up the sap for us—and I want our water barrel full before we start. Any volunteers to hose down the fumes?"

"I don't reckon there's an easier way to do it?"

"Not until we get us a nozzle to spray it down for us the way I want. I don't have the knack for that kind of thing. Maybe I can get the smithy to do something about it; I don't know."

"What's the kiln for, anyway? I never got that figured before I got the boot."

"For roasting all this pyrite we've got stockpiled," Bill said. "There's sulfur in there, and it'll smoke off with enough heat and some bellows. Melissa, save the glass jars for the shop. You can put that in the plastic sour cream tub. I tell you Omar, it's a whole 'nother branch of chemistry, but if I ever figure out polymers, we got it made. That stuff's built to last."

"But what do you do with the smoke from the pyrite?" Omar asked.

"Oh, yeah. We catch that smoke in our fancy new lead chamber out yonder; that's when we can hose it down with water and some oxidized nitrogen. When it dews up, we've got middling-wrought sulfuric acid."

Omar crossed his arms and leaned up against the doorpost. "How do you make the oxidized nitrogen?"

"Burn stuff. The oxygen and the nitrogen are already in the air. Most fires will put out some in the smoke."

Omar nodded. "Pretty clever."

"Naw, folks were using this method three hundred years ago. The clever thing is that the oxidized nitrogen I use for this, I can also use to make the nitric acid."

"Sounds like it works pretty smooth."

"It's doggone wasteful. The chemistry books I've studied told of several ways, and I had to choose the worst one. I don't have fine-cut tools or stainless steel or pressure vessels or vanadium. I wouldn't even know where to get most of that stuff."

"When will we reload the old bullets for the old guns?"

Bill laughed. "Whoa, we're *way* off from that, yet. I've got enough brass stored up, and I reckon the Taylors have got the tools for it, but you'd need a primer you can touch off with a hammer, not a simple flint spark. I'd need to react mercury with nitric acid, and I don't exactly have mercury lying around. I don't have much of anything lying around since we've used up so much fighting the Greenbriers. Right now, let's just focus on getting the nitrogel stores back up."

If Bill didn't think a chemistry discussion this early in the morning was out of the ordinary, Melissa might have. Omar caught an askance look cast from her direction, but she said nothing.

"What, uh, what fighting against the Greenbriers?" Omar asked. A change in subject might not hurt.

"Yeah, you were gone for that, weren't you?" Bill said, taking a bite of breakfast and talking with his mouth half-full. "It's been a bad—"

A knock at the front door interrupted Bill and pulled his attention around the corner and down the hall.

"That had better not be a customer coming in before Ricky, that good-for-nothin' farmboy." Bill said, sliding back from his steaming pile of nearly untouched eggs. "I expect ten solid hours out of my apprentices, and if I have to get those hours on the back end—"

It wasn't a customer. It was Sam Chambers.

Which meant Bill wasn't the one chewing out, but the one getting chewed. "Look, I didn't forget about the water tower. I'll send one of the boys out as soon as—"

"It's not that. Is Omar up? I have to get him ready for the initiation."

Bill slapped his forehead. *The initiation!*

Sam Chambers tugged at the collar of the sports jacket he wore to clan meetings and special occasions as he waved at various townsmen and elder farmers coming into the relative cool of the clan meetinghouse. Most folks mocked the ostentation of the jacket and tie, especially on hot summer days like this, but Sam knew his role among the clan elders and what it took to maintain that role. Elvin always brought with him a gun or a sword and his narrow-eyed scowl as a way to establish his authority; Sam brought with him more intangible—but no less powerful—markers of authority: confidence, stability, diplomacy, and intelligence. A little sweat under the arms was a small price to pay for keeping the clan from slipping into illiterate barbarism.

He took quick note of the elders in attendance: Shane Bunton, the carpenter, known for his temper in quiet times and his cool head in danger; Job Brody, a mediocre farmer, as farmers go, but a crack shot; Clyde McDaniel, a wisecracker with a superstitious bent; Arnold Brody, the only man in town who could talk Elvin McDaniel back from a ledge. Hite Evans, a reticent fellow who only seemed to have a firm opinion when the weather came up. Then, of course, were the reverend and the watchman, who had firm opinions on everything. Many of the surrounding farmers and town elders were too busy, it looked like. Johnny Grierson, the crusty prospector a couple miles out in the backhills, hadn't even responded to the message sent out about the drifter's redemption and initiation. With so few elders present, with the addition of Miss Holland and a couple folks from that part of town, the backroom of the meetinghouse across town would serve their purposes well enough. Those that had come, Sam ushered into the hallway down the center of the "new" wing of the old high school. Sam followed the last of them into the meeting room on the inner side of the hallway. The three sides of the meetinghouse bracketed the empty courtyard right outside the windows. A nice, private ceremony.

Once everyone was seated, Sam took his place, adjusted a pair of scratched reading glasses he didn't really need, and began. "Do you, Omar Walking, swear to serve and protect the Tucker clan as long as you live? To obey our laws and submit to the elders? To join clansman and clanswoman alike in bonds of friendship, loyalty, duty, sacrifice, and generosity? To share in the wealth of all salvage—well, wait, strike that last part." Sam Chambers paused to make a note to amend the fifty-year-old pledge of allegiance. "To make war against our enemies and to do no harm to our friends? To employ yourself productively so as to never be a burden on the clan? To forsake your ubermenschian heritage and the bloody legacy of your species?"

"I do."

"Elders of the Tucker clan, you have met this man and reviewed his case. Are you willing to accept Omar Walking as a fellow clansman?"

"We are," the elders in the room murmured in assent.

"As the spokesman for the Tucker clan, I welcome you to our kinship. You will be tattooed as a reminder to us and to all other clans that you are, and will forever be, ours."

A smattering of applause erupted—enough to be polite. Folks had other business to attend to, and the non-elders were already leaving.

There was another small matter to attend to first, though.

"Miss Holland, if you would care to come forward?" Sam Chambers waved her up from where she sat at the back of the room.

Ella waited, looking about her as the last of the town Tuckers left. When only she and a bare minimum of clan elders remained, Sam cleared his throat and said, "Okay, Reverend, you have the floor."

The hook-nosed Reverend rose with all the gravitas due his station and addressed the sparse gathering as he would a packed congregation. "The clan faces many threats, for which we have a watchman to guard our borders and marshal our militia. Some threats, however, cannot be countered with a rifle or spear. Some are diseases of the body, for which we thankfully have Doctor Bernhard to safeguard us. And then we have diseases of the mind. It was a disease of the mind that seized the old world and twisted it into the fallen one we see today. It is a disease of the mind which lies dormant, waiting to spring up and infect us all, to divide us, to drive us to the same madness which consumed the ubermenschen.

"It was to protect against such diseases that the founders of our clan established the Strictures, and a Keeper to enforce them."

Elvin McDaniel rolled his eyes, already slouching in his seat towards the back of the room. Sam fought the temptation to do so himself and continued listening like a dutiful churchgoer.

"As my father before me taught me to keep the Strictures, so I will train a new Keeper to watch for heresy and corrupting thought in my stead. I have taken in Ella Holland as my apprentice. Any new reading materials, any news from the outside world, any contact with the nomads, will pass through her as it would through me. Her approval or disapproval will carry the same weight as my own words. If she invokes the Strictures, you must accept her judgment as you would mine, and to disobey her will carry the same consequences.

"And if she fails in her duties," the Reverend said as he turned his severe gaze from the elders to Miss Holland, "whether through negligence or betrayal to her oath, may God have mercy on her soul. Do you understand what I'm telling you?"

Sam wasn't sure if the Reverend had directed the question at Miss Holland or at the elders. Perhaps both. The office of the Keeper was, by design, one rarely considered and even more rarely discussed. It likely served the Reverend well to show everyone the Keeper still had teeth, lest the elders disregard the role completely. Sam was apt to buck the Strictures himself—the siren call of hidden knowledge pulled at his scholar's heart more strongly than most—but the clan had nearly banished a widow and her toddling son for what was almost certainly Keeper skullduggery.

No coincidence, then, that the girl who had come to Mrs. Daly's rescue now stood in front of them as the new Keeper's apprentice. Miss Holland knew something dangerous. The question was whether the girl was using this knowledge against the Reverend, or if the Reverend was using it against her. Sam had always thought of knowledge as power, but the Reverend seemed to think of it like a death sentence.

Normally, Sam kept a list of items to bring before the elders whenever he could get enough of them together to have a meeting, with the others itching to leave before he could see to all the pressing business. This time, however, he found himself stuck listening to one thing after another, wishing he were elsewhere, while other elders went on about matters he couldn't openly shrug off.

Elvin McDaniel, his floppy hat still on his head inside just the same as outside, gave his update on the hunt for the unbred-tamer who'd hit the Holland home. The strange fellow was gone, as far as anyone could tell, not that anyone could tell much. Not so much as a puff of breeze had cast them a scent of any sort in days, and he wasn't banking on a change in the weather to tell their noses anything new. The scouts and farmers had seen trifling unbred signs around the clan, but given the attack within the clan walls, the still-boiling feud with the Greenbriers, and the limited amount of nitrogel powder they had, Elvin recommended keeping up doubled roundswalks for at least another couple weeks.

It was a nuisance—but a necessary one, Sam had to admit.

When the meeting dismissed, Mr. Chambers left, crossed over the currently dry streambed that bisected the town, and made for his schoolhouse. When he finally arrived at his next engagement there, he found Ralph McDaniel working with a homemade mechanical compass and a chalked string for making lines.

When Sam broke the studious silence with his entrance, Ralph made straight for the framed slab of slate hanging on the wall as a chalkboard. Sam had dug that slab out of a mountainside by himself and dragged it into town years ago, when he first became schoolmaster. It had felt momentous at the time. He wondered when his young disciple would carve out his own chalkboard.

"Been workin' on the proofs you told me to, and for the life of me, I can't figure this one out," Ralph said.

"Well?"

"Well, I was wondering if you could help me."

"Did you draw it out like I told you?"

"Yes, sir."

"Still can't see it?"

Ralph shook his head.

Sam shrugged. "Well, keep thinking on it. You don't solve problems by giving up after one night's hard thinking. How do you suppose Bill Puckett invented his nitrogel?"

Ralph hung his head. "It's... mighty hard to think over at my house sometimes. I'm always afraid Pa's gonna get after me for something. I'm worried he'll up and tell me I can't go to school no—*any*more."

Chambers sighed. "It's okay, Ralph. I know you try, and I know you have a tough situation."

"I just can't keep up with it all. I'm supposed to keep up with the patrols, but also the garden, and caring for the horses. I've got to mend my boots on my own time. We had a day off, and Pa got after me for not playing soccer with the other guys. As if the other guys would want to have anything to do with me even if Pa let me hang out with them. Nigel's fine, but the rest... Ricky Brody thinks I'm a wimp, even though I've been in battle, same as him. *He* gets to apprentice for Bill Puckett, but me?"

Sam sat down next to Ralph. "When I was your age," he said, "the clan, as we know it, was still pretty young. Stability was... delicate. I had to learn that from an early age. I also dealt with other boys who didn't see me as a valuable member of the clan. It seemed like, even if I could shoot or use a spear, it only mattered that I could read well and do my figures. And that made me someone to be ignored at best, and ridiculed at worst. If it makes you feel better, most of them either change as they get older or die."

"Who says I'm not going to die before they do?"

"Ah, but what they don't realize is, the smart ones live the longest."

"But my pa is dead-set on keepin' me dumb."

"We can meet in the evenings if you like. After your day chores are done. You *are* a smart young man, Ralph. And smarts always win out over brawn. Don't you forget that. Diplomacy, democracy, reason, innovation: *that's* what made this country great in the past, and *that's* what will make it great again in the future. It's what will one day make you a leader in this clan." Chambers leaned back with a smile. "Which is why I won't tell you the answer to your proof problem."

Omar was pedaling on the foot-powered pump under the town's water tower when Ella joined him. "Need to rest a spell?" she asked.

"I'd take a break," Omar answered, dabbing his face with the back of his sleeve while rivulets of sweat streaked down his neck to disappear beneath his half-unbuttoned shirt. The black walnut ink of the fresh tattoo on his arm stood out red on his skin.

Ella took his place and leaned into the tattered foam of the backrest support. "I needed to talk to you about this," she said, pulling a ceramic talisman from her pocket as she started pedaling.

Omar examined the white chip. "This the same thing I left behind when they banished me?"

"The very one. It's got something to do with how the shadowers control other unbreds. Old-world technology. It chirps like a cricket whenever a shadower's close, even a dead one. Like a bee finding its hive, I guess."

"Wasn't chirpin' when Amos and me bagged the shadower general last winter."

"Yeah, well, I wonder if it don't do more than sniff out shadowers. Makes me wonder why the Reverend planted it in your travel pack when you was banished."

"He's the one who done that, huh?"

Ella didn't answer immediately—or directly, for that matter. "I've had the chip tucked into the back of my chester drawers ever since. Could just be the way the wind blows, but the screevlers hittin' my house, of all places..."

"You think the unbreds can sniff out that chip?"

Ella nodded, panting now as she toiled on the pedals. "If the Reverend wanted to get rid of the chip, he coulda just broken it, right? So, when he put it in your pack, was he tryin' to get rid of it, or was he tryin' to make sure you..."

"I wouldn't put it past him."

"Or maybe it's too dangerous to break."

"That little thing? Even packed with nitrogel, that chip wouldn't do more'n ring your ears if you took a hammer to it."

"All the same, I'd feel safer if we destroyed it outside of town," Ella said.

"'We?'"

"I don't want to do this by myself. What do I look like? Becky?" She got up from the seat.

Omar's eyes flicked up and down her figure before he caught himself and looked away. "I don't know how to answer—"

"Anyway, this business is all secret, and you can bet your britches I ain't bringing this to the Reverend. Which leaves you, and you need a break anyhow. Come on." Ella waved for Omar to follow her.

With the town surroundings under such close watch, a sentry at the western gate flagged them down and asked where they were headed. Out to do an experiment for Bill, and no, you can't come and watch, and yes, we'll be back in about a quarter hour, and yes, come looking for us if we're not back by then.

"You've got a knack for fibbing," Ella said once they were beyond earshot. "Sounding irritated so you don't have to stop and answer too many questions."

"That's because it *is* irritating," Omar replied. "It just so happens that it keeps our real reasons safe. A good fib always has some truth in it."

"Huh." Ella went silent as if pondering some amazing new revelation.

They went on together in silent fellowship until they reached Bill's proving ground out in the old town, where Omar looped a nylon rope over a tree branch and raised a steel weight Bill used for impact testing. Underneath it, Ella squared the white talisman on a flat stone and backed away. "Okay, Omar, let 'er go."

He released the rope holding up the weight. The heavy steel rang a bit as it bounced off the stone, sending the white chip rocketing into the grass. Ella scrambled into the foliage, rustling through the grass with her fingers until she found the chip. "Still in one piece. This thing's tougher than I thought."

"The stone's not quite flat. Put 'er right on that hump there in the middle," Omar suggested.

Ella squinted with one eye level to the plane of the stone. She nudged the chip a bit to the side. "Hoist your smasher a little higher, too." She backed up again and signaled Omar to drop the weight. The steel came crashing down, louder this time, with an audible crack and a puff of white powder as the chip crumbled.

"I think that got it," he said. "Didn't reckon it would—" He looked over from the white residue on the rock to Ella. She wasn't moving and wasn't looking his direction. "Ella?"

She fell to the ground.

"Ella." Omar scrambled over to check for a pulse and found it, a steady tap at her throat. He swept the hair away from her face and pried one eyelid open. An insensible iris stared up at nothing. Her breathing quickened, but her eye remained fixed. "Hey, wake up," Omar said, holding her face in his hands.

Her eyes opened, clouded with fear and confusion which slowly gave way to relief as she looked up at him. "Wh-what's going on?"

"Are you all right?" Omar asked before realizing he was too close and pulling back.

"I'm fine. I—" Ella shooed him away.

"You went down like someone had dropped a rock on you. Your head hurt?"

"A little, but not from falling, I think. Did you"—she looked around—"hear anyone... you know what? Let's get out of here," she said, rising to her feet. "Let's get back to town before that doggone thing does something else."

Ella hurried back towards the gate, and Omar followed, but not before scattering the remnants of the shattered chip into the grass with his foot.

Doctor Bernhard knocked at the door to gain admittance to Phil Holland's sickbed. "How you feelin'?" he asked.

"Lousy," Phil answered.

"Feverish?" Doctor Bernhard took out a jar of his garlic-and-honey extract and gave it a vigorous shake, ignoring the young boy who poked his head through the doorway. The doctor set a small metal pendulum up on the dresser next to the bed.

Phil shook his head. "My stomach hurts."

"You don't say," the doctor said, touching Phil's head with the back of his hand, then pressing a hand against Phil's chest as he flicked the small pendulum and counted softly as the metal ball swung back and forth. "You been eating like I told you? Drinkin' your garlic?"

"Yeah. But last time I took a crap, it felt like I was rivin' in twain. I wonder if I ain't pulled a stitch or two."

Doctor Bernhard leaned over and lifted Phil's shirt, then carefully undid the bandages wrapped around his middle. The stained shroud lifted to reveal the ugly scar bristling with black sutures.

The doctor sighed. The harsh red blossom of infection radiated out from the wound.

A young boy gasped from the doorway.

When he was done with his geometry exercises, Ralph McDaniel hurried home to finish his chores before his father noticed any discrepancy between his academic interests and his household duties. He tended to the chickens beside the house as the last patrol came in to give their report to the watchman. The creak of his father leaning back in a rocking chair out in front came before the clomp of boots on the front porch. Ralph peeked around the corner. His father sat stitching a pocket torn loose earlier that day, waiting to hear the report from the patrol leader—in this case, Amos Taylor.

Amos removed his hat from his head. "There's been some stuff going on out there, no doubt," he explained. "We spotted some unbreds here and there, but they're acting really skittish. Victor Fillmore says he's seen traces of humans, but it's all mixed up with unbred tracks. I don't see how, but this drifter has a pack of unbreds working for him."

"Amos, I want you to give notice to the next roundswalk to shoot anyone, and I mean *anyone*, they spot wandering around these woods. I don't know how he's done it, but this feller's as dangerous as they come."

"Sir, mind if I do a little thinking out loud?" Ralph heard Amos ask.

"Go ahead," Elvin said with the kind of easy open-handedness Ralph rarely heard from his father.

Ralph pulled the rusting wire fence serving as a gate back into place and turned from the chickens in the yard to peek at the two warriors on the front porch. Still shy of seventeen, Amos Taylor stood before the watchman as handsome and confident as ever—the crush of every girl in the clan and the envy of every boy. But he looked harder now, less prone to smile, and quicker with a cutting word. *Understandable*, Ralph thought, considering how he'd lost his younger brother.

"I wonder if we shouldn't try to catch this guy and figure out how he's done it. Tamed the unbreds. If we could do it ourselves, we'd never have to worry about unbred attacks ever again, *and* we'd have a weapon to keep any nasty jaspers away from our territory forever."

Ralph didn't hear his father answer for some seconds. "Sounds a mite risky to me," Elvin said presently. He pulled a thread through the next stitch on the pocket. "I'm not sure all the elderfathers would go along with the notion either. But I like your gumption."

"Just a thought, sir. And—I'd like to sign up for the next roundswalk."

"Things must be moving slow at the gunsmithy with your master laid up and all. How's he faring?"

Amos looked at his feet. "An infection's set in. Doesn't sound good."

"I'm sorry to hear that. But in the meantime, I could use an extra hand on the roundswalks. Maybe you could tag along with me sometime. Learn a few of the watchman's tricks."

"I might like that, yeah."

"I ain't tryin' to poach you from the apprenticeship. Just—with the way things are right now, with the Greenbriers, and the unbreds, and low-down drifters running around... you know how it is."

"I get your meaning, sir. Whatever the case, I wouldn't mind taking up some watchman-like skills where I can."

Chapter 6

In Which Mr. Puckett Considers a New Business Opportunity

T he highway passing through the area cut a swath through the nigh-impenetrable woods, and though the stubborn shoots of spry young trees had encroached on the cracked asphalt from both sides and into the median, the road provided enough of a break in the terrain to allow for lookout points on the artificial cliffs overlooking the road. Three people manned one such lookout under the shade of a tattered billboard proclaiming a lawyer's willingness to represent whoever laid eyes on him.

Amos paced through the underbrush atop the cliff, as he had done since he and Omar and the watchman's boy, Ralph, had arrived. For an occupation so dangerous, most roundswalking duty was taken up by waiting and brain-crushing boredom.

"There's a radio tower or something way down south of here," Amos said, shading his eyes and peering at the far-off steeple jutting up from the hills.

"We're already a mile out from town," Omar said. He lay leaned up against a tree, a cushion of moss covering the rock beneath him, a floppy hat pulled down over his eyes as if he were napping. "Ain't no cause to get out that far."

"You're a lazy son-of-a-gun, you know that?" Amos said.

"My motto is 'Work smarter, not harder.'"

"Yeah, well, that radio tower's to the south," Amos said, as if the mere direction were enough to explain his reasoning.

"I ain't followin' you."

"I'm not saying we need to head out there right now, Omar. No need to get all huffy about it. Sheesh."

"No, I mean I don't know why it matters there's a tower to the south."

"Oh. Well, that's Greenbrier territory, that direction."

"Y'all didn't care this much about Greenbriers two months ago."

"Ain't nobody told you yet?" Ralph McDaniel said, incredulous.

Omar shrugged. "I just heard there was fighting."

"The Greenbriers attacked us." Amos turned to face Omar. His voice was a banjo string wound too tight. "Raped, tortured, and killed our clansmen. They got my little brother."

Omar sat up, lifting his hat. "I'm sorry to hear that."

"And if Greenbriers weren't enough, now we've got this unbred-taming drifter on top of everything. The more warning we can get, the better, is all I'm saying."

"Hmm. Maybe we'll ask the watchman when—wait, you smell that?" Omar went rigid.

The three lookouts turned east, squinting into the sun as the distant foliage in and around the highway stirred. The stirrings gradually resolved themselves into the dark shapes of men, animals, and pedal-powered vehicles—nomads.

When the caravan had reached shouting distance, Amos hailed them. "How's the road?" he called out to the mounted caravan guards, who were always the first people you addressed when opening up communication with a nomad clan on the road.

"Not bad," the apparent head of the guard answered. "Who goes up there?"

"Tuckers. You're about a mile out yet."

"Would you mind riding in with us? We've got some ride-alongs wanting to see your powdermaker as soon as they can."

"Sure." Amos waved at Ralph and Omar. "Let's go."

"You two go," Omar said, his eyes flicking to the distant cell tower to the south. "I'll keep a watch out here."

Melissa Daly stood on the palisade, looking into the sagging, overgrown ruins of the old town and the forest that had overtaken it. It had become something of a ritual for her. Little Earnest walked around the ladder below, whacking various weeds with a stick he'd found. Folks didn't care to ask her what she was doing all alone on the wall these last few weeks since her husband had been killed, and she didn't care to answer. As long as she stayed out of trouble, maybe things would work out.

"Mrs. Daly?" a voice asked her from behind.

"Ewwa!" Little Earnest cried. He had taken quite a liking to Miss Holland in the time since Ella had redeemed both Melissa and her anklebiter.

"What's the matter?" Melissa asked, turning to look down at Ella.

"Nothing's wrong," she said, but her brow remained knitted with care. "Just wanted to see how you're doing." She climbed up to stand next to Melissa on the palisade walkway.

"How's... how's your pa doin'?"

If Melissa was guessing, she'd guessed right. Ella's face screwed up. "Oh, Melissa, he's taken an infection. Doctor Bernhard's got him eating garlic by the fistful, but I don't think... if I lose him, I'll be the last one out of my first family left. I—I love my step-mama, and Clive and Margaret both, but..."

"Whatever happens, you'll always have a family, Miss Holland," Melissa said.

"I just... don't know why it never gets any easier."

The town bell rang, and a moment later came the news it bore, carried by the impromptu heralds running the streets. "Nomads! Nomads from way out east!"

Bill scratched at the tuft of hair clinging to what technically still qualified as his forehead as he finished up his notes on the latest iteration of the formula. He scrawled out an item on a long checklist of stages in the process he wanted to revisit. Circled at the top was *Nozzle for water spray*. Maybe he'd see what the Taylors could do about it, or maybe he'd play around with a length of pipe himself.

He rubbed his eyes, and for a moment, was still. Always a mistake in times like these. Never stop to catch your breath, because it'll always turn into more than a breath-catching. He sighed.

Poor Leah Holland. Soon to be a widow, it looked like. Seemed like widows and widowers were becoming awful common. He supposed a widower like himself, who hadn't yet given up on the idea of a second hitching, ought to be grateful for more eligible females. Yippee. He stood, thrusting his hands into his pockets with more force than necessary and kicked his chair back into place next to his desk. This was why a body had to keep itself busy, lest a fellow find himself sucked into the muck of melancholy and wistfulness.

He closed his book and grabbed the lantern by which he was working. He turned to find Amos standing in the door of his study. "Amos! You heard of knockin'?"

"I did. Nomad clan's come in, and they've got some ride-alongs wanting to see you."

"Ride-alongs? Where they from?"

"Out east. They say they're junkers from somewhere called New Ashburn."

"The heck? What do a bunch of trash-pickers want to go around sight-seein' for?"

Amos shrugged. "I figured you'd ask them. I'm just dropping them off. I need to head back out; I left Omar watching the highway out east."

Bill closed his book of notes, pulled down the roll-top cover of his desk, and locked it. "Let's go see what they want, then."

The ride-alongs stood out from the rest of the nomad clan in about every way a body could stand out. They were both too well-dressed for nomads used to a life on the road, yet also more stooped and spent than their far-ranging guides. The old canvas travel bags they carried were already lying in the dusty street, the riders heaving over the handlebars of the bicycles they rode into town. The nomads themselves kept their own distance from the low-down, landfill-living trash-pickers. The junkers all wore athletic shorts and sweat-stained t-shirts, which might have made sense given the work and the weather, but it only made them look even stranger.

There was a man, a woman, and a girl of apprenticing age, all following young Ralph McDaniel, who waved them over to Bill.

Bill took a moment to overcome his bewilderment before he squared the hunch in his shoulders and made himself presentable. "Howdy there. I'm Bill Puckett, the powderman. So...." Bill bypassed the half-erected nomad stalls on the edge of the clan main while still keeping a safe distance from the visitors and the landfill stench they surely carried with them. "What brings you all the way out here?"

The woman of the group, a sandy-haired lady old enough to be a respected matron but young enough to endure a long jaunt on the road, spoke first. "I'm Cora Compton. This here's Mayce Salazar, our archivist. And this is Mr. Salazar's apprentice, Jody Perkins." Cora gestured to the girl, who lowered her head so as to better obscure the discoloration that ran down one side of her face to her collarbone. Some kind of chemical burn or a birthmark, Bill guessed.

"We heard tell from the nomads of the chemistry operation you've got going on here. We talked to your watchman out at the east gate. He seemed to have a solid grasp of what you're doing with flash powder," Mrs. Compton said.

"You interested in buying?"

"We're interested in the making," Mr. Salazar said. "Mr. McDaniel told us you made everything from scratch. We figured he was puffing up the story for us a bit."

"What I can trust to get from elsewhere, I buy from the nomads, and that mostly amounts to the basic feedstock, baking soda, glycerol, and ethanol. Everything else, I make in-house."

Mayce Salazar looked confused. "We're not talking regular gunpowder here, though, right? You—you made nitroglycerin from scratch?"

"It's not the same formula exactly. But yeah, it's a lot. The whole thing takes..." Bill expelled a breath as he rubbed his neck, gauging what was safe to tell strangers. "At least sulfuric acid, nitric acid, other sundry nitrates."

Two jaws dropped in unison. "From *scratch?*" Mrs. Compton said.

"Well, like I told you, not *everything*. And it wasn't exactly a breeze to come up with all this stuff. I've got two whole different setups for making the sulfuric acid, depending on what stuff I've got on hand to work with."

"We've got some folks in our neck of the woods who'd very much like to learn your craft," Mr. Salazar said.

"Huh. I... I never thought about folks from other clans comin' in to apprentice. It'll have to go through the elders, but they've already okayed a scruffy young drifter..."

"Boss?" Ricky Brody cut in after giving the junkers a thorough looking-over. "You sure you want to let trash-pickers in on our doin's?"

Bill waved him off. "Ricky, ain't you got crap to shovel? If you're worried about losing your apprenticeship to some foreigner, keep your nose to the grindstone where it belongs." He turned back to the junkers as Ricky slunk off. "I reckon I could use the help, but you can see I've already taken in some apprentices from other families in the clan. And I'll warn you: I've hit some mighty big snags in the past few years, and what with spreading the business, don't be surprised if any learners you send end up doing more work of the bricklaying and nail-hammering sort."

"I'm sorry; I think you misunderstand," Mr. Salazar said. "It's not that we're not interested in sending you helpers, but we're really here because we're interested in something more... collaborative."

"How so?"

"We're chemists of a different sort. Coming from work in a landfill, we've had cause to become masters of different tricks—distillation in parts, filtering, salvage and reuse, spectroscopy, toxicology. We figured we could help you with your production in return for giving us a market for some of our stuff."

"What kind of stuff of yours would I need?"

"Well, what's your process for making nitric acid?"

"That's a trade secret." Bill shot a glance back at Ricky Brody, who hadn't quite gotten around to leaving just yet.

"Fine, fine," Mr. Salazar said. "But if I were to guess, I'd say that whatever you do, you tend to end up with a lot of oxidized nitrogen floating around, am I right?"

"Couldn't really find an easy answer to that."

"You realize too much nitrogen dioxide is very dangerous, right?"

"I always do that bit outdoors with a damp breathing mask."

Mrs. Compton frowned. "Wouldn't the water in your facecloth react with the NO_2?"

"The product is weak, and my breathing mask has an offset frame to keep it off my face."

"The point is, Mr. Puckett, if you want to ramp up your output, you need to start thinking of what chemicals you're letting out into the environment. We think we can help you."

"Yeah?"

Mr. Salazar came in again. "Have you tried running your nitrogen dioxide through a palladium mesh? Under pressure?"

"That's how the books say to do it, but palladium was a bit easier to come by when the books were written."

Mr. Salazar got a rascally look in his eye. "Where do you think all that stuff ended up?"

Bill found the rascally tone catching as his face lit up. "In the landfills."

"The smart 'uns in our clan done figured out how to salvage all sorts of valuable old-world minerals and metals—rare earths, platinum, iridium, palladium, tungsten, lithium. And we've spent years laying the pipework for the cleaning and processing. The problem is, 'til now, there's never been much of a demand for what we were pulling out of old circuit boards. 'Til now, it's been a hobby at best, a waste of time at worst."

Bill laughed. "That's what folks were sayin' about my experiments." He looked between Mr. Salazar and Mrs. Compton. "And you can make some sizable pressure chambers?"

"We got several old tanks from an old dairy farm. Once you outfit them with the right rubber seals, I expect they'll work fine."

While the adults talked, Ralph glanced at the girl out the corner of his eye. She was a pretty little thing, in spite of the spotty blemish on the side of her face. Maybe because of it. He blushed the moment he allowed the thought free rein, the red deepening when she looked up and noticed him staring.

When he looked up again to find her still glancing his way, he sauntered up in what he hoped seemed a relaxed manner and knew wasn't. "Uh, hey." Ralph raised an awkward hand in greeting before fiddling with the strap of the rifle slung over his shoulder. "Nice weather, ain't it?"

She dead-eyed him for what seemed like a full minute before she said, "The burn's from the leachate. It's whatever liquids get squeezed out of the landfill over time. Even after fifty years, can still be mighty potent."

"Ah," Ralph said. "I wasn't—"

"It's fine. Best to get it out of the way. It was my fault. Wasn't following protocol."

"So, uh, Jody, is it? What kind of apprenticin' work you do for the mister yonder?"

"After that disaster with the leachate, I mostly stick to the library."

Ralph jumped. "Wait, what?"

"Oh—my family's archivists. Or archeologists. Whatever. We preserve whatever historically valuable items we dig out of the landfills. Any knowledge material. Usually books."

"Out of—landfills? Is that possible?"

Miss Perkins's initial stiffness cracked. "Oh, you wouldn't believe what people would throw away back then."

"But it's been fifty years in a trash pit!"

Jody's eyes brightened at his astonishment. "Landfills are sealed, which makes them an anaerobic environment. Stuff inside stops decomposing past a certain point. When we open a new section, we find food in there you could eat." She crossed her arms, then added, stuttering, "N-not that we eat it. Not *everything* folks say about us junkers is true."

"And... books?"

"Literally tons of books. Mostly garbage. People liked to read bad romances, mostly. Don't quite know why. But we've got thousands of manuals, and textbooks, and classic literature—"

"And newspapers? Do those make it?"

Jody turned to face Ralph fully, making no effort to hide her burn. She threw her hands wide. "We've got *stacks* of them. Like new. Organized by date. We've found a few newspapers dated three months *after* the Outbreak."

Ralph's hands shot to his head. "What?! That's impossible! That means, even after the Pandemic, not only were folks still making newspapers—"

"They also had people still willing to dump their trash in landfills." Jody grinned from ear to discolored ear.

"And you preserve it all?"

"Painstakingly. My family has an honorable profession. Every day is like walking right into a picture of the old world."

A harsh voice shattered their conversation. "Ralph!"

Ralph jumped and moved away from the junker girl as if she'd suddenly burst into flame. He turned to face his father's stern gaze.

"Your job's to watch the newcomers, not jaw at 'em."

Ralph looked down, his cheeks the color of apples. "Yes, sir."

"Git on over here. We've got to check up on something outside of town," Elvin called to his son and walked off, his command hanging in the air behind him.

"Coming, sir," Ralph called. "Sorry, Miss Perkins. My pa—"

Miss Perkins picked up her canvas travel bag and began to move away. "I'd best be setting up camp, anyhow," she said. "I'll talk to you later." She cast a glance over her shoulder as she left, her burned side facing him. "Ralph."

Ralph watched her walk away. His rifle slipped from his shoulder without him much noticing.

Only his father's harsh command pulled him back to himself and away from her.

Bill paced. "If you've got the tools and the know-how, how come y'all ain't tried to do something useful on your own?"

"Some folks can't see past their own nose," Mrs. Compton said. "And those folks always wind up running the clan. The junker way of thinking is, 'Why make it when you can just dig out something better from the landfill? And if you can't find it in the landfill, you probably don't need it.'"

"It's not quite as bad as all that," Mr. Salazar said. "Mrs. Compton's husband is an aspiring pharmacologist. He's made himself some—"

Mrs. Compton kicked Mr. Salazar quiet.

"What?" Bill asked. "Made himself some what?" His voice raised in pitch despite himself.

"We were saving that last little bit for negotiation," Mrs. Compton said through gritted teeth. "We don't need to get everything out in the open just yet."

"A pharmacologist makes medicines, don't he? What kind of medicines he done?"

"Aspirin and penicillin," Mrs. Compton began. "But we'd have to insist on setting up all operations at our current site before—"

"I'll go wherever you want! Penicillin's an anti-bi-otic, right?" Bill said, stumbling over the unfamiliar word. "If you got any on you, I'll—"

"Bill, you ain't makin' any deals with nobody without the elders' say-so!" Elvin hollered.

"But what about Phil?" Bill hollered back, then turned again to Mrs. Compton. "I got me a hundred jaws from Omar, and a sick friend. Any penicillin you got handy—"

"Just a few grams' worth. Enough for three or four doses, nothing more."

"I'll pay for what you got."

Mrs. Compton sighed. "Can I see him?"

Doctor Bernhard ushered both Bill and Mrs. Compton into the Hollands' home, but by the time they'd entered, Ella had caught wind of the rumor, too. The whole household had.

"Did you get medicine for Papa, Uncle Bill?" Margaret asked. "Is he gonna be all right?"

"Get these kids out of here," Doctor Bernhard snapped, though he himself trembled with excitement only tempered by a fifteen-year-long career of losing patients despite his best efforts. He didn't open the door to Phil's sickbed until Ella had shooed her half-siblings safely away.

Phil was already pale and feverish, but he had enough sass left in him to wonder aloud if the doctor were taking in an apprentice.

"Let's not get our hopes up, but there's some nomads coming through town who might have some medicine for you." They lifted Phil's bandages to see tomato-red skin blossoming around the wound. "I give him a day or two before he goes septic," Doctor Bernhard said.

"Give him a dose right away," Mrs. Compton said. "It will be enough to fight the infection, but he'll need a stronger dose. For that, we want some sort of agreement that whatever factory gets set up, we set up at our settlement in New Ashburn. We can still split the profits or products evenly, but our council won't let our equipment—"

"I'll agree to it. Get you a heap of penicillin and get on back here as soon as you can."

"*The elders* will see whether or not Bill's going *anywhere*," Elvin said. "We can meet right after this."

Mrs. Compton scratched her forehead. "Mr. Salazar can head back right away, but it'll be at least two weeks before he can return. I'll need to stay and help ration the antibiotics."

"I can do whatever needs to be done," Doctor Bernhard said.

Mrs. Compton shook her head. "The body won't take in the full dose of penicillin. If you want him to survive the two weeks it'll take to get his next dose," she said with grim certainty, "he'll have to drink his own piss."

The elders didn't bother sitting down in the circle of folding metal chairs. They paced in and out of the shafts of light that streamed in the windows above the bleachers, milling around the gymnasium, restless and testy. None more so, apparently, than Doctor Bernhard. "This is ridiculous," he said. "I've got a patient with a life-threatening infection, and now that we've got the medicine to treat him, I have to wait for the elders' say-so before I can do my job. You're putting a clansman's life at risk, McDaniel."

Elvin stood leaned up against the far wall with his arms crossed. "I put a clansman's life at risk every time we go to war, Doc. I'm fine doing business with foreigners, but they're taking our powderman with nothing but a pinky-promise to trade for him. We're walkin' a ridge without lookin' where we put our feet."

"Whoa, we're gettin' the cart clear out of sight of the horse." Bill Puckett raised a finger. "Who said they're taking me?"

"That Compton woman did," the watchman said, unmoving. "Any medicines they trade us would be part of the powder deal. Meaning not for sale."

"Fair enough, Elvin," Sam said. "Let's talk about it. What's so wrong about striking up a trade partnership with New Ashburn?"

"No." Reverend Brody swept the very notion aside with his hand as if clearing a messy table. "The Founders' Strictures forbid it."

Sam ran a hand through his hair. "Reverend, I respect what you're trying to do, but we have a democracy here. You can't invoke the Founders without an explanation whenever you don't like the direction the clan's taking."

"The Strictures warn against too much contact with the outside world. To have a clansman *living* in a foreign clan is to expose him, and thereby the rest of our clan, to ubermenschen ways. If we take a common course with them, we put everyone in danger."

"So, what's the alternative, then? We cut off all contact? What do we do with the nomads? Where do you think they get their wares from, huh? Are we going to start asking every caravan that comes through whether they've done business in New Ashburn?"

"What about the medicine?" Bill Puckett hollered above the din. "We need to decide what to do about the medicine before we—"

"I say we keep out all the nomads except for the Schneiders," Elvin said. "We're acting like we ain't stretched ourselves too far when we likely stretched ourselves too far a long time ago. We've been free-wheelin' with foreigners in the middle of a goddamn *war* with the Greenbriers. We never did track down that eyeless drifter. We initiated that Omar Walking without a full vote, we took in these junkers without giving two thoughts about it, and now, we're fixin' to give up our powderman and his nitrogel. I'm with the Reverend. You ask me, he should've 'voked the Strictures a lot sooner."

"Now, see here," Bill Puckett said, his face reddening. "I don't cotton to all the nasty rumors been a-stickin' to my apprentices, Omar in particular. And I don't like being ordered around like I don't got no say about what I do with my own doggone business. And that junker woman offered to stay behind to help my friend. Seems to me foreigners been doin' us quite a bit of good so far."

"Oh, sure." Elvin sneered. "Let's say, outta six foreigners, only one of them turns out to be a cutthroat. Unless there's only five folks in New Ashburn, we've got ourselves a problem."

"Okay, one: you're making up numbers." Sam waved his finger in the air. "Two: that isn't how odds work. What's really going on here is that *some* people are afraid of progress. It's all fear-mongering isolationism, is what it is. Open a history book and tell me when that's *ever* worked out in the long run."

"Hold on a second." Arnold Brody, the butcher, spoke up. "We're gettin' distracted by ideas, and there's nothing like ideas to keep us from figuring practical notions. Like, what happens if the New Ashburn-ians pal up with the Greenbriers instead of us?"

The room went silent.

"If these junker guys made it out to us," Arnold continued, "who's to say they can't make it out to the Greenbriers? And what would happen then?"

"The Greenbriers would gut any travelers headed out their way."

"Oh, that's hooey, and you know it, Elvin. If they were that dumb, we would have wiped 'em out by now," the butcher said.

"What's your point?" Shane Bunton, the carpenter, asked.

"Not sure I've got one yet, but I suppose if the Greenbriers makin' war against the junkers was a dumb move, it would be a dumb move for us as well."

"No one is talkin' about starting a war."

"Then what are we talking about, Elvin?" Sam asked.

"We're talkin' about medicine for *my* friend," Bill Puckett broke in, nearly shouting. "They've brought penicillin, and they're waiting to see if we agree to their terms. We need to decide *now* if we agree to their terms, or if we need to talk things over more. But *my* friend and *your* clansman is sick, and if we don't get him the medicine *today*, the elders ain't nothin' but a brood of clucking hens."

"Bill's right," Sam said, exhaling slowly. "We need to reach some sort of agreement with the junkers."

"How do you expect them to hold up their end of the bargain once they've got Bill?" Elvin asked, his arms still folded. "Just trust 'em, I reckon?"

"No," Sam said, his voice teetering on the edge of exasperation. "We treat them like any common-sense businessman: We make a trade. If they take Bill on loan, they have to leave collateral."

"Co-what?"

"A hostage. Someone important, or the son or daughter of someone important. For now, the hostage can be Mrs. Compton. If they want her back, they have to give us someone equally important to them, or useful to us, or else give us Bill back in return. Under no circumstances will either clan have sole sway over the other's clansman. Is that a fair enough addendum to answer the junkers?"

Nearly all hands went up in unison.

When the elders accepted the junkers' proposal with the added stipulation of exchanging a hostage, Mr. Salazar and Mrs. Compton went to confer by themselves. It did not take long before they returned, agreeing to the arrangement. Mrs. Compton would of course stay to administer the penicillin to Mr. Holland, and as a further show of good faith, Miss Perkins would remain to assist her, as well as tend to what counted as the Tucker library. Their only insistence was that if Mr. Salazar was to return to New Ashburn and leave his companions, Bill Puckett had to go with him.

Bill immediately agreed, and his apprentices not out patrolling helped him pack his essentials. Once he had a better idea of what the junkers had on hand, he'd send for more of his specialized equipment and stocks. He said a quick, tearful goodbye to his daughter Sophie, saying that he had to go save his friend. Ella waved goodbye to her not-quite master, not-quite uncle with her own tears of both sadness and hope before going to help Sophie cook dinner.

Mr. Salazar and Bill departed soon after, and the Tucker elders and surrounding clansmen scattered to complete their put-off tasks. Reverend Brody stalked at the edge of the meetinghouse, staring at the two junker females.

Chapter 7

Truth and Other Dangerous Infections

E lla and the Reverend stared across the church room at each other. When the town had been much more populous, this building had been the high school. Now, with fewer people in need of advanced education, but with everyone in the clan needing a shepherd, the high school gymnasium was the church room, while the little steepled church building on the other side of town had become Sam's domain. Motes of dust meandered through the natural rays of sunlight coming down through the smudged windows high above, and the lone voices of the Keeper and his apprentice echoed in the solemn emptiness. Though once a gymnasium, the space now bore all the sanctity of a cathedral.

"I don't want to spend any longer on this than necessary," the Reverend said. "You will watch the Compton woman and make sure she sticks to her tasks and speaks to no one but you, your father, or the doctor. Don't ask her what she knows about the unbreds, the plague, or the breedcrafting."

"What about the windows Tuckers have in their minds? How'd I see what your pa heard years ago?"

"I told you not to ask me about that," the Reverend snapped.

Ella sighed. "How am I supposed to keep dangerous truths out of people's heads if I don't know what's dangerous and what's not?"

"It's evil. Don't go looking into it, don't ask questions about it, and never, *ever* try to do it again."

"I didn't *try* to do *it* at all. I don't even know what *it* is." Ella threw up her hands in frustration. "And what makes it evil in the first place?"

"I want you to treat the mere *curiosity* about what happened to you and my father as you would the sound of a screevler at your door. Don't even look."

"What if these junkers know about this sort of thing, and they spread the idea among the Tuckers? I won't know they're doing anything wrong!"

The Reverend paused for half a second. "Most ubermenschen children got the same sort of man-made breeding—protection against different diseases, more smarts, a few special tricks the body could do when given medicines we obviously don't have anymore. Some ubermenschen were designed for more special purposes. Many of the Tuckers are descendants of that special class. That's all you need to know."

"Would the junkers know that?"

"We must hope to God they don't. No one must know. Not them, not your fellow Tuckers, not even you."

"But you just told me—"

"The first thing you need to know about being a Keeper," the Reverend said, interrupting her, "is that you must hold yourself to the same truth as everyone else."

"Even if it ain't true?"

"Reminding yourself it isn't true is how you let something slip. The Pandemic happened; there's no way to deny that. But *we* are the survivors. Even if the rest of the unmodified humans were scoured away, it only makes us *more* special. What you *think* you know is nothing more than a passing stench in the face of our sacred truth: our clan carries the banner of unsullied humanity against the ubermenschen's war of extermination. *That* is what you will tell Mrs. Compton. We are a clan of purebred humans. We tolerate ubermenschen, but we will not tolerate any ubermenschen twisting of history. No superior race nonsense, no pining after the old world, and not a breath about the so-called extinction of naturally stocked humans. That is the story you will tell her."

"Won't she know better?"

"I don't care what she knows. This is what you will tell her, and this is the story she'll have to stick to if she wants to keep this shameful treaty with us. Same with that drifter and the adulteress you've decided to shelter."

"I don't know what Omar does or doesn't know, and I'm pretty sure Melissa doesn't know anything." Ella leaned forward with a hard look at the Reverend as she spoke of Melissa.

"I have my reasons to suspect every one of them." The Reverend paced, his hands behind his back. "The junker woman, the drifter, and the whore are *your* responsibility. If you want to protect them, and thereby this treaty, and thereby your own father, forget the evil truth, and then teach them to do the same."

You make me responsible for protecting secrets, but you hoard them like a miser yourself, Ella thought.

"We shall meet again, and you will tell me what you have observed from those you have been tasked to watch over," the Reverend said, having regained his composure in the stretch of silence that had passed through the space between them. "Now go. You wouldn't want to miss anything important."

Reverend Brody was a busy man, despite what many of the clan's working folk may have thought. Sure, he delivered sermons once a week. But nearly everybody in the clan worked more than one job. The Fillmores brought in meat and forage from the woods, but they were also the tanners. Shane Bunton did rough and fine carpentry and also fletched arrows. The Taylor smithy reclaimed scrap, and Phil Holland was the clan's most skilled machinist and gunsmith before his injury laid him low. The miller was also the baker; the farmers were all the keepers of the outer posts; the schoolmaster was the diplomat, and so on. Everyone did patrol shifts, everyone helped with the harvests, and everyone helped salvage material from the old town, bit by bit.

Reverend Brody's job was no exception. He differed from the rest in that most of his work went unseen. It was his unseen work that harried him as he slipped out the back door of the "new" wing of the meetinghouse. He crossed the wide open space beyond the meeting-house—it had once been an intersection, and the automobiles of the past had required outrageous amounts of space—and passed by his younger brother's slaughterhouse barn on his way to Doctor Bernhard's house. It was not by accident that Arnold lived so close to the Bernhards. He had wanted to study doctoring under Dr. Bernhard Sr., long ago, but he didn't have the knack for book learning. The reverend remembered how crushed his brother had been when Bernhard Sr. had dismissed him from his apprenticeship. Arnold had taken up as the butcher then, serving as a surgeon's assistant whenever the need arose, but nothing more than that.

Were it not for the reverend's squeamishness around the general messiness of the profession, not to mention the greater importance of his own, Reverend Brody might have made a fine doctor himself. He'd gone through many of Doctor Bernhard's books to check for dangerous knowledge. In some ways, simply based on the problematic pages he'd ripped from Bernhard's anatomy textbooks, the reverend knew *more* than the good doctor about the breedcrafted body and how to treat it.

The doctor likely knew, or at least suspected, what the Tuckers really were. He was smart. His books said nothing about adult teeth regrowing, and yet, scarcely two months since Deek Evans took an arrow through the jaw while battling the Greenbriers, here he was with three new pearly whites poking through his gums. The old books mentioned many diseases common to "the unmodified." And yet the Tuckers, even the half-breeds, never suffered from any such ailments. There were many blood types among the unmodified, yet the Tuckers, according to Dr. Bernhard, Sr., were uniformly O negative.

Most Tuckers, even the reverend's own brothers and sisters, didn't know any of this or never paid it a second thought. The doctor, however, surely knew. But he'd never aired his knowledge, probably, the reverend guessed, because he was smart. He'd likely remembered the "ubermenschen" the clan had banished in a purge back when they were all young and anti-ubermenschen fervor was at its strongest, back when the clan was dominated by the fearsome Paul McDaniel and the quieter, but no less ruthless, Sal Brody—the reverend's father. The clan had even expelled the half-breeds, though they almost certainly knew nothing. It had taken significant compromise to allow them to settle up at the mine and not wipe them out entirely. The doctor would remember all that. Reverend Brody certainly did.

Bernhard's wife answered the door, her familiar hair shot through with early gray.

"Helen. Is Doctor Bernhard—"

"Jake's out back." She jerked a thumb over her shoulder. She'd known him when they were younger, and she never responded to his formalities in kind. Or kindly.

He nodded and, as awkwardly as every time they spoke, took his leave and passed her by. Doctor Bernhard was tending to his poppy garden. The greenhouse he used to keep his poppies growing all year long stood nearby, its roof open for the summer. Bernhard was on his knees, pulling weeds.

"Can I help?" the reverend asked.

"If you don't care to soil your church clothes. Sure."

The reverend kneeled and got to work. Helping would make what he had to say go down easier. He still had a hard time getting it out. "How are your patients?"

"I've got to pull an ingrown toenail this afternoon. I've used up most of my laudanum on Phil Holland, and I don't have another section of poppies to harvest for at least another week. I've been... agitated."

The opium was a powerful anesthetic, and Bernhard's ability to grow, extract, and concentrate it could have made him a rich man. But he'd inherited the Hippocratic instinct and refused to put up for market a substance so dangerous. It was hard enough to produce it just for the clan's needs, given how much space the doctor had used to grow the flowers. It probably didn't help that, likely by testing dosages on himself, the doctor was addicted to the stuff.

Having a drug addict in the clan would be grounds for banishment in a normal set of circumstances, but no one, least of all Reverend Brody, was about to suggest they banish their only doctor. It was one of many such calculations a discerning elder had to make.

"I wanted to ask you about the poor gunsmith. What are Mr. Holland's chances, in your professional opinion?"

"Now that we've got him on penicillin?"

"Yes."

"As long as we can get that second shipment of antibiotics in time, he should make it."

"And if it doesn't get here?"

"The infection will look like it gets better, but it'll come roaring back. When you douse a fire, it ain't safe until the coals is wet."

"So we have to have that second shipment?"

Doctor Bernhard shifted to the next plant with a grunt. "That's right."

Reverend Brody plucked some crab grass from the soil. "What are the chances Mr. Holland survives until the junkers return?"

The doctor paused, looking over at the reverend with keen eyes. "As long as they get here within two weeks, I'd say his odds are good."

"Certain?"

"Well, no, not certain."

The reverend chose his next words carefully. "I pray every day for Mr. Holland's recovery. But I also pray we will not be forced to treat with ubermensch junkers who aim to lead us astray."

"That sounds like God's area of expertise. Not mine," Doctor Bernhard said, his voice growing chilly.

"I'm merely asking you whether, given his grievous injuries, it would be so surprising if he slipped away in the night?"

Doctor Bernhard stood. "I'm a doctor. I can't guarantee anything except that I'll do everything I can to cure my patients, up to and including selling my soul to the devil himself. Have a nice day, *Reverend.*"

As Reverend Brody left, he supposed he hadn't expected the meeting to go much better than it had. There had never really been any love lost between the two of them. Of course Doctor Bernhard had interpreted his question in the most uncharitable way possible, as if the reverend would *actually* suggest such a thing!

He needed advice, and he also needed to go check in on someone. He headed north and back east, his eyes fixed securely on the pavement as he walked. Summertime grasses wormed their way through cracks in the street, and no amount of grazing or treading could keep the weeds from forcing their way into the tiniest crevices, like a thief's fingers finding a gap in the window. He might work that illustration into his next sermon: beware the weeds of foreign ubermenschen, which, having taken root in our soil, will grow and drive us apart, forcing open our divisions and making us weak. Speaking of infection might not have its intended effect. Perhaps he could speak on addiction.

A host of worries assailed him. On the face of it, it looked to come from the junkers, their greed, and whatever dangerous ideology they carried with them like fleas on mangy dogs. But that was just the fruit and leaves pushing past the surface. At the root, it was Miss Holland. She was the one sheltering the drifter. She was the one who'd kept the hussy and her—his—bastard child on the clan's dole, always threatening him like a sword hung over his head.

He cursed himself, as he did almost every day, for his weakness. Melissa had seemed so helpless at the time, married to a nasty rascal of a man, bearing scars and bruises everyone noticed but no one dealt with. The watchman would go straighten the fellow out from time to time, but it never stuck. Her husband had always denied touching her, and in the end, she'd always confirmed it.

He'd tried to help the wretch. Eventually she'd confided in him, told him Bert Daly hit her often, that he blamed her for not producing children, that he either didn't know how or didn't care to make her feel like a woman in bed...

The reverend had fallen for her. Stupid. She'd tried, as soon as she was able, to get her husband banished. But now she was pregnant, and folks would wonder. Folks would talk. He couldn't have come out as a married man, let alone as the reverend, to stand as a witness at a time like this. Go to the watchman, he'd said.

Oh, but the watchman didn't understand, she'd answered. The watchman thought she was a liar. The girl who cried wolf. He thought Bert and me were both scum; we were both leeches on the clan. If the watchman banished Bert, he'd banish me, too.

As the reverend had listened to it, he'd realized that he'd been tricked. She hadn't cared for him. She'd needed someone to keep her fed in the lean times, and she'd needed someone who couldn't expose her without risking his own neck. Someone like him.

That Miss Holland was being used just as callously didn't matter; what mattered is that Miss Holland didn't see the danger of half-breeds like Melissa Daly, or of drifters like Mr. Walking, or of the seductive deals offered by foreigners.

Reverend Brody knocked at the door of a small house next to the northern wall. An old man answered it.

"Father." The reverend bent his head forward.

"Oliver."

"Are you well?"

"I'm fine."

"Do you need help with..."

"Everything's fine. Come inside. You sound like you need something," his father said.

"Have you painted over the message?"

"Not yet."

"May I see it?"

"Go ahead." Sal Brody gestured to his bedroom.

Reverend Brody walked into the bedroom and immediately saw the claw-scratched taunt on the wall: *I require sacrifice.* "This is the same one who attacked you and Miss Holland earlier, I suppose. It would explain why it went for the Holland home first."

"I'm sure of it. It's getting stronger. How is Miss Holland as your new apprentice?"

"I'm not confident in Miss Holland's commitment to her vows as a Keeper. She does not yet understand fully what it means to hold this position. The very impulse that led her to save you from the shadower cabal is now leading her to subvert my authority as a Keeper. I can see it already. She's more loyal to individuals than the clan."

"You should have killed her," the old man said, rubbing his hooked nose.

The reverend bristled. "I'm not a monster."

The old man shrugged. "What's done is done. But you can't complain about her not being ruthless enough when you don't have it in you either."

"What I need," Reverend Brody said, "is to decide what do to about her *now*, and what to do with these two junker women we have in our midst. Two *weeks* among us is too long. And if Mr. Puckett sets up a factory with them... it's a matter of time until..." He shook his head.

"It always was. The world changes. It gets bigger. Harder and harder to keep the forbidden knowledge out."

"Then why did we ever start such a scheme, if it were hopeless?" the reverend asked.

"You know. You know just as well as I do, Oliver. We either put them in the garden with the forbidden tree and tell them not to taste the fruit, or we hide the tree from them and don't tell them the fruit exists. We all decided we would last longer with the second choice."

"But to think that we've... that *I've* failed so soon. The junker women are sure to violate the Strictures before the others have even returned from their trip east. Wait." The reverend froze in the grip of a sudden inspiration. "I know what to do."

Chapter 8

Doves and Serpents

Ralph shoveled the beans and potatoes into his mouth almost before his family had finished saying grace. His father had yet to take a bite. His little brothers and sisters were giving him sidelong glances without asking the question they knew was coming.

"What's your hurry?" Ralph's father asked, his small eyes squinting in that wary way of his, his spoon hanging halfway between his plate and his mouth.

"Tutoring with Mr. Chambers," Ralph answered. "We've had to move the time around since the junkers come in. His day's been taken up working with that archivist apprentice on his—"

"That girl with half her face painted a different color from the rest of her?"

Ralph winced at his father's disapproving tone. "Yes, but—"

"I don't want you hangin' around her, understand? I can abide that Compton woman staying behind to strain mold dust or whatever outta Mr. Holland's pee. But gettin' a scribe to go over our books, overstandingly a trash-picker from who-knows-where... I don't cotton to it. And I won't have my boy gettin' his head filled with junker notions. It's bad enough I went along with that schoolteacher's mollycoddlin.'"

"She works with Mr. Chambers during the daytime. That's why we moved my tutoring time. I don't need to see her at all if you don't want me to."

Elvin stuffed the spoonful of dinner into his mouth and stabbed his empty spoon at Ralph, his mouth still half-full. "You done your chores? Gave the horses a brush-down?"

Ralph nodded.

"I'll be up until you get back. Don't keep me up late."

Jody Perkins was walking along Sam Chambers' wall of books in his inner sanctum when Ralph came over for tutoring. Of course she was there, and Ralph knew full well the hell he would pay if his father found out his lie.

Jody didn't seem to notice him entering. She tapped a piece of chalk in the air along the spines of various titles on the shelf before making a mark on the slate she cradled in her other arm. Then her slender arm raised again to catalogue Sam's collection, her lips moving silently as if chanting some sacred invocation.

Ralph came to himself and cleared his throat. "Hey, there, Miss Perkins. Is, uh, Mr. Chambers around?"

Jody turned fully toward him and offered a simple smile. "He ran out to fetch something. What is it you want him for?"

"I come to Mr. Chambers sometimes for tutoring. I thought maybe, since we've got some out-of-town folks around, I might do a little studying up on what you and Mrs. Compton do."

Jody shrugged and set down her slate. "Mr. Chambers has me lookin' at his library, countin' and sortin' and such. It's not a bad way to pile things up if you've got a small collection you plan to use by your lonesome, but much bigger, and you've got to get yourself a system. If you plan on havin' people *read* your books and get any use out of 'em, you've got to separate things that are useful *now* from what might be useful to our grandchildren. Mr. Chambers has got six manuals on different vacuum cleaners, and underneath them, he's got an illustrated book for kids on how a bunch of different machines work."

Ralph gasped when Jody showed him the battered copy titled *The Way Things Work.* "I was wondering where that went!"

"See? That's why you need a system. That's a good book. It'd be a shame to lose it."

"You had a copy where you come from, huh? I never did understand the part about computers. Seemed like magic to me." He flipped through the book. "I was younger then, though."

"I always thought the basics of computers were real simple," Jody said. "Could be the archivist in me comin' out. All the old world ever did was figure out a system to organize a mountain of knowings. Nothin' magic about it."

"But they had computers what could talk to you like a person and read your mind, I heard. How's that got anything to do with organizing stuff?"

"My master, Mr. Salazar, told me, 'How do you eat a bullhusker? One bite at a time.' He meant you can take nearly any complicated thing, like talking or thinking, and break it down into small enough bits that any silly old thing could do it well enough to shake a stick at. Here—I'll show you. Give me those two books." Jody pointed at a couple old hardcovers next to Ralph.

He handed them over and watched her set them upright, side-by-side. Then she picked up a hefty old dictionary and set it up so the two smaller volumes overlapped it in a sort of V-shape. "You can see if you tip any of these books over, it won't be heavy enough on its own to tip over the big one. I have to tip over *both* books to get the big one to fall over. The old computer scientists called this a logic gate." Jody cleared her slate and drew a quick little table with Ts and Fs in the boxes. "The little books here are what you're puttin' in. These can either be true or false. The big book is what your computer or whatever's puttin' out. If your put-ins ain't both true, your put-out's always a-gonna be false."

"Wait—this is a little like the proofs Mr. Chambers had me practicing a while ago," Ralph said, his hand shooting up to his temple as he thought. "It's like... a statement, but with books falling over instead of words."

"Right." Jody pointed to the books and tipped the first two over. The dictionary tilted, then thumped over from its own weight. "This logic gate was called an AND gate, because it had to have this book *and* the other book falling over for the next statement to be true. But if you switch this big book out for a smaller one..."

Jody replaced the dictionary with a fourth book. "Then either of the first two books will be big enough to tip it over and keep up the logic chain. This is called an OR gate. 'Cause either this one *or* this one is all you need. There's a few other logic gates that do the same sort of thing. And if you decide to say 'one' and 'zero' instead of 'true' and 'false,' then you can start *counting* with logic. We're used to counting to ten because we have ten fingers, but computers need numbers broken down into smaller bites. Computers, in a way, only have two fingers for counting. Think about what we do with the numbers we use when we get to ten."

"Well, we have to move over and use a zero to hold our place. So... I reckon counting with ones and zeroes would be the same, right?"

"Right. Try it."

Ralph took the slate, and listed the numbers *0, 1, 10, 11,* pointing to each one as he counted. "Zero, one, two, three."

"You pick it up quick, Ralph," Jody said, looking up from the slate between them. "Can you write four?"

Ralph scratched *110*.

"Nope, not quite," Jody said. "You do need three digits, but it should actually be…" She erased it and started to write in the correct answer before Ralph asked to try again.

He wrote *100* on the board. "Is this right?"

"Got it."

Ralph set down the slate and blew out a lungful of impressed breath. "Mr. Salazar taught you all that?"

"He even had me make a simple calculator out of dominoes."

"What are those?"

"Adding machines."

"No, dominoes."

"Oh. Little ceramic blocks. Doesn't matter. If you string these logic gates together the right way, you can get 'em to add up ones and zeroes for you."

"Could you make a real computer? Or fix one up to work again?"

Jody shook her head. "Just because I know the basics, it don't mean I could make a real one. And anyway, what would I do with one? Folks back in the old days had a heap of uses for them, I guess, but the best use I can see is doing sums and keeping track of books and such, and I can do both just fine with chalk and slate. Most of the folks I know back home couldn't hardly care less what a computer's for."

"Do folks back home see much of anything your way?"

"Not many, no."

"I don't suppose, then, there'd be, uh, a lot of fellers back yonder for you to go a-courtin' with?"

"There's guys there, sure, but not a lot who'd put up with this ugly scar. They like as not think whatever got on me's catching."

"Miss Perkins…" Ralph swallowed. "I do believe you are the prettiest girl I ever did see."

Jody blinked. "Shucks, Ralph, you don't mean that."

"I surely do."

Jody laughed, but Ralph looked as serious as a hangman. She stammered, "B-but I live quite a ways from here, and courtin' ain't a likely thing—"

"Your clan wants Mr. Puckett to set up a factory out yonder. I can get a job out there. I got me the know-how. You'll see."

"It... it don't sound to me like folks here are too keen on the idea. One of Mr. Puckett's own apprentices—"

"Oh, Ricky? Never mind him. He's just jealous, is all. He's the kind of feller what can't stand someone else doing something better than him. If he don't want to cooperate, there's plenty in this clan who can take his place."

"But... you're the watchman's boy."

"I... who cares about what my pa thinks?"

"It ain't that. It's... you seem like an awfully nice boy. But I don't know if I could court a... violent man."

"I... I ain't that a-way. I know how my pa is, but I ain't—"

"I've never known the son of a watchman to be a peaceful sort."

An image, scarcely a month old, flashed through Ralph's mind—a man's eyes glassing over as Ralph held the bloody knife that killed him. "I—"

The door to the study opened, but instead of Mr. Chambers, in came Ella Holland, slipping the door shut behind her as she did. Even with such a mild entrance, both Ralph and the junker girl jumped a little.

"Howdy, Miss Holland," Ralph said, swallowing.

"Howdy," Ella answered in a low, breathless tone, straining to sound convivial. "What're y'all up to?"

For a question that should have sounded idle, Ralph's cheeks flushed at everything held in it. "We was talkin' computers and such, waitin' for Mr. Chambers."

"Ah, well, I don't think Mr. Chambers will be makin' it tonight. Which means, I'm sorry to say, Ralph, but you'd oughta hoof it back home before your pa finds out."

Ralph cast his eyes downward. "I... I wasn't..."

Ella put her hand up. "Never said you was anything. Just don't want folks to get the wrong ideas, is all."

Ralph nodded. "All right, then. Well... goodnight, Miss Holland. Goodnight, Miss Perkins."

When Ralph had gone, Ella sat down with a sigh and dimmed the coal-oil lamp a mite. "Folks around here are awful touchy about outsiders. There's a lot they don't know about the world and the past, and they don't want to know."

"Ralph don't seem that a-way."

"He isn't. That's the problem. Believe it or not, our clan has rules about what folks are 'lowed to know. And if you break those rules, even on accident, there's some who'd like to burn our treaty before it's had a chance to settle."

"Did I do something wrong?"

"No, not at all. I only wanted to head off trouble before it—"

Both young women turned to see the dour visage of Reverend Brody emerge from the entrance. "Evening, Reverend," Ella said.

"What are the two of you doing in here?" The Reverend's keen eyes narrowed.

"I was watching over Miss Perkins here, letting her know how we do things in the Tucker clan and such," Ella said, her hands folded in her lap.

"That was not your responsibility."

"I didn't suppose you would mind it if I took care that every foreigner knew the state of things."

"And you left the others to their own warp and weft?"

"I'm not worried about *them*, Reverend."

"And why not?"

"'Cause they weren't the ones you were trying to trap." Ella kept her hands folded in her lap and her calm gaze on the reverend throughout the stunned silence that followed.

"You think I was trying to trap this young lady?"

"I know it."

"How?"

"When you told me to watch over Mrs. Compton and the others," Ella said, "you never mentioned Miss Perkins. I thought about asking why until I realized she'd be the one most likely to violate your Strictures, or at least seem likely to have done, by your say-so."

The reverend shook his head, staring back at her with silent umbrage.

"Now, I figure an honest Keeper would find that a mite confounding. Why would a Keeper want anyone to violate the Strictures? Unless it helped him get rid of something he hated more, like this treaty with the junkers. So, I've been watching you all day.

"At first, I thought you'd try to use Mr. Chambers as the one to trip the snare. He's a curious man, and the treaty is his darling. Getting caught swapping texts with a foreign girl would take him down a peg in the eyes of the clan and put one more nail in the treaty's coffin.

"But when you stopped Mr. Chambers in the street on the way to his own tutoring session, I realized you were after Ralph McDaniel. No one more curious in the whole clan, and the son of the watchman to boot. Imagine the scandal. 'See how these foreign women lead astray even the sons of our respectable watchman?'

"You'd likely try to get the treaty struck dead right there, on the grounds the junkers didn't hold up their end of the bargain by respecting our ways. Does that sound about right?"

"No, it doesn't," Reverend Brody said. "This sounds like brazen... *spitefulness* from a girl too used to getting her way."

"Then I apologize, Reverend. All I want is to follow the Strictures and keep good feelings alive between us and New Ashburn."

"It's too late for that, girl. Look what she's done." Reverend Brody stabbed a finger at Jody Perkins, who had shrunk back into the darkness with the chalk slate clutched to her chest for protection. "In our library, amongst our writings, carrying her own dangerous ideas like a disease."

Ella stammered. "Are you… going to invoke the Strictures here, on the job already given her?"

"I must."

"I don't know if you can, Reverend."

"Don't tell me what I can and can't do, girl. As Keeper and Reverend, it is not only my ability, but my duty to invoke the Strictures when they've been breached."

"I am a Keeper, too. I don't think they've been breached." Ella's knuckles went white as her fingernails dug into her palms.

"Impudent slackard! Who will the elders believe? Me, or you?"

"Please, Reverend. Don't make this into a fight out in the open."

"Why not? Because you've already made yourself the clan's gawk-a-poppet by throwing yourself at the feet of the town whore?"

That cut deeper than Ella had been expecting, and this was hard enough as it was. She was supposed to be a shy, agreeable gal, handy around the house and in the shop, but with the sense not to stick her nose where it didn't belong. She could feel the clan's collective disappointment still lingering on her like skunk spray. Against the respectability of the reverend, her reputation was tawdry at best.

"It don't matter what the clan thinks about me," she forced herself to say. "It matters what they think about the junkers, about the treaty. 'Bout the medicine. They won't care what you say about the strictures 'less they got no other choice, and I can squeak quiet as a mouse and still give them another choice."

"You make it sound like the decision wasn't a near-run thing. Many were opposed to or unsure about yoking ourselves with the junkers."

Ella's voice trembled, but she kept going. "Your biggest supporter is the watchman. If you dropped his son into a heap of trouble by laying a trap for him, how do you reckon he'd feel?"

"I have done no such thing, and Mr. McDaniel wouldn't believe you if I had."

"He'd believe Mr. Chambers if he said you'd stopped him on his way to tutor Ralph."

At that moment, the very man nearly bumped into the reverend as he walked through the door behind him. "Pardon me!" the teacher exclaimed, hardly noticing how the reverend recoiled from him as he brushed past. "Sorry I'm late. Let's—where's Ralph?"

"I'm sorry. I sent Ralph back home when you didn't show up," Ella said. "As a Keeper, I couldn't leave Ralph alone with an outsider. I hope you'll forgive me. Can I ask what kept you?"

Mr. Chambers shrugged. "Ran an errand for the Reverend here. Took some vegetables to his father across town. Speaking of which, what are you doing here, Reverend?"

Reverend Brody never broke his stare away from Ella. "Only what my eager young pupil took upon herself to do in my place."

Sam looked between the two, his brow furrowing. But he kept his speech light, disinterested. "Well, I suppose we can get to cataloguing the library if I'm not tutoring Ralph," Sam said, setting one of his own books on the table amongst those Jody had pulled off the shelves.

"No need," Reverend Brody said. "The junker girl was just about to turn in for the night. Isn't that right, Miss?"

Jody agreed and promptly left out the back way. Sam stood up and cleared his throat. "Is"—he cleared his throat again—"everything okay here?"

"Yes, quite," the reverend said, his gaze still locked with Ella's. "I just need to talk with my pupil. I'll put out the lantern before I leave."

Mr. Chambers nodded and, with one last glance in Ella's direction, ducked out the door the way he'd arrived.

When they were alone, the reverend's words came through clipped and crisp. "Nothing good will come of this treaty."

"Something good already has. My father would likely have died in a couple more days."

93

The reverend's shoulders sagged as he sighed. "I suppose it doesn't matter anymore either way. You win, Miss Holland, if that gives you any satisfaction. I didn't think you had it in you."

"Jesus said to be wise as serpents and innocent as doves."

"What's next? Do you aim to expose me to the watchman? Drag my name through the mud?"

"If I wanted to destroy you, I would have waited until after you'd sprung your trap, when you couldn't take back your finger-pointing. I don't imagine Miss Perkins thinks highly of you, but I don't reckon her opinion was too high in the first place. As far as I care to say, everybody mixed up in this little story did everything they was supposed to, you included. I don't need to drag you through the mud. So, I won't."

"Why?"

"Because," Ella said, looking at the reverend as if he ought to have known better before dropping her gaze again, "he didn't *only* say to be as wise as serpents."

Chapter 9

A Fox Amongst the Hens

Omar Walking tested the firmness of the logs and rusting scrap metal comprising this section of the palisade. It was an idle task, but after the incident the other day with one of the Carters, checking the integrity of the patchwork wall—overstandingly those stretches equipped with a catwalk—seemed worthwhile. Even if he was supposed to be keeping his eyes on the woods.

His nighttime sight wasn't as keen as the Finches' or the Fillmores', so he saw little point in putting him on the nighttime roundswalks. He'd said as much, but his sayings bore little weight in the face of short hands and strange unbred doings. He was set to patrol out east tomorrow morning as well, and this task, he didn't protest. It had been three weeks since he'd left his Greenbrier clansmen at the cell tower lookout, and they were likely to wonder what had come of him.

Tonight, he'd have to spend most of his time up north around the Brody farm, and he'd stay out there until Ricky or his kid brother or one of the girls got up to milk the cows. That he'd been among the Tuckers long enough before his banishment and since his return to gain not only Ricky Brody's familiarity, but also the familiarity of his kin, was not lost on Omar.

It was right when Omar jumped down from the wall and started up the game trail leading into the dark woods that the first whiff of unbreds hit his nose—unbreds, and at least one human. The scent was strong. *Close.*

Omar's body sprang into action almost of its own accord. Not bothering to try to climb back up with danger so close and yet still unseen, he sprinted back along the wall toward where the streambed bisecting the town ran under a protective grate. Victor Fillmore stood on the wall, guarding the juncture, his long, craning neck leaning over the top of the palisade. His bright blond head whipped Omar's direction as he jumped clear of the treeline.

"What happened?" Victor called out, his head already swiveling this way and that to look for whatever might have spooked Omar.

"The blind drifter, I smelled him—he's in the woods," Omar called.

Victor helped Omar back up onto the wall and relative safety. "You still smell him?" he asked.

"Yeah. The wind hasn't changed. He's out north-west. Between us and the Brodys. Let's ring the bell."

"Naw," Victor said. "Let's not warn that feller off if we don't have to. I bet we can nab 'im, us twain."

Omar turned his head from the woods to look at Victor. "I don't think that's a smart idea."

"You scared, Omar? Your nose and my trackin' can't handle a blind man? If he's between us and the Brodys', he's within rifle range. Hurry up. He could slip away any minute." Victor dropped down to the other side of the palisade and plunged into the woods.

Omar cast one last look over his shoulder at the comforting lantern-light on the post in front of the meetinghouse, grumbled to himself, and followed the tracker. Victor pressed on ahead of him, his head bobbing up and down and side to side, birdlike, as they slipped through the deepening shadows.

He suspected they were making less headway through the woods than it seemed. His nose didn't lie: the human had to be beyond sightline of the wall at least, which meant his earlier sense of being watched had been his own imagination. Was it his imagination now?

A canebrake rose to take up the space the trees left unoccupied, and seeing no quick way around it, Omar plunged in and through. The foliage pressed in close around Omar, like black fingers sometimes stroking his face. Something rustled the hill cane somewhere in front of him. "Vic? Victor?" Omar whispered.

"Shhhhut the hell up," Victor hissed from the dark to his left, much farther away than Omar had expected.

Whatever it was rustled in the brush again, and Omar glimpsed the eye-shine of something not fully human. He should have had his spear ready earlier, but he wasted no time slinging his muzzle-loader over his shoulder now that an unbred was within sneezing distance. He two-handed his pike and squared off against the creature.

Even in the dark, he could see the characteristic apelike hunch of the pigman making it seem smaller than it really was. He waited for the pigman to growl or make some kind of threatening noise, but it sat there, silently watching him, waiting. Omar flicked his eyes left, then right—pigmen were known to sneak around looking to snag a flank. He retreated a half-step.

Then the pigman advanced. Omar lunged forward like a coiled spring and caught the unbred right in the middle of its half-crouched ambling. A trained pikeman could cover nearly ten feet with a proper thrust, and it was easy for an unbred to misjudge the distance in the dark.

Omar also misjudged how much force he'd need; he spitted the creature through both sides of its ribcage and found his spearpoint trapped in there. The pigman gasped its life away as Omar tried to yank the shaft free. In a panic, he let go of the spear and unsheathed his matchet just in time to catch the scent of another pigman's frenzy sweat insistently close. He sensed, rather than heard, the unbred's leaping attack.

Omar's wild swing didn't so much catch the pigman's neck as pass cleanly through it. The pigman's momentum carried its body on into him, knocking him off his feet, but it fell promptly to the side. In the moonlight, he saw its head twist around backwards on its spine, the only thing still keeping the head attached to the torso. Something warm and wet covered him. It had pissed on him; he knew it.

He got up to one knee and made a quick scan around him. *No further on-hand threats. No spear, neither.* Further ahead, he saw something moving into a small clearing—the first pigman, the spear shaft protruding upward like a grotesque flagpole. The thing was still hobbling, canted to one side like an oxcart in a rut. Its quivering forepaws sometimes grasped impotently at the spear and sometimes reached up to the moon as if in supplication. Its breaths came in shallow, agonized gasps.

Omar crushed the twin sensations of pity and revulsion with a quickness born from years of grim experience and finished the creature off with his matchet. Checking to see if the coast was still clear, he planted one foot on the pigman's neck and heaved the spear free of the warm corpse.

There was silence.

Then a moan. It was low at first, wavering, then warbling, rising in pitch and volume. Finally, it became a scream before weakening and dying out. Omar couldn't tell how far off. His nose hurt, and he couldn't smell right. "Victor?"

There was no answer.

Omar looked back toward where he knew the town lay, then forward again to where he'd heard the screaming. He looked back to town and back the other way, into the trees. He bit his lip and, tasting blood that wasn't his own, spat vehemently and charged back towards town through the trees. *To hell with this.*

He watched for pigmen, and their absence multiplied their hiding places. He suspected, then was certain there were pigmen everywhere, waiting for him to walk right into whatever ambush they'd set up for him on his way back to town—*There!* A form, too upright to be a pigman, stood silhouetted uphill of Omar, motionless. Omar unslung his musket and brought the butt of the stock to his shoulder, but he didn't line up a shot. He stared right back at the form, transfixed for a moment.

The figure burst into motion, sprinting straight for Omar.

Omar lined up his sights and pulled the hammer back, full-cocked. At the last instant, though, he recognized the figure running towards him—Victor.

Victor tackled Omar in a mad dash, sending the two of them tumbling down the slope head over heels. Omar felt two hands grasping his neck, squeezing. He wriggled a knee up into Victor's stomach and pushed hard enough to feel the strangling hands slip away for a moment.

"Doggone it, Victor, it's me!" Omar hollered, scrambling away from his assailant.

Victor sat on his haunches, panting, for what seemed like an hour. "Omar?" he said at last.

"What the ever-burnin' blazes got into you?"

"I thought—I... what happened to you?"

"Did you get the drifter?" Omar asked. He rubbed his neck. Victor could crack hickories with a grip like that.

"I was close. I liketa had him, then I heard you screaming."

"I weren't screaming. I thought that was you."

Both of them looked to the north. "Want to head back?" Victor suggested.

"Let's get out of here. Get the teeth tomorrow." Omar picked up his rifle and spear. "Been a heck of a night."

With Bill Puckett gone off to New Ashburn and his powder shop temporarily shut, Ella insisted Melissa Daly come along with her to the weekly Tuesday afternoon cooking misadventure at the butcher's house. Ella could hear Becky's mother, Charlotte Brody, hollering somewhere inside about something or other, but it was Becky who answered Ella's knock.

Becky Brody had her mother's temper and neat auburn curls, but her father's delicate nose and high cheekbones. In short, Becky was the kind of untouchable beauty few young clansmen dared approach with confidence—the sole exception being the golden boy, Amos Taylor.

"Hey, Ella... and uh, Melissa," Becky stuttered, lacking her usual conviviality. She put a hand on her hip and exhaled slowly. "Sophie's gone over to the miller's to fetch some flour and a batch of starter, and then... we can get some bread going."

"Doing okay today?"

"Yeah, I just..." she waved Ella's concern away and took a seat. "You've got your own stuff to worry about. How's your pa?"

"Infection's going down real fast. I hope the junkers get back soon with more of them antibiotics. Now," Ella clapped her hands as if ready to get down to the serious business of ruining food, "what's eatin' you?"

Becky exhaled through her perfect nose. "It's just... no. I'm not sleeping well. The heat, you know."

Ella sat down next to her and put a hand on her knee. "Becky."

"I don't want to sour the milk."

"Come on now, Becky. You'd never let this slide with me."

Becky sat down and stared between her knees. "The Greenbriers. I can't stop thinking about what they did back on the Newell farm."

"It's only been a couple of months, Becky. It'll get better."

"I... I never did say what all happened back there. It weren't the Greenbriers who shot Jesse Newell. I did. They was torturin' him." Becky shook her head. "What kind of folks do that? What..." she shook her head again.

"Becky, I'm sorry."

"Do you..." Melissa started. "Do you reckon that's what happened to Bert?"

Neither of the two young women answered. Bert Daly's death was not one mourned greatly in the clan, not even by his disgraced widow. But the murky nature of his death allowed for more than a little dart-throwing amongst those with an imaginative bent.

"I don't know how long it'll take me to stop hearing Jesse's screams. A grown man like that, wailin' like a three-year-old."

"Like a coward?" Melissa's face had taken on a hard look, clearly thinking of her late husband.

"Like a snared rabbit. Wild. I had to listen to it right along next to his mother. She heard it, too. Lordy, I wish Sophie would get here already so I could punch up some dough."

Melissa turned to Ella. "Maybe I should go."

"Hogwash." Becky took a deep breath and waved Mrs. Daly away from the door. "Ain't nothing to bring the clan together like grousing about the Greenbriers."

"Now Becky, I understand completely why you're upset," Ella admonished, "but maybe you should take your mind off—"

"Okay, okay. What about these junkers? I heard my cousin say they're just trying to swindle us out of Bill's secrets. We ain't never had deals like this with foreigners, you know."

"I... don't know if this is so much better. How about something else?"

"Fine," Becky said, half-annoyed, half-impishly. "Now that Bill's gone, I don't expect you and Omar have got much to keep you busy. Or do you?"

Ella's already wide eyes looked like they were about to pop straight out of her head. She buried her rapidly coloring face in her apron and squealed.

"*There* we go." Becky crossed her arms.

Ella steeled herself against the wave of embarrassment washing over her. "Ain't nothing going on between me and him. Bill's got all the apprentices a list of jobs to keep the shop standing until he gets back. Gotta keep turning the niter beds and pulling out the saltpeter."

"Sure." Becky nodded her head as if this explained everything. "Omar scrounged up a hundred jaws and came back here so he could shovel manure for a living."

"Becky, if Omar ever makes a move, you'll be the first to know."

"Well, *that's* not gonna happen."

"What do you mean?"

"I mean that feller's scared of you."

"Of *me?*"

"That's what I said. If you want to catch him, you're a-gonna have to go to him."

"Sounds to me like you just want a passable reason to go after Amos again," Ella attempted to tease back, but it came out more like an accusation.

Becky's denial came strong and certain. "Ella, I tell you what, I ain't forgiven him for leaving you standing at the altar. That boy's off limits."

"Aw, Becky... I didn't mean... he didn't—"

The door mercifully opened to reveal Sophie Fillmore carrying everything Ella needed to start baking and stop sticking her foot in her mouth.

"Sorry I'm late. I would have had Pa or your ma watch the twins today, but of course Pa's gone out to the junker clan, and I reckon your ma's watching Melissa's kid—hey, Melissa," she nodded to Mrs. Daly, "so I had to run them across town to Victor's folks, and speaking of which,

Victor came in early from his night watch and wanted to have *more* babies, if you catch my—"

"Ew, Sophie, *noooo!*" Becky scrunched up her face as if smelling rotten meat. "I *still* remember when Victor flicked a booger on me in school."

Ella laughed. They all laughed, and they got on with their baking. They gossiped and cajoled and joked as they worked, but there was a discipline to it now, a determination not to let talk of the Greenbriers, or of the junkers, or of Phil Holland's wounds, or of the many recent dead. There would be a time to talk of these things, but this was a Tuesday, and Tuesdays were sacred.

Omar knocked on the door to the gunsmithy.

Amos opened it. "I see you're around bright and early. Not even lunchtime yet."

"Ran a patrol last night. Thought I'd check on the Hollands before I got back to the grindstone."

"It would be a surprise to see Phil in his shop right now, wouldn't it?"

"Yeah, well... I saw you come in earlier. Wondered what you were up to. Seein' how Phil ain't in smithing shape."

Amos shrugged. "Mr. Holland had me cutting threads for silencers before... the screevlers. Thought I'd give the lathe a few spins before I went out with the watchman."

"Whereabouts you going today?"

"Won't know until I go see him. Why? You want to come along?"

"I'm moving out east to check the highway into town later today. But you and McDaniel might want to check things out to the north."

"Why?"

Omar stared at the ground, measuring his words and finding them wanting. Omar sucked his teeth. "You been walking the watchman's game trail ever since I got back."

"So?"

"There's likely trouble that-a-way, and you're more liable to have the watchman's ear."

"We've got plenty of trouble to the south, unless the Greenbriers worked their way up to come at us from the other direction."

"I'm talking about a tougher nut than all the Greenbriers put together."

Amos scoffed. "I can't think of anything I'd rather spend my time on than killing Greenbriers."

"Is that the real reason you've been running with McDaniel?"

Amos shrugged. "I've been getting the taste for that line of work. These days, the clan could use an extra matchet-hand. Or a fellow who knows his way around a bow."

"I got better sense than to chase the watchman's trade. That's a hard life and an early grave."

Amos' face darkened. "A hard life's the only one on the cards for me. The only question is how hard I can make it for those who've got it coming to them."

A muscle in Omar's jaw twitched. "I... know how it is, Amos. Losing kin is hard. Mighty hard."

"You ever lost kin because they didn't want you anymore?"

Omar spread his arms out in front of him. "I was a drifter, wasn't I?"

"Fair."

"Thing is..."

"What?" Amos asked.

"I don't know if I ever thanked you proper. For sticking up for me, back when everyone else was set against me. I know it had to cost you. Don't quite know why you done it."

"You saved me and Dale from the pigmen."

"That can't be the whole reason."

"Once I've thrown in my lot with someone, I'm in it for good. I can't stand the wheeling and dealing the elders get up to. Besides," Amos cracked a grin in a hint of his old humor, "you're more interesting than these other townies who've never traveled more than twenty miles beyond the walls. You uh, you kept up that fencing arm of yours?"

"Ain't hardly touched a matchet for anything more than brush-hacking. Listen, about that patrol with the watchman up north—"

"Is it the Greenbriers?"

"That's not what bugs me."

"You haven't dealt with the Greenbriers, have you?"

"Listen. You think I'm interesting 'cause I know things I'm not supposed to. Things the elders want hid. It's one of those hidden things what's bugging me." Omar turned to the side, thrusting one hand deep into the pocket of his trousers. "The eyeless drifter."

"What about him?"

"He ain't gone."

"How do you know?"

Omar hooked one thumb through the twine serving as his belt and exhaled through his nose. "I was on patrol with Victor last night, north of town. Caught a whiff of 'im. We went after the jasper, but his unbreds jumped us. He liketa got us both."

"Why didn't you tell Elvin about this?"

"He wouldn't understand."

"Why not?"

"That blind drifter? His kind aren't supposed to exist, as far as your lore cares to know."

"So what is he, then?"

Omar answered neither immediately nor directly. "Dangerous."

"I'll see if I can't get Elvin to check it out."

"If anyone knows I told you about this, I'm out on my ear again."

Amos stared at Omar until the drifter met his gaze. "I won't tell anyone."

Omar extended a hand, which Amos clasped in a firm grip. "Thanks."

"Whatever happens, you can count on me."

Omar strolled across the open road to the cell tower in the broad light of day. He leaned up against the steel frame of the tower with the confidence of a man in his own home and waited.

Minutes passed, and he grew tired of waiting. He banged on a metal crossbrace with the flat of his matchet like he was ringing a dinner bell. It would not normally be a good idea out alone in the woods, but he knew he wasn't alone, and he needed to get back to his post.

A young man climbed out of the culvert under the road, rubbing his eyes. "Omar," he said. "Caught me in the middle of a nap. You did it? Is it done?"

"You'll get snuck up on one of these days, drowsing without someone watching your back."

"Jacks ran to get some water. It's so boring out here. Please tell me you're done."

"I'm not done."

"Why the heck not?"

"I've run into some snags."

Before the young man had a chance to groan, another Greenbrier emerged from the woods, a couple full plastic jugs hanging from one shoulder. "Omar!"

Omar didn't bother with any howdy-dos. "I don't have long, so here's the news: they're short on the fancy ammunition, and the powderman's got himself a tough time making enough to replace what they used while also building new cookworks at the same time."

"That's good news," the first Greenbrier kid said.

"Except we ain't the only ones been hearing about this nitrogel. A nomad clan just come the other day with out-of-town folks asking for the powderman. He's done run off to their clan and took most of his notes with him. I've been taking down my own scratches, but I don't know what he does to make the nitric acid, which might be the foremost part. I don't think he's done playing around with the recipe, so if I leave too early, he's liable to make it better than whatever we end up making. If he stays with these new folks, I might have to come up with a way to get myself out there with him. Which means I don't know rightly when I can make it back here to check in. It's all so twisted-up, it makes my head spin."

"Okay," the second one said. "Tell us what you've got so far, then."

"Pile up whatever nitrates you can, saltpeter and such, just like with regular powder. They'll come in handy. And then as much iron pyrite as you can get ahold of."

"Iron pyrite?"

"Fool's gold. There's plenty of it around if you know where to look. The Chapmans'll likely know what it is. You can get what you want from the right coal, too, if you know what you're doing. Wash it out and sniff for rotten eggs."

"Anything else?"

Omar looked down, thinking. Should he tell them? "There was a... screevler attack. A weird one."

"Weird how?"

"I saw... an unbred shepherd."

"That's their problem, not ours."

"Yeah, well..." Omar trailed off, casting an unsure gaze away from his clansmen as he scratched at his jaw. Then he froze, suddenly wary. "Someone's coming."

The three Greenbriers scrambled off the road, off the south-facing embankment, then further on up the hill. They stilled after casting just enough enshrouding brush over their backs to break up their outlines.

"You got some field glasses?" Omar asked.

"Here." The older Greenbrier passed him a set of binoculars they should have used to spot him coming earlier.

Omar scanned the road and woods opposite them, eventually finding movement, then the source of the movement. "Damn," he said. "It's Amos. He was supposed to be up north."

"I'll wait for a clear shot." The older Greenbrier primed his pan.

"No. There's more." Omar squinted into the binoculars. "The watchman. And his boy."

"We can take 'em if we get the drop on 'em."

"And blow my cover? How's it gonna look if I'm the only one to come back alive from patrol? Stop thinkin' with your balls and stay put." They didn't seem to like Omar's instructions, but they nodded when he'd finished.

Omar heaved himself up and crept back and parallel to where he'd spotted the Tuckers. He gradually made his way back down to the road, where he crossed behind a bend, went back over to the Tucker side, and picked up the pace through the woods. He worked it out so that he came up roughly behind the Tuckers, who by now had reached the road and were inspecting the radio tower and culvert.

"Psst," Omar said to Ralph, who whirled in surprise.

"Omar! You're a doggone *ghost*," Ralph said. "What're you doing here? Amos said you were back at the highway."

"Yeah, well, Amos was wanting to check out this tower the other day, so I decided I might as well swing down here on my way out."

"That's what Amos was wanting to do."

"I thought you guys were going to check things out up north of town."

"Why would we do that?"

Omar blew a sigh into the mossy forest floor. "You fellers found anything?"

"Amos was sure he heard something a while ago," Ralph answered, pointing up ahead. "He's taking point."

Omar moved up through the woods to talk to Amos, stepping out into the clear next to the road. As soon as he did, though, a shot from the hill to the south rang out, ricocheting off the asphalt not ten feet away.

Omar ducked back into cover as a second shot rang out, and he found himself next to Elvin McDaniel. He took a moment to inwardly curse his clansmen's impatience before he brought himself back to the part he had to play. "I guess Amos was right to want to check this place out."

Elvin didn't answer, too busy scanning the woods for the source of the gunsmoke drifting through the brush like fog.

Seconds passed, and then another gunshot spat from the forest, this one landing close to the watchman. Omar swore. They were supposed to be gone by now. He looked over the edge of the embankment and saw movement in the woods. Elvin did, too, and lined up a shot.

Omar lined up a shot of his own. The father was right there, and the son not far beyond, well within a quick matchet strike. Only one problem. "Wait, where's Amos?" Omar asked.

A final shot thundered in the woods, audibly different from the others—a nitrogel charge—followed by a scream.

Omar rose from his crouch and sprinted across the road. He ran back up to where he'd left his clansmen and found Amos leaning over a Greenbrier kid who tended to drowse on watch. The kid clutched his bleeding hip, growling in pain through clenched teeth. "While you guys drew their fire, I snuck around to catch a flank."

"Good instincts, Amos," Elvin McDaniel said, coming up behind Omar. "Good instincts all around."

"I think I saw another one who ran off," Amos said. "Think we should chase him down?"

"Too risky. There could be more." Omar fought to keep his voice even, to keep his gaze from drifting toward the kid.

Amos laughed without humor. "I know someone who could tell us for sure." He turned toward the kid and put a foot on the wound, drawing forth a sharp scream. "What about it, huh? How many Greenbriers are there around here? How many?"

"Amos..." Omar began before he locked eyes with the kid. He knew the kid's father.

"Look at *me*, you sonofabitch," Amos said to the Greenbrier. Omar had never heard such bile from Amos before. "You want my foot to move, you better start talking."

Omar reached for his rifle.

A gunshot crashed, and a massive hole opened up in the side of the Greenbrier's head in a gory spray. Amos jerked to the side to see Ralph McDaniel holding the rifle.

"I can't abide somebody suffering that a-way. Not even a Greenbrier," Ralph said as he lowered his smoking gun. His stone-faced grimness never wavered, but his voice cracked, boyish and weak.

Chapter 10

Harvest Time

Job Brody surveyed the field of wheat, savoring the sun-toasted heads stooped over with the weight of the grain they held. He closed his eyes and inhaled the warm aroma wafting up to him in the lazy midmorning breeze. He swore it almost smelled like bread baking. The trills and buzzing of the katydids and junebugs and cicadas always reminded him of the wheat harvest.

He reached down and plucked a head from the field. The chaff around the kernel yielded to his calloused fingers, drifting to the ground like snow. He pressed a fingernail into a kernel and found it hard.

He'd never told anyone this, but he was thankful for some of the "CRISPR-fy-ing" that had gone on back in the old days. Years of scientists fiddling with the wheat's germline had given him a hardy winter wheat that could be mighty thrifty with water when the weather didn't cooperate. Of course, the idiots had also made many crop varieties infertile past one planting, so he had to admit folks had a point when they talked about the foolishness of the past breedmongers.

They'd also created the pigmen, the descendants of which had run amok in his field, lodging large swaths of his wheat and potentially rendering it un-harvestable. He'd have to go out and check the lodged wheat to see if its time spent lying flat had set it to rot yet.

The pigmen had never made sense to Job. Even if he thought the idea dumber than a box of rocks, he could at least see the point of making seeds that couldn't reproduce themselves outside a breedmonger's magic house. But the pigmen, and the bullhuskers, and the shadowers and screevlers... there didn't seem to be any point to those monsters other than causing an awful nuisance. His brother said the unbreds were an accident, but Job didn't buy the explanation.

The old scientists had made crop seeds designed to go extinct on purpose, and then turned around and made fast-breeding pests like pigmen on accident? And *then* turned them loose into the wild?

Nobody was that dumb.

Sophie Fillmore looked in on her sleeping husband from the bedroom door. He'd been leery talking about his night patrol, but he'd sure come in all stirred-up. He looked peaceful enough now. She hated to wake him, but word had gone around: harvest time. The whole clan had to turn out to get the cutting and threshing done safely.

She shook her husband's shoulder. "Hey, darling. I'm sorry to get you up, but the wheat cuttin's starting up at the Brodys' at noon, and Mr. McDaniel wants you as a field watcher. I got that opossum you caught cooking over the sassafras. Us and the twins can walk up together after... Vic?"

Victor responded neither to her gentle shaking nor her gentle voice. He didn't respond to her more vigorous shaking or her panicked voice, either.

"He's not the sluggardly type, Doc!" Sophie said, leading Doctor Bernhard up to the door of their little home. "When the babies are caterwauling, he gets up before me, but he was as limp as a rag doll this morning!"

The two entered the house nearly at a run and already breathless, crossed the living area cluttered with half-stitched leather items, and opened the door to the Fillmores' bedroom. Their bed lay empty, the covers thrown back.

"Wha—he was just—" Sophie stammered.

Victor wandered in from the kitchen, the bowl of eggs and bean paste Sophie had made for him in his hands. "Hey, hon," he said. "I was wondering where you were. The little ones are up." He looked at Doctor Bernhard. "What's going on?"

If planting was a chore, harvest was brutal, particularly the wheat harvest. The soybeans they would plant in the wheat's stead wouldn't be harvested until October, and the corn and potatoes in September. Wheat had to be harvested in the punishing heat of a midsummer sun. Planting took a lot of hands; harvest took every able body. The town emptied to cut and bundle the shocks of grain, tend to the workers, or patrol the rounds, often taking turns between the three jobs.

If the weather held, the work crews would make the trip to every crofter's wheat field, then take the sheaves inside the safety of the clan walls. After drying them on the wide-open clan main, there'd be a threshing bee. For that, they would use what had once been a combine harvester, which had been disassembled into a threshing machine and then further disassembled into a simple rotating threshing cylinder and fanning mill, all of which had to be powered by animals and operated by multiple clansmen. What had once been a single machine had now become, either by the need to retrofit or through a lack of replacement parts, a carriageable factory stored in the meetinghouse in the fallow seasons.

When she wasn't working the huge vats of porridge for the workers, Ella usually had to follow the harvesters, collecting and tying sheaves by hand with straw plucked from the bunch. She paused for a moment to stretch her sore back and wipe the sweat from her head. She looked around. "Have you seen Omar?" she asked Melissa Daly, who by no accident was working the next windrow over.

"I ain't seen anything but straw and field stubble. I can't even keep track of Earnest," Melissa muttered.

"He was headed back south," Becky Brody said.

"Who, Earnest?" Melissa said, straightening up and looking around.

"No, Omar," Becky shouted back.

Ella shielded her eyes from the sun. "Towards town?"

"Why should you care? Unless you're makin' googly eyes at him." Becky may have meant to sound teasing, but what came out was something more akin to annoyance as she grunted from behind a shock of wheat.

Ella thought for a minute, a hand on her hip. "I'm taking a break," she said, finally.

"But we've just started—"

"I'm going to check on my pa. I'll be back."

Omar slipped into Bill's workshop through the back door facing the palisade wall. The town was nearly empty, but nearly empty and completely empty were two different things. Once inside, he stepped past a huge jar holding the liquid filtrate from the bucket of sludge they'd pulled out of the hopper outside. Beyond stood the door to Bill's office, and inside, in the upper-left drawer of Bill's rusty metal desk, lay a jumbled mess of papers and parchment at various stages of degradation. Some pages were neatly printed reference materials ripped from their previous housings and annotated with various writing implements. Other pages were stained with chemicals and frayed from constant handling. The most up-to-date stuff had gone off with the powderman who penned it, but these notes would make a good starting point.

Omar retrieved the folded paper from his pocket and spread it smooth on the desk next to a quill and inkwell. He removed the stopper from the inkwell, dipped in the quill, and, finding the black walnut ink too thick, left the office to get some water to thin it out.

He returned from the kitchen sink with a beaker full of water and stopped in the middle of the shop. Ella stood in the front hallway, staring at him, her mouth hanging open as if in the middle of asking a question she'd forgotten halfway through. "Omar?"

"Hey, Ella." Omar took a couple slow, deliberate steps to the workbench and refilled the basin atop Bill's filtration system with an even slower, more deliberate motion.

"What are you doing here?"

"Forgot to do this this morning. And it beats working the grain cradle." He turned to face her. "What are you doing here?"

"Wanted to check on Pa."

"Yeah? How's he doin'?" Omar asked, as if he hadn't heard the moment he got up that morning.

"The infection's going down real fast, but Mrs. Compton—you know, from the junker clan—she don't think she can recycle much more of the medicine. I hope Mr. Salazar can get back with a big dose soon."

"If you were checking on your pa, why'd you come over here?" Omar asked, still frozen to the spot where he'd wandered under Ella's gaze.

"I heard a noise next door, and after what happened last time with Bill's shop, I thought I'd check on it." Ella flicked a hand towards the leaching nitrates. "And I guess this beats gathering sheaves."

"Yes, well..." Omar cleared his throat.

"Yeah." Ella nodded. "I guess I'd better... you know." She tilted her head back in the direction of the front door.

"Ah. Yes. Back to the old grindstone."

"Would you care to... you know..." It looked as if Ella's arms couldn't decide whether to hide themselves stiffly behind her back or fold over each other stiffly out in front. She chewed her lip, which only showed her prominent front teeth more. "Walk me back?"

Escorting her back to the fields was the least terrifying of all the things Omar thought she might have said. "Oh. Sure."

"Unless you've got more stuff to do here—"

"No, no, no. Forgot what I was doing when you came in, is all. It'd be my pleasure," Omar said, moving to the door and taking her arm with a sudden vigor. "Let's get a move on."

Outside, they followed the stream up through the middle of town to the northern gate. Ella made as if to start talking, but stopped herself. After a few false starts, Omar asked without looking her way, "Somethin' on your mind?"

"Well, I just think... that is, I was a-thinkin', what with your comin' back so sudden and all... it's kind of a curious thing, you know?"

What was she sniffing after? "Yeah, I reckon so."

"Oh. So, you thought so too?" Ella's breathing grew somewhat more belabored. It was probably the walking.

"Sure."

"And I just figured it might be a good idea... to, uh, get everything, you know, sorta..." she made an impotent gesture like she was trying to push the words out—"to get everything out in the open. Whew. You know?"

"How so?"

"Well—I was thinkin'... I could ask you a question." Ella's head bobbed to one side. "Then you could answer it." Her head bobbed back the other way. "Then you could ask me a question, and maybe I could catch you up on everything, and—"

"Ella, you're weavin'."

"Oh." She corrected her course and straightened herself up. "I was just thinking we could sort out where everybody stands. And then we can—know where everybody stands. What do you think?"

"Sounds like a plan. You go first."

"Okay. Uh, well, why did you come back? Ugh, that didn't sound right. What I meant to say, was, well, 'Why *did* you come back?'"

Omar took a long time to answer, knowing Ella would know if he laid it on too thick. "I suppose..." he said, looking away from her as he spoke. "I suppose I came back to figure out where I stand."

Ella took a longer time to answer back. "So... with the Tuckers, or with us Pucketts and Hollands, or... someone more specific?"

"Well... I reckon you make a real nice mess of beans."

Ella bowed her head and looked away. "Aw, ain't no one ever said that about my beans!"

"You pick the hairs out, they'll whole-and-hale clean you through."

Ella laughed as she slapped his knee. "You are a beast and a half, you know that?"

Omar grinned. "I know it."

"So that's it? You came back for my cookin', is all?"

"Anything's better than raw crawdads."

Ella's laugh rounded out her stern scolding. "You didn't used to tease me like this, Omar."

"You didn't know me none too well, then."

Ella calmed her laugh. "I guess not."

"Can I ask a question now?"

"After your shim-sham of an answer? Hardly. But I reckon I'll allow for it."

"Did you get around to forgivin' me?"

"For what?"

"For bein' so low-down and not telling you everything about Grierson and me. I coulda been more trusting."

"Oh, Omar. Don't you fret yourself about that none. I'm just glad you're back. Forgiveness gets easier with practice. Takes a different way of thinkin' to start out, though."

"I hear you."

"But I'm gettin' better about it."

"You don't need to get better about nothin'."

"Always room to grow. That's the joy about life. Always can go a little higher."

It was Becky's turn for a break, and she made her way over to the line of coolers set up on a folding table. Every square inch of free space was taken up with the cups folks had brought with them to drink. Not far off, her mother and father roasted several goats on spits. The smell of cooked meat dangled the promise of a tasty reward at the end of a hard day's work, and almost gave the harvesting a festive feel. Almost.

Amos Taylor came up for a dram as well, shirtless and glistening with a sheen of sweat. His leanness was less boyish now, more muscular. Becky rolled her eyes.

"Afternoon, Miss Brody," Amos said with what would have sounded like humorous over-formality a year ago. Given everything that had happened since then... it fit.

"Good afternoon, Mr. Taylor."

"Would you like to sit next to me come dinnertime? I can walk you home after."

Becky took a long sip of water. "I'd like that," she said. "But I'm not sure... what all this is supposed to mean."

"What all what is supposed to mean?"

"Walking me home, and talking to me. All personal-like."

Amos shrugged. "Whatever you want it to mean."

Becky kept her gaze forward. "It ain't that simple."

"Why not?"

"If I see it one way, but the clan sees it another, it don't matter what I say."

"Like it didn't really matter what happened between me and Ella?"

She turned toward him. "You're really going to stand there and tell me you weren't courting her?"

"Sure. I courted her. I took her dancing *one* time. We never even kissed."

Becky forced her mind from the thought of kissing Amos Taylor like she was pulling a stubborn mule from a bushel of oats. "Ella had high hopes."

"She told you?"

"I could tell."

Amos sighed and took the drink he'd been nursing. "Ella's a fine gal. Really she is. After the pigman siege, after Omar and I took down that shadower... I had every girl in the town after me. I got distracted."

119

"Well, it's nice to finally get a little honesty out of you, at least," Becky said, crossing her arms.

"If it helps any, I lost my standing with about everybody once I got my brother killed. My own mother still won't speak to me."

"Now don't go making me feel bad for you." Becky groaned. "I'm sorry. It ain't right, Amos. You weren't the one who shot him."

"Does it matter? Like you said, if the clan thinks it's so, that's the way it is." The hardness had crept back into Amos' voice. "Killing the Greenbriers in the ambush made the womenfolk afraid of me. Not what I aimed for, exactly."

"I ain't afraid of you, Amos." Becky inched closer.

"Becky!" It was her mother, shouting from over by the goats in a louder and harsher voice than was necessary. "You quit lollygagging and help me carve this goat up."

"I'll—I'll... see you, Amos," Becky said before going to her mother. She cast a look over her shoulder at the young man returning to the fields.

"I don't want you hanging around that boy, you understand?" Mrs. Brody said in a low voice.

Becky let loose an exasperated sigh. "Oh, Mom—"

"You quit chasin' after him, y'hear? I mean it. You're old enough now you oughta be looking for marriageable folks, and he ain't one."

The goats were not ready to cut up; not close to it. Becky balled up her fists and turned to face her mother. "First of all, Amos and I are friends. I got enough sense to know he's a skirt-chaser, but *you* think that's all there is to him."

"Becky, I won't have you—"

"Second," Becky continued, "I'm good and able to pick a husband on my own just fine."

"You can't hardly pick an apple out of an apple tree. There are plenty of fine men in the clan, already out of their apprenticeships, some of 'em master tradesmen."

"Unmarried? Like who, Ma?"

"Mr. Puckett, for one."

"*Bill?* He's old enough to be my pa!" Becky stood aghast.

"And he'll take care of you."

"Maybe I don't need taken care of, Ma."

"Then you're ready to move out on your own then, huh?"

"If I don't have to deal with you telling me what boys I can talk to in broad daylight, I'm *beyond* ready."

Mrs. Brody wasn't about to let Becky have the last word, even if it took her a mite longer to come up with one. "As long as I'm your mother, you best mind me. That boy Amos is trouble."

Sophie Fillmore woke to find an empty space in the bed where she'd expected her husband to be. She got up and looked out the window. It was still dark, and in the middle of summer, that meant it was no time to be up if there wasn't a night watch to tend to. Victor had already done his night watch last week, so he wouldn't be due for another couple months. Where had that man got off to?

She stopped at the sound of a keening hum, almost a whisper, coming from the twins' room. She went to the door and peeked inside.

A couple bureau drawers had been made for the twins' respective cribs and packed with straw and blankets. Victor kneeled over them both, absently patting their chests as they slept. But he was talking to them quietly, and not like a doting father. "Fine little specimens. Keep growing, little ones. Still too tender, not yet ripe..."

"Darlin'?" Sophie said.

Victor's head jolted up, his eyes gleaming while the rest of him remained shrouded in the darkness. "Did I wake you, Sophie?"

"Come to bed, darling. It's the babies I'm worried about you waking."

121

"Sure, sure," Victor said, stepping out of the nursery and crawling back into his depression in the mattress. "Couldn't sleep. The heat, you know."

"I do. I do know, Vicky," Sophie said. But she didn't drape her arm over him as she was used to doing. She curled up on the opposite side of the bed, away from him, and pretended to go to sleep, as she knew he was pretending.

Sleep eluded her for some time, and she knew Victor lay awake for every moment she did.

Chapter 11

Americans

Between gaps in the forest canopy, a view of the distant crinkled blanket of green Appalachian hills peeked through. Ralph, his father, and his father's all-but-in-name apprentice had nearly reached the highest point for many miles around. It was a chore to reach, but a valuable one to undertake every now and then. Ralph's father valued it for tactical considerations. Ralph just liked the view.

Ralph wiped sweat away from his babyish face, still sporting little more than peach fuzz in the way of facial hair. He looked over at Amos, who, though barely a year his senior, held the hard look of seasoned cast iron.

"Sometimes, a watchman has to take a loss and fall back," his father said, ducking under a branch. "A dead watchman ain't no use to the clan, nor a dead war party neither. You gotta pick your fights. But fallin' back can never be the last thing you do. Your clansmen won't tolerate it, nor unbreds, Greenbriers, marauders, none of 'em." He spoke loudly enough for Amos, spaced a safe distance to his right, to hear, but no louder than necessary. Ralph could also hear the instruction while tailing the two, but of course his father wasn't talking to him. "If *anybody* gets the idea you turn tail or cry uncle when the shootin' starts, it's only a matter of time before you'll have to do it again. Once the enemy has a grip, they ain't gonna give it up until you're unbred food. So, you never let them have the last word. If you fall back, you better have a plan for how you're going to make them pay for every foot you withdraw, every rotten potato they steal, every goddamn *twig* they snapped on your watch. Make them regret the day they ever crossed you."

"Then why haven't we finished off those Greenbriers?" Amos asked. "I counted twenty-eight dead among the war party we trapped. That must be a sizeable fraction of their best men, gone right there in one battle."

"'Cause the clan comes first. I'd wipe the Greenbriers off the map if I could do it without losing a Tucker. But I don't know that. You go to war, you're liable to sacrifice the lives of your clansmen. It's okay to sacrifice them if you need to, but it's against a watchman's honor to sacrifice them if you don't."

"How will I know if I need to, then?"

"The clan," Elvin answered. "Always for the good of the clan. When the Greenbriers attacked us, we had to hit back, even if it meant losing our kin. But the Greenbriers done lost their fangs. The clan is safe, or at least it will be once we kill that eyeless drifter."

The descent from the high point came much easier than the ascent, and by the time they found their way on the other side, they'd come in a roundabout way to familiar territory. They came out of the woods and stepped into the narrow killzone around the little settlement nestled in the crook of a mountain slope, the rusty mineshaft hoisting-tower poking above the palisade wall like a raised fist. "Ho, there!" Elvin hollered. "Who's wardin' the wall?"

"Me," answered Edward Grierson through a gun port cut into the wall.

"Any news from the highway? Figgered those junkers would've showed up by now."

"We can't have somebody watching the road all day, every day," Grierson complained. "We don't got enough hands to keep this mine going like we ought to, let alone runnin' errands for you everwhich way."

"Or pitch in to help with the harvest like you ought to, neither," Elvin said.

"You've got enough hands to spare three town Tuckers and send 'em all the way out here to pester us about a road hardly anybody ever uses."

"You're picking up your brother's ornery streak, you know that, Eddie?"

"Yeah, well, we're running a business out here, not an army outpost, and ain't neither of us cotton to you trying to turn us into one."

"Eddie, we killed us a Greenbrier scout not two miles from here just the other day. I want you out to that highway every morning. If I have to go all the way out there myself, I'm a-gonna be pissed."

"See? There you go again! Why we gotta waste time on the lookout for a friendly clan like they're a shadower army?"

"'Cause I don't trust foreigners, no matter how nice they talk. I told you, they shoulda showed up two days ago."

"Could be any number of reasons they ain't—"

"Eddie!" someone called from the other side of the settlement, loud enough for Elvin, Amos, and Ralph to hear. "Caravan come up the road just now. It's the junkers, but they've got soldiers with them this time! Army guys, with machine guns and all! I hear tell they've come all the way from Washington D.C.!"

"*Dadgummit,*" Eddie hissed from behind the gun port.

125

Right outside the eastern gate, in the open space where the brush had been cut back from the road and the wall, the junker visitors, their new armed escort, and the ever-growing crowd of Tuckers faced each other. The soldiers, some twenty-five or thirty of them, milled about and thumbed the safeties on their sundry automatic weapons, regarding the Tuckers with equal parts amusement and wariness, as if the clan members were a tribe of unsophisticated apes who may or may not be man-eaters. But out of deference to the watchman's orders, the man in charge and his heavily armed comrades remained outside the eastern gate with a full dozen vigilant Tucker guards watching over them while someone went to fetch Sam.

The Tuckers showed more interest in the strangers than the strangers did in them. Amongst the armed guards, but well separate from the junkers, was a simple mule-drawn cart with a canvas-draped body on it, an odd burden to bring along when most travelling folks buried their dead on the side of the road. But it was the Americans' weapons which drew the Tuckers' overstanding wonder. Not many Tuckers could accurately identify the different guns, but the light machine gun, with an underslung ammo box like a treasure chest full of priceless jewelry, spoke for itself. All of it looked pristine—no duct tape anywhere. The troops wore camo fatigues and looked like they had stepped right out of the early days, when the military had scrambled together, too late, to exterminate the unbreds. Elvin waited with his arms crossed, not yet saying a word.

The butcher, Arnold Brody, leaned over next to Elvin. "They've come with the junkers... ain't too likely to be an ornery bunch, right?"

But they weren't themselves part of the junker clan, which meant the elders would have to figure out what to do with this armed escort, which meant fetching Sam Chambers, which was why they had to wait out here watching the trees grow while Sam came out from his schoolhouse to hear the dad-blamedest nonsense Elvin had ever heard. *Washington D.C., my ass.*

When Sam finally did turn up, he did it with a line of eight-year-old dust moppers in tow.

"Absolutely fascinating. Class, this is... what's your name, sir?"

"Chitman. Lieutenant William Chitman," the leader answered. He carried himself strangely, straight up and down, never smiling, but never frowning either. It was hard for Elvin to tell what the man was thinking, other than exercising strict control over his thoughts and feelings.

"This is William Chitman, class, and he and his men are from Washington, D.C. How many of you know where that is?" Sam stepped forward and moved around the stranger like the man was a statue.

One of the little McDaniel girls—Elvin's niece—shot her skinny arm up faster than the others. "It's over east, next to the sea."

"Good. Now why is Washington D.C. important?"

"It was the first place that got nuked."

"No, that's not why it was important, and it wasn't the first place anyway, Wallace. Someone else want to try?"

"It was the capital."

"The capital of what?"

"Of America!"

"Now why was America the greatest country that ever was?"

There was a silence before a Bunton boy raised his hand. "Because they had freedom!"

"And cars!" one of the Craines added.

"Everybody had cars, stupid!"

"Don't say 'stupid,' Wallace. Can anybody tell me why freedom was such a big idea, and why it's important to us?"

The students couldn't come up with an answer.

"America was free because its founders said that all men are equal. America spent a long time trying to make everybody equal. There was a time when some of us here would have had to go to different schools and live in different towns because of what we looked like and where we came from. But that sounds silly to us now, doesn't it?"

The students nodded in unison.

"It used to be that everyone looked the same around here. But when the unbreds took over, people got mixed around everywhere. If it weren't for the idea that we are all equal, the Tucker clan might never have survived. We'd be too busy fighting each other to ward off the unbreds and enemies."

"What's it like where he comes from?" a child asked, pointing to the American.

"Raise your hand, Wallace. I don't know what it's like out there; we have heard nothing directly from that area in thirty years or so, so let's all pay attention and hear what he has to say."

"Later, Sam," Elvin inbroke, his forbearance finally worn out. "I need to talk to him."

Sam sighed as if *he* were the one losing time. "Okay, fine. Everybody say bye!"

The children erupted in a chorus of cheerful goodbyes and filed back in through the gate.

"Ralph, would you take the class back and watch them while I'm gone? Have them practice their figures."

"Ralph's on duty. He stays with me," Elvin snapped.

"I'm on duty too, Elvin," Sam said in that irritatingly laid-back way of his. "If you need me to discuss things with these new folks, I need someone to watch the kids in my place."

"Can't you send the kids back home for the day?"

"Not unless you want to explain to all the tradesmen in town what clan emergency required you to set loose a bunch of kids in their shops."

Elvin looked like he might prefer that to letting his son dodge patrol duty for some limp-wristed babysitting. But these newcomers were still waiting, and this spat had already gone on longer than it should have, as Sam had likely planned. "Go on, git in there," Elvin growled at his son.

Ralph slid past his father like a rat hoping to snatch errant crumbs.

Elvin turned and gave William Chitman the tongue-lashing he'd been saving up for the better part of an hour now. "Okay, Chitman. If you're really who you say you are, what the heck took you so long when the folks you're supposed to be bringing here have medicine we need? You tryin' to get my people killed, or are you just lazy?"

Chitman took Elvin's attempted dressing-down with an air of detached professionalism. "I apologize for taking so long," he said, "Heavy geemo activity on the road slowed us down."

"Geemo?" Sam asked.

"Geemo. G.M.O. Genetically modified organisms."

"Oh. We call them unbreds around here." Sam sounded like he wanted to sit around a fire and swap stories. "Is that what did in your unfortunate companion there?" He pointed to the shrouded body on the small cart.

"Hmm?" Chitman turned to the body before waving the question away. "Don't worry about him. Not relevant."

"Okay, Mister Chitman," Elvin said, clapping to keep Sam to the matters at hand, "I want to hear it straight from your mouth. Why you here?"

"*Lieutenant* Chitman. We're the escort for Mr. Salazar and the other representatives from New Ashburn."

"Where's our powderman?" The early wrinkles around Elvin's eyes stood out as he squinted at the officer.

"He elected to stay at New Ashburn. He didn't much care for travel, and he's found himself busy inspecting the facilities around the junker clan." Lieutenant Chitman pulled a thick sheet of fresh, white paper from a pocket on his uniform and passed it to Sam. "I'm sure he explains everything satisfactorily in this letter, which he asked me to give you."

"Where did you get this?" Sam asked, staring at the unfolded letter.

"From your powderman, Bill Puckett," Chitman repeated. "He signed it at the bottom."

"I can see that. I meant the paper."

129

"From our paper mills. Steam-powered." A flurry of whispers sprinkled down on them from the town Tuckers looking down on them from the palisade. Real paper!

"Looks like this checks out," Sam said, scanning Bill's letter. "He sounds excited. He says he needs any help he can get out there. He mentioned Melissa, Ricky, and Omar specifically."

"When the colonel heard you'd cooked up smokeless powder, she wanted to make sure nothing happened to the delegation. Which is why I'm here."

"What colonel?" Elvin asked, his squinty stare never wavering.

"Colonel Armstrong commands the Western Appalachian Expeditionary Force."

"And you call yourselves the 'New American Federation,' huh?" Elvin sneered at the term.

"We've secured the Chesapeake Bay, and we've recently added Norfolk to the south and Philadelphia to the north. We safeguard some two hundred thousand souls, with more joining every day."

"What about the junkers? They part of your Federation?"

"They're in the process of joining us. Naturally, different settlements and enclaves have to adapt somewhat to the way we do things. We have to make sure they're aware of our laws and agree to follow them."

"Okay, that settles it for me," Elvin said. "You and your men can camp outside the walls. You can pick up your junkers when we're through with them."

Lieutenant Chitman came up short. "I have to stay with Mr. Salazar and the other Ashburnites. My orders were—"

"If Salazar didn't think we'd keep them safe, he wouldn't have left his womenfolk with us while he went to run errands. You may run things out east, but you don't run things here. I don't care how much you think you need to watch the junkers, I won't have a mob of strangers totin' chatterguns around town."

"You made a treaty with the junkers, which means you made a treaty with us," Lieutenant Chitman said. "And any problem you make for them, you make with me. They are under my protection."

"Now, Elvin," Sam said, "I think any reasonable—"

"I want an elders' meeting before we do *anything* else. Deals, business talk, anything. We didn't sign up to become part of any federation or foreign government or whatever."

By now, Lieutenant Chitman had retrieved his firearm, which he now held across his body. "Maybe I didn't make myself clear," he said, ticking off the safety on his gun. "You *did* sign a treaty with the American Federation. I would not advise going back on it now."

The on-hand folkward watching from atop the palisade raced to load and prime their weapons. The attending American soldiers spread out from their knot on the road, finding cover—and firing positions—for themselves.

Elvin's stare darkened. "Who the hell—"

Sam cut him off with a snap of his fingers. "Zzzzt!" He stepped in between Elvin and the American lieutenant. "Elvin, we've made a treaty with the junkers, and any friend of theirs is a friend of ours. You *cannot* shoot unless they start shooting first, do you understand?"

Elvin didn't answer, or even look at Sam. Sam stepped closer, blocking Elvin's view of the American. "Watchman. Do you understand?"

Elvin's gaze darted to the American soldiers, or rather their guns and uniforms, and his shoulders slipped downward ever so slightly. Sam saw his face twist even at so small a falter. "I hear you," Elvin growled.

"Mr. Salazar!" Sam called while still keeping his eyes on Elvin. "Are these so-called Americans escorting you in good faith?"

"Yessir," Mr. Salazar answered.

"And is your clan in good standing with the American Federation?"

"We're... we're actually part of the American Federation."

"They lied to us!" Elvin hissed. "These trash-pickers done tricked us into a treaty with a whole state. This deal is off. They can turn right back around and bring Bill back to us. They ain't gettin' their ladyfolks back until they do, I tell you what."

"Calm down, Elvin," Sam warned before turning to Mr. Salazar. "Why didn't you disclose your relationship with this 'American Federation?'"

"Because it doesn't matter. Our treaty is a trade deal: Our penicillin for your powderman, and then the agreed-upon shares of the profits going forward. Whether the Federation takes a cut of the profits or not, it would come out of our end, not yours. Your clan's sole responsibility is to keep up your end of the bargain."

"Which you are trying to back out of," Lieutenant Chitman said.

Sam sighed. "Do you have the penicillin?"

Mr. Salazar raised the satchel he carried at his side.

"That was the deal. Penicillin for the powderman. Deliver the penicillin to Doctor Bernhard, and Mrs. Compton and Miss Perkins will be packed and ready to go with you by tomorrow morning. Any armed personnel, I'm sorry to say, will have to remain outside the clan walls."

"No deal," Chitman said.

"The deal's already been—"

"You're trying to get the medicine out of our hands without giving us what we agreed on in return."

"You already have our powdermaker. Did you not hear me when I said Mrs. Compton and Miss Perkins would be ready tomorrow?"

"I heard what you said. And I have a good idea how tomorrow will go. You will say, 'So sorry; we've thought about it some more, and we don't want to go through with this deal after all, but we're not giving the medicine back either, so you can either go back empty-handed or become geemo food.'"

"Even assuming any Tucker would *ever* be that back-stabbing, why would we do that when you have our powderman?" Sam shook his head.

"My job isn't to predict what an uncontacted hill tribe will or will not do. My job is to protect New American citizens, two of whom you are holding as hostages."

"They agreed to it!"

"I'm sure they did. If I thought they were in imminent danger, we would not be having this conversation at all."

"You tryin' to start something?" Elvin snapped.

Lieutenant Chitman shook his head. "Exactly the opposite. I'm stating precisely what needs to happen for things to end well for everyone. If I don't come in there with my weapons in my own hands to make sure the deal goes through, then the deal's off. No medicine."

Sam turned back to Elvin. "Have your men stand down," he said in a low voice.

"The hell I will."

"I said *stand down*, watchman," Sam said, his voice rising. "They'll be gone when the deal's done. They need this as much as we do, and they're in no position to pull a fast one on us. We outnumber them twenty-to-one."

It felt like a full minute before Elvin waved the folkward to come down from the palisade and open the gates, but wave he did. He shook his head as he watched the soldiers march in, and several of the surrounding Tuckers could hear him mutter, "With guns like those, they can do whatever they want inside our town, twenty-to-one or fifty-to-one."

In the evening twilight, Reverend Brody looked over the paper on the table between him and his protégé. The paper was worth a fair amount of money, but the contract written on it might be worth quite a bit more. That was—it might cost quite a bit more.

"Residents of New Ashburn and Tucker County may travel freely between each others' settlements, while still obeying the laws and customs of their hosts," the Reverend read from the contract. "While the agreement is in effect, at least one member of each party will remain within the other's territory as a guarantee of good faith. The business arrangement may be terminated at any time by either party. In the event of such a termination, all equipment and workers will return to their place of origin, and all products and profits will be distributed between the parties equally. While operating, any profits or products will be split evenly between the two clans, represented by Mr. William Puckett and Mr. Mayce Salazar."

"Seems like fair terms to me," Ella said.

"It's a *hook*," the Reverend spat back, pushing the cursed paper away from him. "The promises of wealth and prosperity—perhaps. But already we are less of a clan because of it. Bill Puckett—*gone.*" He blew dust from his fingers.

"You make it sound like he died."

"He may as well have. He's joined them now. He won't have cause to come back here. And who do we have in his place? Junkers. They're leaving one of their number behind, with a bodyguard of these Federation people to remind us that this isn't a guarantee of our rights. *Sam Chambers* is coming out there with you. He says it's to make sure the deal is kept, but he'll do everything he can to push for more, more, more. Soon, this place will be crawling with foreigners, and *you* will be responsible for keeping our secrets safe when I am gone. How will you manage that, hmm? You've been a Keeper less than half a year, and already, you've failed."

Ella was aghast. "How have I failed? I done everything you asked me to."

"This contract will undo everything I've done as a Keeper, and you saved it."

"And what would have happened to my father if I hadn't?"

"Everyone makes sacrifices for the clan."

"I lost my mother when I was ten years old. I lost my brother when I was eighteen. Mrs. Puckett, who was like an aunt to me, died when I was fifteen. How many kin have you lost, Reverend?"

"It doesn't matter. There's not a single one I wouldn't give up to keep the rest safe. Now, they're all in danger because of your carelessness."

"That..." Ella shook her head, blinking as if she'd opened up a jar of spoiled food. "That don't make any sense at all. Why... with thinkin' like that, why send out roundswalkers to watch for nomads and unbreds? Why tend the fields if it puts our farmers at risk? Why not stay locked up inside this town like we were during the pigman siege?"

"We *are* in a siege. And you've opened the gates for them. You're not fit to be my apprentice." The Reverend sounded like he was moving on to other business. "I'm meeting with a couple pertinent elders to finalize it, but you will be leaving with the other apprentices."

Ella gasped. "You're banishing me?"

"Not officially. But I don't expect you back as long as this affair with the junkers continues. You, or the drifter, or the harlot. You're all going with him."

Chapter 12

On the Road

The procession stood ready to leave, this time with all of the junkers and a few of the Tuckers. Some of the clan had come out to see them off, one such being Ralph McDaniel.

"So long, Miss Perkins," Ralph said, tipping his floppy hat while doing his best to hide his forlornness, both from Miss Perkins and from the ever-watchful eye of his father.

"I thought about what you said the other night—about watchmen and their sons and such," Jody said, her hair covering the discoloration on the side of her face. "I didn't mean to sound the way I think I sounded."

"Ah." Ralph waved her concern away. "It didn't bother me none." Then, upon a moment's reflection, he added, "Not that I don't care. I do. But I... I know how things are. You were right. Right about my pa. He wouldn't let me take a job out yonder. I let myself get carried away. You're... what were you going to say?"

Jody stopped to measure her words before speaking—an admirable quality among many Ralph lacked himself. "If I had more time, I'd... you pa just seems so scary, is all. I'm sure he's a nice feller, even if he is a... oh, that don't sound right, either. If it were any other way—which I'm not saying it isn't... or maybe it is..."

"What do you mean?" Ralph asked.

Jody took a deep breath. "I'll write to you," she said at last. "Maybe as early as the next nomad clan come through."

Again, Ralph watched her leave, gobsmacked. A letter? For him? How could he afford the paper to write her back?

The caravan made good time on their first day of travel, by Ella's guess. It was remarkable how much difference a road made—even a broken, overgrown, occasionally obstructed road. They made two or three miles for every one they would have taken going through the brush, so even if the road meandered more than she'd have liked, she could see why the nomads used them. There was no telling how fast you could make the trip if you had yourself a fresh horse under you. Their ox pulled the cart in which they'd stored whatever essentials left over from Bill's shop and in which Melissa stored Little Earnest. Earnest thought the journey was quite an adventure for the first quarter-mile, and then a tiresome bore from then on. When he could no longer stand sitting in the bumpy oxcart, he rode on Ricky or Omar's shoulders. Neither seemed to mind. Omar in particular bore the burden with more verve than Ella would have expected from a stoic drifter who'd always referred to Earnest as a "bothersome ankle-biter." Omar occasionally bade Earnest to quit yanking on his hair, as this was not a horse ride and his hair "weren't no reins," to which Earnest responded by saying "giddy-up" and pulling that much harder.

Ella smiled and allowed herself a low chuckle. When Omar looked her way, she covered her mouth to hide her front teeth, but she no longer broke off her gaze and stared at the ground like she used to. Not with Omar. He cracked his sideways smile her direction.

Melissa kept within arm's reach of her son, occasionally offering to carry him, but not so often that she was in much danger of actually having to tote him. *Nothing wrong with that,* Ella supposed. This was turning out to be more difficult than a Sunday stroll, and the toting might best be left to the menfolk.

Nearby, Ricky Brody walked alongside the oxcart, his ever-vigilant eye on Omar and Ella—she didn't see why it was Ricky's concern where the drifter chose to walk—and on the precious glassware packed between sacks of saltpeter and straw. He shooed the Ashburnites away from the cart as a hen would ward off a cat from her chicks. He especially snapped at Jody Perkins, whether because of her discolored face or because she seemed to worry about the books she had stored on her side of the cart.

"I don't see why we gotta do everything these trash-pickers tell us to," Ricky grumbled once they'd all gone far enough for their feet to hurt.

"Ricky, we're soon to be their guests. 'Trash-pickers' isn't polite," Sam Chambers said to the Brody boy. He picked up little Earnest off of Omar for a spell, who rubbed his sore shoulders before picking up his muzzle-loader from the oxcart and slinging that over his shoulder where Earnest had sat. Sam drifted back over to Mr. Salazar and Mrs. Compton, to continue their near-incessant conversation, likely doing his best to keep moods high and attention away from Ricky Brody's grousing.

Sometime past midday, when the trek had long since passed from adventure to drudgery, a growing awareness pricked the hairs on the back of Ella's neck. Maybe it was something in the woods—but no, she noticed it first in the people around her, in Ricky Brody and Sam Chambers. Conversation ceased, and the pace slowed to a stop.

Ella, pulled free of her one-note drumbeat tread, scanned the forest and underbrush around. The birds had gone silent. Something big moved in the woods and pulled Ella out of her own ponderings. It came closer, and the gigantic crashing in the brush left no doubt what approached. She felt the thud of its footfalls rumble through the pavement under her.

"Bullhusker! Bullhusker comin' out through the trees!" Ricky hollered to the American guards.

Lieutenant Chitman waved away Ricky's worry with an annoyed flick of the wrist. He pulled wax molds out of a satchel at his side and stuffed them into his ears with unhurried efficiency as he signaled to his men to fan out along the edge of the treeline.

"Lieutenant!" Ricky Brody hissed. "You ain't got enough guns to take on a bullhusker toe-to-toe! We gotta get off-road, fasten up on those cliffs up there!"

Chitman didn't bother to shush Ricky a second time. Instead, he waded into the nearly chest-high weeds and young trees at the edge of the road and bellowed into the woods without a single thought for his own safety.

The rustling in the woods picked up, and soon, they all saw the flickering movement of a great hulking thing approaching through the undergrowth, branches and vines snapping under the inexorable onslaught of its strength and growing rage. Chitman had issued a challenge, and the bullhusker had taken it up.

Its two gleaming tusks emerged first, curved upward and sharp enough to spit a horse. Then came the rest of its head, the whites of its eyes shining out, human-like but for their animal stare. Its face sagged around its massive tusks and millstone teeth like the jowls of an old glutton. Its whole body was a mass of heavy folds and tumorous bulges, but all that thick hide concealed the muscle and concrete bone underneath.

The beast was not yet fully clear of the forest when Chitman opened up with his assault rifle. The percussive blasts from the muzzle made Ella blink with each shot. The tall summer grass shivered and bowed before the gun as if from the gusts of a thunderstorm. The bullhusker began its charge, but no sooner had it moved than it felt the sharp sting of jacketed rounds punching through its iron hide like stakes driven into the ground by a heavy post driver. Chitman squeezed off shot after shot, the coiled springs of his arms and shoulders bringing the weapon back to zero every time.

The pigmen who'd accompanied the bullhusker piled up behind the massive corpse and collectively locked eyes with Chitman. The Federation lieutenant waved his hand at the pigmen in the same way he'd waved away Ricky's concern. The pigmen bowed as one, turned, and fled back into the woods.

"I suppose now is as good a time as any to take a break," the lieutenant said, slinging his gun and stooping to pick up his spent brass as if he hadn't just performed an entire series of miracles. "Grab a bite to eat while my men cut this thing up. We'll pull every bullet we can out of the carcass, and once your factory's up and going, we'll be able to reload our spent ammunition for the first time in decades."

They made camp that night with the western hills behind them sprawling like knees curled up under a bedsheet. The road, no longer paved in any meaningful sense of the word, skipped along the headlands through intermittent patches of woods and grassy glades, wagon ruts in the dirt here and there deepening to gullies. A swath of footworn earth branching off from the main path led them down the slope to a spring of icy water guarded by the hanging branches of hunched willows. Everyone refilled their canteens as the setting sun winked at them between the knuckles of stony hillocks. Ella marveled at how far they'd come in just one day. "The Tucker clan must be clear on the other side of them mountains," she said to Omar as the two of them got off their sore feet.

"Huh?" Omar said as he laid down his gear and started tying the net he used as a travel pack into a hammock well off the ground.

"I think I recognize those hills, but they always seemed so far off east to me. And now I'm looking at them from the other side."

"Never been this far out?"

"Never. I don't suppose this distance means much to you."

Omar shrugged. He passed her a blackgum twig. "Brush up."

"Thanks." She took the twig and started chewing. "Why you tyin' your hammock up so high?"

"Safety. Don't want an unbred gettin' at me before I can get full awake."

"I think you've spent too much time on your own. We got plenty of watches to warn us if it comes to that." Ella pointed at the four Federation soldiers already fanning out into the woods, laying claim to this part of the wilderness for the night.

"I ain't in a habit of trusting other folks with my life," Omar said. Then, in a low voice, he added, "Overstandingly not these jaspers."

Ella looked around her with the sudden new wariness of her surroundings a deer might have when sensing a predator. The few junkers with them, as well as Sam and Melissa and Ricky, went about their business like the clan-bound ignorant travelers they were, but the soldiers... the soldiers were different. Not just hardened. They were dangerous. She hadn't noticed it before because... well, because it seemed like Omar was always there, standing between her and the guards, and because Lieutenant Chitman seemed so orderly and proper, and he kept his men on a tight leash, or so it seemed. They didn't speak, but when Chitman wasn't looking, the guards passed knowing glances between each other—smirking, silent mockeries of their commander, or their orders, or the ones they were charged to protect, and maybe of all of them. The blackgum twig frayed into strands between her teeth, but she kept on chewing.

The uniforms they wore were nothing but a layer of whitewash. These were thugs and brutes, and if they were loyal to anyone, it wasn't the Tuckers. They'd likely protect Bill because they had to, but everyone else was worth no more to them than a tooth to use in a trade.

One must have seen Ella staring, because he abandoned his companions to sidle up next to her, uncomfortably close. He was chewing on something that stank. "See something you like, girl?" he asked.

Ella popped the blackgum toothbrush out of her open mouth and looked down. Her reputation for staring was coming back to her in the worst way. She stepped backward, and the soldier stepped forward, closing the space between them further.

Then Omar wedged himself in between them, his own blackgum twig clenched between his teeth at the corner of his mouth. He stood nose-to-nose with the soldier.

The soldier's smirk turned into a scowl. He rolled whatever he was chewing into his cheek with smacking lips and tongue. "Hey there, kid. Trying to show your splicing in front of your girlfriend?"

"No," Omar answered, his voice flat, even bored. "I'm trying to get to my bunk. There's twenty square miles of empty land around us, and you chose to stand right where I need to be."

The soldier's jaw clenched, and for a moment, it looked like he was about to hock whatever he had in his mouth all over Omar's face.

Lieutenant Chitman's voice snapped the taut silence between them. "Starkman! What are you doing?"

"I'm getting sick of these goat-fuckers staring at me," the soldier answered without looking away from Omar.

Lieutenant Chitman walked up, his autorifle still slung down in a carry position. "I don't give a shit. Choke down your rations and go to sleep. You're on the second watch. Don't waste your sleep time."

When the soldier was gone, Lieutenant Chitman turned to Omar and Ella. "I suggest you leave my men alone." He gave a meaningful glance to Ella especially.

"I was just... I was wondering how the nomad clans manage the travel, with it being so dangerous on the road and all. Y'uns have guns, but even if the nomads have automatics, they can't get into the habit of using old ammo every time a pigman swarm gets after them." Ella had to scramble for a reasonable-sounding question, and this one worked exactly because she'd wondered about it for some time.

"Most of the ones I know train in the phalanx." Chitman waved a hand to swat the details away like so many pesky mosquitoes. "It's hard to keep together, and a bullhusker will knock them over like bowling pins, but it works against the smaller geemos, most of the time. And several of them have a neurocaster with them."

Ella's eyebrows bunched together. "A what?"

Now Chitman looked at Ella as if she were some funny curiosity. "Huh," he said to himself. "Never mind. See to your things. We'll get back on the road tomorrow once the sun's dried the dew."

When they were alone again, Ella looked over at Omar. "Is there enough room in that tree for both of us?"

Chapter 13

New Ashburn

Three days later, the small caravan came around the bend as evening approached to see the gates of New Ashburn within shooting distance, nearly a full day earlier than Ella'd hoped for. *Hallelujah.* She didn't think she could hack the life of a nomad. Her feet were killing her.

Two torches burned brightly over the gate in the summer twilight. A tall wall of riven trunks and sundry salvaged materials surrounded an old compound by the river—once a utilities station, perhaps.

"Home sweet home," William Chitman said to his Tucker escorts after calling out a pass phrase to the sentries.

Bill Puckett came out to greet them with open arms. "Welcome to New Ashburn."

"Bill!" Melissa Daly cried out before running forward to catch him in a quick embrace.

"Oof! Uh, good to see you, Mrs. Daly," he said, his cheeks flushing. "I've been out here the last three days looking for anyone coming from out west. Is everything settled? Oh, Sam's here, I reckon you got some cud-chewing to do? Ah, never mind. Follow me. If you're headed to the citadel, I can show you on the way where I'm thinking of setting up the factory." Bill didn't let Sam or anyone else to get a word in edge-wise as he pointed out the various old-world structures and the newer edifices further up the winding trail that roughly followed the contour of the river downhill to the left.

Omar whistled to himself as they entered New Ashburn. "Take a look at those." On either side of the gate, covering the approaching party, loomed two light machine guns with ammunition belts curling out of the receivers./

Inside, the distinction between the junkers and their American protectors stood out like whey separated from milk. All the Americans wore military camouflage without any of the gaudy bangles that warlike marauders and ostentatious nomads were apt to wear. The junkers who swarmed out to receive them wore the weathered clothes and looks of workmen.

A score of American guards patrolled inside the walls, nearly all armed with pristine automatic rifles. The Tuckers stared. Most of the families of the clan had some old hunting rifles and shotguns, with maybe a pistol here and there. Automatic guns were special prizes claimed by the wealthiest Tuckers, and only used in the direst emergencies.

"Just what did you get us into, Bill?" Melissa asked.

"Hopefully, the best thing that's ever happened to our clan."

"What's that big pile over yonder?" Ricky Brody asked.

"Reclaimed scrap from the surrounding area," Lieutenant Chitman answered. "Standard procedure."

"I didn't figure there was that much scrap metal still around that hadn't rusted to bits," Ricky wondered aloud.

"Our recycling program has reached a scale that even the junker clans can't match."

"How do these junkers feel about that?" Ella asked.

"Why do you think they joined up with us? Or why they wanted to set up a factory? 'Make yourself useful or die.' It's the same rule since the geemo Revolt, one level up."

"That don't sound like the deal they got when Mr. Salazar talked it up to us."

"There's two ways to look at it," Mayce Salazar said. "Our clan saw it more as 'Progress or die.' For the first time, we're seeing people coming to us looking for work. You'll have plenty of labor to get your factory up and going, Mr. Puckett. And the Federation's protection frees up our fighters to do other jobs. It's amazing what you can do when you don't have to worry about pigman raids or shadower armies."

Just beyond the massive heap of rust-pocked metal, a smithy bellowed smoke into the sky. A smattering of grime-encrusted workers toiled to forge links for a set of chains that coiled out of the smithy and hung from the overhanging ceiling. The acrid smell of pine tar and coal smoke hung in the air. The Tuckers had never seen so many chains. "Your factory is a small part of what we're starting out here. If we can produce enough scrap around here," Salazar continued, "we might start up a steel-mill or something, which would bring in *more* workers. Thanks to a wealthy backer from out east, we pay in teeth at the end of every week—real money."

Ella found herself wandering from the group, examining the forge and the throng of laborers. It was nearly evening, past time for the workday to wind down. They didn't look like Tucker workmen. They looked more tired and... scared. There was a young woman there, not much older than her. Their eyes locked for a moment before an American guard turned the young woman back to her work with a heavy hand on her shoulder.

"Don't want to wander away, now," Chitman said from behind Ella.

"Those folks ain't paid." Ella didn't turn to face the lieutenant behind her.

"Smart kid."

"Y'uns keep slaves?"

"Not slaves. Prisoners."

"They don't look like criminals to me."

"Not that kind of prisoner. Don't you know there's a war on?"

"War?"

"Oh, I guess you wouldn't know about that out here. Stick with the group if you want to learn something."

Ella sped up to get close to Bill. "Did you see those raggedy folks yonder?" she asked in a low voice.

"I seen 'em." Bill kept his gaze straight ahead, his jaw set.

"We ain't gonna use them in the factory, are we?"

"Don't you fret about it, none. I'm sure there's some kind of explanation for it."

"But Bill, did you *see*—"

"I told you I seen it." Bill sighed. "Any workers of mine get treated proper, you'll see. I don't care who they is."

The group wove their way through the town. In contrast to the Tucker town, newer construction dominated the settlement. The various recycled materials gave it a jumbled, run-down look, but evidence of careful planning told Ella this was a place where people lived rather than merely survived. Except—

"Where are the houses?" Ricky asked, speaking aloud what Ella had wondered.

"These are all shops and salvage depots. Recycling, processing, our tradesmen."

"And our library," Jody Perkins said, pointing to a boxy, windowless metal building with a rusting metal staircase leading up to a second-story exterior door.

"Yes, and our library. All of this used to be zoned for heavy industry and transportation, so it didn't take much effort for our founders to make the switch when we used it for processing salvage."

147

"We used to have something like this around the Tucker clan," Bill said, "but we left it all out in the old town. The Founders didn't think it was worth the saving, I guess."

"That's not the junker way of thinking. Next year or in a hundred years, we'll be glad we saved it."

"But you can't save *everything*," Ella said.

"Well, no, I guess not. We tore up the asphalt to clear ground for our community garden up yonder. And we couldn't exactly move whole houses out here, so the houses about a mile away, we left to rot."

"Then where do you *live?*" Ricky Brody asked, the disgust in his tone suggesting he wouldn't be surprised if they stretched out a tarp and called it home.

"Up the hill a bit. Our foodstores and housing"—Mr. Salazar pointed uphill, away from the grim rusty crush of industry to the towering corner of the distant edifice—"are all in there."

"That?"

The blocky, square building was immense, stretching almost beyond their field of view. The uphill slog suddenly flattened out into a vast clan main, some of it indeed a large garden, some of it home to more shops and storage, but the rest of it a wide sweep of asphalt. The clan main, Ella realized, had once been the parking lot for this massive structure. The giant construction intruded into the hillside that swaddled it on three sides. It was as if some mythical titan had cut a slice out of the hill and used a half-mile wide building to patch the hole.

"It used to be a super-mart," Salazar explained. "It's got enough square footage to comfortably house our nine hundred souls. It's nicely compartmentalized. We have year-round refrigeration in the back, electric lighting, and indoor plumbing. And it's wonderfully defensible."

Indeed, on closer inspection, the entire clan's layout bore evidence of careful planning. Except, of course, for the walled-off slums next to the super-mart where the slaves were clearly kept. There was no room for them in the luxurious expanse of the Ashburnite quarters.

"I figured it would smell around here," Ricky said.

"If the wind moves the wrong direction, it does," Mr. Salazar explained. "When the town was founded, we found this made for an ideal setup. The super-mart was the kind of shelter we needed. The river gave us a clean water supply and, until the dam failed, hydroelectric power. The landfill's further to the east, a safe distance from both the town and our drinking water, but not so far it's hard to get to."

"How safe is your drinking water? You ain't ever had the landfill leak into the river?"

"The landfill is downhill of the river, and the old-world engineers made doggone sure groundwater always flowed toward the landfill instead away from it."

"Wouldn't that flood your landfill, though?" Sam Chambers asked.

"That's the beauty of it! They installed drains, basically wells, to pull off extra flow from groundwater before it can reach the landfill. We get clean, ground-filtered water right out of those drains, and it keeps our landfill worksites dry at the same time. If you want, I can give you a tour of our landfill worksites sometime—"

"Maybe, but remember, I'm not here for a tour," Sam said.

"Right. You'll need to talk to Colonel Armstrong. Not even Mr. Puckett here has gone to see her yet."

"Where is she? In the super-mart?"

"What? No, no, no. The Americans don't live with us." Mr. Salazar pointed up the winding path ascending the steep mountainside behind the super-mart to the fortress above their heads. "It used to be our citadel for last-ditch emergencies. Colonel Armstrong's using it as her base of operations now."

"You have accommodations already lined up here at New Ashburn. You all can hit the sack as soon as Colonel Armstrong debriefs you," Chitman added.

The citadel overlooking New Ashburn was a circular wall of wooden stakes topped with twisted locust-tree branches used for barbed wire. In its middle sat a preexisting concrete monolith of a structure. Likely it used to be the base and maintenance building for some huge broadcasting tower, but rusting metal shards poking up at the sky were all that remained of such a spire. The squarish building, meanwhile, had what looked to be a couple guards on the roof. One guard, however, lay stretched out on a lawn chair with a pair of binoculars around his neck, while the other waited at the side, hands clasped behind his back.

Upon admittance to the small courtyard, Lieutenant Chitman hailed the seated watcher, "Captain Carlson," who answered back without getting up, "Go in. Colonel Armstrong is expecting you." Upon a closer look, Ella saw the soldier bore some kind of insignia on his shoulder. He had the square, pugilistic face of a brute, but bright, quick eyes. For someone so slouched and lackadaisical, he carried a sharpness about him.

Ella blinked at the chill brightness of the concrete hallway inside. "Y'uns got electricity here?" she asked, incredulous, shielding her eyes at the garish brilliance. "And enough to use on lightbulbs?"

"They're LED's," Chitman answered, leading them on. "Most efficient lighting you can get. The solar panels we've salvaged are more than enough to keep the fort going."

"And the town down yonder?" Bill asked. "Electricity would make things at the factory a lot simpler."

"And a lot more complicated at the same time," Chitman answered. "Infrastructure is the name of the game. We have enough difficulty keeping the refrigeration units in the super-mart working reliably. The tradesmen have to make do without power most of the time. We don't have the materials or the available experts to wire up all of New Ashburn without burning through all our resources or frying careless workers. Or both. But you can ask Armstrong for a requisition if you decide electricity is necessary."

The party waited under guard in a narrow hallway while the lieutenant stepped into an inner room and closed the door behind him. A few minutes later, a soldier ushered the Tuckers into the room, where a woman dressed in uniform paced in front of an office desk as if in the middle of solving an urgent problem. The other occupant—a wiry, pale man with a head so hairless it shone under the bare lightbulb in the ceiling—stood at the side, an antithesis to the woman's sharp intensity. His vacant stare and slack jaw remained unchanged as the visitors entered the room.

The office, like the rest of the building and the whole settlement, felt like a mix of old and new. The harsh electric light laid bare discolored walls and worn, cracked laminate flooring, and the room had the faint musty odor of the kind of dark, abandoned buildings in the old town Ella had learned to avoid as a child. Yet patches of the floor shone through gleaming and untarnished, suggesting the recent cleaning and rearranging of the space, and a hole in the wall at the back of the room was one apparently made on purpose, with the revealed wall studs reinforced with new-cut timber and a mess of patched wiring coiling out of it. And all around the room were stacks of clean blank paper in sheets and whole spooled rolls—more paper than Ella had seen in her entire life.

The woman pacing the room was around Bill's age—dark-haired, stern, and shockingly beautiful. She had none of the wrinkles that most Tucker women her age had developed. She wore two holstered nine-millimeter pistols and an inscrutable face that commanded attention and was probably accustomed to commanding much more. In her hand, she held a glass decanter with a drink cooled by fresh ice. The beads of sweat on the outside of the glass reminded Ella of how

151

worn-out she was, and how much she might like a taste of that cold water.

"The representatives from the Tucker clan, Colonel Armstrong," Chitman said, entering the room behind Ella. Then, upon seeing the bald man in the corner of the room, he lost his composure for the first time since Ella had met him. "What's *he* doing here?" Chitman demanded.

"We can discuss why I requested Jarvis' transfer out here when there aren't civilians present, Lieutenant," the woman said.

"Sorry, sir." Chitman bowed his head.

The woman took a drink from her glass, the ice clinking to tantalize the parched travelers. "I'll handle the new arrivals, Lieutenant. Get your men out to the barracks and rest up. I'll debrief you and give you your next assignment in an hour."

Chitman nodded and left the Tuckers with the woman just as the square-faced man from the roof entered from a back door and leaned up against the wall next to the man called Jarvis.

"The Lieutenant tells me your clan has some reservations about dealing with the Federation," the colonel said, though Ella couldn't decide whether she was accusing, questioning, or merely stating a fact.

Sam Chambers seemed to take it as an accusation. "We agreed to a trade deal, and we kept our end of the bargain. No more, no less."

"Then why are you here?"

"Bill Puckett is here, and has been here, to start up a nitrogel factory in New Ashburn, like he agreed to in a contract signed by both him and Mr. Salazar, the junker. *I* am here to talk to you about closer ties to the Federation. Lieutenant Chitman was helpful in getting us here, but he was a little vague on the details."

"Fine," Armstrong said. "As it stands, you are already in an alliance with the Federation. New Ashburn is now a Federation city, and the junkers who started it are now Federation citizens. You have a trade partnership with them; therefore, you have a trade partnership with us.

There's nothing left to discuss. You're under Federation authority and protection as a trade partner."

"Whoa, now. We're trade partners. Fine. But that's... a pretty limited alliance," Sam said. "By the terms of our contract, we're exchanging workers, equipment, and materials related to nitrogel production. That's it."

"What about the penicillin delivery I authorized?" Armstrong asked.

"It was a good deal, and an honest one. It was all stipulated in the contract."

"So, here's what happens," Armstrong said, placing her now-empty glass on the desk. "When you, by whatever mechanism you choose, decide to apply for admission to the Federation, a review detachment will survey your settlement to screen for problematic elements. We don't want bands of marauders or beggars latching onto the Federation. Upon your approval, which I have the authority to give, your settlement will move to probationary provincial status."

"What does that mean?"

"It means your clan will have access to trade deals exclusive to Federation allies and the Federation-approved nomad clans running our trade routes—things like penicillin or paper. Your nitrogel will also be sold exclusively through these channels."

"The nomad clans we normally trade with won't like that deal."

"They can take it up with me. That's why I required this factory set up here: so other parties can't bully a clan on the fringe of our territory into a trade partnership I don't like."

"What about laws? Will we still be self-governing?"

"As far as it concerns local matters, yes. All our provinces have a high degree of self-determination. There are a small number of statutes we insist on—like not starting any wars we're obligated to help you with—and there will be a temporary enforcement detail to see these statutes are followed, but it's all a formality, really."

Sam sighed. "I believe in keeping everything above-board on the negotiating table, and so I have to tell you we're already at war with another clan to the south. Greenbriers. We've given them a bloody nose, but I can't honestly say they're out of the fight. Our clan has no further offensives planned, but I can't say what the Greenbriers want other than that they haven't sent us talks of any kind of peace."

Ella saw the bald man called Jarvis twitch out of his apparent stupor at the mention of "Greenbriers." She looked at Colonel Armstrong, who also froze for a moment. But it was no more than a moment, as likely to have been about the mention of the ongoing war as it was the name of the opposing clan.

Either way, Armstrong was quick with her response. "The Federation is very tight-fisted with its military resources, so don't expect assistance, material or otherwise, in your local conflicts. Among other things, we're very near to eradicating all hostile genetic chimeras in a hundred-mile radius around the District of Columbia. In the future, we're looking at expanding our safe zones, securing our roads, and building out new infrastructure."

"To where? To us?" Sam asked, his eyebrows raising at so ambitious a statement.

"To whatever provinces prove most valuable. Which brings me to you, powderman," she said, turning to Bill. "I want you to show me your formula."

"Uh, I—well—" Bill stammered.

"I'm afraid his formula is a closely guarded secret," Sam explained.

"I'm a representative of the New American Federation," Colonel Armstrong said as she crossed her arms. "I'm the most trustworthy person in these hills. And I will accept no production deal if I don't know exactly what is being produced."

Reluctantly, Bill fished out a sheaf of loose yellow papers and passed them along. Armstrong looked at them with distaste. "I don't understand any of this," the American commander said, examining the stained notes.

"Well, of course not; I wouldn't expect you to," Bill said, then corrected himself at a sideways glance from Armstrong. "That is, a powdermaker would have to give it a close lookin'-over to get it all figured out."

"What kind of formulation is this? Is this the same gunpowder that vintage ammo has?"

"No. Most stuff you have in your guns has some sort of double-base propellant. Most old ammunition uses nitroglycerin in some form or another."

"Why don't you just use nitro-whatever, then?" She swatted at the air with one hand as if to wave away the useless jargon.

"Too hard to make, and too dangerous once you do. I switched to single-base powder when we had some pretty bad accidents a few years back. My nitrogel is closest to an old French formula—nineteenth century stuff—but it will do the trick, I expect. You can get about the same pressure output for the same cartridge size. The differences would be little things, like how long it will keep and how stable it is."

As Ella watched the back-and-forth, her eyes locked for a moment with the man called Jarvis. The man's eyelids shuttered, and Ella felt a curious, almost spoken urge, like someone breathing down her neck: *Look behind you.*

It was after she had turned and seen nothing that she wondered what had put such an idea in her head. Even then, she might have thought nothing of the passing paranoia, except Sam Chambers had turned as well.

"Is something the matter?" Armstrong asked.

"Sorry, I..." Sam brought his attention back to heel. "I thought I heard something."

Across the room, Jarvis stared at Ella with an expression she couldn't quite read. She couldn't, however, shake the feeling that she herself were being read like an open book.

#

Everyone else had retired to their temporary quarters in the super-mart on their first night in a different clan, and Melissa Daly sat on a rock wall outside, wrestling with a caterwauling Earnest in the dark.

It was the first time either of them had been so far away from home, but it had not made his stir-crazy fussiness any less grating, and her efforts to get him to calm down inside the supermart had backfired. In a matter of minutes, he was pitching a fit that drew the ire of everyone within five units. So she'd hauled him outside and tried to settle him down there.

Earnest was still whining when Melissa heard footsteps behind her. She turned with a gasp, her hand darting to her heart. It was Bill, coming up with his bedroll.

"We'll get you a better sleeping set of stances in the next few days, if the one you got ain't to your liking."

"Just about scared me half to death, Bill!"

"I'd be jumpy out here alone, too. That's why I thought I'd join you."

"You don't mind his bellyachin'?" she asked, wrestling against Earnest's thrashing.

"Can't hardly stand it," Bill grunted as he dropped his sleeping mat next to a sturdy tree and sat himself down. "But I can't stand my ap-prentices getting kicked out of their shanties more."

"I'm used to it. Ain't nothing but a low-down half-and-half, you know."

"I won't abide you talkin' about yourself that-a-way," Bill said. "You can't help who your parents was, or what the ubermenschen did."

"I also can't help how the rest of the clan sees me."

She saw Bill nod in the dark. "Yeah, I reckon."

Earnest had finally lessened his wails to whimpers, and tired ones, at that. He no longer kicked at her, thank goodness. Bill shifted into a more comfortable position with his back to the tree. "Say, how come you and Bert, God rest his soul—"

"His soul ain't resting with God." It was all Melissa could do to keep her voice flat.

Bill cleared his throat. "I didn't want to speak ill of the dead, but I reckon you knowed him better than I did." He coughed. "I was just a-wonderin'... how come the two of you never went out to join the other half-and-halfs at the Grierson settlement? Wouldn't y'uns have been welcome there?"

"The Grierson settlement wasn't really somewhere the half-breeds chose to go. It was more where they were sent."

There was a long pause before Bill spoke again. "I thought they all wanted to go."

"They all *agreed* to go. Peaceful-like, so they could go with supplies and such, instead of out on their asses with naught but their clothes on their backs. It was a nicer banishment that worked out better than the elders thought it would. Likely that nasty ubermenschen breeding made them harder to kill; I don't know."

"I thought... huh." Bill said.

"You'd know if you were a half-and-half."

"How come you weren't kicked out with the rest?"

This time it took Melissa a while to answer. "I got a reputation what saved me and Bert both. Folks thought I was the sort of woman... you don't want too close, but also don't quite want to send away, either."

"I see."

"But I ain't that kind of woman. I never was."

"I didn't think you was."

"All a pack of rumors what keep going around and around."

"And I never did care for the rumor mill."

"But the rumors kept me in town. Rumors might could hurt some men near as bad as they hurt me." Melissa didn't say more. There weren't many men in the clan who would have been more than annoyed at getting charged with adultery, outside the Reverend, and even now she didn't quite want to expose him. "Weren't ever any men who thought

157

anything of me. My own daddy liketa kicked my teeth in when I was little."

"I'm—I'm sorry to hear that."

Earnest had quieted down to the point where Melissa could lay him down on her sleeping bag without riling him up again. His eyes drooped.

"Do you ever get lonely, Bill?"

"Yeah. Sometimes I do."

"I reckon I shouldn't feel lonely all the time. I ain't been a widow long. But Bert weren't a good husband to me. He left me lonely an awful lot."

"I'm... sorry to hear that."

"You was married once, too, weren't you?"

"To Martha."

Melissa scooted closer. "Tell me about her."

"Most folks didn't know I was working on smokeless powder. Those that did thought it was a waste of time. Martha believed in me. Right up 'till the end. Explosion in my shop killed her, but I got to hold her hand before she slipped away. She told me the accident was her fault, so I wouldn't... wouldn't feel as guilty."

"I don't... I don't reckon a lot of women measured up too well to her."

Bill snorted. "You got that right. N-not that I meant any offense to you in particular." He cleared his throat. "You're a... right handsome woman, Mrs. Daly."

Melissa hugged her knees. "I'm cold."

"Huh? This air is downright *wet*, with all the rain we've had. I don't know how you ain't sweating through your shirt."

Melissa got up and sidled up next to him. "Maybe you could warm me up some more."

"Well, I uh..." he started to put his arm around her shoulder, then tensed up like a coiled snake. "Hang on, now. Hang on one doggone second." He stood up and faced her. "Just what the heck do you think you're doing?"

Melissa didn't answer. She was suddenly grateful for the dark masking her face.

"You little... you listen here, little missy... little 'Lissa," he tripped over his words in his indignation. "I'm past ten years older than you, I'd bet. Another ten years, there won't be a hair left on my head. I'm a grumpy 'ole widower, and ain't no changin' that."

"Maybe I don't care about none of that."

"Or maybe I know enough about your... reputation to know what comes next."

"I ain't that kind of woman."

"Oh, ain't you? Then let's get one thing straight, right here. I aim to do right by you as your master, and that's it. I expect you to keep your mind on your work and your learnin'. I don't want none of this... tomcattin' nonsense, or whatever this is." Bill left her, pacing the periphery of the supermart as if on patrol.

Now that Earnest had fallen asleep, Melissa brought him back inside to the privacy of her living space, but she stayed far enough away from those still awake to hide the tears on her face. Stupid. She was long since accustomed to her reputation as the town whore, and she didn't care what one widower thought about her.

Then why couldn't she stop crying?

Chapter 14

A Captain of Industry

B ill Puckett stroked the huge stainless-steel cylinders piled together in what amounted to another big storage shed. The Ashburnites had given him several choices for where to set up his factory. All of the possible factory sites were currently being used for this or that storage with the hope of being useful someday, but with the nitrogel formula promising to be useful now, Salazar had expressed a readiness to make almost any number of accommodations if Bill thought they were needed.

"The tricky thing here is how to step up the cooking," Bill said, taking in the space around him and imagining how he could make the most use of it. "I got us a batch already cooked up with the stuff I had on-hand, plus some ingredients I scraped together over here. And I could keep that up pretty easy—small batches every week or so, as long as I can set up a steady supply chain of glycerol and alcohol. But if I'm gonna come all the way out here, I'd better have more output to show for it. Which means I'll sorta be starting things from scratch here."

Mrs. Compton, who'd been giving him a tour of New Ashburn's various storage sheds full of salvaged goodies, turned to him and scratched her head. "How so?"

"When I first got the idea of doin' the smokeless powder, I knowed I'd need much higher nitration than you get in regular black powder. For the high nitration, you need nitric acid. For the nitric acid, I thought I'd use the Ostwald process I'd read about. But even without the platinum catalyst, I'd need ammonia for feedstock. So that's two things I didn't have. Platinum—"

"Which we have," Mrs. Compton said.

"And ammonia," Bill finished. "Since ammonia's a gas, it's hard to get ahold of in bulk. So, I looked into the Haber process for the ammonia, and I just didn't have anywhere near the money, manpower, know-how, or dadgum *piping* to get started on it. So, I did it the way God intended: pulling the nitrates right out of mountains of crap, which I had to do for black powder anyhow. Then you mix it with sulfuric acid, which I get from iron pyrite. Thing is, my way don't step up too well. But I know how to do it.

"If I were setting up a factory, though, I'd want to do it the *right* way: Get a ton of ammonia, cook it in an oxygen-rich box with some platinum in there, then bubble the gas through a big ole tank of water. Distill that, and you've got a lake's worth of nitric acid. And since the reaction makes a ton of heat and steam, we could get a steam-operated mill or something running off all that extra energy.

"Problem is, I don't know how to make a steam engine, and I ain't comfortable working with the kind of pressure you'd need, and for the Haber process, I'd need hydrogen, which means I'd need coal or oil or methane for that, and I'll be honest: I ain't too familiar with that bit of chemistry." All the roadblocks should have had a stultifying effect on

Bill's enthusiasm, but with all the new toys at his disposal, he relished a challenge.

"Hold up," Cora Compton said. "We'll see about the Haber process, but I think we can run around it entirely. Remember, we're sitting almost right on top of a landfill. Landfills produce tons of methane *and* ammonia, and we've got systems already built to collect them. Do you know what these are?" she asked, tapping the steel cylinders. "We've used them for distilling alcohol, but originally, they were bioreactors for producing ammonia. Genetically modified bacteria were used to help recycle plastic waste, which apparently was a real problem back then. Chuck some plastic bags in there with a healthy culture of this bacteria, make sure they have enough water, and watch your tank fill up."

"Huh. Neat," Puckett said, examining the piping going into and coming out of the tanks. After thinking for a moment, he turned to the junker woman. "Y'uns have salt around? Like, a lot of it?"

"Depends on what for. How much you need?"

Bill pursed his lips and squinted, calculating in his head. "Fifty pounds, maybe?"

"We cure meat, same as everyone else. I could scrape you up some. Why?"

Bill waved a hand at the tanks and tubes. "Gettin' ideas."

When Mrs. Compton saw he didn't intend to elaborate, she shrugged and moved on. "What I'm concerned about is safety. We're going to be dealing with acid, poisonous gas, pressurized vessels, and explosives. Miss Holland said you've blown up your shop twice?"

Bill shifted from one foot to another, looking down. "Once was sabotage. I'll be careful."

"It's not enough for *you* to be careful. We'll need some fifty workers in here, and they'll all need to be trained. Protocols," Mrs. Compton said, as if the very word sent her into religious ecstasy. "Our clan knows about the need to guard against creeping dangers like toxic waste. Walk me through every step of the process, and we'll look at each failure point.

And all of this"—she waved at the entire array of pumps, valves, pipes, and tanks—"will be inspected daily."

Mrs. Compton had set up the Tuckers a couple days ago in a wing of her own apartment, which, by the look of it, was a roost not many Ashburnites could aspire to. The astounding thing, though, was not the floor space. It was that though it was hot enough outside to bring out a sweat standing still, the entire indoors felt cool, and not like a nice-breeze-through-an-open-window cool, but a deep-inside-the-Grierson-mine cool. It was unnaturally, refreshingly cool. Ella hadn't really known what it meant until she'd felt it for herself—air conditioning.

"Who would have thunk banishment would've made life easier?" Melissa Daly had said, sprawling out on the real-foam, mostly stain-free mattress, and Ella had to admit she had a point.

But now, with Bill caught up in the planning, and workers—slaves—toiling simply to clear the space for the factory equipment, Ella found herself without much to do. She settled on seeing the town, and Omar and little Earnest wordlessly elected to come along with her; Earnest, because the little boy had taken on a bald-faced infatuation with her, and Omar likely out of some notion she needed protection out there. Given the tense four-day journey from home, maybe she did.

Indeed, she did need someone with her, even if not to ward off hateful soldiers. Wandering through the town, unsure of whom to talk to or where to go, Ella felt with great acuity her status as an outsider. Most of the junkers seemed friendly enough, but they all gazed at her and Omar with a curious scrutiny she had never borne before. They stared at her, holding the hand of a small child who was not her own, walking around somewhere she clearly didn't belong. When Melissa Daly caught up with them and took Earnest away, Ella imagined she might have been taking more comfort from the boy than he was taking from her. She finally had enough of the stares and marched out from the safety of the walls towards the wilderness beyond, at which point Omar certainly had to tag along to protect her.

She examined the low hills hugging close to the river wending its snake-like path around New Ashburn. Narrow dells, fenced off for growing potatoes, scooped here and there into the woods. On a stretch of flat land to the north lay what looked like New Ashburn's version of the old town—a rotten scattering of an industrial district, some of it perhaps connected to processing landfill waste long ago.

"How did you cope with it?" Ella asked Omar.

"With what?"

"Feelin' like a horse on auction in the middle of a clan you aren't kin to."

"An army of hungry pigmen has a way of making any company tolerable."

"Well," Ella said with an affected huff, "I suppose I'm happy you find my company more tolerable than an unbred's."

Omar smirked enough for her to notice. "Just barely."

Ella gave him a shove, which Omar took with that ornery half-smile of his.

A nearby American soldier up on the palisade followed them both with his eyes, and it wasn't until they were out of his sight that Omar continued. "You'll get used to the stares. Most folks don't mean nothin' by it."

"I'm a stranger to everyone here, though. Makes me miss the home folks already. I wonder if Pa's gettin' better by now."

"You'll get past it. I figure we'll be too busy to worry about lonesomeness, anyhow."

They passed under a barely intact railroad bridge. Though some of the stones had fallen away due to erosion, graffiti covered what remained of the underside. Ella looked up at the crude drawings and misspelt scrawls. "How much longer you reckon this bridge here will stand?" Ella asked.

Omar reached out a laid a hand over an inscription describing some long-dead girl's loose morals. "Thing's made of stone. Dogged if I know. Hundreds of years, maybe."

"Quite a thing of cleverness and hard work, I'd say. And what would you bet that all this," Ella pointed to the paintings, "will stick to its underbelly until the very end."

"You sayin' it says a little something about humans?"

Ella sighed. "Yeah, I reckon, but I just realized sayin' anything about it is so tiresome I'm liketa bash my head in with this here rock."

Omar laughed—not a thing he often did, and then only alone with Ella.

"What do you think about New Ashburn keeping slaves?" Ella asked without preamble, her smile fading.

"I know they want us to call them prisoners of war."

"And what do you think about that?"

Omar ran a hand through his hair. "I think if a feller looks at a turtle and says it's a bird, it's either because he's crazy, or he wants you to think you are."

"But what should we do about it?"

"Not sure that we can do much about it. Take it from me. There's more evil in the world than we can ever hope to fix."

"But that don't mean we ignore whatever evil we can fix."

Omar drew a long breath. "Yeah, you got me thinking that way sometimes. Against my better judgement. Bill might be able to get some pull for the slaves."

"Yeah." Ella brightened up a bit, having some hint of a plan to put her mind at ease.

"Want to head on back, then?"

"Sure. I needed some space from people for a bit, is all."

They reentered New Ashburn and explored the sundry shops round the backside of New Ashburn's warehouses. "It ain't all too different from home, I reckon," Ella said. "Folks busy with their work, trying to scrape a living, helping each other out as best they can."

"It's the bad 'uns you gotta watch out for," Omar said as he scanned the various junker and American faces along the way. "Folks are the same all over, but there are always bad 'uns here and there."

"Is that how it was with your own clan?"

"It's been a long time since I left home. But yeah, I reckon. We had us some bad 'uns."

"And some good 'uns, apparently," Ella said, turning toward Omar.

Omar stopped and turned to face her, as well. "I—"

"Omar! Ella!" It was Ricky Brody, coming down from the direction of the supermarket. "Bill's been looking for you. Don't go wandering off. We can't trust these trash-pickers. Omar, Bill wants you to go with Melissa and me to tote a bunch of glass tanks. Ella, he wants you to wait for him up at the supermart." Ricky headed back up the way he came.

"Well, the break was nice while it lasted," Ella said.

"I'll see you later," Omar said, meeting Ella's eyes with his warm, if almost imperceptible, half-smile.

She returned the smile, and for a moment she had no thoughts to spare for her mule teeth, or her long face, or her scraggly hair. "Yeah, I'll see you," she answered. He left without another word. No other words were necessary.

Ella watched Omar go and heaved a long sigh before she went her own way. She did not, however, make straight for the supermart, but rather took a detour to scout out the planned area for the factory.

Along the way, Ella drifted to a halt at a slapdash cowpen crammed into an out-of-the-way excavated hillside. Except the pen didn't hold cattle. It teemed with people, mostly resting in the dwindling shade of the steep rock wall at the back. There was no other shelter from the elements.

She felt the urge not to stare too long, to move on before the guard on duty there noticed her... too late. The American walked towards her.

Ella didn't move or look directly at the approaching guard. There was a woman standing out in the sun, her hands clinging to the chicken-wire stretched over the aluminum fence panels. She had stinking rags for clothes, and her face was lined with hardship. Their eyes met. Ella saw grief, pride, and baleful hate mixed together in her face.

"No civilians allowed here," the American guard said, yawning.

"Are these the workers we're supposed to use for the factory?"

The American took a closer look at Ella. His face took on a nasty, low-down, Bert Daly kind of look.

"I'd like to talk to that lady there," Ella said.

"What's a cute little bitch like you want in the slave pen? You want to join them?"

Ella stammered at the guard's harsh turn. She'd never thought a smile could look so wicked. "They... they said these people weren't slaves. They said the workers were prisoners of war."

"They are."

"A bunch of these are women, children, and old folks." Ella pointed to the woman leaning against the fence. "Is the Federation fighting an army of mothers and their kids?"

The guard's leering smile never wavered. "Look, honey—you're from that powdermaking shithole, right? This new factory's going to make your clan rich. Don't bite the hand that feeds you."

Ella looked back at the woman behind the fence. "If this is where my food comes from, I'd rather go hungry."

She walked away. She'd get answers for this, one way or another.

Lieutenant William Chitman waited while Colonel Armstrong put the finishing touches on her letter, "Concerning the Pacification of the Hill Tribes of Central Appalachia."

"Is this for the extra reinforcements, sir?" Chitman asked.

"Had to get them somehow."

"What about the Pied Piper?"

"He can wait." Armstrong folded the paper and dripped some wax from a nearby candle onto the fold.

"But, sir, if I may—"

"You may not. I understand our mission better than you do, especially how to accomplish it. The higher command didn't give me enough resources to go after the Pied Piper, and I've found a way to secure those resources."

The American lieutenant kept his gaze focused at an invisible spot on the wall above and to the left of Armstrong's head. "Permission to speak freely, sir?"

"I know what you're going to say, Chitman. But people are resources just as much as anything else. You of all people should know that."

"I regret what I... had to do."

"But you had to do it." Armstrong rearranged a couple items on her desk, signaling the end of the discussion. "I'm placing you under Captain Carlson's command for now. If and when I receive the reinforcements from back east, I'll send for you to retrieve them. Get me Captain Carlson on your way out."

Chitman left, frowning, to be replaced by Captain Carlson. Royce Carlson was a big man, but his weight was all muscle and bone. Unlike Chitman, Captain Carlson didn't look all business. He slouched a little, and his mouth carried a perpetual grin, as if some secret joke lay sealed behind his lips. But Armstrong had seen him execute an insubordinate sergeant without batting an eye.

"Royce, normally, I would ask you to start putting together some direct assault and envelopment scenarios for a conflict with the Tucker clan. This time, we may have to use kid gloves."

"We already have their powdermaker, sir."

"It's not the powdermaker I'm worried about. It looks like the Tucker clan falls under... Jarvis's area of expertise."

Carlson's mouth formed an 'O' as his eyebrows nudged toward the ceiling.

"Take Jarvis and his neuronet, as well as any men you feel necessary to get leverage over the clan without making it look like an invasion. Their schoolteacher will help you get your foot in the door if you keep him on our side. Take Mr. Salazar back out there, too. Have Jarvis survey the clan for the shine and await further instructions from me."

"And if it comes to shooting?"

"Then respond appropriately. Just remember: I want the bulk of the population left alive until Candice gets here."

Royce smirked. "Are you going to use Chitman as a courier again? Is he causing trouble?"

Armstrong's eyebrows arched. "I sent Chitman to D.C. because we're dealing with an extremely dangerous hostile mountain clan, and I need more men to put down an open rebellion. And Royce..." she said.

"Yes, sir?"

"We *do* have their powdermaker. In the interest of keeping his focus on gunpowder production, you would do well to monitor any correspondence he has with his home clan."

Captain Carlson nodded and left.

Later, at her office window, Colonel Armstrong lifted the binoculars to watch Captain Carlson and his detachment below lead the Tucker schoolmaster out the western gate back toward the Tucker clan. In their entourage, they carried more penicillin and a few other tempting surprises to help with negotiations. It felt like a waste of time she couldn't afford, but neither could she afford to be hasty when delicacy was required.

But that was why she'd sent Royce to manage things. Royce Carlson was one to get things done efficiently, and if there was anything to the reports and rumors, he would get to the bottom of it. She'd sent Jarvis along as well. Again, if the rumors were true, Jarvis was the one with the right stuff to take advantage of it. Lieutenant Chitman was an honor-and-duty soldier, perfect for certain tasks; Captain Carlson was a different animal entirely, to say nothing of a wild dog like Jarvis—different tools for different challenges. Armstrong had a sensitive nose for valuable human resources, the advantages they offered, and the accommodations they required.

Which was why it didn't surprise her too much when the Tucker powdermaker requested an audience with her regarding labor at the factory. "No slaves."

"It is in both of our interests," Armstrong said, "to have the factory up and running as soon as possible. You're not in a position to reject free labor."

Already, the mountain chemist looked unsure of himself. He was used to being a big fish in a small pond, of tinkering with toys and calling it invention. Now that he had actual *responsibility*, he didn't know what to do with it. "I went into this as a businessman, not a slave driver."

"You won't be the one driving the slaves. My troops can handle the discipline."

"I... that ain't the point. They're sleeping right out in the open, with nothing more than dirty sacks for bedding and an open pit for their toilet. I didn't agree to set up a business for folks to be done that a-way."

"Mr. Pluckett—"

"Puckett."

"Whatever. You're a powdermaker, for Chrissakes. You're not in a position to lecture *anybody*, let alone *me*, on right and wrong."

The powdermaker stumbled over himself trying to keep up. "I ain't a bad... I ain't that kind of a feller."

"Oh, you *ain't?* What do you think this stuff is used for, fireworks? We have a national emergency on our hands. A confederation of hostile city-states collectively calling themselves Sylvania has overrun a swath of territory stretching all the way to the coast, and we don't even know how far north. They are a threat to the Federation's security. If you're wondering where your nitrogel's going to be used, it's going to go towards killing Sylvanian fighters. And we need that nitrogel fast. So far, we've been able to outgun them thanks to a sealed weapons-and-ammo depot we cracked open in southern Virginia, but our ammo reserves will run dry by the end of this year, and that's barring any catastrophic geemo attack."

"Geemo?"

"G.M.O. Forget it. We've got a crisis on our hands, and we'll only come out of it if everybody does their part. If that means forced labor from prisoners we've taken from northern aggressors, so be it."

"But... but if I'm going to run a powder factory, I don't want prisoners working around dangerous chemicals and explosives. I've already been sabotaged once. It ain't hard—"

"Fine. We'll limit the prisoners to construction duties, and all main factory personnel will be vetted, trained, and *paid* workers. Satisfied?"

The powdermaker didn't appear satisfied, but he didn't have the leverage, or the aptitude to use it if he did.

"Here." Armstrong reached around and grabbed an ornate wooden case. "Got these on my promotion, but I don't smoke." She opened the hinged lid to reveal cigars as big as sausages.

"I... what?"

"The tobacco was grown in the Carolinas. Fine smokes, I've heard, but again, I don't smoke. In spite of this fretting you've insisted on, you're doing a satisfactory job with the deadlines. Consider this a bonus."

"I... shucks. Thank you, ma'am," Bill said, eyes wide. A hillbilly like him had likely never *seen* a real cigar before. He accepted the box gingerly, as if unworthy of such an expensive container, let alone its contents.

"If you don't have anything else for me, I have other things I need to attend to." Armstrong opened up a fresh sheet of paper for a message to send out east. The powdermaker bowed his head and retreated to the door. "Also, I expect you to keep a tighter rein on your apprentices. My guard caught a girl of yours fraternizing with the prisoners. They're not safe. I'll be assigning Lieutenant Harlow to act as your bodyguard going forward. I don't want you near the prisoners without him there."

"I—yes, ma'am."

Melissa Daly climbed the uneven wooden stairs to Bill's office overlooking the warehouse floor, which was rapidly becoming the soon-to-be factory floor. The light was on inside. She cradled a steaming kettle with a thick hot pad. "Bill?" she asked, opening the door. "Bill, I made you some tea if you—"

It wasn't Bill in the office, but Omar.

A mess of papers littered the desk and floor. Not Bill's kind of mess—that of a distracted genius—but a more haphazard one born of haste. Omar stood frozen at Melissa's intrusion. His hands held a binder full of Bill's personal notes. She saw it all in the moment before Omar clapped the binder shut.

"Bill's not here—"

"What are you doing?"

"I'm..." Omar swallowed. "Miss Perkins thought Mr. Puckett needed to get his stuff sorted. Copies made and such. I agreed to help her."

"Where's Miss Perkins? Why're you up here so late?"

"Look, I... you gave me a start, coming in like you did. I... this is extra work I thought I'd get done after hours."

"Does Bill know about this?"

"Yeah. He's got business up in the citadel with Armstrong, so he had me get started without him."

Melissa nodded slowly, then backed away out the door. "Okay, then. Tell Bill I've got some birch tea with honey for him in the cookhouse if he comes back."

Chapter 15

Milling Tales and News

Tucker Territory

The old mill, uphill and upstream to the east of town by nearly a mile, waited for its annual refurbishment in drab silence while the brook from which it drew power bubbled along below. The dam reservoir festered as a fetid pond overrun by mosquitos and gnats. Gaps where paddles had fallen out of the water wheel stood out like missing teeth. The two-story building carried the faint odor of dry rot. It had been a spacious home in the olden days, with a deck overlooking what had likely been a fine view past the stream. It wouldn't serve as a home these days, with unbreds and marauders on the loose and no cars on hand to shoost one to town in sixty smart seconds. As a mill, however, so close to a stream and a nice drop in elevation, the place was ideal.

An armed troop of clansmen sauntered up the long path to the mill, a contingent of their elder sons and daughters trailing with mules and carts laden with tools and supplies. The clan had not checked up on the place since the end of the pigman siege six months prior, and even then some repairs had demanded attention.

Unbreds had licked clean all the hog grease lubricating the mechanisms, tearing out some parts and scattering them over the hardwood floor. Birds had found a way to nest up inside, as always, so there was that whole mess to clean up as well. The water wheel and its giant shaft needed inspection, as well as the dam.

Deek Evans closed the lower sluice gate to get the reservoir filling again. The rainy days previous meant ample inflow, and the red sunrise this morning portended more rain tomorrow, Deek prognosticated with a contemplative hocking of phlegm. Best to get the burrs ready for milling while the weather cooperated.

Shane Bunton dropped a satchel of woodcutting tools where the wheel shaft extended from the building and hollered at his son to get up on the roof and take a gander at the shingles.

"How's them there shingles keeping on?" Clyde McDaniel, the clan miller and baker, asked.

"A couple of 'em's curling, and..." Nigel Bunton stabbed at those within reach with a screwdriver, "these here have gone awful soft."

"Figures," Mr. McDaniel sighed. "I'll rive some new ones."

The Taylors had brought nails for the occasion, which Shane used to attach new paddles he'd shaped beforehand to the waterwheel. Mr. McDaniel heaved out a set of heavy cowhide belts with the hair still on them for grip and started hauling them inside to link up the shafts and pulleys.

Some of the fathers set their girls to cleaning out the nesting birds and sprucing up the floors, then sat on the sacks of grain they'd carried up and set themselves to jawing. The presence of folks like Job Brody, a couple of the Hadleys, and one of the Newell men, having all come in from their respective farms, exposed the gaggle of unoccupied clansmen for what it was: a porch-jury chewing the cud over the latest unforeseen bend in the river.

"So them Americans what just come in the other day," Mr. Finch began. "What do you reckon about 'em? They're saying the junkers belong to them someway."

"The junkers *are* Americans," the butcher explained, passing up a crowbar to young Nigel Bunton on the roof.

"They seem different from the junkers. 'Specially the bald one what talks to himself."

"They're milit'ry folks," the miller said. "Leastways the ones with guns are. Can't speak for the bald 'un."

Deek Evans climbed up out of the now dry streambed downhill of the dam. "Shucks, I'm blamed took up with that paper and printing press," he said, massaging the healing scar under his chin where a Greenbrier arrow had taken him. "I never did see paper so white. Gives me half a mind to go back to Sam Chambers for my letters."

"I don't know how I feel about 'em," Job Brody stroked his hooked nose with his usual air of grave sagacity. "My boy Ricky went off to the junker clan with Bill just to keep his apprenticeship. He's got a head about him, but I don't like him being gone, me not knowing if I'll see him again or not. Ain't no telling what all could happen."

"Becky!" the butcher's wife shouted at her daughter from inside the mill. "We forgot the hog grease! Take Shooshie back to town and fetch the bucket! And don't tarry with that Amos Taylor when you do!"

"Oh, Ma..." came the exasperated reply.

"Why'd you bring up your old sorghum mule, Arnie?" The elder town-side Craine asked.

"Traded my stout one to Johnny Grierson," the butcher replied.

"For what?"

"Got me a good coon dog, a jug of whiskey vinegar, and a barrel of hickory chips." The butcher rubbed his thin nose as he smirked at his well-made deal.

"Wait a second." Shane Bunton's head poked out from between the broad spokes of the water wheel. "A coon dog? Did you trade out that coon dog?"

"To Fillmore, and half the whiskey vinegar, too. But I got me a load of wood chicken, a basket of dried morels, fresh huckleberries, and a tobacco pipe."

"That ornery devil..." Shane muttered.

"What?" Arnold asked.

"I traded for a coon dog with Fillmore. Worked all morning rolling logs for his son's place to get it, and threw in my wife's stitching to boot. And then comes Johnny Grierson a-lookin' for a coon dog."

Shane's tale lacked any jocular tone, but all the gathered men burst into laughter, even those who had up to that point been actually working.

"What did you trade for it?"

"In return for the dog and a full fifteen fresh-fletched arrows, he gave me some huckleberries, a watered-down *quart* of whiskey vinegar, and..." Shane shook his head in begrudging awe, "a stitching pattern what looked awful similar to my wife's."

His listeners erupted into laughter again. "Are you telling me," the miller said, "that one-eyed half-and-half came to town to trade his coon dog, and got his own dog back with arrows, fresh berries, and vinegar besides?"

"At least."

That did the menfolk in for a bit before Mr. Finch, ever one to bring up politics for entertainment, turned the topic back to the Americans. "Did you see the bald one?"

"Every time is step outside, I get me the itching behind my neck he's the only one I'll ever see," the butcher said.

"What's that supposed to mean?"

"He has a way of popping up. Like he's following me," Arnold Brody said.

"I ain't seen 'im around overmuch."

"I almost could swear I hear him whisper to me, clear from the other side of the street."

"I get the same feeling," Job Brody agreed with his brother. "Seems like a steep trade for little magic pills."

"That there penicillin's a wonder-drug," the broad-shouldered Clyde McDaniel answered. "I seen myself how quick Phil Holland's healing up after that screevler pert near tore him in two. I heard tell from Doctor Bernhard he'd give his right arm to have the stuff. Don't tell my cousin, but I might go with Chambers on this 'un."

"This shaft is warping," Shane said upon inspection of the massive hickory impeller. "We can brace it with some boards for now. I'll put this one up on my to-do list, like it ain't long enough already."

"Feels like things is changing awful fast, don't it?" Mr. Finch said in total disregard to the work at hand. "First the junkers, then a month later and bam! New America. And they talk fancier than the schoolteacher, just about."

"We don't cotton to foreigners 'round 'ere," one of the other men grumbled. "We keep letting these folks run 'round, we'll start to lose what's holding us all together. Ain't that right, Shane?"

Shane's answer came sharp as his arrows. "You gonna hand me a paddle or keep jawing in my ear?"

A rustling amongst the heath sent every Tucker bolting for a weapon.

A voice carrying stern authority called out from the greenery, stopping the Tuckers in their tracks. "What's going on, here?" Captain Royce Carlson emerged, followed by three soldiers and the bald American who sometimes wore a uniform and sometimes wore gaudy nomad cast-offs.

"Uh, howdy there," Arnold Brody said when no one else spoke. "Fixin' up the mill for some meal grindin'."

"Don't you know it's dangerous out here?" Carlson asked.

"Well, sure. But we always come out well-armed. Mr. McDaniel here, he's our miller, see, and come millin' time, he and his kin make this a little outpost up here. Saves the rest of us on patrol time."

Captain Carlson smiled. "But you have us here to do the patrols now, and we've got better guns to do it with."

Arnold nodded. "Much obliged. But the thing is, we uh," he chuckled with a shrug of his shoulders, "we like bread."

"But it's such a nuisance, isn't it? Coming up here to grind grain for days on end. It's a lot of trouble for some biscuits."

"I'm sure we'd take any easier way if we could. But it's not so bad—"

"You know, as part of the New American Federation, you'd get exclusive trade deals with nomad clans running our routes. That means bargains other people can't get. You could sell your grain directly to them when they came to you, instead of coming all the way out here every time you wanted to bake something."

"But where would we get our bread?"

Royce laughed. "From the nomads, of course! I'm sure you're used to trading only for... specialty items. Novelties. But the New American Federation is industrializing again. Nomads are more and more trading in commodities. You'll have plenty of fine flour, or even ready-made bread, if that's what you want."

"But—"

"But what?"

"Well, the thing is, millin' time is such an occasion for the clan. The millstones grind terrible slow. Folks get to telling tales, or singing, or sawing at the fiddle, or dancing, just cuttin' capers and such. Even marryin'."

Captain Carlson's smile softened as he shook his head in good-humored bewilderment. "You have to come up here and work in order to recreate? Wouldn't it make more sense to separate labor and recreation, so you can get more work out of your labor, and more fun out of your recreation?"

"Well, uh, when you put it like that, I... the thing is—"

"Listen, I don't want to disrupt your way of life here." Carlson reached out and clapped a firm hand on Arnold Brody's shoulder. "It may not make sense to me, but my orders right now are to protect New American interests and look after your clan, not to tell you how to run things. You can go on with your milling. My men and I will watch over the operation to make sure everyone's safe."

The soldiers took up their places around the dell, with the bald American—some jasper who only went by Jarvis—going through the working men and sniffing at their collars.

The Tuckers finished their repairs before noon, and started the grinding even before that. Work was quick when done in utter silence.

Chapter 16

The Enemy Within

Amos Taylor knocked again at the door of the Fillmore house. Here it was, almost mid-morning, and no one had seen either Victor or Sophie about yet. Forbearance had never been Amos's strength, and the last few months had done nothing but sharpen the hasty streak in him. He knocked once again. "Victor, you'd better get outta that bed, or I'm coming back with a bucket of water."

The door finally opened, but it was Sophie who stood in the doorway, bleary-eyed.

"Mrs. Fillmore." Amos tilted his head as if Sophie were twenty years his senior, rather than two. "What's your husband up to?"

"Goodness knows." Sophie threw up her hands. "I was havin' a hard enough time with the twins, but these last few weeks, Victor's been all a-skelter, too. Up all hours of the night. Something's shook him up, I think."

"I might have just the thing for him. Omar's gone out with the junkers, and Elvin won't go along with what I'm wanting to do. The Americans sure won't like it."

"What are you wantin' to do?" Victor came out of the dim house behind his wife, stretching.

Amos grinned. "Get up to some mischief."

"Why this hushing-and-whispers stuff?" Victor asked as he followed Amos out the western gate. "What are we doing?"

Amos waved at a bored-looking Becky Brody sitting atop the wall on roundswalking duty. When they were a fair distance out of earshot, he muttered, "There's something up with that blind drifter. The elders know something about it they aren't telling. I want you to help me track him down. Figure out what he's done to the unbreds."

Victor stopped. "I don't know, Amos. If the elders are keeping something under the bushel, maybe they got a good reason for it."

Amos groaned. "That's what Omar said, too."

"Omar?"

"Before he left. He told me you two caught wind of the drifter back in June."

"You know how he is. He didn't want to tell the elders about it."

"Do I look like an elder?" Amos said. "He used to be a drifter, and he doesn't take chances he doesn't have to. He's a good guy, but he doesn't know how to take the bull by the horns."

Victor shook his head with a humorless laugh, picking up his stride again. "You're gonna get yourself killed someday."

"Everyone keeps telling me that. But we didn't catch that shadower or beat the Greenbriers by sitting on our hands."

"Fine, fine. Keep a lookout for me." Victor kneeled and examined the ground and leaves, looking for telltale disturbances among what, to Amos, looked like undifferentiated vegetation.

Together, the two went off through the woods, picking their way up and down steep slopes. They were more likely to spot footprints where the going was rough; Amos at least knew that. And he had the good sense not to run his mouth. He kept an eye out for dangerous animals or unbreds, throwing occasional looks over his shoulder.

Victor, for his part, kept all his attention on the immediate ten-foot radius around him, gradually leading Amos north.

They'd been combing their way through the forest long enough for Amos to work up a good sweat when he finally spoke up. "Okay, Vic. That's far enough."

Victor stopped and turned around, confused. "Huh?"

Amos held his rifle pointed down, but his thumb was on the flintlock and his finger on the trigger.

"What's going on, Amos?"

Whatever kinsome bearing he'd had before, Amos had snuffed it out. "I don't like it when people lie to me. Omar told me he lost track of you, that he heard screaming and thought it was you. Your wife says you haven't been acting like yourself lately. You saw something in the woods that night, didn't you?"

Victor didn't answer either way. His eyebrows pinched together, either in concentration or contempt, Amos couldn't be sure.

"It's just you and me out here, Vic. Now, I asked you nicely what you know. I expect to get what I want. What did you see that night you went after the drifter?"

"I-I saw..." Victor began.

"What? You saw what?" Amos stepped forward, huffing with impatience.

Victor started to panic, his breath coming in rapid gasps. "I saw... I saw..."

"Spit it out, Victor! What was it?"

Victor sank to his knees and collapsed—out so cold Amos had to stop him from rolling down the hill.

"What the heck is this about?" Amos said, pulling him up by the suspenders. He hooked his hands under Victor's armpits and hauled him into an awkward, half-seated position against a nearby hickory tree. He looked around, bewildered. He'd hit on something, some loose thread of the truth, but he didn't know what it was.

Amos shook Victor's limp body. "C'mon, guy. What's going on with you?" He laid a hand on Victor's chest and felt a heartbeat. He pried up an eyelid to stare into an unmoving, unseeing eye. "Are we gonna have to carry you all the way back to town?"

"I can only live in one body at a time," said a voice from the crest of the hill behind him.

Amos froze. His heel was a millstone grinding years of broken hickory shells into the dirt as he turned.

Two shadowers, a mere stone's throw uphill, stared down at him with too-wide eyes, their milky, translucent skin stretched too tightly over their skulls. They were bent over like slaves, supporting with their gangly arms something—someone sitting on their shoulders like an ancient heathen king. The king they carried had no eyes.

The man with no eyes was not old, and his smile bared straight white teeth. His eyelids drooped, half-closed, deflated, sagging into the empty sockets they covered.

Amos brought up his rifle, but the eyeless man fell limp before he could draw a bead. Then Victor tackled him from behind. The two of them tumbled down the hill, each trying to pin the other against the hardscrabble earth. When they rolled to a stop, Victor was on top, his eyes wide open now with a furious, bloodshot frenzy and a wild grin.

Victor planted his knees on Amos's elbows and seized Amos's thrashing head between both his hands. "I can't assimilate new ones with a proxy," he grunted into Amos's ear, close enough Amos could feel his breath, warm and wet, against his face. "Not yet. But you can see."

Amos saw flashes of a snow-dusted forest, a smoldering campfire, and himself, hung up in a pigman snare, calling out for Omar. It was last winter—a dead shadower's memory.

Amos squirmed under the weight of Victor's body, but he couldn't get free. "You... what are you?" He gasped.

"I am the Pied Piper. Just you wait, little one," Victor muttered, his voice giddy now with anticipation. "You have a powerful light within you. More than the rest."

Amos saw the shadowers approaching with their eyeless charge. He thrashed against his assailant with renewed terror. "*Help me!*" he shrieked.

Victor went suddenly rigid, his head snapping up to look around for a new threat he sensed. The iron grip on Amos's head slackened for a moment, and a moment was all he needed.

Amos worked his knees up under Victor's belly and shoved him off, then pulled his hunting knife free of its scabbard and rolled to a half-crouch, anticipating an attack from the two oncoming shadowers. But no—they were retreating, pulling the limp drifter back up the hill, up and away.

Amos scrambled after his fallen rifle. The drifter couldn't outrun a bullet.

But before Amos could reach the stock with his outstretched hand, he felt Victor's grip on his foot, pulling him back down the hill, away from his weapon. He slashed at Victor's hand with his knife, and the blow connected. The flesh peeled away from Victor's white knucklebones like a gruesome smile, but his grip remained tight around Amos's ankle.

"You quit that right now!" a female voice shouted from further down-hill—Becky.

"The drifter!" Amos shouted back. "The drifter's up yonder! Shoot him!"

Victor's iron grip finally released, and Amos got a hold of his rifle. But when he looked up the slope, the shadowers and the drifter they carried were gone. He looked back to see Victor had gone limp again.

Becky came running up, her curly hair springing loose of the bandana she'd used to tie it up, a rifle in her hands and a shotgun slung across her middle.

"What the hell took you so long?" Amos said.

"You told me to follow at a distance, so I did. I saved your hind end, didn't I? Come on; we got that drifter on the run." Becky reached down to help Amos to his feet.

"No, we've lost our edge. I'm not walking into a pigman ambush," he said, cutting lengths of ivy tendrils creeping up the sides of a nearby tree. "Help me tie his hands and feet. We're gonna haul him back to town, you and me." He pointed at Victor.

"What happened to him?"

"I aim to find out."

Amos was already tired by the time he and Becky had dragged Victor's slack body back to the palisade, but the ensuing chaos drained him further. His own irritable snapping batted away a few of the buzzing clansmen rushing up with pretenses of helping, but once Sophie Fillmore had caught the rumor on the wind, there was no keeping her away.

"What's wrong with Victor?" she said, already in a breathless panic, cradling his unconscious face in her hands. "Stay with me, darling, stay with me!"

Amos caught a look across the street—his stepmother, standing in the door to the smithy, her arms crossed and a frown on her face. *Another dead clansmen you drag home,* she seemed to say. Amos tore his own gaze away, irritation boiling to rage. He pushed Sophie Fillmore aside. "He's alive, goddamnit! Help me get him in the meetinghouse or get the hell outta my way!"

Elvin had arrived by now and more authoritatively dispersed the gawping onlookers. "Get ahold of his feet, Becky. I got him by the shoulders. Get the door for me, Clyde. No, you can't come in, but you can go fetch the doctor if you'd like to be something other than a pain in the ass," he growled.

Amos was grateful for the relative cool and darkness of the meetinghouse interior, and some on-hand help looking to get things done before asking questions. They managed to haul Victor through the main hallway to just inside the main gymnasium doors. "Lock the door behind us, Elvin," Amos said once they were safely inside. He stumbled in the dim light, before Sophie came in from behind with a lantern in hand. Together with Elvin, Becky, and Sophie, he got Victor propped up in a chair.

"Don't leave me, darling," Sophie begged, crying in the darkness. "You have to stay for me and the little ones!"

Just you wait, little one.

"Becky, give me your bandana. Go fetch some rope or twine or something. And a lantern. I can't hardly see," Amos said. Once the sweaty bandana was in hand, he slung Victor's wrists behind the chair back and tied them together as best he could manage.

"Why you tyin' up Victor? What's going on, Amos? His hand's bleeding. What's happened with my husband?"

Elvin grabbed Sophie firmly by the arm and guided her to the door, his respectful words belied by his clipped tone. "How about you stand out here in the hall for a spell, Mrs. Fillmore? Don't you fret none, for now, leastways. Once I know somethin', you'll be the first I'll pass it along to."

Once the door closed, leaving Amos and the watchman alone with an unconscious Victor, Elvin let out a slow, tense breath. "What. In. Holy. Hell?"

"Sorry, boss," Amos grunted. "I had an inkling, but I couldn't go to you until I was sure."

"Sure about what?"

"Victor saw the drifter and didn't report on it. He lied to Omar and kept him from telling the elders. I thought I could find out why, and maybe bag the drifter in the process." Amos shook his head. "I... think the drifter did something to Victor."

There was a knock on the door. "Better be the doctor," Elvin muttered.

It wasn't. The door swung open to reveal Reverend Brody holding a lit lantern, with Becky Brody following behind with a length of rope. "What happened?" Reverend Brody said, setting the lantern on the floor and squaring off with Amos. "Did you say something about the drifter and Victor?"

Amos started to explain again, but the reverend cut him off when he mentioned the drifter appearing atop the shadowers. "Did the drifter touch you?"

Amos shook his head. "No. Victor wrestled with me, grabbed me by the head. Said some weird stuff, but Becky came along before the drifter could—"

The reverend seized Amos with both hands, just as Victor had done. "Reverend, what's going on here?" Elvin protested, reaching out to separate the two.

"*Back off, watchman,*" the reverend hissed with unusual viciousness.

A brief, blinding pain stabbed Amos behind his eyes, and through the haze, he perceived the reverend's voice, or something that felt like the reverend's voice. *Don't you try to lie to me. I'll scour your mind away if you think you can hide among us.*

Just as suddenly as the pain had come, it calmed, and Amos was on his hands and knees, panting, a fuzzy blackness retreating to the corners of his eyesight.

Reverend Brody was already pacing the floor. "Amos Taylor is clean," he declared. "But that one"—he nodded towards Victor—"is not. We'll have to kill it."

"Excuse me?" Becky said, aghast. "'*It?*'"

"What are you doing to my Victor?" Sophie cried out, standing in the open doorway behind Becky.

"Who let her back inside?" Elvin shouted, moving to shove her back out into the hallway.

Sophie pushed back. "I'm not leaving him! I'm not leaving my husband! He ain't done nothing!"

"Sophie, he jumped me back in the woods," Amos said, trying to explain.

"You're lying! Victor wouldn't hurt a fly!"

"*Shut up!*" Reverend Brody shouted, pushing past Elvin to grab Sophie by both shoulders and shake her. "Victor Fillmore is gone. *Gone*, do you hear? That *thing* tied to the chair is nothing but a husk, a scarecrow. It's a puppet being used by the most evil kind of ubermensch ever to walk the earth. I'm sorry, Mrs. Fillmore, but your husband is already as good as dead."

"Just what is this all about, Reverend?" Amos asked. His head was spinning. Everything was happening too fast.

"This is all forbidden knowledge." Reverend Brody stamped his foot into the floor. "Watchman, bleed that thing and be done with this whole damnable business."

"Now, hold on, Reverend," Elvin retorted. "I ain't gonna kill a clansmen just on your say-so. I—"

"Sophie?"

Everyone went quiet and looked at Victor. He was awake, peering through the dim lantern light, searching for a friendly face. "Is that you, Sophie?" he asked again.

"I'm here, sweetie." Sophie pushed her way past the reverend, who had spread out his arms as if to protect the rest from Victor's seated, bound form.

"How did I get here? Why'd y'uns tie me up?" Victor asked, his voice hitching high and pathetic, as if he were on the verge of tears.

"Quiet, devil!" Reverend Brody stabbed a finger at Victor, but still from a safe distance.

"Vicky, they say... they say the drifter hurt you somehow. They say you're gone."

"Honey, I'm right here," Victor said, pleading. "You know me. It's *me*, Sophie."

"If it's really you, you'll be able to tell me something only you and me know."

A silence stretched out between them. The air in the room felt heavy. "We're gonna... we're gonna have us another baby, Sophie. You and me."

Sophie turned to the reverend. "It's my Victor, I'm telling you!"

Reverend Brody's look of disgust grew stronger.

Sophie ran to her husband, but stopped short. Victor's desperate, pleading face had twisted into a gleeful smile. "The reverend is lying," he said, his voice a hop and a skip short of a laugh. "Victor isn't gone. He's still in here, in bits and pieces. I even let him out sometimes."

Sophie's hand jumped to her mouth as she and Victor locked eyes. She stepped back.

"I made him watch," it said.

Amos watched as Sophie looked down, horrified, at her belly, then back up at the thing that had once been her husband. She crumpled in on herself, a whimper escaping as she withered under Victor's gaze.

"Enough of this, watchman." Reverend Brody grabbed at Elvin's shirt. "I tell you to *kill it*."

"Hold on—wait," Amos said. "I need to figure out what the drifter was up to. I need to ask it some questions."

"Absolutely not! There is nothing to learn from it but how wicked the ubermenschen are!"

Victor laughed. "Still trying to spin your webs, old man. How are you going to keep the lid on this one? You were never as good at keeping secrets as you thought. Half the clan suspected you were the one shagging Bert Daly's wife. The thing that'll really keep you up at night, though: Could you have saved Victor if you'd told everyone the truth about what that eyeless drifter was? About what you are?"

A thunderous flash blasted Amos's ears to a ringing daze. When his shoulders relaxed and he opened his eyes again, Victor's head was slowly sagging down towards the bloody, ragged hole in his chest.

Across the smoky room, Sophie Fillmore stood with Amos's rifle, the now-empty barrel drifting toward the floor. "Goodbye, darling." She dropped the rifle and collapsed, her head buried in her hands.

Chapter 17

The Friend of My Enemy

<u>New Ashburn</u>

The sun was setting when Ella brought a tray full of food down to the prisoner pen. The workers lay sprawled out on the ground inside the fence, exhausted. The same guard she'd seen before was still there with the same yellow grin. She made for the gate without looking his direction, but an extended rifle butt stopped her before she attained it. "The slaves have already eaten. And you're not on the cooking detail."

"Mr. Puckett thought they'd done awful hard work today and thought a little treat would suit 'em."

"Any outside contact with the prisoners has to be cleared by Colonel Armstrong. And she hasn't told me anything about extra rations."

"It's only a batch of biscuits and plum jam. I don't see why that's such a big deal. You're welcome to have some yourself... to inspect, you might say. And if it passes your inspection, I don't see why Colonel Armstrong needs to hear about this at all." Ella dared to look up and meet the guard's eyes.

The American's eyes looked at the tray of food, then wandered up and down her figure. "I would accept other forms of payment."

Ella fought to keep her composure. "I'm sorry, Mister. A biscuit and jam are all I have to offer, and you'd be a fool not to take it. My treats are the envy of the clan every harvest and planter's eve."

The guard scratched his dirty beard, hocked a wad of phlegm into the dust, and swiped a biscuit from the platter. With the available spoon, he scooped a great blob of jam onto his biscuit, then, with hungry eyes still boring holes through Ella, licked the spoon clean with sensuous extravagance before returning the spoon to the jam jar. "Enter." He opened the gate with one hand, shoving the biscuit into his mouth with the other.

Ella had grossly underestimated the demand for the food she brought and overestimated her own supply. The prisoners swarmed her, threatening to knock the entire tray and its contents on the ground. She tried to stem the onslaught with promises that, one way or another, she would provide a helping for everyone, that folks needed to be patient, to share. But the pleas and cries and outstretched hands were too much for her, and she found herself backed up into a corner of the fence, the locust tree barbs poking at her back, until—

"*Enough!*"

The slaves reaching out to Ella stopped and subsided at the sound of a woman's voice. The crowd parted, and Ella beheld the woman she'd seen earlier at the fence—the woman who seemed always to look outward, proud even in a prison camp.

"Back up and form a line." The woman spoke with authority, honed to a keener edge by their collective hardship. "Children in front, day-workers next, oldsters in the back. Now."

The slaves did as they were told, heads bowed. Ella, though she'd worked at a great clay oven for hours, barely had enough biscuits for all the children. "I'll come back later with more, I promise," she said to the groaning slaves, some of whom cursed their misfortune, while others trembled with desperate gratitude.

"Thank you kindly, Miss."

"An angel. You're an angel. Thank you."

"We're so hungry. Please, Miss. Tell the colonel we can't go on like this."

The woman, the de facto leader of the slaves, shooed them away, children and adults alike.

Ella breathed a sigh of relief. "How are things in—"

"*What do you think you're doing?*"

Ella blinked, nearly dropping the tray she held. "I... I'm sorry?"

The woman didn't touch her, but she drew close enough Ella almost would have preferred a slap in the face. "It's not enough you imprison us, rape us, starve us, and force us to build your factory? Now you'll have us grovel, too?"

"I saw your people were hungry. Folks here at New Ashburn had some extra vittles, so I did a little cooking. I aim to keep cooking until I run out of food to share, or your folks ain't hungry no more."

"Armstrong didn't put you up to this?"

Ella shook her head.

"The powdermaker?"

"No, but he's been fighting to get you better treatment. I was the one who put *him* up to it."

"I see," the woman said. "A bleeding heart. A pawn of the Colonel, without even realizing it."

"What?"

194

"When you've brought people so low that giving basic necessities looks like a kindness, that's when you've truly enslaved them." The woman's scorn cut deep. "Did you see how they simpered for you? For a scrap of bread and a smear of jelly? Make them forget, even for a moment, how they've been abused, and they'll worship the ground beneath your feet. And they'll build the factory for you with glad and eager hearts. And the factory will make gunpowder to supply the Federation, who will go out and kill *my* people still out there." The woman pointed out to the horizon, angry tears in her eyes now. "People I haven't forgotten, even if the rest of these slaves have."

Ella reached out to put a hand on her shoulder. "Ma'am, I'm so sorry—"

The woman swatted Ella's hand away. "Don't you touch me! If you had seen what that guard did to an eleven year-old girl..." She shook her head and clenched her fists. "And you *fed him.*"

"So I could get in here. To you all."

"You fucking hypocrites. You work with the powdermaker. You help him make the ammunition to kill innocents, and you think you can buy your way out of it with some *bread?*"

"I ain't your enemy."

"Yeah? Prove it. Do something that matters. Free us from Armstrong."

"You know I can't do that."

"Sabotage the factory."

"Ma'am—"

"I don't care about kind words if there's a knife behind them. I don't care about what you intended. Armstrong is evil, and the American Federation is evil, and you're working for them. Helping them spread their evil."

"So you say. But even if—"

"Are you *blind?* You don't think Armstrong knows what's done with us slaves? You don't think she ordered it?"

"Even so," Ella said. "You can't fight evil with evil."

"Spare me your bullshit moralizing. You've picked your side, and it's on the other side of this fence. Go. Your guard friend is waiting. Your friend Armstrong might start wondering what you're doing here, pretending to be one of the oppressed."

Ella walked to the gate, but turned at last before she left. "I ain't Armstrong's friend. But I ain't her enemy, neither. I ain't your enemy. I ain't no one's enemy."

"The world doesn't work that way, little girl. If you try not to be anyone's enemy, you'll find yourself everyone's enemy."

Ella walked back to the supermart with her pan hanging limp at her side, her head down. She almost missed Omar sitting up on the split rail fence with a piece of straw in his mouth.

"What happened to you? Someone taste your beans?"

Ella looked up, and for once it looked like he was the one in a good mood and she was the wet blanket. "You might say that."

Omar looked down the hill where she'd come from. "Did you take dinner to Bill?"

She shook her head. "The slaves."

Omar chewed at the piece of straw. "How'd it go?"

"Like sneezing on a brush fire."

"Hmm."

"They hate me, Omar."

"Then they've got a couple shingles loose up top."

"I never wanted to be the evil one, Omar, but it feels like I'm put in that spot no matter what."

Omar shrugged. "Well, that's enough of that." He slapped his knee and reached back behind him.

"Enough of what?"

"Enough hand-wringin' about what you can't do nothin' about. I want to show you something." He produced a banjo and laid it across his lap. "These junkers got everything here."

Ella felt her eyebrows arch skyward. "You play?"

"It's been years, but..." he plucked a string and turned a tuning knob. "There was a little while I noodled around on any stringed noisemaker I could lay hold of."

"Can you play anything?"

"Used to tear up 'Miss Sadie Blue' pretty good."

"Don't know that one. How about 'I've Been Walking a Skinny Trail?'"

Omar turned a did-you-really-ask-me-that look her way. He started picking at the familiar tune as if he'd been practicing that very morning.

"Can you sing it, too?" Ella asked.

Omar hit a wrong note and frowned. "Never was much of a hand at singin'."

"Well, there's your trouble right there. Singin' ain't normally done with the hands."

He smirked and scratched behind his ear before darting a quick glance in both directions. "Here goes nothin'." He played the intro, then again to get a running start, then started in a low, breathy, unsteady tone:

I been walkiiiiin, a skinny traaaaaiiil...

A generous opinion would not have deemed it good singing. He broke off with a cough, then started again, just as unconfident as ever.

But by golly, he was *trying.* Because she'd asked him to.

I been walkiiiiin
a skinny traaaaaiiil—

Ella came in to harmonize with him, salvaging the song before Omar could quit.

—for yooouuu, my deeeeaaar.
And I been keepiiiin
My eyes out for yooouu

This rough ole' road
Ain't 'nough to keep me
From findin'
My way
Back to you

Ella coaxed him into the end of the song, and Omar let out a gentle sigh. "Please don't make me sing the second verse."

"What you talkin' about? That sounded fine."

"*You* sounded fine. I sounded like a bullhusker humping a sorghum mill."

"Ew, Omar, watch your language."

"Sorry, Miss."

Ella tapped the neck of Omar's banjo. "You're a fine hand with that there twanger. We ever get back to the Tucker clan, one of the Craines can match you on the fiddle."

"My pappy taught me to play. He was better at it than me. Could play 'pert near anything. He got the work done when he needed, but he always had time for music. I swear he would've packed us all up and joined a nomad clan if he didn't love home so much." He plucked at the strings, searching for a pleasant riff like a man luring fish in murky water.

"Is your pa still... around?"

"Maybe. I don't know. It's been a while."

"Do you expect to see him again some day?"

Omar played a twinkling of harmonic notes that rang through the air like wind chimes. "Dunno. Kinda doubt it. Bill Puckett's apprenticeship is the closest thing I've had as a home since..." Omar shook his head.

"Why? What happened?"

"Give me another song, why don't you? Something you can sing along to." Omar's voice wasn't grim, but he'd made it clear he had abandoned the former topic with finality. "If I had my druthers, I'd leave the singing to you. I reckon we make ourselves a fair match, musically-speaking. Fair enough to beat the nomad pickers."

"Oh, I don't much care to sing in front of folks."

"You got the voice for it."

"Omar, have you been trying to cheer me up?"

He turned his ardent gaze from his banjo to her, ending his picking with a comical discordant strum. "Is it working?"

She smiled at him. "Yeah, I reckon it is."

Dear Ralph,

I suppose you'll be getting this message from Mr. Chambers when he gets back to you. Lieutenant Chitman (that was the fellow who guarded Mr. Salazar during my stay with your clan) says the journey will get easier and faster with each passage as the pigmen and marauders get cleared out. I look forward to getting a letter back from you, and I've included some blank paper to that end. I know how scarce good paper can be.

Maybe it's a little too forward to ask about it, but how do your people feel about race mixing? Miss Holland told me you are a clan of unmodified stock (I thought that a little surprising (I thought the Plague pretty much wiped out the unmodified)). Not to put too fine a point on it (you've guessed by now already, I'd bet), but me and my clan are all modified. Ubermenschen, I guess you'd say, though my folks say it's an ugly word. We don't seem so different, though. It makes me wonder if maybe the scientists didn't mess around with our breeding as much as I thought they did. I used to think unmodified humans were a bunch of hairy ~~halfwits and psychos~~ *(sorry, I didn't mean it to sound that way, I just tend to think different about people I've never met, and I thought your kind were all extinct anyway). I know before the Plague and the nuke attacks, modified and unmodified humans weren't getting along too well. I understand if your kind bears some sore feelings on the subject, but I want you to know that I don't. What I'm getting at is if you think your clansmen would go along with you and me, well, <u>you know...</u> (I'm blushing!)*

199

Mr. Puckett cooked up his first full batch of his new nitrogel. Some of the Americans (I suppose we're all Americans here at New Ashburn, but I still haven't gotten used to the idea) have already started reloading cartridges for their old automatic weapons, and the tests so far seem like the nitrogel works as well as the old ammunition. Some nomads came from out east and bought the whole lot. I expect your clan will get their cut along with this letter.

Things are busy here. The apprentices Mr. Puckett brought with him are working hard (Ms. Holland has been tending to the prisoners of war the soldiers brought with them, I think 'cause Mr. Puckett's got a soft spot for the workers), and I'm watching for leaks in the piping with Mrs. Daly. Mrs. Daly seems nice, but I don't know what happened with her husband, and I'm afraid to ask. She leaves most of the work to me, because she has to look after her son. It doesn't make much sense to me why Mr. Puckett would want to bring her along with a little one to keep after, but maybe she has a special knack for powdermaking (or he's got a soft spot for her, too). The fellas, Ricky and Omar, do a lot of the toting. There's more than enough work for us. We've got leaks everywhere, and we had someone pass out the other day from the fumes, even with the doors wide open.

I think that's enough for now. It's late, and I'm running out of coal-oil for my lamp. I'll await your reply whenever you can get it sent.

Warmest Regards,
Jody Perkins

Dear Jody,
I received your letter. Forgive me if my letter-writing isn't as fine as yours. It's hotter than blue blazes, and I can never sleep with the sun going down so late. As I write, I'm deprived of sleep and sweating like a bullhusker.

I'm afraid I write to you with some bad news for some of the Tuckers gone out to New Ashburn with you. Victor Fillmore was killed in a hunting accident a couple days ago. His widow, Sophie Fillmore, has been taking the loss mighty hard. Becky Brody has been looking after her, but I think she's shook up pretty bad herself, since she was in the hunting party when he died. You'll need to tell Miss Ella Holland and Mr. Bill Puckett the news. Sophie is Bill's daughter, and she and Becky are both pretty close to Miss Holland.

I'm glad you were so frank in your questions as to my clan's breeding. I was wondering the same myself, but I didn't have the guts to ask. We have some confirmed ubermenschen among us. Omar Walking, an apprentice to Bill Puckett, comes to mind. Mrs. Daly and her late husband were both half-and-halfs. Same with most of the folks up at the Grierson settlement a couple miles outside town. I can't say our clan is too fond of such people, and maybe that same prejudice says something about the chilly welcome you got from some of our townfolk. I don't think it's any accident our half-and-halfs and ubermenschen either live with the Griersons or went with Bill Puckett to the nitrogel factory. Ella went with them, and everyone around here knows the heart she has for foreigners and half-breeds. I'm not saying it's right, but it's hard for a lot of Tuckers to let go of their history with modified folks. On the other hand, Johnny Grierson, who's about the most unpleasant half-and-half I've ever known, is a man of high standing in the clan. I don't know. To be honest, I'm not sure I ever thought much about it until I met you. Now that I do give it thought, and speaking for myself, I don't give a broken tooth for what my clan thinks about your breeding.

I'm more worried about my pa. I'd hoped he might come around once the factory was up and running and let me do at least a month out there working with you, especially once the money started coming in, but it's gone the other way. Sam came back with this Captain Carlson and a company of soldiers, and not a tooth of profit. Pa didn't want to let in so many men with guns, and for a while I halfway thought it might come

201

to shooting again. But this time around they came as Sam's personal guests, and Pa couldn't do much about that without risking the elders turning him out. But he's spitting mad. There's talk of making a treaty with the Federation, same as your clan did, and my pa's set himself against the whole notion. He won't allow talk of anything to do with the Americans or anyone allied with them, including you.

Aside from that, he can't stand the idea of his firstborn doing anything other than beating around in the woods looking for something to kill. Not that he thinks I'm cut out for that kind of work. Quite the opposite. In fact, he's pretty taken in with Amos Taylor, who never seems to get anything wrong. You would think, since Pa's got himself a preferred successor anyway, he'd loosen up on me a bit. But no. He just tightens the harness another notch. He won't even let me talk to Mr. Chambers now, who's trying to get the elders into a deal with Captain Carlson.

Our business with the Federation has got everyone riled up. With you folks from New Ashburn, I think most of us Tuckers liked the idea of starting something together, as partners. These American soldiers, though, they don't look at us like equals. It might be because of our breeding. I'm starting to see what the Reverend meant when he talked about how racist the ubermenschen were. Which isn't to say he was talking about you. The Americans are different, somehow, even if you are one of them. I'm not sure if that makes sense. It's really hot right now.

Sam's in favor of an alliance, and he makes some strong points. The Americans didn't bring any money or nitrogel, but they did bring a cartload of paper and an honest-to-goodness printing press. The whole town is papered with news, announcements, and a load of hurrahs for the Federation. I think most Tuckers are more impressed by all the paper than by what's actually printed on it. I don't know which way things will swing, but I expect the elders will decide one way or another by the end of this week.

I'd like to see you again, Jody Perkins. Write soon.

Best,
Ralph McDaniel

Chapter 18

Each Man to His Trade

<u>Tucker Territory</u>

Royce Carlson tore a mouthful from the freshly baked loaf, the miasmic stink of a day's patrol settling around him. He chewed absently, his boots up on the teacher's schoolhouse desk, Ralph McDaniel's open letter in his other hand.

The schoolmaster knocked on the door. Again. "Enter," Carlson said, making no move to remove his feet from Chambers's desk or hide the fact that he was reading someone's mail.

Whatever Sam Chambers had come in to say, he forgot it as soon as he saw the open letter. "Are you reading our clansmen's mail?"

"Yeah."

The schoolteacher reached out to snatch the paper away, but Captain Carlson was too quick, and he pulled it back. "This concerns Federation security."

"I don't see how." Sam said. "If we're starting negotiations for admittance to the Federation, and you're already poking your nose into strictly clan business, how is this going to—"

"This is from the watchman's son, right?" Carlson held up the letter. "The watchman is our biggest opposition. Why wouldn't he use any means at his disposal to sabotage our talks?"

"Including using his own son's letters to poison relations between us and New Ashburn? That—" Sam looked away, shaking his head. "That doesn't sound like Elvin."

"You don't think he'd stoop that low? He's an elder, right? Which means he's got to know something about politics. How long has he been an elder, Mr. Chambers?"

"So you think he forced his son to—what, write anti-American propaganda in his letter?"

"I don't know." Royce rubbed his chin. "Have a look. You tell me."

"No," Sam said, turning away from the offered letter. "Seal it and send it on its way. If you want to keep anti-American feelings tamped down, spying on clansmen isn't the way to do it. And it's not enough to wow them with fancy toys. They expect results, and frankly, some answers. Is the factory working or not? If it is, why haven't we seen anything from it? If it isn't, why can't I go back with Lieutenant Chitman to see for myself how things are going along? Who is this Jarvis guy you decided to bring along with us, and why was nobody allowed to look in that covered wagon he drove all the way out here?"

"All of this is privileged information pertaining to Federation military objectives."

"But you never tell me what those objectives *are.*"

"Why should I?" Royce washed another bite down with a draught of tepid water. "Your elders delay, and delay, and delay on a vote. There is no formal agreement between our governments, *as you demanded.* I am under no obligation to divulge privileged information to foreign clans. Are you going to tell me what happened to your, what? Trapper? Tanner?"

"That was weeks ago! I was with you when it happened. I know as much about it as you do."

Captain Carlson did not look convinced. "I heard several stories going around, and 'hunting accident' isn't even the most popular."

"Oh, and you give more credence to 'possessed by the devil?'"

Royce shrugged. "Or he saw something he wasn't supposed to."

"Like what?"

"You tell me."

"I don't know! I feel like you're fishing for something, but you won't tell me what it is. Everything has been one-sided since we've gotten back. You get here and tell me Mr. Salazar is leaving, which was not by the terms of our initial agreement, which stated that both of our clans would hold at least one of each other's clansmen as security. What do we have to make sure New Ashburn holds up their end of the deal if our only Ashburnite returns to them?"

"You've got all of us," Royce said.

"That," Sam said through gritted teeth, "is *not* the same. Unless you're willing to give us your guns."

"The guns are for your protection."

Sam shook his head. "You and your men are getting free room and board and have been for two weeks now. I've insisted we accommodate you until we can decide on a more formal arrangement, but with all give and no take, it's going to be hard to convince fence-sitting elders an alliance is what's best for the clan."

"Have you talked to Mr. Grierson? I went out today and talked to him myself. He's agreed to vote in favor of a deal. From what he's told me, he's gotten more attention from me than he's ever had from any of the other clan elders."

"That's because Johnny's an eternal grump. And he won't be enough to sway the vote. I've delayed because I wanted to wait for a shipment of nitrogel, or an ounce of profit, before calling for a vote. But we haven't seen a thing, and the Reverend is pushing for a vote this week. If you want something formal, we need a better deal."

Royce sighed, then took his feet off Sam's desk and sat upright. "I was afraid you were going to say that. What are your terms?"

"Talk of 'provincial status' and 'probationary period' sounds like crafty double-talk to us."

"Why? Because most of you Tuckers can't understand words longer than one syllable?"

"No," Sam huffed. "Because it comes with too many obligations and no guarantees. We have to agree to an occupying force, to obey your laws, but no support or assistance?" He shook his head. "No. Any treaty we sign, we'll expect full representation in your federation. I won't let my clansmen become second-class citizens in their own country."

"There are five hundred people in your clan. Our delegates represent populations of five thousand, at least. You'd have to roll together several area clans and build a representative district, and as far as I know, you're on speaking terms with..." Royce counted on his fingers. "One."

"I'll worry about that. What I want from you is guaranteed representation, and whatever coalition I build, the representative for our district will come from the Tucker clan."

Royce didn't look like he wanted to take the deal. "You realize you're fast-tracking a process designed to make the transition easier for your people? That speeding this along will make things more complicated for your clan?"

"Fair deals tend to get complicated."

"And I suppose *you* expect to be the representative?"

Sam smiled. "A man can be expected to know his trade."

Elvin McDaniel paced inside the butcher's home with an outraged gait. "This Carlson character is worse than Chitman was. This sumbitch is *asking* us to start a war. I can't *believe* he's sending Salazar on his way without so much as sayin' 'please.' I've a mind to put a gun to Salazar's head until these Americans lay down their arms."

"Easy, Elvin. Not so loud," Arnold Brody said, making a calming motion with his hands. "I've got my kids around, and we don't need something like that to get spreading around."

"I'm fine, I'm fine." Elvin looked about as fine as a thunderhead about to spill over a mountain range. "We ain't at war yet, and I can't say I'm too eager to start one with the Americans *already prancing around inside our walls.*" He shook his head in frustration. "That Jarvis character they brought along—he says he's taking a census of the clan, but I think he's just sizing us up, and it don't help he looks at my daughters like he's sizing up cuts at your shop. And with them Greenbriers a-stirrin' up trouble to the south, it's too much."

"Not good timing."

"Which makes me wonder."

"What? You reckon there them two things is tethered?" the butcher asked.

"I don't know. But they're doing their own patrols now and keeping our folkward from doing ours. They say the southern farms are protected, but how am I supposed to check on that? They say I've got to stay cooped up in town because they don't want 'friendly fire.' Can't go to the Grierson settlement. I'm out of a job, and we ain't even signed any treaty with these play-acting 'New Americans' yet. And I never heard tell of 'New Americans' before in the first place. I don't know. If these folks are really everything they say they are, how come none of the nomads ever talked about 'em?"

"What are you thinkin', then? That they could be Greenbriers?"

"No. If Greenbriers had firepower like that, they'd just ride in, shoot us all full of holes, and be done with it. But who's to say they ain't working together? Or at least that they haven't met each other?"

"I don't know, Elvin. Seems an awful lot like sniffin' for a downstream trout."

"Maybe. But I don't know what they're about, and I'd bet my right hand that they're about more than what they say."

"Ubermenschen?"

"Well, of course they're ubermenschen. Ain't nobody but an ubermensch would be that high and prancy. Something else."

"What?"

"Don't know. That Jarvis character gets me feeling funny."

"Me too. The other day, I could swear he said something about my daughter Becky. But when I looked over at him, he weren't moving his lips. Most uncanny feller I ever did see."

Elvin rapped his knuckles gently against the butcher's worktable in confused frustration. "Can't put my mind to it; can't put my mind at ease. If it comes to shooting, I'd like to take one alive and beat it out of 'em."

"If it comes to shooting, we lose," Arnold warned. "Just the ones here can likely out-shoot us, and then what'll happen to the folks who went out to New Ashburn? And there will be more Americans where they came from."

New Ashburn

"'Lissa, come in here," Bill said, leaning out the door of his study, the lit cigar in his mouth garbling his speech. He was clearly pleased with himself. "Come take a look at this."

Melissa Daly entered Bill's sanctum. The powdermaker had made himself at home. Glassware and oil burners and vials and discolored papers littered the desks and worktables along the walls and in the middle of the room. Even the floor had received stacks of supplies, chemicals, and sundry items Melissa couldn't identify. Bill had his own sleeping quarters, but she could see he'd used the couch in the study for sleeping instead of, well, for studying. For now, the couch served for an empty-enough space to hold the tray of lunch she'd cooked for him.

Bill didn't look the least bit interested in food. "Look—look at this," he said again, pointing to the mason jar full of salt sitting next to an open chemistry textbook. Except it couldn't be salt; he wouldn't get excited about something as simple as that.

"Nitrate?" Melissa guessed.

Bill shook his head. "Baking soda. The nomads would have charged a full jaw for this much, and even then, it would have been some old garbage they scrounged up from who-knows-where. This is fresh. Made it with a brine of salt and ammonia, then bubbled carbon dioxide through the brine. I get the carbon dioxide by stoppering off one of the methane furnace chimneys."

"So... I reckon baking soda... is good for baking?"

"It's good for all sorts of things! Cleaning, deodorin', settling your stomach. You can brush your teeth with it. Not to mention all the chemical uses. It's a right handy base to have whenever you're surrounded by acids, which..." He indicated the laboratory.

"Bill, I..." Melissa was impressed, but he always impressed her. She didn't understand why he felt the need to keep showing off. "Why now? Why here?"

"It's all this ammonia we've got all of a sudden. All-fired useful. If we ever get the Haber process figured out... eh." He made a dismissive motion with his hand. "It would take years."

"Go on. Years to what?" Melissa wasn't exactly interested—she was more of a keep-your-feet-on-firm-ground kind of person—but Bill seemed like a young man when he got like this. And, now that she thought about it, he really wasn't more than a few years older than she was.

"The Haber process pulls nitrogen right out of the air to make ammonia. A lot of it. If we can step up to a real truckload of ammonia production, there's all sorts of things we can do. Not just gunpowder, but other explosives, like for mining, demolition, clearing roads and whatnot. How you think the old-time road builders cut through whole mountains for their highways like that? And not just explosives, and not just baking soda. Fertilizer. What did our farmers get last harvest? A measly twenty bushels per acre, maybe? I bet we could double that. Any other clans get a taste of it, or the Federation, and we'll be *rich*, I tell you. Ain't none of our kids ever gonna go hungry again."

Melissa blinked. "*Our* kids?"

Bill cleared his throat and went red as a tomato. "You know what I mean—Tuckers. Y'know..."

Whether the knock on the door saved them both from embarrassment or made it worse, Melissa couldn't be sure. It was Ella, her eyes rimmed with tears.

"Uh-oh. What's going on?" Bill asked.

"It's those Sylvanian slaves the Americans got working. One of the older ones keeled over today, right on the factory floor."

Bill looked old again in an instant. "Ella, I know you're upset, and I'm not saying it's right—"

"It's awful, Bill! Ain't nothing been done for the slaves! You said there'd be better food, shelter... *something!*"

"I talked to Armstrong. What else am I supposed to do? Look." Bill pointed to the mess of papers on his workbench. "So far, we haven't been able to put out one part in five of what I'd expected. Not out of a single batch. Yesterday, our sulfur dioxide leak got so bad, Cora Compton had me shut the whole operation down for the day. Meanwhile, I'm chasing down my own notions on how to make this operation better and more profitable." He swallowed and cast a look at Melissa. "But none of this is easy while Armstrong's been breathing down my neck every second—"

"I don't care! It doesn't matter! You've been so busy solving little problems, you forgot who you were working for! The slaves are hungry, and they still ain't got a roof over their heads, and they're working themselves half to death building this factory of your'n." Ella waved a hand at the new building around them.

"I don't like it, Ella, but there *is* a war on—"

"Don't give me that excuse. Ain't no reason to take those folks from their homelands and lock 'em up."

"You don't know what reasons the Federation's got any more than I do, and don't go pretending like you do."

"I know the American soldiers have been using the womenfolk for—" She stopped and looked at Melissa. "Beastly things. Can you tell me what good reason the Americans might have for that?"

Bill stabbed out the cigar he'd been puffing on. "Now you listen here, missy. I didn't do none of that. I'm just doing my job."

Melissa spoke up. "Maybe I should just—"

"You picked this job," Ella said to Bill. "You wanted it."

"Because I'm good at it! I'm doing what I'm good at. You know what I ain't good at? Runnin' an army or ruling a town. And I sure as hell ain't good at ordering around someone who is."

Melissa inched toward the door. "I left you some lunch, Bill. I'll see myself out."

Ella folded her arms. "Armstrong's got you scared. That's what it is. Too afraid to lose what you've got to stand up for someone else." She shook her head and turned to leave.

"Melissa, Ella, hold on, now. Let's get this figured out, here," Bill called after them both, but that wasn't what stopped them.

It was the sight of Jody Perkins in the door, her hair half-covering her downturned face.

"Jody! What... what is it?" Ella looked at the crumpled letter she held with both hands.

"I got news." Jody's eyes remained fixed on the ground. "Sophie Fillmore..."

Ella's hands shot up to her mouth, and Bill rose from his seat, face pale.

"Her husband, Victor... there was an accident."

"Is he..." Ella said.

Jody shook her head.

Ella turned back to Bill, tears already welling up in her eyes. "Oh, Bill—"

"Ain't nothin' we can do," he said.

"I—I need to go back to her—"

"You *can't* go back to her."

"But the two little ones!"

"You got a little one here to worry about already, always following you places and gettin' in the way. *I'm* the one gonna provide for 'em all. *I* will make sure Sophie has the teeth she needs to be cared for," Bill said, his jaw clenched tight. "Go on, git. I got work to do." He turned back to his desk and pawed absently at the jar of baking powder. His hand brushed up against the box of cigars Armstrong had given him.

Ella crept up and laid a hand on his shoulder. Melissa fought the urge to do the same.

"I said *git.* You can go on mewling and sorrying all you want, but it ain't gonna cook the porridge."

213

Ella left him to his work. Melissa followed, but gave one last look back before she closed the door. He wasn't a young man, not by any stretch. He hunched over the desk like a brooding crow, the electric light garish on his balding pate.

Chapter 19

Having a Heart to Heart

Ella Holland entered the common area of the bathing rooms in the super-mart and stopped short to see Omar in his undershirt, polishing the mirror on the wall and applying a healthy layer of hog grease to his stubbled face.

She felt the heat in her cheeks in spite of herself, but she managed a "Don't mind me" as she walked up to the mirror next to him. Omar bade her good morning and tested his knife on a fingernail.

Ella washed her face and combed her hair. She looked over into Omar's mirror to see him holding a knife to his jaw, but his eyes were looking her way. His eyes flicked back to his own mirror a jot before Ella's snapped back to hers. She bit her lip and darted a glance back at him. Land's sakes, he was looking at her again. She reflected on her own appearance as she gathered her hair up and tied it back how she did whenever she worked with Bill's chemicals: tight, but with at least a sop to winsomeness.

"You look bright-eyed this morning," Omar said, his knife creeping along his stretched-out neck.

"Yeah?" Ella seized at the unruly strands of hair seeking to escape.

"Yeah."

"Lotta work to keep yourself trimmed up like that," Ella said.

"Mmm-hmm." Omar scraped at the whiskers under his nose. "For now, it's worth the hassle. Unless you'd prefer me with a beard."

"I'd prefer you any which way. I mean, uh... shoot. Uh, I like you with both. I mean, do you care? Never mind. I... see you later!" Ella left him to finish shaving so she could go tear out her own hair in peace.

Omar's voice from behind Ella stopped her in her tracks. "Hold on there a minute, Miss Puckett," he said.

She obliged for what felt like a fair sight longer than a minute. "Wha—"

"Care to go for a walk with me? Chew the fat up on the palisade maybe?" Omar scratched at the clean side of his face, looking down.

"Why, Omar, I... now?"

"Don't have to be now. After our shift, maybe. I reckon we've been so busy with the work Bill's got us doing... we ain't seen as much of each other as we used to back with the clan. That bein' the case, and keeping in mind I'd like to get to know you better, I figured I'd ask you rather more directly than I've been liable to before."

"Why, Omar," Ella stammered again, her cheeks flushing and a smile spreading as wide as her narrow face would allow. She couldn't help but notice, however, that Omar's eyes didn't meet hers the way they used to. It seemed like Omar had to work himself up to asking her out. But it wasn't unusual for folks to feel uncomfortable putting themselves out there like this. He was a shy fella. Heck, Ella had fallen over herself too often around young menfolk already; she wasn't about to repeat the same mistake she had when she'd briefly courted Amos Taylor. "I'd be right pleased to, young man," she said in a teasing effort to liven what increasingly felt like a dour mood.

Omar nodded to her and turned back to shaving. "After our shift, then. Out by the eastern gate, near the river."

Ella left, unsure whether she felt giddy or... wary?

Omar Walking cleaned up his knife and strop before making his way back to his bunk through the myriad apartments subdividing the super-mart. His living space, parceled off along with Bill's and the others, made for a small but comfortable place to sleep. He dressed for work and stepped out of his apartment to head for the factory.

He never made it past their suite of apartments.

Melissa Daly blocked the way. Her son was playing not far off. She stared at him with piercing eyes. "I asked Bill if he'd wanted you to organize his notes. He didn't."

"Bill's got a lot going on. He must have forgot. All the more reason to—"

"No." Melissa shook her head. "You're up to something."

"Yeah? And what do you reckon that is?"

Melissa's silence betrayed her uncertainty, but her face didn't. "Bill's picked you to deliver news and teeth back to the clan. That gives me a while to find out while you're gone, don't it?" She pulled out a wax-sealed envelope and held it out to Omar. "Miss Perkins wanted this delivered to Ralph McDaniel."

Omar stood with his arms crossed. "I'll get going first thing tomorrow morning."

"Bill wants you to go today."

"I've got a meet-up planned."

Melissa cocked her head and squinted at Omar as if trying to guess at what he was made of. "Ella. What do you want with her?"

"Maybe I like her. Ever thought of that?"

"You ain't foolin' me. And you'll just have to dodge your meet-up, 'cause Bill wants you to get a move-on while there's still daylight."

Omar took the envelope and scratched behind his ear with the corner. "Did you volunteer me for the job?"

"I ain't got that kind of pull with Bill. But I—"

"You don't? With your tea and honey? Cooking his breakfast for him? Washing his dishes? What's next? Fixin' to start bunking up with him soon? I bet Puckett will be nice and ready to hear whatever you have to say about me then."

Melissa scowled. "I *ain't* that kind of woman."

"You husband was Bert Daly, weren't he? He tried to put the finger on me, too. Might want to remember how that turned out. Puckett does. Not sure there's anything left to the Daly name other than finger-pointin' and shadow-chasin'."

"*I ain't that kind of woman.*"

"Your husband sure was that kind of man. Did you put him up to that frame job on me last spring? I don't reckon a little worm of a man like that was smart enough to do it on his own. Keep tryin' the same tricks, and folks will start to wonder."

"You *low-down—*"

"I'll get headed out today," Omar said, stone-faced as he pocketed the letter. "While I'm gone, you might want to think real hard about what tree you want to bark up."

An Ashburnite worker staggered away from the mess of piping, eyes watering from the stench of ammonia fumes.

"Okay, everybody out!" Ricky Brody called out in exasperation. "Shut it down again! Let 'er air out!"

"How long did we have the pumps running?" the Ashburnite asked, undoing the handkerchief tied over his mouth and nose.

Ricky looked at the bell tower clock face peeking over the other side of New Ashburn's industrial district. "Better part of an hour, I'd say. Not much better for how much time we spent going over the seals." He didn't say it, but it was these trash-pickers. They acted like they knew everything there was to know about airtight this and watertight that, like their brains weren't mush from all the chemicals they'd been sitting in all their lives.

Still, a break was a break.

Ricky went back up the hill with the other workers—those who weren't slaves, anyway—to the super-mart and basked in the refreshing cool of the air-conditioned interior. He got himself a cup of water from a large tank held next to the Hibernates' big refrigeration unit and felt the cold seep into his hand as he held the cup. He sniffed the water, as was his habit in these strange parts, and had a sip.

"You don't need to keep smelling it, you know," said a voice from behind him. It was one of the young Ashburnite fellows brought into the factory to help pressurize the system. "This here water is likely about the safest you'll ever find."

Ricky took another sip of water to sidestep the need to answer.

"So, why'd you come all the way out here to New Ashburn?"

"'Cause I was Mr. Puckett's apprentice, that's why."

"Mrs. Daly said there was an apprentice who didn't come."

"He wanted to stay home. Most of us Tuckers aren't keen on traveling."

"What about you? You get homesick much?"

"Oh, well, I..." Ricky looked at the Ashburnite. "What do you care?"

"I'm curious. No one talks about what the Tucker clan's like. I mean, a feller like me can't exactly walk up to Mrs. Compton and ask her, and the Perkins girl is as like to tell me about the way y'uns sort your names in the clan registry as anything. And there ain't *no* way any of us are gonna ask the Americans about it."

"Ain't you Americans?"

"Everybody says we is, but I think we're Americans the way an unmodified is a human: we've got all the basic parts covered, but that don't mean we're gonna get the time of day from our betters."

Ricky bristled a bit. "Who says ubermenschen are better than the 'unmodified?'"

"The Americans do. And if we want to keep their traders coming through with food, we better keep nodding whenever they nod."

Ricky let the matter drop. "Why not grow your own food?"

"You see a lot of cropland around here?" the Ashburnite asked. "What acreage we got, we grow potatoes in, but we just don't got the space for much else."

"How in the world have you guys not starved these last fifty years?"

"We never come close to it. Whatever it is, there's always been somebody, somewhere, who's had extra food and wanted something we had. Thing is, most of those folks have been far away, which means the nomads and traders have to cross more land, which means they take a bigger and bigger cut from any trade we make. Which is why most folks here in New Ashburn were pretty excited to find you Tuckers with something useful right in our own backyard. I reckon we'll get us some nice trade between the both of our clans, and leave out all the middle-men."

"Huh." Ricky took another sip of water, wiped his hand on his shirt, and reached over. "Ricky Brody. I worked on my pa's farm before I went to work with Mr. Puckett."

The Ashburnite shook Ricky's extended hand. "Tom Jenkins. My pa is a Keeper of the Compressor. He makes sure the heating and cooling of

220

the main building stays in working order, as well as our clan refrigerator. It's a pretty high place in clan professions, and he weren't too happy to see me go over to the factory."

"Was it hard for you?"

"A bit," Tom answered. "It ain't a bad trade, but my pa's kind just want to keep something going. What we're doing is starting something new."

Ella stared out across the river from atop the eastern gate, leaning up against the palisade parapet. The sun had dipped below the hills, and the valley in which New Ashburn sat now glowed with ever-softening amber light. The summer heat lost its stifling pressure, mellowing to a fuzzy warmth accompanied by the buzzing of night bugs. Her shift must have ended more than an hour ago, and so therefore must have Omar's and yet here she waited, alone, without Omar. Her stomach growled at her. She shook her head at her own impatience and thought about what she would say to Omar when he showed up.

She struggled to find the right words to say what she wanted, and when she'd found them, couldn't bring herself to get them out. And yet Omar, who never seemed like much of a talker himself, got the words out when he was around her. She used her time waiting to prepare herself for what she would say. This time, she would get it all out in the open. Everything she knew, everything she felt.

Her dadgum stomach growled again.

She turned at the sound of footsteps, her face brightening, then falling somewhat when she saw it was Melissa Daly and not Omar.

"Mrs. Daly, I... what are you doing out here?"

"Looking for you. What are you doing out here?"

221

"Oh, I was..." Ella leaned against the parapet, her cheeks going red. "enjoying some time alone, I reckon."

Ella felt Melissa's deadpan stare from the ground below. "Omar couldn't make it," she said.

"I wasn't—why not?"

"Had to head back to the Tucker clan, carry letters, supplies, and such."

"He didn't come to say goodbye?"

Melissa sighed and climbed up the ladder to join Ella on the palisade walkway. "I could tell you he had to leave in a hurry and didn't have time to say goodbye. But you done me a good turn. You done me a lot of good turns. So when I say a feller like him is only going after you 'cause he wants something outta you, it's because I know from my own life, and I'm letting you know as a friend. 'Cause I want to do you a good turn. I don't want you getting hurt."

"Do you know when he'll be back?" Ella asked.

"Hon, did you hear what I—"

"I heard you. Do you know when he'll be back?"

Melissa shrugged. "If he goes quick, a week or two, maybe. I don't know how fast one guy can go alone."

"I hope he's careful."

"I'm sure he can take real good care of himself." Melissa scoffed.

"Mrs. Daly, I know how this sounds, but you don't know him like I do."

"I felt the way you did, once. Maybe more than once. Every time, it got me in trouble. I didn't get my reputation from nowhere."

"I'll be careful."

Melissa rested her forehead on her hand. "You want to head back, or be alone for a while, or..."

"You can stay, I reckon. I don't mind your company."

The two women watched the river trickle by and listened to the droning insects. The wind shifted enough for them to catch a brief whiff of the landfill further east, a thankfully rare occurrence because of the shape of the valley and the prevailing winds.

"Ella, mind if I ask you something?"

Ella turned to look at Melissa. She was rubbing her hands together in slow meditation.

"Sure," Ella said.

"Do you think... Bill likes me?"

Chapter 20

The Factors of Production

The stench of the landfill was not what overawed Bill Puckett, a man long familiar with the odor of decomposition. The thick aroma of the cigar he puffed on masked the smell anyway. Rather, as Bill surveyed the wide swath of the landfill, which loomed over him like a man-made mountain, he wondered two things: one, how humans ever made enough trash to fill up so great a space, and two, how the Ashburnites ever managed to tend to all this junk before they had the prisoners to toil for them.

A collection of newer buildings abutted the main landfill. Materials and waste processing, he'd been told. The largest of the buildings was a forge for iron, copper, and aluminum scrap. Closer to him sat six massive steel drums mounted on an axle running down the middle of each. These were for composting biological waste, and his heart raced at the thought of all the nitrates held inside.

The landfill itself mostly lurked under a skin of unbroken, grass-covered soil. The junkers had carved out no more than narrow slices from the landfill, either to control the release of pollution, slow the deterioration of valuable salvage, or both. Once again, he found himself admiring the careful planning that went into managing something as chaotic as a gigantic trash heap.

Bill turned and beckoned his attendants forward. The first one was the Ashburnite girl, Jody Perkins, who both knew her way around the landfill and knew how to take proper notes. Bill had yet to see her around any worksite without a clipboard and some freshly printed ledger in hand. She scratched one end of the ballpoint pen against her burn as she stared out at the landfill worksite. Bill imagined the scar likely itched. He had a few minor burns of his own that troubled him from time to time.

His other attendant was a burly American bodyguard Armstrong had assigned to him, name of Harlow. Bill had intended to protest, but the bodyguard reminded him that these *were* prisoners of war doing the bulk of the labor, after all. There wasn't much Bill could do about it either way. The orders came down from Colonel Armstrong, and he hadn't seen a guttering candle's glimpse of her since she'd given him a box of cigars and told him to get back to work. She was a busy woman, and the army had subordinate officers for a reason. Bill wondered what Lieutenant Harlow would report to Armstrong about their progress and hoped the reports would be good. He suspected they weren't.

"Can't keep getting off-track," he said, partly to himself, partly to his assistants. "How many workers do I got?"

Jody tallied up the ledger. "Menfolk, or—"

"Anyone."

"325. Half men, a little less than half women, and a few kids."

"The factory ain't going up fast enough with that many. I need more workers."

"Just lengthen the working day," the American bodyguard said.

Bill turned to Lieutenant Harlow. "We've already got them doing twelve hours a day, seven days a week. Hard labor, too. We can't go much more than that without workers getting hurt or sick."

"We can get more. These are prisoners of war. We can always get more."

Bill grunted in frustration. He puffed on his cigar, then waved at the smoke in his eyes. "But that's just not efficient. I'd still have to wait for more hands to come in, and I'm tired of waiting. I couldn't keep them working any more than... I'd say, two hours extra without losing efficiency. I've got to keep them tolerably well-rested and fed. Can I hire more Ashburnite workers?"

"How are you going to pay for them?" the American soldier asked, folding his arms over his chest.

"Colonel Armstrong's got plenty of jaws to-hand. All I need is the means to get production up to where *she* wants it."

"If it helps," Jody said, "labor's mighty cheap right now. It's been hard for most of the workers in New Ashburn to keep up with free labor. It's been getting hard for some folks to buy food."

"Junker grievances are not our concern at the moment," the bodyguard said with more authority than a mere bodyguard would have had. "What is our concern is the increasing hostility between the prisoners and the Ashburnites."

"Because the junkers are losing work," Bill explained.

"Which means the Ashburnites have every incentive to start something the moment you start them working together. We've already had complaints."

"Good Lord, how did I end up with not enough labor and too much at the same time?" Bill threw his hands up, but still kept a grip on his cigar. "Okay, we can keep the workers separate. I've already got some

226

Ashburnite workers on the specialty work. I need extra bricklayers, but I reckon I can split the work into shifts. I'll need to split the factory's daily doings into shifts anyway."

"I still don't see how you're going to pay for the extra labor," the bodyguard said.

"I'd be able to pay for it, easy, if I saw any money for the nitrogel I've cranked out so far."

"It was all in the contract. You get paid once the delivery has been confirmed, minus a portion to pay for the financing of this whole operation. This sort of thing takes time."

"But Armstrong—"

"Colonel Armstrong," Lieutenant Harlow corrected.

"Colonel Armstrong has the money *now*," Bill said.

The bodyguard mused. "I'll ask her. Recruit whatever Ashburnite workers you need."

"What if she says no to the payments?"

"Everyone will be paid. Eventually."

"We all *have* to be paid," Jody said. "This clan can't survive without the nomads, and nomads don't accept I-owe-yous."

"Don't worry about it," the bodyguard shrugged off the concern. "You all worry too much. This is just a cash flow problem. This operation is a valuable asset to the New American Federation, and we're not going to let this operation fall apart over something as stupid as money. As long as you *can* get the kinks out of your production line."

"I'm as eager as Colonel Armstrong is to get this cart rolling," Bill said, "but I think maybe I was too eager. I done tripped over my own apron. We cranked out some acids, we got the new process prototyped, we even got us some actual nitrogel output to show for it. But tryin' to get all the parts in place at the same time ended up just spreading me thin and gauming up the works. We've got a whole line of pressure chambers set up, but it's all there right out in the open. We're having to run the compressors and pumps on mule-powered treadmills, and that ain't going to last. What's worse, it will take *extra* work to convert it all over to electric or steam power. Also, I don't have enough glycerol to keep up nitroglycerin output at this scale. The nomads I used to trade with got plenty from some soap-making clan somewhere, but—"

"Only Federation-sanctioned nomad clans are permitted," Lieutenant Harlow said.

"Then let's hope someone in your Federation makes a lot of soap, or else we start getting plenty of slaked lime and start everything from scratch here." Bill scratched at the back of his neck as he looked skyward. "The bottlenecks are just piling up. Bottlenecks mean downtime for the machines and workers. It means the system gets depressurized. It means inputs pile up on one end and outputs stop on the other. Downtime is money we're losing. Money *I'm* losing. I need me a system. A running checklist of tasks for whenever folks are waiting for the different steps to finish cooking, like in the catalytic chamber or the absorption tower."

"What happens if a worker leaves the... the cookery unwatched?" Jody asked. "Ain't that dangerous?"

Bill puffed on his cigar, and again he blinked and waved at the smoke in his eyes. He echoed Mrs. Compton's maxim with somewhat less relish. "Protocols. We can put one overseer in each section. Make sure they're Ashburnites, well suited to it. And we'll need something better than just the gauges, though I'm right pleased with the ones your people got hooked up. I'm thinking a bell, or an automatic shutoff."

"We get electricity hooked up there, it'll be doable."

"How are we going to do that?"

"Same way we usually do it. Salvage some cables, run 'em out there. Test 'em for shorts and cracks in the insulation and such."

"Will they work?"

"You'd have to ask the electrician about it."

"I noticed the power ain't always steady to some of these buildings you already got hooked up, and sometimes there's sparks when the wind's blowing right. Could be a problem in a gunpowder factory."

"We could make it fresh," Jody said. "Draw copper into wires, cover 'em in fat, harden it up in an oven. It'll take longer and be more expensive, but I seen it done."

"Eh. We don't have the time or money for it. We've got to start cranking out a crapload of nitrogel soon, and for cheap. It'll have to be salvage, for now. Same with the building materials. How's the absorption tower coming along?"

"Mrs. Compton says it's working better," Jody reported, flipping through her notes. "The last time we ran it, Miss Holland said she didn't think any nitrogen dioxide was escaping. Unfortunately, she found that out because some of the prisoners were sucking the tail gas."

"Ah, good Lord." Bill shook his head.

"What's wrong with that?" the bodyguard asked.

"NO_2 is a toxic gas," Bill explained. "We've got to soak it into the water in the tower to make nitric acid. What's left over in the tail gas should be N_2O, which is... laughing gas."

"I see." The bodyguard cracked his knuckles.

"Don't worry about it; leave it be," Bill said, his voice rising a notch, "I'll just give a warning about how dangerous it is to breathe in the exhaust."

"Mrs. Daly has asked for lighter duties so she can watch after her son."

Bill sighed. "I swear, kids are what make us old. She can leave him in the supermart and take regular breaks to go check in on him. He's three years old, and there ain't much trouble he can get to up there as long as someone looks in on him every hour or so."

"Also, the workers have requested—through Miss Holland—for Sundays off. She would have told you herself, but you've been hard for her to get to lately."

"I'm sorry, but I'm busy. Too busy. And I can't afford to let the works run cold for a full day, not right now. I don't like it none, but we're close, Miss Perkins. Close to getting this factory set up proper and some real production going. Once the factory's ready, we'll let up a little, and things will get better. You'll see."

Chapter 21

Like Father, Like Son

Tucker Territory

Ralph crawled over a mountain of bloody severed limbs to see a screaming woman caught in a mess of vines and thorns. He knew, somehow, the woman was a Greenbrier, and when he skewered her with the spear in his hands, he felt nothing. Blood spouted from the wound, turning the spear shaft slick and red. The woman screamed, louder this time, shrill as a screevler.

Ralph pulled loose a curved knife and pounced on her, slashing and stabbing. Still, she screamed. Blood flecked his face and clouded his eyes, and still she screamed.

He went frantic with the knife. The woman turned to bloody, unrecognizable mincemeat underneath him.▯

And still she screamed. Why couldn't he make her stop?

Ralph woke, thrashing, sweat coursing from every pore in his body. God, it was hot.

The droning of the cicadas and crickets told him it was nowhere close to morning, but the thunderous beat of his heart had driven sleep far away. He stumbled out of his room, aiming to wet some rags to cool himself, but he marked someone outside the kitchen window.

It was his father, sitting in a rocking chair, sipping something from an earthenware mug. Ralph shrank back, but from the darkness outside, Elvin called, "Who's there?"

"Just me, Pa," Ralph answered, trying not to wake anyone else in the house.

He heard his father rise from the rocking chair and lay his hand on the kitchen door. "Couldn't sleep either, huh? Come on out," Elvin said, grabbing an extra kitchen chair from inside. "I'll give you something to help."

Ralph followed, knowing any objection would be useless, even if he had one to give. Elvin returned to his rocking chair, and Ralph sat down in the chair put forward.

Elvin picked up something off the ground and poured a teacup for his son. "Take yourself a dram 'o this."

Whatever was inside the teacup wasn't tea. Ralph nearly gagged at the unexpected astringent taste.

"A watchman can't make a habit of it. No mor'n once a month, I'd say. Esspenssive. You can get hooked on it. Blunts yer brain. But sometimes you gotta blunt the brain a bit, er else you'll go crazy."

Ralph looked down at his teacup. Whiskey, then. He tossed back what was left in the cup and reached for a second helping from the brown jug his father extended to him. It was worse than taking medicine.

"Did I ever tell you 'bout my first kill, Ralph? Think I was twelve, maybe. Someone takes a shot at me from who-knows-where. This was back when lots of folks still had real guns with real ammo. I get a tree between me and the shooter, and backed on up from it, nice and slow. Was on mossy ground, see, so's could move quick without bein' heard. So, I move, find a better spot, and wait." Elvin's eyes glinted in the dim moonlight. "Along comes this jasper in a ghillie suit and a huntin' rifle. I had him. Just wait for a clean shot and drop 'im."

He took another swig from his mug and sighed. "Turns out it was a woman. Some kind of drifter. She had a camp on down the hill, a carved-up human hanging from a tree for eatin', and a half-starved kid who thought he could fight me with a little butcher knife."

Ralph had the sense not to ask what had happened to the kid.

"I'll tell you, son: I loved it. Loved it even when I was scared. That jack-racker comes into my sights, and I know I've got 'er..." Elvin fired a finger gun at a target hidden to all but his mind's eye. "The feeling you get when you nail some sucker who wanted you for lunch. Someone you've been hunting for hours, days even." He swallowed, though he hadn't lifted the mug to his lips. "But I never forget their faces. 'Specially the women. The young 'uns." He tipped his mug over and found it empty. "I gargle enough of this stuff, I might forget. But then I wouldn't be much use as a watchman anymore, would I?"

Ralph stared at his own empty teacup. The dainty cup handle felt oddly like a rifle's trigger guard in the dark. "Think you might have somebody take over for you someday?"

"While I'm still alive? What'd I do then?"

"I don't know, Pa. Tend a garden like Old Man Brody."

Elvin gave a derisive snort. "Yeah, and who'd take over fer me, huh?"

It was a rhetorical question, but Ralph chased it down anyway, against his better judgement. "Well... seems like you got more choices than you ever had. Amos Taylor might be the best watchman who ever was."

Elvin struggled out of his seat. "You tryin' to dodge your duty again, Ralph?"

Ralph sighed in frustration, the alcohol giving him more boldness than he was used to. "I ain't tryin' to dodge nothin', Pa. I'm only saying what's already out in the open. Everybody's thinkin' it."

"Thinkin' what? How my good-for-nothin' son ain't no match for the blacksmith's boy?"

Ralph ignored the barb. "If you want what's best for the clan, choose the best man for the job."

"Then what'll *you* do, huh? Fritter away your time with that—schoolteacher?"

Ralph got out of his seat. "No, *Dad.* Maybe I'll get work at the factory. *Build* something for a change."

The sway left his father's shoulders. "You want to follow that trash-pickin' girl."

"What difference does it make? Why does it matter to you what I do?"

"Because it ain't about what you want." Elvin advanced on the boy with each sentence, jabbing a stiff finger into Ralph's chest to emphasize the pertinent points. "'Cause everybody makes sacrifices for the clan. I did, and so will you. You'll crawl through the mud just like I did, and you'll get the nightmares same as me, and you'll be *grateful* for it. You're a Tucker, and more than that, a McDaniel, and more than that, my eldest goddamn son, and I won't have you turn your back on all that just because some potlickin' bitch batted her eyes at you."

Ralph's eyes flared. He seized his father's accusing outstretched hand and twisted it to the side. Elvin stumbled, off-balance, while Ralph pulled his father into a wild right haymaker that split Elvin's lips open on his teeth and bruised his cheek.

Elvin stumbled back, stunned, to the ground.

Ralph stood with raised fists, ready for more, even as he fought back tears.

Elvin wiped the blood from his mouth and struggled up from the ground where he'd fallen, but he didn't make a move toward Ralph.

Ralph bolted into the night.

Elvin watched him go, his mouth hanging open, blood dripping down his chin. It was a punch he should have been proud of—certainly, Paul McDaniel would have swelled—but he couldn't muster the pride. Maybe he should have given Ralph a good thrashing for it, but he couldn't seem to muster that up, either.

Elvin staggered a couple faltering steps after his son, but didn't give chase. The anger was now drowned out by something else. It wasn't his father; he couldn't be sure what it was. Perhaps it was the blow to his head, or the whiskey. Ralph—he'd never thought...

How many times had Elvin wanted to slug his own pa like that?

Ralph stumbled through the thick darkness, hacking madly at the grasping undergrowth with the matchet he'd hastily grabbed in his headlong flight from town. The hiccuping sobs rising from his chest barely escaped his mouth, as if unsure where to go once out in the wild. His face and brain felt fuzzy, dazed. Was he running away? He didn't know.

He didn't know anything except that he couldn't go back.

His halting, wending path led him into the old town, which a saner Ralph McDaniel would have avoided even in daylight. He wasn't aware of the unconscious pull drawing him inexorably through the abandoned buildings and dark, wrecked basements; all he felt was the push to get as far away from his father as he could. He didn't take stock of his surroundings until he heard hushed voices.

Ralph had thought death would have been preferable to the prison his father had made for him, but now, in the dark, his mind returning to itself, he found his hand tightening on the duct-taped handle of his matchet. Who was talking in the old town in the middle of the night?

A voice rose higher, close by, to his right. Ralph moved forward with tentative steps, struggling to keep his sobs under control, a new emotion seizing his heart. With the outstretched blade, he swept aside a vine-choked tree branch to see a coterie of human shapes in a trampled clearing under pale moonlight. A burly form paced back and forth, a second leaned at the edge of the clearing with crossed arms, and a third sat in the center.

"...leave us alone when it's done. We can take care of ourselves." Ralph recognized the burly man's voice—one-eyed Johnny Grierson.

"We can't guarantee your safety like we can the rest of the evacuees."

"Don't care. This is home."

"Then why help us with... the others?"

"'Cause they banished me from my home just for hearing the truth. One threw actual crap at me as we walked out the gate. I'm returning the favor. And if what you say is true what really happened to the trapper, it *will* be a favor. Better they settle wherever you put them out east than let this Pied Piper character you're talking about have his way with them."

"The schoolmaster didn't seem to have any idea."

"None of 'em do. Always made sense to me to have the truth out and guard against any Pied Pipers out there, but I guess the Reverend was more afraid of his own."

"The reverend's a scared fellow."

"A guy who looks for spiders in every dark corner is usually a spider himself. He'll fight you to the end, and if you aren't careful as a tomcat on a milk-shelf, it'll be an actual fight."

"If I wanted a fight, we'd have already killed them all. These Tuckers don't have what it takes to go toe-to-toe with a single platoon. But I don't want to waste valuable human resources."

Mr. Grierson stopped pacing for a moment to look at the man leaning against the tree, then to the figure kneeling on the ground. "How does something like the Pied Piper happen, anyway?"

"Not our fault. Most neurocasters are well-controlled, but every once in a while, you get someone a little crazy."

"Crazy like your friend here?" Grierson pointed to the seated figure in the middle of the group.

Carlson didn't answer. "What we're doing out here is damage control."

The seated figure suddenly moved. "There's a neurocaster close."

The man at the edge of the clearing chambered a round in his autorifle. "Is it him?"

Ralph's throat hitched, and he took a half-step backwards.

"No." The figure in the center of the clearing stood with closed eyes and pointed directly to Ralph.▯

I see you.

"It's the watchman's kid."

Chapter 22

Backroom Deals and Front Porch Quarrels

It was midmorning by the time Elvin had his horse trotting to the southern gate, and for the first time since the Americans had come in force, a sentry manned the battlements. But, to Elvin's displeasure, the sentry was no Tucker. Worse, it was Royce Carlson, and he seemed much more interested in watching the people inside than whatever lay outside.

Carlson leaned with one knee propped up against the palisade, the easy authority he commanded unruffled by Elvin's glower. "My men tell me you've been busy this morning. Knocking on doors, shouting at the schoolmaster. Care to tell me what's going—ouch, looks like you took one on the chin. Don't tell me the schoolmaster did that to you."

"Ain't none of your worry, *Captain.* I'm busy, and I've got me a headache."

"With your face in that condition, I bet you do." Carlson laughed. "But if you're planning on leaving town, I'm afraid it is my business. My scouts detected unusual geemo activity outside the walls, and I don't want to put any clansmen at risk."

"What about the farmers?"

"Already recalled to town. I've got my boys bringing in the last of the livestock right now. Too dangerous outside the walls for civilians. Wouldn't want another 'hunting accident,' would we?"

"That'll be my problem." Elvin shook his horse's reins and continued to the gate.

"Maybe I wasn't clear. You're not going out there until I know why." Carlson remained relaxed, amused at Elvin's bullheadedness, but he slung his assault rifle a little higher, a little closer to ready.

Elvin clenched his jaw against the ache pulsing through his head. "My boy done run off in the night. He ain't come back, and nobody in town's seen him."

Carlson appeared surprised. "I'm so sorry to hear that. Do you know why he would have done something like that?"

"I aim to find out, once I've drug him back home by the scruff of his neck."

"I'll send out new orders to be on the lookout for a young Tucker wandering the woods." Carlson stood up. "I'll let you know the moment we find him."

"He's *my boy, not yours!*"

"Elvin." Royce shook his head. "If we're going to get along, you're going to have to learn to trust me."

The Tucker watchman pulled up on his horse, who'd started snorting and stamping at Elvin's tone. "You can pull this shit with Sam, but I ain't fallin' for it. I wouldn't trust you to clean my outhouse. I ain't under your orders."

"But you are under the elders' orders." Royce pulled out a paper from a pocket on his tactical vest. Fresh, mechanically printed letters stood out on the paper like charcoal on snow. "The Tucker ambassador, with a quorum of four clan elders, grants provisionary authority to Captain Royce Carlson and the company under his command to patrol and pursue military objectives essential to New American Federation security in and around Tucker clan territory without hindrance or aid required from Tucker clansmen, et cetera, et cetera."

Royce folded the paper again and returned it to his pocket. "You have a problem with it, take it up with your elders. Today's the day to do it, too. Don't you have an elder's meeting this afternoon? You wouldn't want to miss it looking for a kid playing hookey."

Elvin looked back at the clan meetinghouse, then out the gate. The leather reins strained in his white-knuckled grip before he swore with bitter vehemence and wheeled his horse back around, away from his missing son.

"Let's get started. I have good news and bad news. The bad news is that the trade deal we currently have going with New Ashburn sits in violation of the New American Federation's trade laws. Colonel Armstrong, whom I met out there, forbids trade agreements that don't go through inspection from the central trade authority. This would explain why we haven't seen our share of the profits come in yet."

There was a loud slam as Elvin McDaniel jumped to his feet and pounded his fist into the table in front of him. "Those slippery little devils! They run off with our clansmen and our nitrogel, and there ain't a single goddamn thing we can do about it!"

"Easy, everybody, easy," Sam said. "The good news is that Colonel Armstrong has sent this detachment of troops to fast-track our clan through the admittance process into the Federation."

"What's that mean?" Shane Bunton asked. "We're gonna... what?"

"Become part of the New American Federation. Which, besides restarting the trade deal with New Ashburn and getting us the money we're owed, means we'll also get representation with the national government. We get a say in how the whole country's run. I don't think I need to explain how beneficial this would be for the Tucker clan."

"This would be the worst thing I could imagine!" Reverend Brody exclaimed, a look of genuine horror on his face. "Apart from the total destruction of the clan, I can think of nothing worse than to be swallowed up by these people."

"You've seen that Royce character already traipsin' around like he owns the place. Says he's lookin' for somethin' in the woods, but won't let me go with him. I feel about as useless as a spoon at a threshing bee. We sign a treaty, he'll have run of the whole place," Elvin said.

"Let's back this whole thing up for a gosh-darned second," said Phil Holland, who was now able enough to come out for an elders' meeting, though unlike most of the rest, he remained seated. "I'd be in my grave by now if it weren't for the Americans and their antibiotics."

"You'd be dead if it weren't for the *junkers*, and we already got a deal with them," Job Brody said. "I'm thinking we've gone fishing for trout and hooked us an alligator. My boy's *and* your daughter's gone out to New Ashburn with Bill, and I don't like the idea of them being a bargaining tooth in all of this."

"I'm not sure how much of a bargain there is to have," the butcher said, leaning back and scratching his head.

"What do you mean?" Job asked.

"If we don't make treaty with the Americans, what happens to those we sent out to New Ashburn? It's plain to me the Americans don't have to give them back, and they wouldn't want to."

"I will never, *ever* let a single Tucker stay in the thrall of a foreigner while I'm still breathin'," Elvin said.

"So, if we don't make treaty with the Americans, it's war?" Phil asked, his voice rising in worry.

241

"No, no, no." Sam waved away the concerns with all the vigor of a man trying to command the waves of a storm. "The bargain is already laid out for us. We go through the process; we become part of the Federation; we get representation and all the special privileges that Federation territories enjoy."

One of the Finches raised his hand. "Like this paper?"

"And the army. Are they going to take over protecting the clan?" Johnny Grierson asked.

"Now, hold on, now," Elvin said, rising from his seat again. "Are you saying you *like* these Americans taking my job? Did I screw it up so bad you're thinking of backsteading me the first chance you get?"

Sam's voice was strained, even if his words were encouraging. "No one's saying that, Elvin. All they're saying is not all change is bad, and the Americans bring some real advantages with them."

"Think about it," Shane Bunton said. "No more night patrols. Or any patrols. No more feuds or raids on our farms. No more unbred raids or pigman sieges. The Americans take care of all of it. That's a heap of hassle I'd rather not have on my plate."

"And the paper! We could get ourselves a newspaper going, or start reprinting old books!" Sam said, though this admittedly did not draw as much of a cheer from the gathering.

"I can't believe the lot of you," Elvin spat through swollen lips. "A passel of fancy-pants out-of-towners wave some paper and chatterguns, and you offer your own backs as a stepstool!"

"It isn't like that, and you know it," Sam Chambers said. "Folks, this is our big chance. We've gotten used to the idea that our kids and grandkids will have to live the same way we did: dying young, fighting unbreds and other clans, always one bad harvest away from starvation. But it doesn't have to be that way. We could be a few years from electric power, plenty of food, and every expectation of a longer and happier life. And in exchange? A piddling amount of tax. Heck, I'll pay the tax out of my own pocket if that's your worry."

"It ain't about teeth! It's about who we are. We join up with the Americans, even if everything happens just like you say it will, then we lose everything what matters. We'll get settlers out here, with their eastern ways, and they'll outnumber us, and our kids will go soft, and before long, we'll forget where we came from, what we had. We'll forget every Tucker who died fighting the Greenbriers. We'll lose our edge. We'll be helpless babes sucklin' at the Americans' teat. You want it to be like the old days, Sam. I don't. The folks of the past age got what was comin' to 'em, sittin' around and eatin' sweets all day, and their time's all took up. A million of their lives didn't count for as much as one *drop* of our founders' blood."

"I work and I strive, same as you," Sam Chambers rejoined, advancing towards Elvin, his face reddening. "But what's the point of striving if you're not striving *for* something? What's the point of suffering if that's all we're ever destined to know? You want the clan to keep beating its head against a tree to remind itself what it means to feel? Or is it fear, Elvin? Are you afraid what will happen if the Americans can protect the clan better than you ever could?"

"You shut your mouth!" Elvin shouted, stepping forward to meet Sam's challenge. Arnold Brody tried to calm the watchman, but Elvin shook him off.

"Or what? You'll get more Tuckers killed? Looks to me it's all you're good—"

Elvin broke Sam's nose.

Arnold Brody and Shane Bunton seized Elvin on either side, dragging the spitting, cursing watchman back as the elders erupted into a tumultuous ruckus.

"Good God, man!" Doctor Bernhard said, leaping to Sam's aid.

"Arnold! Shane! Lock him in the back room!" Johnny Grierson shouted, stepping in to chair the meeting in Sam's stead.

Together, the two clansmen dragged Elvin McDaniel, screaming curses, from the room.

The door to the meetinghouse basement room creaked open, and the watchman blinked at the lantern light spilling in.

"Hey, Elvin," Sam Chambers said, his voice nasal and weedy.

Elvin said nothing.

"Ralph still hasn't shown up. Do you know where he might have gone? I can pass it along to Captain Carlson."

Elvin was silent.

Sam sighed. "Think of your son, Elvin. Where is he?"

"He's my son. If he's alive and don't want to be found, he won't be."

"Why wouldn't he want to be found?"

Elvin didn't answer.

"Some of us think he might have run away to New Ashburn. Did he say anything to you about it?"

There was still no answer.

"Can you at least tell me who gave you that busted lip?"

"You did. You busted my lip, my family, and the whole clan."

Sam sighed. He turned away, delicate fingers feeling the new shape of his nose. "The clan respects you. Heck, even I do, even now. I have no personal interest in bringing you low. But I couldn't have you sit through the whole elders' meeting. You'd find a way to swing enough folks to your side. I also know you're the kind of man to solve things with your fists, and the American question isn't one you can use your fists on. A broken nose is a small price to pay for the clan taking the right path."

Elvin curled his lip at Sam and looked away.

"If you were curious, we still ended up with a tie. We decided to put the issue to a general clan vote. All adults, fifteen and up, get a say in whether we join the Americans. We'll have to send out to New

Ashburn in the event of another tie, but I don't think that will be a concern. Democracy is the way forward, and people in a democracy only want what's best for themselves and their children. You'll come around eventually. This really is the best way."

Elvin didn't meet Sam's gaze.

"You'll be let out in a couple of days, once things are settled. Is there anything you'd like in the meantime to make your stay more comfortable?" When Elvin remained silent, Sam sighed and turned to leave.

"Wait," Elvin said. "Leave me the lantern, a quill, and some of that American paper."

Sam sat counting the two piles of black-and-white stones a second time when the captain entered. "Those piles look more even than I'd expected," Royce said.

"It's because of the airs you and your men have been putting on," Sam snapped. "Lots of clansmen don't like the way you talk to them. Elvin said you were here to put us under your boot, and his words carry a lot more weight when you act all high and mighty." He tossed another black stone onto the pile and sighed. "We're behind. I can't—I thought a popular vote would work for us, not against us."

"Yeah, I was afraid of that," Royce said, motioning for the two soldiers behind him. "That's why we went up to the Grierson settlement and collected their votes as soon as they got their polling finished."

"I thought you were out looking for Ralph McDaniel."

"I can multitask." Captain Royce gestured to the men following him. The two soldiers heaved a box full of white stones onto the table.

Sam looked up. "All 'Yes' votes?"

Royce shrugged. "Johnny Grierson's on our side, and whichever way he goes, they all go."

"Are there that many folks up at the Grierson settlement?"

"Sure, why not?"

Sam said nothing for a full minute. Then he reached over, plucked a white stone from the Grierson pile, and chucked it in with the rest of the 'yes' votes. "If we win, we'll still have to deal with all the people who voted 'no.'"

"Oh, I'll deal with them."

"I didn't mean it like that!" Sam slapped the table in front of him. "We've got to show them this was in their best interest. And I want you and your soldiers gone as soon as this treaty is settled."

"'Due to the increased threat of hostile genetic chimeras, all Tuckers are to shelter within the town walls, only to venture out with an armed military escort.'" Amos read the posted notice in the town square with a voice that rose in anger the longer he spoke. "'For the safety and internal security of the clan, all gunpowder-based weapons are hereby impounded, and all security and law-enforcement responsibilities will be passed on to Captain Royce Carlson and the soldiers under his command. Signed, Samuel Chambers, Tucker Provincial Governor.'"

"I can't believe it." Becky paced behind Amos. "I ain't never seen a body get so full of himself so fast. We ain't hardly finished counting stones before he got himself set up as governor. I don't even know what the job calls for, other than staying in the meetinghouse and sending out orders on paper. And they *still* haven't let Elvin McDaniel out—"

"There's a draft."

"A what?"

"A draft. They're carving off a slice of the clan to go off and fight in the war."

"Like slaves?" Becky sounded as if she could kill somebody. Amos reminded himself that she already had.

"We're on the draft list."

"What?"

"Look." Amos pointed to the long sheet nailed to the post beneath Sam Chambers's various accrued proclamations. "There's your name. And mine. Some of the Finches. Most of the Brodys. Even Old Man Brody! And Noah Hadley! What is he, six years old? What kind of war are they expecting to use us for?"

"I ain't fighting nobody's war but my own. I don't care what the Americans say; I didn't vote for this. They ain't taking me from my home without a fight."

"Quiet down, Becky." Amos looked around and saw an American soldier watching them. He'd seen this particular soldier—if he could be called a soldier at all—often in the past week—Jarvis.

Folks thought of him as a soldier, but he wasn't like the others. He wore a uniform, and his shining bald head seemed the model of military tidiness, but he only barely took orders from Captain Carlson, and he almost never carried a gun with him. And yet the Tuckers feared him more than any other. He went from giddy to stone-faced as if feelings were muscle twitches. The soldiers said his official job was a census taker, but for all the paper the Americans had, he never wrote anything down. He didn't seem to be interested in most of the Tuckers, often walking past them or shoving them out of the way like furniture that got in the way. The ones he did find interesting, he followed with predatory alertness. People like Old Man Brody and six-year-old Noah Hadley.

He peered at Amos now, arms folded, butt resting back against a hitching rail as if he were listening to Becky and Amos's conversation from clear across the square. Even when they stopped talking, he continued staring.

Finally, he got up and approached them. He'd found them interesting.

Dear Ralph,

I received your letter, and the news of your fellow clansman's death was hard to take in, and even harder to pass along to Miss Holland and Mr. Puckett. Mr. Puckett has his work to take his mind off things, but Ella seems less and less focused on her role as a powdermaker with the news. She's taken to caring for the slaves (I suppose she has permission from the Americans; us Ashburnites aren't allowed to talk to the prisoners), and the news of Mr. Fillmore's death has shaken her deeply. She has sent a letter to the widow along with my letter to you, and I would very much appreciate it if you could ensure the letter reaches its intended destination!

I have no desire to drive a wedge between you and your father, but secretly I hope this talk of an alliance with the Federation bears good fruit. I would very much like to call you a fellow citizen! (Officially, that is. I felt our kinship almost from our first meeting.)

I do understand concerns folks might have at so big a change, but if our experience can be generalized, I expect your clan would adjust well. New Ashburn only joined the Federation last year, but already things are changing. Colonel Armstrong oversees our integration, as she puts it, but apart from taking over our citadel (Mr. Salazar was not happy about that), she hasn't interfered with most of our day-to-day doings. They did end up confiscating most of our firearms, but I suppose it's hard to keep law and order when everybody's packing heat. The Americans say it helps smooth out the integration. Armstrong hasn't done too much with Mr. Puckett's nitrogel factory, other than manage the slaves she brought in from the war. I think she's got other concerns. She is a colonel, after all, and there is a war on.

The factory is going up fast. Faster than any construction I've seen our folks take part in. They ran wires out, and we've got electric pumps working in parts of the factory. Ricky Brody, though he is scarcely an apprentice himself, has already taken upon himself the training of many of our young Ashburnite learners, and he and some of the local boys have become thick as thieves. Mr. Walking keeps to himself, likely because his bookish turn has made him the operation's resident scribe, and there's enough work to keep him busy for ages, what with Mr. Puckett's constant tweaking and experimentation.

This letter, I believe, will arrive with Mr. Walking. I look forward to reading your reply,

Warmest Regards,
Jody

Chapter 23

Infliltration

Tucker Territory

When Omar passed through the eastern gates of the Tucker clan on a cloudy day in mid-September, he found the town quiet—the kind of quiet you get when a rotten rope's just snapped and all your timber is dangling by the last strand of the other rope while you're wondering if it will hold. The guard at the gate made him identify himself and offer proof, then confiscated his rifle—Sam Chambers's orders—and waved him on through without another word.

As Omar looked at the quiet American guards watching him come in through the gates, and the quiet Tucker farmers loading a train of carts with the clan's wheat stores, and the quiet dogs whining at the feet of their quiet masters, he wondered what that first snapped rope had been, and how long this quiet would hold.

The Americans had put up posters on every tree, fencepost, and door. *We Believe in the American Way!* and *Restoring the Glory of the Past for a Brighter Tomorrow!* and *Are You Worthy of Your Genes?*

It wasn't until he reached the steps of the meetinghouse that the first person came up to greet him—the American captain, Royce Carlson. "You from the factory? What's your name?"

"Omar Walking."

"What do you have from New Ashburn?"

"News, teeth, some letters..." Omar dismounted and checked his saddlebags. "Where's Mr. Chambers? I thought I'd be giving these to him."

"He's busy with administrative tasks. I'll get these to him."

Omar held the bundle of pigman teeth in one hand and a few letters in the other, but didn't hand either over to Royce. "You sure? I can deliver the letters; I know who they're supposed to go to."

"I'll have my boys take care of it. You'll need to get back to New Ashburn soon, right? You have a place to stay? Go get some rest; I'll have someone tend to your horse, too." Royce took the stuff and disappeared back inside the meetinghouse, leaving Omar with his horse.

He took the horse to the shared stables on the west side of town and found most of the stalls taken up with the farmers' animals. On the way, he walked past the butcher's place and saw Arnold Brody outside, carving up an entire hanging beef for a mob of American soldiers. He wandered into Bill's house and found the Newells living there.

"Psst." It wasn't the Newells camped out in Omar's old hovel who hissed at him, but Becky Brody, waving at him from the side door connecting the Puckett home with the Hollands'.

Taking his traveling things with him, Omar followed the Tucker beauty across the narrow alleyway separating Bill's house from the Hollands', where he found Amos Taylor and Phil Holland stringing up bean pods

251

in the kitchen. "What's going on?" he asked, finally crashing down into a chair at the Hollands' kitchen table with an exhausted sigh and stretching his legs.

Amos answered first. "I'm spitting mad, and I don't know who's got me irritated more—the Americans, or Sam Chambers. I don't know where to start."

"They've turned this entire town into a prison," Becky Brody said, looking out the window at the palisade catwalk overlooking the back of the house.

"How'd they manage that? You got 'em outnumbered ten-to-one."

"They've taken all our guns, and it was Sam Chambers who ordered it," Amos said. "If it were just the American captain, we would have told him to move along at the other end of a shotgun, but nobody wants to go against the schoolteacher."

"Not the watchman?"

"Elvin McDaniel's been clapped in irons since he laid Sam out on the floor of the meetinghouse, and the elders have been following Sam's lead since the clan voted to join the Federation."

"Ah. Well, that *is* news."

"Except almost none of the adults I've talked to actually voted for it! Since the results came in, everybody's been whispering: 'Did you vote for it?' 'I didn't. Did you?'"

"I didn't even vote for it," Phil said, a hand on his scarred belly. "And that's the story over the whole clan! Sam's in cahoots with these Americans, and I think they put their thumb on the scale!"

An American soldier knocked on the back door and let himself into the kitchen. "Meeting about something?"

"Just drying out some shuck beans for winter," Becky said.

Omar grabbed a handful of beans and started to string their pods up to give his hands something to do.

"How many pounds is that there?" The soldier stuck his hand into the bushel, either gauging how deep it went or feeling around for contraband.

"Not this, too," Phil complained. "You're gonna starve us."

"You Tuckers worry too much," the soldier said as he took a turn around the kitchen, examining everything and dwelling the longest on the real metal cutlery. "I told you—our traders run the most regular routes in the world. Nobody in the Federation goes hungry." He grabbed a handful pods from the bushel, shoved them into a satchel slung over his shoulder, and winked at Becky before he left.

"Looks like they have about the same attitude here as they do back in New Ashburn."

"Is it that bad?"

"Not for the Ashburnites."

"How's Ella?" Phil asked of his daughter.

"Not bad. She's, uh—taken after some hard-up folks."

Phil rolled his eyes. "Of course she has. You keeping her outta trouble?"

"I've been trying to, sir. I aim to get back before trouble can come to her. She had a letter for Sophie, but the Americans—Carlson or whoever..." Omar slapped the empty pocket at his side. "Are the Americans coming and going whenever they want now?"

Amos chucked a bad pod into a nearby bucket with more force than necessary. "When the Americans went door to door taking our guns, no one had the guts to stop them. Then we *couldn't* stop them when they started raiding our food supplies, or when they issued 'Draft Summons' to people all over town. Shane Bunton tried to step in, and they roughed him up pretty bad. They can't get away with this." He glared into the floor. "They're not going to get away with it. If these were Greenbriers, we would have staked their bodies out as a feast for the crows by now."

Omar looked at Amos. "I don't see how you'd do it without firepower."

253

Amos looked over at his old master. Phil Holland shrugged. "Can't expect them to get everything from the gunsmith. I had a couple pieces I was working on that weren't put together in a way they figured was dangerous. And I got me a handful of them silencers I been working on."

"That's still not enough."

Amos leaned forward. "They've got the guns and just about everything stored in the meetinghouse. I'm willing to bet they haven't locked up the courtyard access."

Omar's hands dropped into his lap with a limp *thud.* "You're cracked. This whole clan is crawling with soldiers."

"Not tomorrow. Not if you help me."

It was Sunday. In normal times, folks were expected to show up for Sunday morning church, regardless of their actual religious convictions. Now, they simply had nowhere else to go.

In normal times, the clan meetinghouse was the only building large enough to hold services in, while what had once been the town's church building was Sam Chambers's schoolhouse. These were not normal times. Sam and the Americans had set up the meetinghouse as an administrative center, jail, fortress, and barracks for the ever-increasing number of Federation soldiers. Sam or the Americans—the distinction between the two had ceased to be meaningful—had declared, for security purposes, the meetinghouse off-limits for everyday clan functions, including church services. The clan had to make do with the open street in front of the schoolhouse on the east side of town, across the creek.

Chambers had declared attendance at Sunday morning services compulsory, likely not because he had been gripped in a new wave of religious fervor, but because it gave the Americans a handy way to keep a weekly headcount. The Americans kept a fine-cut tally, with certain Tuckers exempt, one being Phil Holland, whose pesky gut wound often kept him bedridden. Mr. Holland had found that his convalescence afforded him the time and space to do his own record-keeping. In normal times, he was not much of a note-taker. These were not normal times. These past few weeks, the gunsmith had looked out from his upstairs bedroom window with chalk and slate in hand, a view of the broad clan main at the intersection of Market and Main, and a new eye for peoplewatching.

Because of such a confluence of factors, Amos found himself with a rare opportunity. His old master had relayed, through casual-but-hushed conversation, that eighty-four American Federation soldiers occupied Tucker territory. If last Sunday was any predictor of this Sunday, about thirty or so soldiers would watch over the gathered Tuckers in the Sunday-morning service. A further twenty would patrol the walls, as they did every day, while maybe another twenty struck out into the wilderness, likely in search of the eyeless drifter. This left no more than two dozen soldiers within the meetinghouse, and most of them would be off-duty and resting in the gymnasium, which the Americans used as their barracks.

The sparse number of alert Americans around the meetinghouse, however, wasn't what gave Amos his big opportunity. It was Omar. He had taken his leave early that morning, departed from the eastern gate, then doubled back around and snuck in under the drainage grate Amos held up for him. Then, when the Tuckers all swarmed out for their Sunday service, Omar went along in Amos's place. With five hundred Tuckers to count, the Americans wouldn't remember or care about faces as long as their ledger showed up the same as last week's.

Now free for several hours, Amos's goal was simple: slip in through the meetinghouse's courtyard access, find where the Americans had stashed the Tuckers' guns and ammunition, steal it back, and re-arm the folkward.

The shade cast from the multistory, U-shaped meetinghouse sheltered Amos as he made his quick sprint across open ground. Feeling the cool stone against his hand, first mortared in place nearly two hundred years ago, steeled his nerves. The first step was done. A crude wooden paddock stretched across the space between the two wings of the meetinghouse to close in a courtyard area where the clan could keep its livestock during a siege. He peeked through gaps in the planks and saw no one in the courtyard area. He jumped up, grabbed hold of the top of the enclosure wall, and vaulted over.

The Americans had closed the steel shutters over the lower windows, and they had likely locked the main basement courtyard entrance. But this building was old, and there was a long-disused coal chute to the boiler room which the Americans had likely overlooked. The entrance was overgrown with dry weeds, and Amos had to struggle to remove the sheet metal concealing the gaping hole, but once he had cast the aluminum covering aside with as little noise as possible, he looked down a narrow rusty concrete and stone tunnel slanting down into the meetinghouse foundation.

Amos slipped into the hole and wiggled feetfirst until the coal chute hatch at the bottom stopped him. This final door had a simple latch on the other side, but no lock. He wouldn't be able to slip the latch with his fingers but... he unsheathed his matchet and crouched down as far as his knees would allow in the cramped space.

He fought back against the claustrophobia as he tried to work his blade into the space between the hatch and the bottom of the chute. It was dark, and everything was rusty, and he really should have brought a shorter tool for this. Sweat ran into his eyes. There! He felt the latch and pushed up with his blade. Again, the rust fought back against him. He wiggled the matchet backward and forward, side-to-side, up and down, and then the blade seized, stuck on the rust and pinched at a bad angle.

The claustrophobia came roaring back. For a moment, it felt like his stepmother was crammed in there with him, excoriating him with words that felt like claws. *Look at you. Foolhardy little boy with aims bigger than his years. Never will be a man, not a proper one. A real man doesn't get his little brother killed. You let Dale die. Didn't try hard enough. Can't do what's needed. Stay here and smother. Better than getting more clansmen killed.*

Amos swore through the salt running through his teeth and kicked at the matchet: once, twice, three times. The latch popped up, and the chute hatch swung open with a heavy, metallic creak. He slid down into the dim boiler room and sucked in a breath of cool air. Second step, done.

Amos crouched in the dark, a single shaft of light from the open coal chute behind and above him glinting off the matchet he held in one hand and the sawed-off shotgun he drew out with the other. The shotgun, however, he had loaded with a single slug and threaded with a silencer Phil Holland had made these last few months. It was an ugly, inaccurate weapon, but one that would do in a pinch for short ranges without alerting nearby guards... hopefully.

As far as hoping went, he hoped he'd get lucky and find the weapons stashed down here, but no—it was nothing but the various odds and ends the Tuckers had stored before the Americans had arrived, at least here in the boiler room. The basement extended under most of the school, as far as he knew, and there may have been some nooks and crannies down here that even he didn't know about.

The place was a catalogue of changes wrought over generations. The walls were weathered stone and crumbling brick. Much of the original equipment had been removed, even before the Pandemic, but a mass of corroded metal lay piled in one corner. Above, wires and pipes of different compositions ran through holes cut through the joists, many of which had been replaced before Amos' grandparents were born. Amos wove through the steel support columns toward where the basement wall on his right made a right turn.

Amos followed the turn to a basement hallway which served as part of the central foundation. In the receding dimness ahead of him, the hallway split at a right angle: concrete stairs going upward on his left, what was once a janitor's office on the right. He peeked through the slitted window in the door to the janitor's office and saw only darkness. He tried the door. Locked. Why?

He looked up the stairs, listening for any movement, then brought up the butt of his gun and tapped the wired glass window a couple times with increasing force. He counted in his head: *one, two, three.* The strike was enough to crack the glass, but not enough to break it in. Amos placed the butt of his gun against the spider-web crack and leaned into it. The window crunched inward, with shards tinkling on the concrete floor on the other side of the door. Amos stuck his matchet through the hole and levered it around to bend the wires out of the way—they would cut up his arm just as bad as any glass shards would.

A bustling commotion of soldiers up the stairs behind him froze him in his tracks for a second. When his wits caught back up to his instincts, he pivoted away from the locked door back around the dark corner. The soldiers were talking to each other. Not about him. But these guys were coming from outside the building. He stuck one eye around the corner and glanced up to the first floor where he glimpsed the men. They were very much on duty and occupied with a prisoner they were escorting in.

Reverend Brody. Captain Carlson was leading the reverend in, reciting the charges as lazily as he might comment on the weather. "For promulgating seditious speech, you'll be confined here until the draftees are escorted east."

Amos cursed inwardly. The Federation had chosen to arrest the reverend publicly, during church. They probably thought an open show of force would help put the lid on any flare-ups from cantankerous elements in the clan. More immediately, however, it meant clansmen and previously occupied soldiers were now wandering all over the clan—more roving eyes to dodge.

"No use lying to a liar," the reverend snarled with an unbridled contempt Amos had never before heard from the man. "I know what you're going to do."

"Sure, whatever. If you try to cause trouble, I'll feed you to mine. If I were you, I'd rather be assimilated by a trained neurocaster than a wild man like Jarvis."

"They're all the same."

The voices and footsteps faded into echoes as they climbed the main set of stairs to the upper floors. He turned back to his work and cleared a fist-sized hole through the little window before threading his arm through it with the care of a watchmaker.

As he fumbled for the door handle on the other side, he saw a murky reflection looming in the glass in front of his face. A foot stepped down at the top of the stairs behind him. Amos had laid his gun and matchet on the floor, and he was elbow-deep into a jagged hole in the window. Crap.

At the periphery of his mind, he almost heard: *Nice try, Tucker.*

He craned his neck around to identify the source of the reflection: the wild-eyed man called Jarvis. He stood just below the stair landing, a smug grin on his face and a gun leveled at Amos. *Kick your gun and your sword toward me.*

Amos did as he was told, glaring at his adversary as his arm remained immobilized in the broken window.

You want to see what's inside the door? Open it. The American waved his gun at the door.

Amos found the handle and turned it. The well-greased latch clicked open, and Amos withdrew his hand from the glass trap. He raised both arms in surrender.

Go ahead. Open the door.

Amos nudged the door open with his foot. A large cache of weapons and ammunition lay stacked along the walls and in the corners of the room—except for one spot at the side, to his right. There, just a few feet beyond the door, lay the bodies of several women—not Tuckers, not anyone he remembered ever seeing before—dressed not so much in clothes as in burlap sacks. Motionless, stored down here like canned goods. And they stank, though not yet of death.

He stopped and turned his head to the American. This mind-hearing—it was familiar. He'd felt something similar when he'd killed the shadower last winter. *How did you know I was in here?*

The American's eyebrows arched as if Amos had piqued his curiosity. *Who taught you to neurocast? I thought your preacher kept that knowledge hidden.*

The preacher underestimates me.

Cute, Amos felt the American think. *But you can't hide from me if I decide to look. I can spot a tasty brainshine like yours from a quarter-mile away. What do you think? Do you like my collection? Would you like to join them?*

Amos' face twisted in disgust and confusion.

Tell you what. I bet you're quick on the draw. I'll make it easy for you. Jarvis laid his automatic gun down on the stairs in between them and stepped back. He sat down on the topmost stair, unarmed, and spread his hands wide as if he were a generous host inviting guests to a feast. Then, if that weren't strange enough, his head lolled back, and he went as limp as a fish.

"The hell—"

A hand grabbed him from behind, and he felt a shard of glass press itself against his throat. A woman's voice hissed in his ear. "Come and be a part of my collection, sweeeeeetheart."

Amos drove an elbow into her ribs, knocking the woman straight back onto the floor. He spun to see her unconscious, her feet cut and bleeding on the broken glass, her skinny white legs sticking out awkwardly from her sackcloth.

Before he had time to catch his breath, someone grabbed him from behind again—Jarvis. Amos tried to struggle, but the moment Jarvis' fingers touched his scalp, Amos felt himself somehow paralyzed. A blinding terror or pain—his mind couldn't distinguish between the two—bloomed like a flash of nitrogel and aluminum powder. Then came something deeper than either the terror or the pain—something like falling without an end. It was not unlike how Amos had felt when he had looked at his younger brother, when he'd spoken kind words and carried the boy for miles to find out he'd been comforting a corpse. It was a deep understanding that, whatever happened, things would not be okay. Nothing would be okay. His heart quailed, but before the tidal wave of the abyss could overwhelm him, it broke and receded as quickly as it came.

Amos recognized Captain Royce's voice cutting through the encroaching fog around his mind. "Jarvis! What did I say about assimilating without my permission?"

"Fine, you got me." Jarvis sounded like a teenager who'd lost a friendly game of cards. Amos gasped involuntarily when Jarvis released him.

"Who's this?" Royce asked, coming down the stairs, surveying Amos, the open door, and the interior of the room in once glance.

"Found the kid snooping around in here," Jarvis answered. "Looks to me like we've got a little insurgency problem."

"Nice of him to walk himself close to our jail, then." Captain Carlson turned to look back up the concrete stairs to the ground floor. "Take him upstairs."

"All the rooms in that hallway are taken up."

"Oh, yeah, I guess you're right." Captain Royce closed his eyes to visualize whatever part of the meeting-hall they were using as a jail. "We stuck the watchman in there," he pointed to an invisible room on his right, going down the available rooms. "The preacher after that. Stick

261

him in with the teacher, I guess. Hey! Harper!" Carlson called up the stairs and waited until a soldier responded to his call. "Help Jarvis escort this Tucker kid up to jail. We'll interrogate him when I have time, see if there's anyone else he's working with."

Jarvis spoke up. "It would be quicker if you'd let me—"

"We're saving as many as we can for the *professionals*," Captain Royce said as if this was the thousandth time he'd given the order. "We'll do it the old-fashioned way first."

Jarvis, along with the American soldier, hauled Amos up the stairs to the broad main hallway running down the wings and center of the meetinghouse. With Captain Carlson following behind, they escorted Amos down the northern wing, but before they reached the gymnasium annex bulging off the end of the hallway, they took a hard left turn up the stairs and ascended to the top floor and led him to the end of a dead-end corridor.

The American soldier unlocked the door to a small, bare room, where Sam Chambers sat on the floor with his head in his hands. In the other corner, chained to a metal pipe, sat a shadower with its knobby knees drawn up in front. Amos recoiled from the unbred creature. Sam, however, seemed beyond caring that he was locked up with a monster. When he looked up, Amos could see yellowing bruises on the schoolteacher's face. Someone shoved Amos in.

Jarvis petted the shadower's smooth, translucent head. It turned its catlike pupils upward to him in a weirdly plaintive look. "Who's been a good boy, huh?" Jarvis said as he would to a loyal dog.

"If I can't get anything from him, I'll let you have him," Royce said to Jarvis. "But don't get greedy."

Jarvis smiled at Amos as they closed him in with Sam. Amos could feel the American's strange glee from the other side of the door.

You might be a bright neurocaster, but don't think I can't subsume you. Once there's more than one in a network, it's just a numbers game, and everyone in this fucking clan is an isolated morsel, waiting for me to gobble them up.

Captain Carlson went downstairs, out the double doors, and across the clan main to where Omar Walking stood among the dispersing Tucker congregation. Carlson took him gently by the elbow and walked him to the eastern gate.

When they were out in the open, beyond earshot, Royce turned to Omar as if to bid the dark-haired young man farewell. "Thanks for the tip," he said. Even when expressing gratitude, his smug grin never went away. "Anyone else involved I should worry about? Family members, close friends?"

"No."

"That suppressed weapon didn't come from nowhere."

"He'd been working on those old cans for months. Probably had it hid under his bunk."

"You're telling me that kid acted alone?"

"You wouldn't be surprised if you knowed him."

"But he had to tell you all about his plan."

"I was part of his plan. He needed me to pull it off. I worked it out so no one would get hurt."

"Why?"

"Just... keepin' the peace," Omar said without looking Carlson's way.

"You don't seem like the kind of guy interested in peace." The American rubbed his nose and stroked the horse's withers. "I did some poking around. You're not one of them."

"I didn't used to be. They inked me." Omar rolled up his shirtsleeve to show the tattoo.

263

"Bullshit," Captain Carlson said with the good humor of a man hearing a tall tale from an old friend. "That's not worth more than the ink they used to make it. You know it. I know it. They for sure know it, and I don't think they'd ever let you forget it."

Omar didn't respond at first. "I got my own scores to settle."

"Well..." Carlson patted Omar's horse. "That answers my question. I don't suppose you want to tell me where you're really from, do you?"

"I'm a drifter. Does it matter?"

"If you're from up north, it does."

Omar sighed and looked up at the sky. "Would you believe me if I told you I'm not?"

"I believed you when you said someone would try to sneak into the main building."

"Fine. I'm not. Do I get my gun back?"

"Once you're out of town."

"I don't suppose you're gonna tell me what's gonna happen to the old folks and kids you're drafting?"

"Do you care?"

Omar still didn't look Royce's way. "I don't reckon it matters if I care or not, for all's the difference it'll make."

"That's the spirit. Have a safe trip, Mr. Walking. I'll send a couple of my guys with you to see you off."

Revenge wasn't as sweet as it had often been advertised.

Chapter 24

In Which Amos Has a Little Chat

Amos stood sandwiched between two American guards at the end of a cold room of cinderblock and concrete, stark naked. He tried to turn away when Captain Carlson entered the room with the wild-eyed American called Jarvis. As they came up to inspect him, the two guards seized his arms and forced him to face them.

Captain Carlson looked over Amos, his hands folded behind his back, the picture of detached professionalism. "What do they call you, Tucker?"

Amos hesitated. "Dale. Dale Taylor."

Jarvis squinted at Amos.

"I've got some questions for you, Dale Taylor," Captain Carlson began before Jarvis nudged him in the side.

"That's not his real name," Jarvis said.

Royce frowned, then looked to the guard at Amos's left and nodded. The guard did something both painful and humiliating to him.

"Oh, deeeaar," Captain Royce said. "Looks like we got off to a bad start. The sooner you answer my questions honestly, the sooner we can be done with this."

Amos looked at the floor and tried to calm his breathing. "My name's Amos."

"You have to understand this is for your own good, son." Royce squatted down on his haunches and put a hand on Amos' shoulder. "I don't know what you were thinking, trying to sneak into here, armed like that. Someone could have gotten hurt."

"Don't talk like you're here to help us."

"I know you must not think much of me. Of us Americans. You don't want to join us, though the rest of your clansmen do."

"That vote didn't count for—"

"I know you want to stay independent, to look after your local concerns. Your little harvests. Your little apprenticeships. You worry about little packs of pigmen. About your little feud with another hill tribe. I understand. What we're giving you is a chance for something *big*. Before, you people were only worried about survival. I can give you *purpose*."

"I'll be seeing to my own, purpose, thanks."

"Can I have him now?" Jarvis asked.

"No," Carlson said, never breaking eye contact with Amos. "I still want to ask Mr. Taylor some questions." The American captain produced a white porcelain chip. "I don't want to hurt you. I don't want to let Jarvis hurt you. Answer these questions honestly, and my men won't have to hurt you. Have you ever seen one of these before, Amos?"

Amos nodded.

"Where?"

"Got it off a dead shadower."

"When?"

"Last winter. Late January or early February."

"Had you ever seen one of these before then?"

Amos shook his head. "Turned out the chip was illegal, but I didn't know it at the time. The elders hid stuff from us."

"What happened to that chip?"

"Took it to Mr. Chambers, and that was the last I saw of it."

"What happened to the trapper?"

"Hunting accident. Flintlock slipped at the wrong time."

Royce tsked-tsked and motioned to a guard, who forced Amos to his knees and began twisting his arm into an increasingly painful angle. Amos gasped.

"I know it hurts, I know. Listen closely, now. The trapper wasn't dead when you came back into town with him. Was he unconscious?"

Amos fought back against the twinge of pain in his shoulder. He cursed as the American leaned a knee into his back. "Ah! Yes! Yes, he was unconscious!"

"Who sent you to sneak around in here?"

"No one."

The guard behind Amos forced him down onto all fours while the other American started poking different parts of Amos's body with a sharp knife.

"I told you, no one! You've already locked up the watchman! Who else is there to order me around?"

"Now, Mr. Taylor. A kid like you wouldn't do this on your own."

Amos looked up from the floor to fix baleful eyes on the captain. "I bagged that shadower on my own."

The American called Jarvis stepped forward and kneeled down to get closer to Amos's face. "He's a hotshot, Cap. I can feel his brainshine. It burns brighter than any I've seen."

"I told you, Jarvis, you can't have him. But I suppose we've reached the point where real pain is necessary." Royce sighed as if he regretted admitting it.

Jarvis stepped forward and forced Amos to the floor. He put one foot on the back of Amos' neck, squishing Amos' face into the cold tile. "Not the kind to break easily, huh?" Jarvis said as if he relished the challenge.

"You're not going to get away with this."

"Oh? 'Get away with' what? This?" Jarvis curled Amos's fingers into a ball, then slowly crushed them under his heel until Amos squealed like a girl. "What are you going to do about it? Go run to mommy and daddy?"

"Oh, why do we have to go through all of this?" Carlson asked. "So much useless suffering."

When Amos didn't answer, Jarvis kept up the pressure on Amos's popping knuckles. "What are you going to do about it, little boy? Huh?"

When the bald American had finally let up, Amos cradled his hand and glared at Captain Royce and Jarvis. "I'm not going to give you what you want. That's what I'm going to do about it."

Jarvis blindsided Amos with a punch to the ear. Amos grunted from the stinging blow, and when he looked up, he saw something approaching earnestness on Jarvis's face for the first time. "Who says *this* isn't what I want?"

"I've seen your kind before. The kind who makes a sport out of killing my kin."

"I guarantee you've never seen anything like me before. Not in your worst nightmares."

"Not so different, unless you don't die when I stick a knife in your throat."

Captain Carlson leaned back against the wall. "I'm afraid I can't tolerate threats against my men. Even from a foolish boy with his bare ass in the air."

Amos gritted his teeth. "You keep me like this 'cause you're too afraid to take me in a straight fight."

"Straight fights are for people who don't know they've already lost," Royce said. "Tell me who else I need to arrest and get this over with."

"No."

The guards forced Amos's other hand into a ball on the floor, and this time, he fought back tears as they stomped on his closed fist.

"Why not?" Carlson asked as if curious.

"Because I'd never betray a clansman. Even if I've already lost, they haven't, and they're worth more to me than my fingers."

"Again, you're thinking so small," Captain Carlson said. "Your clansmen *have* lost. They lost without ever fighting, because *all* of you think too small. You people are backwards, uneducated, with corrupt breeding and primitive social practices. It's not your fault, but you can't see the bigger picture. You don't realize how much you need someone like me to look after you and give you purpose. It's for your own good."

"You don't give a shit about my good," Amos spat. "You just have to say something to dress up slavery nicer. It's still slavery."

"And what does it change if I call it slavery?"

"Then my people would at least know the truth."

"The truth?" Captain Carlson shook his head with well-meaning pity. "The truth has been staring them in the face for years, and the only ones who had an inkling about it are safely locked away in this meeting-house of yours. I could go out onto the town square right now and yell the truth at the top of my lungs, and it wouldn't make a difference to you people. I can tell *you* the truth, though you won't believe it: all this honor, loyalty, rights-of-man bullshit—" He snorted. "Fairy tales. Here's the pure truth of humanity, the one law common across all clans, cultures, languages, and ages: The strong do what they want." This time, Captain Carlson leaned his weight into Amos's outstretched hand. "The weak suffer what they must. Which side of the equation do you think you and your people are on?"

Chapter 25

A Shot in the Dark

"Hey, Tucker."

Omar stopped his dun horse and looked back at the town he'd just left. Two American soldiers sat atop their own horses, trotting after him. "Leaving without us? Captain Carlson wanted to make sure you got back to New Ashburn safely."

Omar eyed the two men and the automatic weapons they carried, shrugged, and urged his horse back into an easy gait. The two men followed, several paces behind.

By the time the road eastward disappeared into dense forest, Omar's horse was showing some discomfort. Omar pulled up just outside the tree line and brushed his hand under the saddle pad. "Think I snagged a burr back yonder," he said.

The two Americans slowed to a halt right behind Omar.

"Go on ahead. Don't let me slow you down." He waved them on.

The two Americans looked at each other and took the lead.

Omar mounted up and followed. The three of them made their way down the road for several miles in complete silence, until the setting sun was casting their shadows in front of them. The two Americans started mumbling, but too low for Omar to hear.

Finally, the one on the right spoke up. "Think we should be setting up camp, Tucker?"

"The horses are still fresh. I want to make good time while we can."

After a little further, the soldier on the right spoke up again. "I think I saw something further down the hill, Tucker. You mind riding ahead and checking it out? We'll cover you."

"You two are the ones with machine guns. You catch a fishy smell, I reckon you oughta check it out."

The two Americans looked at each other and exchanged more mumbles. The one on the left turned and looked back at Omar. "Why are you riding so far back? We don't bite."

"Just like my space, is all."

It was almost full dark before Omar assented to stopping for the night. But he forbade lighting any campfire, and promised to get back on the road before first light. One of the Americans claimed the first watch, which suited Omar fine.

"If it 'suits you fine,' why are you lying down with your rifle?"

Omar rested his head on the saddle he'd placed on the bare ground. "You boys ain't done much traveling alone, have you?"

Neither American bothered to answer.

The night crickets chirped away the time as the night air cooled. The horses were whickering and sighing nearby. The American on watch walked lazy circles around the camp, his form fading into and out of the dark of night. Omar's lumpy shape on the ground shifted one more time before going still.

Presently, the Federation soldier on guard walked back into the small clearing, ambled over to where Omar lay, and lifted his firearm. He fired a single bullet into the prone form, shattering the relative calm. The brief flash from the gun barrel illuminated the Federation soldier and the empty saddlebags he'd shot long enough for the hunter to realize his prey wasn't where he'd thought—and for the prey to get a fix on the hunter.

The squealing of the startled horses masked the whistle of the arrow that flew from the darkness. The sharp *thwack* the arrow made came through the night air clear and crisp as it pinned the American's arm to his chest.

The other American was up in an instant, a pistol in hand. He swept the pitch-black forest in vain for the drifter while his mate gasped for air.▯

The horses had barely quieted down when the American squeezed off three rounds into the woods in a fan pattern, setting off the squeals of terror all over again.

To the American's right, a gout of brilliant white flame and sparks again lit the campsite briefly into visible daylight, leaving a still image frozen in the eye like an old-time photograph. And in that photograph, hunched behind a rifle in the middle of all that light, was the drifter.

The American turned to the afterimage and fired four more times. The horses stamped and reared in terror, but nothing more came from the woods—no bullets, no arrows. Keeping the pistol leveled at the woods, the soldier stepped forward and rounded the hulking mass of a great tree.▯

The ringing in his ears subsided just enough to perceive a rustle in the grass—from behind.

The American spun to see movement and one last blinding spike of light. He felt his hip shatter as the bullet from his own rifle passed through him. He didn't have the presence of mind to know whether he still had the pistol in his hand as he fell. He saw nothing but a human form lunging forward, a spear in his grip.

When it was done, Omar cast the spear aside and wiped his brow. He pulled the arrow from the first American, inspected the point, then cleaned it and returned it to his quiver. He hauled both bodies away from the campsite and piled them on top of each other after first going through their pockets for anything that could prove useful. He kept the teeth, a multi-tool, a tight bundle of gauze, and some netting, but left the scraps of paper the soldiers had on them—they weren't valuable enough to risk someone questioning where he'd got them.

He returned to camp and did his best to calm the skittish horses, then collected the firearms and started counting ammunition. The nearly moonless night made all the work difficult and tedious, but he still counted the bullets twice to make sure. There were eight rounds left for the pistol, and for the two autorifles, seventy-two rounds of 6.8 mm ammo—all for an execution he was sure they had been expecting to carry out hours ago.

Omar moved to saddle up again, hiding the holstered pistol under his saddlebags and slinging one American rifle over his shoulder while he carried the other across his lap. There would be little rest tonight. He wasn't meant to be the messenger back to New Ashburn. The two soldiers were the real messengers. If Royce meant to tie up loose ends and found this particular thread free, he'd send scouts after him, or further messengers to New Ashburn to head him off.

Whatever happened, Omar couldn't let an American beat him back. Not with so much work left to do. And he still had a meeting to get to.

It was late morning the next day when Omar stepped out from where the trees grew tall and old into the fresher growth receding into the patchwork mess of the old asphalt road. Down to his left, decades of an untamed stream had carved its own channel around a clogged culvert. He shaded his eyes to look up again at the old cell tower nearby, but his second inspection revealed nothing more than his first. If the outpost was still manned, they were being awfully lackadaisical about posting a sentry.

"Jacks?" Omar called out once he'd reached the other side of the road.

There was no answer.

His new American autorifle, already unslung, went to his shoulder as he scanned the descending slope on the other side of the road for signs of life. The mouth of the box culvert yawned, black even in the golden light of dawn. He caught a fetid stench from that direction.

Movement stirred in the darkness, and Omar froze. A small arm sprouted from the culvert, followed by the tousled, dirty hair of a child. "Hello, Omar," the child said as if he'd known Omar his whole life.

Omar didn't lower his rifle. "Who are you?"

"It's me. Clint. Clint Filby."

Omar's eyebrows drew closer together. "What are you gettin' at, kid?"

"It's the truth. I'm using the kid's body, but it's Clint inside the brain-case." The boy tapped his head. He was filthy, drawn, and worn, but his eyes shone bright.

Omar still didn't lower his gun. "Clint had the wanderlust bad when he took up with that nomad clan. No one thought he'd ever come back to these parts. If you're really Clint, you'd know why."

"Banished for neurocasting."

Omar did not lower his gun. "I reckon your... neurocasting has something to do with this kid you're using?"

The boy nodded.

"Never thought I'd see you again, Clint. Let alone without eyes. I saw you—not the kid you're talking through, but *you...*" Omar struggled to find the words.

"My root, yes. The face you knew when I was a Greenbrier."

"Sure. Except without eyes. Back when the screevlers attacked, when you took that Tucker girl. Almost took a shot at you."

"I appreciate your discretion."

"How'd you lose your eyes, if you don't mind the asking?"

"Gouged them out myself. Little nuisances. Kept me from focusing on my proxies and all the inputs from my para-neuronet."

"So, this... kid you're talking through?"

"Bah." The boy waved away Omar's question. "Some runt I picked up on the way out here. That's how I got most of my proxies. I keep them stored under here. Look." The boy beckoned Omar over.

Omar stepped forward and peered into the mouth of the culvert. This was the source of the smell. The tunnel was packed with bodies—men, women, and many children. Some were clothed, some nearly naked, the thin scraps of cloth they had literally rotting off their frames. But the bodies themselves were not rotting. Indeed, Omar saw their chests rising and falling, as if in deep sleep.

"It's a hassle maintaining this many proxies, but I spend about an hour each day getting each one up, feeding and watering it, pissing and shitting in a hole over there, tending to sores, and going back under. The unbreds keep me well-supplied."

"What... what happened to all of them?" Omar pointed to the bodies.

"*I* happened to them. They're all me now."

"Will they ever be... themselves again?" Omar turned to see the boy shoveling a handful of grain in his mouth—it looked like wild grass seed.

The boy shook his head, chewing. "The organic processes keep going, but the only mind left is mine."

"I don't remember Clint talking like that."

"I've learned quite a bit during my travels." The boy leaned forward, his keen eyes looking right through Omar. "What are you thinking?"

"I'm beginning to see why the clan banned neurocasting."

"The folks you had posted here took some convincing, too. But they saw things my way soon enough. Once I convinced them I wasn't after Greenbrier neurocasters. Once I convinced them I was after the Tuckers. And after the last little run-in they had out here just waiting for you to show up, my way seemed like a better answer."

"So, they packed up and left you to it, huh?"

"It beat sitting around and waiting for you to come reporting in. What's it been? Two months?"

"Mighty hard to get away."

"Mighty hard to wait that long for news. They didn't even know about the Americans until I told them. Speaking of—what are the Americans doing inside the Tucker clan? I've lost my proxy on the inside."

Omar blinked, then understood. "So, it wasn't a hunting accident what got Victor."

"The Americans—what are they doing?"

"The Tuckers voted to join the American Federation. The colonel out in New Ashburn's given orders to draft a bunch of Tuckers, ship 'em out east."

The kid shook his head. "Uh-uh. Not acceptable."

"You crazy? The Americans are doing our work for us. I saw the list. There were dozens of names on it. A quarter of our feudlin's—*my* feudlin's—carted off overnight, and you say that don't work for you?"

"The Americans are hunting for me. Whatever Tuckers they get out of there, they'll use to track me down."

"Are you in this to help us or to save your own hide?"

"Stick with me, and I'll help us both."

"I ain't too keen to pal up with an exiled neurocaster."

"What the Americans want from the Tuckers, they'll want from the Greenbriers, too."

Omar scratched the back of his neck, staring at the tangle of bodies. "How am I supposed to 'stick with you?'"

"Take this." The kid fished into his pocket and pulled out a small white chip. He flicked it to Omar.

Omar examined the porcelain wafer. "What is it?"

"A better way to get a hold of you. If you need to talk to me, take this somewhere high up and wait. What we're going to do might take some coordination. I'll be heading east to take care of some stuff, so I won't be far from the junker clan."

Omar turned the white chip between his fingers. "What do you want me to do?"

Omar knew better than to go sleeping on the ground when traveling alone. When morning came the day after his meeting with Clint, he untied himself from the tree where he'd spent the night and chewed on some of the hardtack he'd grabbed before he left Tucker territory. He stopped every now and then to sniff the air, checking for the acrid odor of unbred sweat.

Along the way, he ran into a stream running parallel to the path. Around noon, his stomach growling, he glanced to where the watercourse picked up its pace. A fine bed of silt lay under the clear flowing water, with tell-tale dimples scattered throughout. He probably shouldn't stop, but river mussels were mighty good eating.

He took off his boots and socks, rolled up his pants, and waded into the shallow stream. He plunged his hand around each dimple, cupping the hidden mussel around its breathing hole and shaking loose the mud and silt as he pulled up on it. He collected a couple dozen and tied them together in the netting he'd taken off one of the American soldiers.

He walked on until he passed some paper birch trees, where he picked up a nice handful of wisp-thin bark, plenty of dry twigs, and scattered deadfall.

Starting a fire was dangerous, but it was the middle of the day, and a small fire on a dry day wouldn't likely attract attention. He could see a ways up the road ahead and behind him, and the collection of fallen boulders would screen him from any observers while he cooked and ate.

He started a little fire and set the mussels to roasting over a mesh of green hickory twigs. When they were done, he fished them out with the American's multitool and ate them while they were still steaming. A little chewy, but nourishing, and not much time lost.

A fair number of miles still stretched between him and New Ashburn. Doubling back for the meeting at the old cell tower, then back again to where he'd stashed the American bodies and the sealed papers they had in their pockets had cost him a lot of time—or given him time, depending on how you looked at it. Plenty of distance to get ambushed by unbreds, or worse, bloodthirsty marauders.

The distance also left him with plenty of time to think and re-flect—plenty of time to plan and remember. It was nigh-on three years back...

Omar had smelled the screevler before he'd ever heard the screevler's screams. His clan at the time had been putting up traps all through those woods, and the snare had scarcely been up for an hour before some unbred got itself tangled up in it.

He'd broken away from the rest of the Greenbriers to reset it and collect the claws. He'd caught a human scent from down in the valley as he approached the snare, however, and he'd known who it had to be this far into Tucker territory. He hid himself just a slip away from the dead screevler and scanned down the hill for an enemy he knew would come and investigate.

Omar saw him soon enough—a young fellow about his own age, a tattered baseball cap on his head and a rifle trained on the surrounding woods. Any foolhardy young kid would have taken a shot at the Tucker right then and there, but Omar waited, testing the air for any other unnatural smells. The Tucker made his way along, and still Omar waited for the right opportunity.

When the opportunity came and the Tucker turned his head away, Omar slithered from his hiding space, drew his bow, and put an arrow between the young man's ribs.

The cry of pain made Omar wince. If a dying screevler wasn't enough to bring all the surrounding Tuckers coming, then a dying man would be.

Omar jumped up with his knife to finish the young man off. The Tucker was on the ground now, a hand around the arrow shaft, but not touching it.

Omar couldn't quite remember what the young Tucker had said before he stabbed him. Something like he was all alone, or go easy on me, or something like that. Omar plunged the knife in and pulled it out, and the young man moaned a little before he deflated. His life sighed out of him.

Omar was still busy stripping the body of any valuables he could carry when he picked up his bow and turned his attention to the forest again. Was he alone? Were there more? He stepped out of the open and moved down the hill a ways. A stream flowed about a hundred or so feet down the slope. Had he heard something, or did he smell something? He waited for any sign of movement or ambush.

When he was satisfied, he clambered back up to the body, took the hat from the corpse and put it on his own head, and cut the claws from the hanging screevler. With the Tucker rifle slung over his back, he made his way back to his clansmen.

When he returned, he'd received a party in his honor for killing the Tucker. His young friends had regarded him with a new kind of awesome respect, and they'd asked him what it was like. Did they get into it hand-to-hand? Did the Tucker get a shot off? Did Omar have to duck behind cover and roll up behind him?

To all of the questions, Omar simply responded, "If you want to fight, you start swinging punches. If you want to win, you sit and wait."

He'd received another party just a few months ago, when fate had restored him to his brethren as if from the grave. The Greenbrier watchman was a crafty devil, and over the course of a few days, the two of them worked out summaries for the key figures in the clan, as well as the layout of the Tucker's town and southern farms. At the time, Omar had figured that would be the extent of it.

And then there was the skirmish out in the Heresford Dell. Two were killed in action, one died later that day, and one more was wounded, almost all by Tucker guns shooting at infernal ranges thanks to that newfangled smokeless gunpowder. Then there was that costly raid on the Tucker farm, then the massacre on the Youngblood homestead. The Greenbriers' ammunition-eating breechloaders had been outclassed.

Since returning to the stronghold of his enemies, Omar had done his share of sitting and waiting. Now the Tuckers had found themselves outclassed, but not by the Greenbriers, and that was the problem. The American Federation, with its open embrace of neurocasting, would not hesitate to engulf the Greenbriers any more than the Tuckers. That much was obvious, with or without Clint Filby's warning.

What wasn't obvious was whether to trust a kid claiming to belong to an exiled neurocaster. If Omar could trust the plan, then the forged letter he carried, with the seal he'd lifted off an American corpse, would draw out Colonel Armstrong and her people into some nasty surprise. If he couldn't trust the plan... no easy solution presented itself.

Sit and wait. Sit and wait.

Chapter 26

In Which Bill Is Burned in a Fire of His Own Making

<u>New Ashburn</u>

B ill paced atop the rickety catwalk overlooking the factory floor, Jody Perkins following with pen and paper, Lieutenant Harlow following close behind her. The support beams now held up the roof at regular intervals, the gaps in the framing were disappearing, and the attached nitration station, whose double-door entryway already bore an overhead warning against sparks and open flames, had been completed in all but the finishing details. The air was redolent of sawdust, pine tar, and grease.

"How has the training been going with Mrs. Compton?" Bill asked.

"She says she's on schedule and aims to go over pressure monitoring with the Sylvanian prisoners soon," Jody said as she glanced at her clipboard.

"I don't want them anywhere near the pressure chambers or the nitration station. Too much danger of sabotage, and I've been burned before. There's plenty of work for them with the feedstocks and such. Any problems with the prisoners?"

"That's not your concern, sir," the American bodyguard said, sounding bored but firm.

"We've got a batt'ry of tests to set up, still. The last batch we had was over-nitrated. It'll work if we want to blow something up, but not if we want to use it in a gun. We either need to dial back the nitric acid ratio or add in some wax, and test our new batch every time we do. But our last experiment broke our bomb test bulb, and now we've got prisoners digging up a pile of dirt shot through with mercury. I reckon it's better for using the mercury to make primers, but the main thing is I need that bomb tester rebuilt, and we'll need another way to check the pressure on these tests. I really thought the mercury would work. What was Salazar saying about piezer-lectric—"

The archival apprentice spoke up. "If you take some kind of crystal, like quartz, and smack it against a piece of metal, it creates a tiny amount of electricity. Attach a wire to that metal, and you've got a signal," Jody said. "Salazar told me we could have a long metal tube and space out these piezoelectric triggers along the way, all regular. We run wires from them to electrical switches on the other end, and then we just look after each test to see which switches they flip. Ones for true, zeros for false."

"How quick can we get that done? I can't make real changes to the acid ratios until I have a way to test."

"Now that the electrician's done hooking up the main factory, I expect we can get it set up in a few days. Maybe a week."

"I also want to set up tests on the pressure chambers. The more psi's we can get out of 'em, the—"

A deep thump reverberated through the factory floor and rattled its way up the catwalk, finally shaking loose a familiar, awful feeling in his gut. An explosion.

It wasn't loud, but he felt it. He didn't hear the screams of the workers. He didn't see them rushing to the nearest exit or gap in the wall. He didn't really note the workers staggering out of the double doors of the nitration station. He only saw the doorway itself, yawning open like some cavernous black maw, billowing smoke into his factory.

Not again. He came to himself, precious moments later, when his bodyguard physically shoved him along the catwalk towards the ladder. Bill caught the last fragment of whatever the lieutenant was saying: " ...have to get out of here *now!*"

Pulled out of his reverie, Bill now moved toward the ladder of his own power, but not so he could escape. He hit the factory floor running and sprinted to the entrance to the nitration room. Standing at the edge of the murky darkness, eyes stinging from the fumes of the smoke, he perceived flames flickering inside. Suddenly his eyes blinked at a flash of blue light. Lightning? Inside? Then it hit him: the dadgum junker wiring.

He coughed on the acrid smoke and waved at the red-faced body-guard coming at Bill, ready to carry him out on his shoulders.

"Get those damn workers back in here and put this fire out!" Bill hollered.

"I'm getting you out of here, powderman," the American insisted.

"If this factory goes, I go with it!" Bill stabbed one finger down towards the ground to drive his point home.

The American swore and charged past a petrified Jody Perkins to find the workers outside the exit.

"Jody." Bill snapped his fingers to get Jody's attention, but she didn't move.

"Jody!" He grabbed her by the shoulders and shook her.

Jody came to herself, and her bottom lip began to quiver.

Bill locked eyes with her. "Put down your damn clipboard and fetch me a damn ladder. We need to unhook the damn water intake from the damn absorption tower." Bill cursed once more for good measure.

"I—I can't... I don't want to get burned again."

He looked to the discoloration on the side of her face. He didn't have time for folks locking up on him. "Then get the hell out of here and fetch me someone who can help me!"

That got her going, and Bill set about trying to unhook the walkway ladder from its scaffolding.

A dozen workers—the expendable Sylvanian prisoners—had marched back into to the building at gunpoint by the time Bill had worked the lever hose clamp free from the tower's water intake. Water spurted, then gushed, as the hose fell away to the floor below. Bill nearly slipped off the ladder, then nearly tipped the ladder over as he struggled to stay upright.

"Get this hose into the nitration room and douse that fire!" Bill ordered the prisoners like a general commanding soldiers as he strode to the exit doors.

"The hose won't go all the way!" one of the prisoners protested.

Bill ignored the slave's near-panicked face. "Ain't nobody leaving 'till this thing's under control. Get some damn buckets, or find another length of hose. Use some gumption, for cryin' out loud!"

Bill stormed past the two American guards at the exit and found the other workers—still only the prisoners—forming some semblance of a bucket brigade under the direction of Lieutenant Harlow.

A ragged woman strode up to Bill, defiant for all of her slight form. "You've got to get them out of there. It's too danger—"

Lieutenant Harlow stepped between her and Bill, stopping the slave with a quick backhand to the face.

"I want this bucket brigade to go in from the other side of the nitration station," Bill said, undeterred by the woman's aborted protest. He turned to scan the factory and attached chemical workshop. "The guncotton stores haven't gone off, or we'd have pieces of us lying all over the place. We need to move them further away, over by the gate, for now. Ricky, you head that up."

Ricky Brody had just run up to check on his master. He balked at his new assignment. "You sure it ain't too dangerous?"

"Not if you hurry. It's wet guncotton. We soaked it in alcohol for a reason. Get yourself five steady hands."

Without any further hesitation, Ricky turned and ran to select five young Ashburnite junkers who had been Ricky's workmates in the factory. Immediately after that, Bill saw Ella Holland come running up. "Bill, what happened? Is everybody—"

"Electrical short! These damn trash pickers couldn't wire up a toaster."

"Did everybody make it out of there okay?" Ella asked, pointing to the smoking nitration lab.

Bill stripped off his shirt with a huff. "I don't know yet, Ella. I'm fixin' to get in there and look." He dunked his shirt in a passing water bucket and squeezed out the excess damp before tying it crudely over his face. He took a couple angry strides toward the outer nitration lab doors before he froze.

Smoke wasn't just coming from the nitration lab now. Beyond the lab, where Bill's study lay to the southwest, smoke and flame crackled and billowed up from the slapdash thatch roof of his office. Right where he kept his notes and personal experiments.

Bill felt his face blanch underneath his hasty breathing mask. He bolted through the scattered workers and shouldered his way through the bucket line, making a mad sprint for his life's work, but Melissa Daly cut him off. He saw his own panic mirrored in her face.

"Earnest! Have you seen Earnest? I can't find him anywhere!"

"He ain't up in the supermart?"

A secondary explosion blew out one wall from the nitration station, and everybody near the factory ducked for cover.

Screams.

Not the screams of grown men, though Bill heard those. Not the screams of terrified women, either, though Bill heard those, too. It was the scream of a child in agony.

In a narrow alleyway separating the nitration lab from Bill's office, a small form ran wild, flames engulfing half its clothes.

"Oh, sweet Jesus," Bill heard someone say, then realized he'd said it.

He wasn't aware of his legs carrying him forward; he seemed to float toward the burning child. He seized the boy and wrapped him in his damp shirt, suffocating the flames. He then stripped the boy naked. His skin was red and already blistering in places, his screams warbling and unabated. Bill wrapped the boy up again in his damp shirt and picked him up in his arms.

He stood up and turned to see workers on fire from the explosion, rolling around on the ground to put out the flames while others came over with buckets to drench them with water. Melissa Daly was running at him. She had a look on her face he didn't care to see and couldn't bring himself to meet.

"I—I—" Bill started, but he didn't know what he was going to say. Earnest was still screaming.

A prisoner came up with a bucket of water. "Flush the burns," Bill said, but the worker was already splashing the cool water over the burns and blisters covering Earnest's right arm and upper torso. The boy's screams weakened to sobs and cries for his mama.

"You did this!" Melissa spat as she wrested her son away from Bill. He reached out to her, to Earnest, but she pushed him away. "You did this!" she repeated through her tears, holding Earnest in her lap. "You and your stupid factory! Your stupid nitrogel!"

When the bucket of water was empty, the prisoner pouring it over Earnest swapped it out for another one. The bucket brigade had become a branching river to the various burn victims, and still the nitration station smoked like a chimney. A couple prisoners hauled a limp body out of the smoldering lab, either a dead or senseless worker. Back well away from the commotion, Jody Perkins stood watching, her face partly covered with her clipboard.

The screams went on. Bill sank to his knees, helpless. Not enough water fast enough. The fire would spread to the factory and his office, and it would all burn. His notes. His formula. The equipment would be ruined. He couldn't do it all himself, and Earnest's screams were all he got for trying. It was too much.

It was the prisoners who finished the firefighting, first entrapping the blaze from both the outside with the buckets and from the main factory floor with the absorption tower hose, then strangling the blaze to flickers, then flickers to tinders, then finally to cold, charred bones. Half his study had gone up before they got it under control, and he couldn't find his papers in the mess. Probably lost to the fire.

There were many injuries from the fire. Aside from little Earnest, the rest were all Sylvanian slaves, forced into the most dangerous parts of the fire and closest to the secondary explosion when it went off. Earnest never stopped crying, and even the adults groaned or wept from the pain, no matter how much cool water their caretakers poured over their burns.

Bill's American bodyguard gave him the news: Armstrong was displeased with the mishap and would soon expect a report. In the meantime, all non-injured personnel were to resume work at the factory, either implementing repairs or resuming construction or production.

So Bill ordered as many workers as he could spare to tend to the absorption tower. The nitric acid, however, he simply stored in a giant polypropylene cask which he carted off to the side once they had run out of ammonia. His concern was the tail gas, which his workers pumped into a rusty handheld air tank. When it was as full as he could get it, he picked up the tank and descended to the factory floor.

"What's that for?" Lieutenant Harlow asked, pointing to the air tank.

"Experiment," Bill answered. "I need a rubber rain boot, a hammer, and an awl."

"What for?"

"Experiment."

Harlow shrugged and barked at a slave to get the required materials. Once he'd received them, he punched a hole through the rubber near the toe and widened it until he could fit the hose from the air tank through it. He stood and walked toward the exit.

"Where are you going?"

"To fetch Jody. I gotta make me a new to-do list. You can stay here. Watch over the workers." Bill left the American with the workers and made his way to the slave pen for the first time since he'd come to New Ashburn.

New Ashburn's doctor was there, treating the wounded, and Melissa and Earnest were there, too, since that's where the doctor was. And of course Ella was there, playing nurse and smearing some kind of ointment over folks' burns. They were all moaning. Earnest was still crying in his mother's arms, an exhausted cry of unceasing torment. Melissa was trying unsuccessfully to make Earnest drink from a cup, promising it would make him feel better, likely willow bark tea. Further off, a man was cursing and crying as the doctor scraped and cut at a white burn with a knife.

"Doc, hold on over there!" Bill called out. "Wait until I get to you." Bill didn't offer any other words of greeting, just sat down with grim purpose next to Earnest and stuck the open end of the rubber boot over Earnest's mouth and nose. Earnest sobbed and swatted at the boot. "Hold his arms down," Bill said.

Melissa glared at him. "Why should I—"

"Just do it."

She obeyed, though her tear-streaked face never changed.

Bill opened the valve on the air tank just a hair, just until he heard the tiniest hiss of nitrous oxide escaping into the hose. Of course little Earnest didn't understand. He thrashed and gasped and sobbed and sucked down the gas fed to him in a stream.

In seconds, Earnest was calm, his breath now hitching as he closed his eyes at his reprieve from the pain. He clutched at his mother's shirt and sighed, his breath hitching again.

Bill closed off the valve. "Don't want to give him too much. See if he'll drink his tea now. I'll come back when it wears off."

Bill moved through the injured, starting with the one the Ashburnite doctor was working on. The slave pulled desperately at the makeshift mask, letting the stuff wash over him, dragging him to near oblivion. He didn't protest, or even move, when the doctor cut the spot of dead tissue away from the burn.

"This laughing gas ain't gonna keep 'em down long. Don't you folks got any painkillers stronger than willow bark?"

"I've got a single jar of morphine I got from the Americans, but it's for combat use only. They'll kill me if I use it on the slaves."

Bill sighed and moved to the next one, putting him under while the doctor scrubbed away at the loose skin of the badly burned arm with some kind of gritty paste. Then the next patient, then the next, and already Earnest was crying again.

"I need to talk to Jody," Bill said as he thought. "Y'all got any chemistry textbooks? I think mine got burnt up."

"I got your stuff out, Bill," Ella said softly. "Your notes and books and everything. I got it up in my room in the supermart."

Bill nodded. "Go get me my books on biochem and organic chem. Meet me in the factory. And bring me some good strong whiskey; I know these junkers at least have that stuff lying around."

Bill set a beaker up under a distillation setup and measured out equal quantities of sulfuric acid and alcohol. He then mixed them in the beaker and set it up over a low lantern flame—very low, since both the alcohol and the product were extremely volatile. He set up another beaker at the end of the distilling pipet and waited until a steady drip came forth. A quick sniff confirmed what the sweet-smelling liquid was: ether. He'd knocked himself out with the stuff once when he was fooling around in his chemistry shop back home, and hadn't touched the recipe since. Now, knocking someone out was just the thing.

He eyeballed additional sulfuric acid and alcohol as needed; the fine-cut ratios weren't necessary, since the reaction would naturally equal out over time as long as he kept evaporating off the ether. He doused the lantern now that the mixture was gently bubbling; ether had such a low boiling point he'd have to put a lid on the beaker to keep the stuff from evaporating before he got to use it.

Footsteps behind him. "It's been hours," Lieutenant Harlow said. "It's getting late, and most of the factory still hasn't resumed operation. The workers haven't even cleaned up the nitration lab."

"It's not safe. I've got to neutralize the spilled acids in there."

"Then get in there and neutralize them."

Bill slapped a plastic lid over the glass beaker of ether and made for the exit. "I've got things that need me more."

The American bodyguard blocked his path. "Will it get this factory running again?"

"Yes." Bill tried to step around, but the American was big, and his bearing bigger.

"Show me. I'm coming with you."

"Folks were injured in the fire. They need medicine."

"Not your problem."

"It'll only take me a bit."

"Give it to me," the bodyguard said, reaching out to seize the beaker.

Bill jerked away. "These are *my* workers, and—"

"These are enemy prisoners of war. You will not waste time or resources on them."

Bill felt his free hand ball into a fist, but he decided he liked his jaw where it was. "At least let me help the kid, guy."

"What kid?"

There was no way the bodyguard hadn't seen or heard little Earnest, and his feigned ignorance burned Bill like concentrated sulfuric acid. "It's the son of my personal helper! A helper I care about, who might never talk to me no more! A helper who's half my reason for keeping this good-for-nothing factory going at all! So if you want to see another *gram* of nitrogel come out of here, step aside and let me get this done!"

Bill's bodyguard stared at him with cold, unsmiling eyes, but he let Bill pass. As Bill reached the exit, though, the American called out, "Colonel Armstrong still wants to know what caused that fire."

"Electrical spark. The salvaged wires are no good. When we rebuild, I want better craftsmanship. I don't care how much it costs."

Bill soaked a rag with ether and held it over little Earnest's mouth and nose. Soon the child was out, and this time he stayed out. He passed the beaker and rag to the Ashburnite doctor. "Go around and knock them all out. Be careful not to give them too much, but... you can handle it." He sat back on the ground and rested his head on one hand. Lordy, he was tired.

"I wanted to say I was sorry. For what I said earlier." It was Melissa, still holding Earnest in her lap. "I was wrong."

"No. You were right," Bill said without picking up his head. "You were right. I did this."

"Doctor says Earnest will heal. Maybe won't even be any scars."

"I'm a-gonna fix this. Ain't any more work at the factory until I fix this. I'm a-gonna have me a talk with Armstrong tomorrow."

Chapter 27

No Good Deed Goes Unpunished

If Bill Puckett had had any confidence when his bodyguard escorted him through the citadel gates at the bottom of the hill, it had all evaporated by the time he reached the top and beheld Colonel Armstrong in her severe beauty. Her jet-black hair was tied back tight, her arms crossed in front of her, her flawless face expressionless. She met him outside the squat concrete citadel, as if she was coming out to make demands of him, rather than the other way around.

The top of the hill was mostly barren of plant life, save for the stubbly, regularly scythed-down grass, now turning brown as the last gasps of summer gave way to the first signs of coming fall. The sunlight reflected off the concrete building and blasted Bill in the face as he stood before the colonel.

Armstrong spoke before Bill could muster the gumption to utter a word. "Lieutenant Harlow tells me that production has completely halted."

Bill swallowed. "Too dangerous."

"Then why are the workers not at least restoring the essential systems?"

"'Cause I ain't figgered out how I want the systems done. I gotta rebuild out of stone or brick, not wood. We had too much burnable material last time. And any electric wires we run out there have to be top-shelf stuff, even made new if we need it. And—"

"You're telling me we have to throttle production and increase our capital costs because you imagine it will make the factory *safer?*"

"Time spent on safety now means less time spent rebuilding later. If you really want to squeeze the most output—"

"I see no reason to waste extra time and resources trying to stop an accident when the danger of intentional sabotage is much higher."

"But the explosion *was* an accident. It was from bad wiring in the nitration lab. I'm sure of it, sure as shootin'."

"So I've heard. Who have you employed in the nitration lab?"

"Only Ashburnites or my own apprentices. The slaves—"

"Prisoners of war."

"The prisoners aren't allowed in the lab, and wouldn't know what to do if they got in there."

"Fine. Until the factory is back up and running at its previous capacity, you will increase the daily working hours for the prisoners to eighteen hours. No exceptions for children or the elderly."

"You'll work some of 'em to death that-a-way!"

"*You* will work some of them to death, Mr. Puckett." Whether it was a command or a statement of fact didn't matter. It always sounded the same with Colonel Armstrong. "And they will make certain their work is quality work, so that there will be no more unfortunate 'accidents' requiring extended shifts in the future."

Bill stammered. "I can't—I can't do this. I came up here to ask for more rations and *shorter* hours for my workers—"

"*My* workers. If you don't think you can do the job, Mr. Puckett, I'm sure I can get a chemist from out east who will be much more cooperative. Once we have your formula, *you* are superfluous as a person. That's a word which means, 'not needed. Replaceable.'"

Bill's hands clasped themselves in front of him. "I want the same thing you want, Colonel. But if my—if the prisoners are worked to the bone, I'll start losing efficiency. It ain't charity I want; it's a proper investment."

"Everyone is replaceable."

"And what if the workers get fed up and revolt?"

"What do you think all these guns are for? I don't see this conversation going any further. I want you and every able hand back to work immediately. I've also heard some of your apprentices have been providing baked goods to the prisoners. That's a security breach, not to mention a loss of efficiency, which you claim to prize so much. No further unauthorized contact with the prisoners."

"My sorries, ma'am, but we'll run into the prisoners whatever we do. You've got 'em at work in the factory, emptying the latrines, and working the laundry for the soldiers. It's hard not to bump into them."

"Lieutenant Harlow and his men will oversee things. And I will be standing by for daily updates from him. Go," she dismissed him with a flick of her wrist.

As he left down the citadel hill, Colonel Armstrong called to him one last time: "You failed me, Mr. Puckett. You do not want to see what will happen if you fail me again."

New Ashburn's Rockhurst boys were, according to Tom Jenkins, an all-fired nuisance. They were always on the landfill-harvesting detail because they were all so lazy they never met their quota, and instead hounded anyone spending less time in the landfill than them, which was everyone, on account of their aforementioned laziness. They may have been troublemakers, but they knew how to play soccer.

So, when the Rockhurst boys started hurling insults across the super-mart at Tom at the end of a very tense shift—the slaves had not been back at work long, and the Federation guards looked like they wanted to take it out on everybody, Tucker or Ashburnite alike—a soccer match seemed the only way to settle the feud without breaking noses.

And Ricky Brody was indeed ready to break noses on behalf of his new friend who'd fought the factory blaze alongside him. Ricky may have done for Tom as much as for a fellow Tucker. Tom Jenkins had found in Ricky Brody a supporter who, once he'd got past his first trepidation, was as boundless a source of energy and charm as ever there had been in New Ashburn. It was the kind of energy the Rockhurst boys would have done well to stay on the good side of./

But Ricky deferred to Tom's better understanding of the way things were done around New Ashburn, and soon understood the challenge they could not ignore and still keep their honor: the grounds were by the eastern gate, the winner was the first to three goals, and the losers would have to tend the landfill's leachate sumps. Tom had some mates—the HVAC guys—to make a team, but he wondered if Ricky wanted to join up as well.

Ricky smiled. "I never pass up a chance to kick some balls."

The game was close, with a goal scored on either side, when a sharp whistle at the gate brought the players to a halt. Nomads, perhaps?

No—it was still more Federation soldiers. Ricky wondered how the American Federation could afford to pay for so many folks whose sole job was fighting and guarding—in this instance, a caravan of strange bald folks who marched in after the armed guards, and a convoy of covered wagons after that. Even with a nose accustomed to the filthy smells of manure piles and open landfills, the stench wafting from under the canvas covers of the wagons nearly knocked Ricky over.

The bald people weren't old. Most of them were young, in fact, and many of them seemed to be women. They all stared at Ricky, and Ricky alone, as they passed.

"Ricky?"

Ricky stared back, slack-jawed, as the last stinking wagon rattled on past.

"Ricky!"

He blinked. "Huh?"

"You gonna play or not?"

"I, uh..." He swallowed. "I'm kinda wore out. Think I could sit for a spell? Who... have y'uns ever seen folks like that before?"

Bill had warned Ella not to knowingly cross Armstrong, which Ella took to mean that she should play dumb and bribe the American guards like she usually did. The bread Ella had baked remained sufficiently unpillaged by the day's end that, when she went down to check on the injured workers, she felt justified in carting the bread down with her to the slave pen as a little something extra to console them for their brutal new work schedule. Melissa Daly came along to help distribute the vittles and nurse the injured, free for the moment since Earnest was still blissfully insensible from repeated administrations of Bill's ether.

The moment Ella rounded the corner of the excavated hillside, however, she knew something was wrong. There were more American soldiers, and the entire slave population watched them from inside their fence. Ella saw the proud slave woman who'd spurned her repeated offers to help—the woman who had led the slaves in quiet rebellion, and who had fought Ella's entreaties earlier that day. She stood not among the slaves, but outside the fence, among the soldiers, her hands bound behind her back. A stepladder stood in front of her, a sturdy tree branch overhead, and—Ella's hand shot up to her mouth—a rope was in the hands of the yellow-smiling guard.

"Take a look at that, boys," the guard said as he looped the rope over the tree branch. "Looks like the chemists brought us a second helping."

A soldier ran up and grabbed the wheelbarrow handles from Ella's limp hands. She looked back to see Melissa's retreat blocked by stone-faced American. Ella reached for the food, but the soldier who'd seized the wheelbarrow shoved her aside.

Ella strode forward, trying in vain to channel the kind of authority Armstrong seemed to exude naturally. "What's going on here? Why are you doing this?"

"Armstrong wanted this woman executed for sabotage, along with the injured prisoners."

"It was an accident! Bill told her so! The burned workers are the ones who helped save the factory!"

"A dozen invalids sucking up time and resources isn't going to save anything. And those biscuits," the guard with the rope nodded to the barrel of food, "are *way* out of line."

"We had a deal."

"We can work out a new deal. You, me, and your friend there," the guard pointed to Melissa, "can find ourselves a nice quiet place to negotiate. How does that sound?"

The other Federation soldiers leered at the two Tucker women, some of them advancing like hungry dogs. Melissa tried again to flee, but the soldier behind her pushed her closer to the armed mob.

The Americans had already tied the noose. The slaves, even the children among them, looked on, dead-eyed in despair.

Ella tried to turn away, but an iron grip seized both of her arms from behind and forced her to her knees. Someone grabbed her chin and turned her face to the makeshift gallows. "Watch." A brutish grunt battered her ear. She recognized the voice as belonging to Lieutenant Harlow, Bill's "bodyguard." Which meant Bill must be nearby.

"Get your hands off my appren—" she heard Bill shout before someone cut him off. She couldn't turn to get a look at him; Lieutenant Harlow kept her facing forward.

The yellow-toothed guard forced the slave woman up the foldable stepladder and was about to kick it out from under her when another guard stopped him. "Wait! Let me do it. My buddies figured this out in Charleston. Someone push up on her feet for a second." He folded up the stepladder and balanced it directly underneath her, so that she tottered near the top of it with her hands tied behind her back.

"Okay. We all take bets on how long she can stay up. I'll count the seconds."

The men laughed. "Spliced! I'll take that bet."

"I say five seconds."

"No way. I say she goes a full minute."

The rotten-mouthed guard took the bets and let the ladder go free. Ella quivered in horror, but the hand holding her face kept her from looking away.

The prisoner struggled to stay upright, but already, she was wobbling. There wasn't enough slack in the rope for her to plunge from the ladder, but the only way to keep from swinging completely free was to use her own neck as leverage to pull on the rope and right herself. She was slowly strangling herself for mere seconds of relief. And all this in front of a gaggle of jeering hooligans.⫽

It was more than Ella could bear. There was no call for this, no call for her to suffer; she'd suffered enough already, couldn't they see that on her face? Of all the heartless—

The woman dropped amid the cheers and hollers of her executioners. Ella's face drained of what little color she had left, but her fists clenched as she watched the proud slave swing.

"Wait, get her up again! If you hurry, you can try it again a couple times!" the guard cried as he picked the ladder up.

"Stop it," Ella breathed to herself. "Stop it," she said, louder this time.

"Get this straight," said Lieutenant Harlow behind her with cold indifference to her pleas. "We don't make deals with you goat-fuckers. You jump when we say 'Jump,' or you become target practice. And your Sylvanian friend is swinging because of your cute little charity."

Ella looked on, helpless, as the woman fell off the ladder a second time.

The slave refused to have her feet held up again, choosing instead to lean into the rope. She got a salvo of rocks thrown at her for spoiling the Americans' game, but she was likely too far gone to notice much when they did. The soldier finally released his hold.

Ella fell to the ground, angry tears streaking her face.

The American bodyguard who'd held her spat on the back of her neck. "It should go without saying, but all extra rations to the prisoners are hereby suspended."

"I'm sorry, Ella!" Bill called, already being hauled away. "I tried!"

Ella crawled away amid the hoots of the Federation thugs as they prepped nooses for the victims she had come to help. Melissa Daly, out of sight of the executioners, set her son down and helped Ella up once she'd retreated to safety. "We did all we could, Ella."

"No," Ella said, wiping the slime from the back of her neck. "*I* didn't. Looks like we'll have to do this the hard way."

Omar's legs ached from a long day on the road, and the effort it took to keep his wits about him when travelling alone had a way of draining his strength at a slow drip. The sight of his destination over the next hill offered some relief, but he wasn't in his bunk yet. He stashed his American weapons—it would be hard to explain to the garrison where he'd gotten those—and trudged across the remaining span, forcing himself to watch the woods and not think about his bunk. But when he finally arrived at the gates of New Ashburn and heard the harsh call of a too-alert American sentry, his fatigue vanished in the face of an unknown sense of alarm.

The stretch of workshops beyond the wall were empty, and it soon became apparent why as he rounded the bend to see the nitrogel factory. A great crowd of people packed together in a huge semicircle in front of the factory as if to hear a speech from a clan leader. There was no clan leader, though; merely Bill Puckett, his back to the sealed factory doors. The factory bore signs of fire: the attached nitration lab looked both more complete than when he'd first left, and also charred to the point of ruin. Fanned out in front of Bill were more American soldiers than Omar could count from his lookout point in back of the crowd. He could hear them, though: shouting commands for Bill to step aside, stop arguing, to open the doors or get a broken jaw.

"What happened?" Omar asked a nearby Ashburnite tradesman.

"Sabotage," the man muttered, not taking his eyes off the standoff. "One of the Tucker girls's been takin' exception to how the slaves are treated. She stole the gunpowder formula this morning and holed up in the rafters in there with some kind of acid. Says she'll destroy the whole shebang if Armstrong doesn't free the slaves."

"Ella," Omar said to himself before turning and swearing softly.

Over the din of the crowd and shouting soldiers, he could hear Bill pleading with the Americans to let him talk to her again. Omar worked his way around the outside of the crowd, trying to find a way to get through, or at least get a better view. He almost missed the American squad coming down from the citadel gate to provide reinforcements. The crowd parted like fat under a sharp butcher's knife. Armstrong was among the soldiers.

Omar tried to get the commander's attention, but she was already standing before Bill. They exchanged some words, and Bill nodded and opened the factory doors for her. From where he stood, he could hear Colonel Armstrong as she called into the empty factory: "I agree to your demands! The prisoners are hereby free!" The crowd gasped as one at such a concession given so readily.

She'd better ask for some security, or—

Ella appeared in front of Armstrong with a sheaf of papers in her hand. For an instant, her eyes found his out of the crowd of onlookers and lingered there. The resolute steadiness in her face flickered as a wordless goodbye passed between them. Omar pushed his way through the crowd, but found his way soon blocked.

Ella closed her eyes, turned away from him as if pulling a knife from her side, and passed the papers over to the American commander's outstretched hand. The papers had no sooner left Ella's hands than two burly Americans clamped on her arms and hauled her off her feet. The crowd stirred again, then dispersed as the American soldiers turned their attention outwards and brandished their weapons.

Bill, unencumbered by the rest of the crowd, stepped forward in protest as Ella was taken away and got a backhand to the face for his trouble—the same for Melissa Daly, who followed after him. From the other direction, east of the workshops, came Ricky Brody at the head of a clump of young Ashburnite men. "What's going on with Ella?" Ricky shouted, his face turning red. Rather than answering, three soldiers seized him and brought him along with her. The Ashburnites they swept aside like sawdust.

Omar kicked his weary legs into motion, fought his way out of the dense crowd, and caught up with the colonel's entourage. "Commander!"

An American soldier tried to block his path, but Omar shouted again past his shoulder: "Commander Armstrong!"

She turned and looked at Omar with cold impatience. "You want to join these two, Tucker?"

Omar cleared his throat. "Uh, no ma'am. I, uh... just come back from the Tucker clan with news."

"What news?"

"All in this letter here." Omar lifted the sealed envelope he'd carried since he'd left the Americans he'd killed.

The guard in front of him snatched the letter and shooed him away. Omar took one step back and watched as the Americans dragged Ella and Ricky away, the colonel ordering a lieutenant to get the slaves back to work by any means necessary.

The gate at the base of the citadel hill clanged shut, and the soldier manning the light machine gun atop the gate waved Omar along. Nothing more to see. Nothing more to do.

Omar shook his head and made his way back to the factory, where the powdermaker sat with his back to the factory wall, his forearms on his knees, his head drooping and his formula notes on the concrete next to him. Melissa stood nearby as if not sure whether to give comfort to him or to seek it for herself.

"She already had my notes in her bunk. She was the one who rescued them from the fire. Didn't even have to break in anywhere," Bill said, dazed.

"Crazy girl," Omar said. "Don't know what she was thinkin', holdin' the formula hostage like that."

"I don't know what to tell the Americans," Bill said without looking up.

"You'll think of something," Melissa said, her voice shaking on a foundation of feigned surety. "I don't reckon Ella and Ricky can get into too much trouble if you stick up for them, right?"

"No. I don't know how to tell them... this isn't the formula." Bill put a hand on the papers next to him.

"*What?*" Omar surged forward and rifled through the cheap American paper scrawled with... gobbledy-gook. Worthless. His hands shook.

"What did she do with the real formula, then?" Melissa Daly wondered aloud.

"Hid it somewhere, or..." Bill shook his head. "We'll never find it. And I can't keep up production with our feedstocks for more than a few weeks without it."

"Can you remember it?" Omar asked. "Fix it up again from scratch?"

"I know the yield-steps. But the ratios, the measurements, the tunings, the timings, the temperatures, the..." Bill threw up one hand. "It'll take... months."

Omar turned and stared up at the citadel overlooking New Ashburn. He swore softly to himself.

Chapter 28

In Which Ella Struggles with a New Perspective

On her second trip up to the citadel in New Ashburn, Ella felt much less secure. It likely had something to do with the two rough Federation soldiers following her with assault rifles uncomfortably close to her back. The men forced Ella back up to the citadel, ignoring her questions and pleas for a gentler handling. She found the cinderblock building busier than she'd ever seen it. Several covered wagons—filled with supplies of some sort—sat off to the side among the weeds. All sorts of strange new people ambled about, but they all stopped and stared at her as the soldiers dragged her into the cool recesses of the cinderblock structure. The strangers were all bald, whether men or women, and she swore she could hear them whispering, though their mouths remained shut. Many of them followed her inside, wordlessly forming two lines like clansmen at a funeral.

Armstrong's attendant led them all into the darkness, around a blind corner, and through a metal door. The room beyond was mostly bare, illuminated by an electric light in the ceiling. Beneath it, Ricky Brody sat in a metal chair. He was unbound, but the guard behind him made any hopes of escape futile. A second chair sat empty, waiting to receive Ella, and the escort to her left planted her there with a firm hand. Ella smoothed her apron, stained more from chemicals than kitchen residue, to calm her nerves.

"Ella! What's going on?"

"I don't know, Ricky."

"They plucked me right from the street. Why are they—"

The metal door creaked open, and Colonel Armstrong stepped from the darkness. Her bald attendant and two of the new strangers followed her.

"These are the only two neurocasters we've found here so far, though I expect a more thorough search of the New Ashburn residents will produce a few more." Armstrong spoke to the bald newcomers as if Ella and Ricky were two prime hogs ready for slaughter. "The real prize, however, is their home clan I told you about."

"One out of four, you said?" one of the newcomers asked.

"I have better news than that." Armstrong held up the letter Omar had given her. "I just received a communique from Captain Carlson. He's located and eliminated the Pied Piper."

"When can we expect the first shipment?"

"Unfortunately, *this* is the first shipment." Armstrong gestured to Ella and Ricky. "There's one small wrinkle left to iron out: Carlson tells me that a settlement of half-breeds nominally under the authority of the neurocasting clan has taken up arms against the draft." She tapped open letter. "Since they control the road in and out, I'll have to send an advance detachment to eradicate them before we can extract any further human resources. It won't take long, though. I'll expect to receive the first real shipment of neurocasters within a month, and the bulk of them before the leaves have fallen from the trees. You can process them all here in New Ashburn. I want additional neuronets out here to soak up the excess brainshine. I'm sending off for the Baltimore enclave."

"So many! Are you certain there will be enough to go around?"

Armstrong smiled. "I have reason to believe there are enough free neurocasters out here for every adept and talent on the Coast."

The two bald strangers merely nodded and stood in front of Ella and Ricky.

A sickening feeling wrung Ella's insides. She looked to Ricky, who had gone wide-eyed and pale. "Ricky, I—" A rough hand boxed her ear, silencing her.

"Permission to subsume the free neurocasters?" the attendant asked Armstrong.

"Permission granted."

The two bald strangers stepped forward, uncomfortably close. Ella turned her head away as if shrinking from hot steel. To her right, the first of the two strangers had already seized Ricky Brody's head in both hands. Ricky jerked away, but the American guard behind him held his arms fast.∥

Ella felt the guard behind her clamp down on her own arms, followed by the stranger's hands on her temples. Fingertips dug into her scalp, and she found herself staring directly into the stranger's cold blue eyes.

A mournful groan, starting out low and guttural and rising to an animalistic shriek, rose into the air like incense. It was Ricky.

Ella tried to look at him, tried to offer words of comfort, of solidarity, but she found herself immobile in a way that had nothing to do with the hands holding her in place. Then a strangely familiar prickling brightness bloomed from behind her eyes, and she knew no more.

The room was not merely empty; it was featureless—neither white nor black, transparent nor opaque. The mind slipped trying to comprehend it, like fingers trying to grasp ice.

The cold blue eyes, however, Ella understood—without understanding how.

The stranger's eyes remained frozen, locked on hers, before their resolve weakened in confusion. "How—how did..." she said, stepping away from Ella.

"You're not the first living creature to peek in the window to my mind," Ella said. "And I don't care for it. It gives me a headache."

"It doesn't matter what you want. I have five proxies in my network. You have none. You are not designed to win this battle."

"Didn't know we were fighting."

"We're not. You are not an adversary. You are fodder." The stranger stepped forward again with new determination, and Ella felt oblivion flicker at the edges of her consciousness.

Memories crackled before her eyes—her brother's lifeless eyes staring at the sky, her tears soaking his shirt, the numbness of shock and grief tingling in her hands as she wandered, lost in the woods, in her bloodstained skirt.

All you are will be mine. I will scour away all that I do not wish to keep.

The memory came back again, stronger even than when she'd first experienced it, and others followed it: Her father weeping over Jim's wooden box, then another box, this one looming larger over a younger Ella, a calloused hand clutching her own small one. Mama was in this box. Ella felt her bedcovers balled into a tangle around her to cover up her girlish wails, understanding Mama was dead, but not understanding at the same time, because Mama was supposed to be there to tuck her in. She felt a soft spark of warmth, and at the same time a searing blaze of pain, when Jim came to tuck her in instead.

Enough of your whinging. Your pain is beneath me.

She saw Omar, framed in the door of Bill's home, a travel pack slung over one shoulder, looking back at her over the other shoulder with more attention than she'd had from anyone in years, speaking in that casual regard of his that always left unsaid what they both understood. "Figured you ought to know. You've got some pretty eyes."

Stop it!

Ella felt her will sharpen to a point, driven like a wedge by a volatile cocktail of feelings she scarcely had names for. *You won't take them from me. Not my kin.*

What is your kin to me? Meaningless. All meaningless. All of it comes to nothing.

As must you, someday. To what end do you scour me away? What possible good is worth this evil?

There is no evil, nor good. Only might.

Then face your own words and despair.

Ella opened her eyes to an electric light in the ceiling above her, the hard floor at her back. Someone was sobbing.

"What the fuck just happened?" Armstrong said from somewhere to Ella's right.

Ella struggled up onto her elbows. The American guard had retreated back against the wall, eyes wide and mouth agape. The bald stranger lay curled into a ball in the corner, her shoulders shaking and shuddering.⟧

The long-cultivated instinct to pity burbled within Ella, and she rose to her feet and went to the miserable creature. She kneeled and laid a hand on the woman's bald head, not to control, but to comfort. "There, there," she said as if to an upset child. "I'm here. It's okay. It's—"

"Get that thing out of here!" Armstrong shouted, and an American guard hauled Ella to her feet.

"Not her—*that!*" Armstrong pointed at the bald woman on the floor. The American guard released Ella and escorted the woman, still sobbing, from the room. "You can feed it to an established neuronet," Armstrong called after him before having the remaining guard right the overturned chair and put Ella back into it.

Ella looked over to see Ricky limp in his chair, the bald person sitting cross-legged in front of him as if meditating. "What did you all do to him? What did you do to Ricky?"

Armstrong ignored her questions in favor of pacing the room. "You have an explanation for this?" she asked her attendant.

"It looks like the Tucker can resist assimilation."

"That wasn't supposed to be possible."

The attendant shrugged. "After a couple generations of unregulated breeding in the wild? Anything might be possible. She could be a valuable asset."

Armstrong looked directly in Ella's direction for the first time since she'd entered the room. The American colonel paced with the focused precision Bill had in the thick of his chemistry experiments. It took the commander some time to distill her thoughts before she aired them to Ella. "I think we're both a little surprised at how things have turned out."

"Was that woman supposed to harm me?"

"Lieutenant Harlow spoke to me a minute ago. You swindled me, Holland. You didn't give me the formula like you promised."

"Did you set the prisoners free?"

"I understand if you're upset, but I don't think—"

"You must think I'm stupid. You think, after all you've done, that I'd trust you just because you said so? I wasn't about to show you the real formula until I was good and happy with the slave situation."

"It wasn't supposed to matter, as long as we got access to your mind, which... didn't go exactly as planned." Armstrong paced as if lost in thought.

"What happened to Ricky?"

Armstrong waved the matter away. "He doesn't matter anymore."

"He matters to me."

"He's *resting*," Armstrong snapped, then regained her composure. "Would you like to talk to him?"

Ella nodded.

Armstrong pointed to the bald person sitting across from Ricky. "Out," she ordered, jerking a thumb over her shoulder to the door.

The remaining bald stranger stood and left, as ordered. A few moments later, Ricky stirred in his chair, standing up as if nothing had happened. "Hey, Ella. I'm okay. Are you okay?"

Something wasn't right about him. He had Ricky's voice, but it was an imitation of the person, the way a screevler could mimic human sounds without making understandable speech. Ella felt her hackles rise. "Yeah, I'm okay. What happened to you?"

He didn't answer right away. "I've become part of something bigger than you or me," he said without meeting her gaze.

Ella stood up, her body frozen between running and hiding, like a rabbit sensing a predator somewhere nearby. "What do you mean?"

"You and I are neurocasters. Our minds can speak to each other."

"How? Is this magic or something?"

Ricky shook his head. "The first rule every trained neurocaster learns is that anything that seems mystical has a rational explanation at the bottom of it."

"None of this seems rational."

"You've seen fireflies, right?"

Ella nodded.

"Genetic scientists identified and spliced the bioluminescent genetic markers from things like fireflies and glowing algae into our DNA. They engineered a bioluminescent organ inside the braincase of a human-derived chimera. That's more or less how we came up with shadowers. They were the prototype."

"There's something glowing inside a shadower's head?"

"Not just a shadower's head." Ricky tapped his temple.

"What's the use of a glowing... bug butt... stuck somewhere no one can see?"

"Some of us *can* see it, just not with our eyes."

"What's that supposed to mean?"

"There are more kinds of light than what our eyes can see. What light our eyes can see can't penetrate very far through body tissues. There's a very specific kind of light, which we call near-infrared, that can reach inside our bodies without cooking us or giving us cancer. The organ inside your head"—Ricky again placed two fingers on his temple as he stared at Ella with a sort of manic glee—"shines at this near-infrared wavelength. It can send signals from the body and sense signals from others close enough for it to detect."

Ricky's gaze intensified. *This is how you hear my thoughts.*

"How come it sounded like—spoken words, almost?"

"Young trainees start out thinking that neurocasting communication will be faster or more efficient because we can somehow transmit the sense of a message without using language. But it turns out language is indispensable, even if restricted to the mind. There have been deaf neurocasters who've adapted sign language for their casting."

"But that bald woman wasn't trying to talk to me. She was—wrestling my soul, or something."

"It's hard to describe what you don't have the terminology for, I know. She wasn't doing anything to your soul, because you don't have one. You—"

"Excuse me?"

"What you call the soul is an illusion. A manifestation rising from a network of information exchange using electrical signals. Your mind is merely the sum of a host of instincts, impulses, inherited and conditioned personality factors, biological drives, and personal habits. A lot of stuff, really, but all individually comprehensible, and together adding up to just that: a lot of stuff."

"I barely understood a word of that."

"The mind, the essence of what we call a person, is merely a pattern that comes from normal stuff doing what stuff normally does. Nothing more. When you want light, you strike a flint to a wick. When you want to think, your brain lights up. Your neurocasting organ can respond to inputs from your brain... or burn a hole in your brain at another's behest. It's tied closely to your frontal cortex, and a neurocaster with a stronger will can permanently override another's executive function. The mind, or the soul, or whatever mystical nonsense you want to call it, is a resource destined to go to those fit to take it."

"So Ricky wasn't—fit to keep his mind?"

Ricky shook his head. "But you were. Which means you're fit to harvest the minds of other neurocasters. Once you've burned out their frontal cortexes, you can occupy their bodies and boost your control over the modifieds."

"You mean... the pigmen, and shadowers, and screevlers and such?"

"It's because of our kind and the neurocasting networks we've built up that the Federation has been able to clear its central territory of hostile modifieds. That was the whole point of the creatures in the first place. The planners behind the Pandemic knew even a tailored virus wouldn't wipe out *all* the unmodified. They needed a sustainable, controllable eradication method that didn't depend on highly developed industry and infrastructure and a long logistical tail to keep going. After the Pandemic, a large number of feedstock neurocasters escaped and fled west, into the Appalachians. You'll be able to find plenty of proxies to assimilate the further we push out. You shouldn't have any problem with the assimilation process once you've—"

"No."

The body that used to belong to Ricky cocked its head at Ella. "What do you mean, 'No?'"

"No, I'm not going along with you to take folks' minds. This is evil."

"Why? What makes this evil?"

"Those are *people*. Ricky is... *was* a *person*." Ella's voice shook in spite of herself. She raised a hand to cover her mouth as the full weight of what had happened to Ricky hit her.

"What does that even mean?" Ricky's body shrugged dismissively. "A *person?* Is an animal a person? A tree? A rock?"

"A human is a person." Tears leaked from Ella's eyes, and she wiped them away with angry intensity.

"What kind of human?"

"All kinds."

"Why? Because you say so? There's nothing special about human DNA, especially after what our ancestors did to it. It's all just stuff. And there's nothing right or wrong about stuff. There's basic reality: You either act on others, or you will be acted on yourself."

"Fine." Ella crossed her arms. "Try it. I reckon I got me some practice on that other gal earlier."

Ricky's body looked over to Armstrong. "Commander?"

Colonel Armstrong unfolded her arms and reemerged from the corner of the room. "Go put your proxy on the meat wagon. I'll deal with her," she said to Ricky's body.

When Ella and the colonel were alone, Armstrong said, "I suppose you believe in God."

Ella nodded.

"Why?"

Ella struggled to answer, taken aback by the question. Whatever she'd braced herself for, it wasn't this.

"I suppose you 'Can just feel it?'" Armstrong said.

"I—no. Well, yes, I reckon I do sometimes, but that ain't all."

"Sure. Let me help you out. Look at the chair. It has four legs and a place for your butt. It must have come from somewhere. Maybe its existence is a convenient accident, but there are enough other chairs around that this accident seems a little *too* convenient. So, it makes more sense to say chairs were designed. And design implies a designer. Agree?"

Ella nodded.

"And so, if something as simple as a chair has a designer, then something like a hand"—Armstrong waved her hand with a flourish—"with all its intricacy and dexterity, why, it must have a designer as well." She affected the surprise and awe of a simpleton having her first original thought.

"Whether by hook or by crook, yeah."

"This Designer—He must have had a purpose in mind when He made hands, don't you think?"

"I reckon so."

"What is a hand's purpose, then?"

"To take hold."

"Would you agree that a good hand fulfills its purpose well, and a bad hand does not?"

"Sure."

"What about people? What's the purpose of a person?"

"He made us for Him. For the one who designed us."

"Why? Is He lonely?"

"Maybe He wanted to do somebody a good turn."

"Judging by history, it seems like He's done us more bad turns than good ones."

Ella shook her head. "Don't you go blaming God for what we done to each other. His good turn was giving us a choice in things. We're the ones who chose wrong."

"But if you create someone to belong to you, and then give them the choice to do whatever they want, did you *really* create them with a purpose in mind? If we have a designer who made us for him, not very many fulfill that purpose. Either your Designer wasn't very good at designing, or you don't know what His purpose was at all."

"I don't expect I know everything about His purpose. I ain't God."

"Well, if you don't know, wouldn't it make just as much sense to say humans have no built-in purpose?"

"The very notion makes me sick."

"Why?"

"Because if we ain't got no purpose, none of what I've suffered means anything. All the people who died, the world that came to an end—none of it matters if there weren't a purpose to any of it."

"Ah, but there *is* a purpose. It's one our species has made for itself, not given from on high. This world is a crucible, made according to a plan set out before you or I were born, designed to purge the irrelevant and refine those who truly matter. There *is* a purpose to your suffering: to winnow out the chaff from the grain. The ones not strong enough to survive? Chaff destined for the furnace. You should be grateful you were selected for the storehouse. You have a purpose. Your purpose is to harvest a rich crop of minds waiting to be plucked."

"I ain't got no say in my purpose?"

"You didn't *want* a say in your purpose. You wanted God to tell you what to do, like a good little servant. It's only after I told you that your purpose is written in your genes that you wanted your say."

"Because a purpose that don't go beyond my breeding ain't no purpose at all."

The colonel looked displeased with Ella's answer, but not surprised. The American sighed. "If you won't fulfill your purpose"—Armstrong examined her fingernails—"how are you different from a hand that can't grasp? If you won't fulfill the purpose you were designed for, what other purpose is there for you than the fire?"

Armstrong knocked on the door, which an American guard opened. "Will you tell me where the nitrogel formula is? Last chance," Armstrong said to Ella.

Ella shook her head.

"Fine." She turned to the soldier at the door. "Clear out a storeroom and lock her in. She can have a bucket. Nothing else."

"Provisions?"

"She can eat the nutrient paste we give to the proxies—enough to keep her alive. I am revoking any special considerations beyond that. She stays in the citadel until she cooperates or until I have a use for her. And fetch your lieutenant. I need to send a company out west to put down an insurrection and secure a population of free neurocasters."

As the guard escorted Ella out the back of the cinderblock building to a collection of smaller shacks, they passed the canvas-covered wagons parked in the courtyard. The canvas covers lay thrown back to show the bodies of men and women, clothed in rags or naked, stacked on racks inside. A soldier stood a few paces back with a hose, spraying the packed bodies with water, which ran off to the ground in putrid streams. Ricky stood nearby.

When the soldier finished, Ricky, or what was once Ricky, gave Ella a parting look and clambered into an empty slot on the wagon, disappearing among the stinking, comatose bodies.

A host of heavily armed American soldiers marched past the outskirts of what was rapidly becoming a town in its own right: Bill Puckett's slapdash nitrogel factory and the rickety shanties serving for living quarters around it. Bill stood atop a catwalk, an American cigar clenched between his teeth, watching the soldiers march past the unfinished brick wall, unsure what the mass departure westward meant. Whatever it was, it couldn't be good.

The absence of so many American soldiers wouldn't lessen the pressure on his people any; the Americans had selected a gang of young rascals from New Ashburn and given them uniforms and guns, and the replacements were just as brutish as the professional soldiers, even if they talked differently. And the soldiers marching past the factory were headed towards Tucker territory. This many armed soldiers weren't going all the way out there to help, that was for sure.∅

Ella and Ricky's disappearance into the bowels of Armstrong's citadel earlier that day had shaken him from his production-obsessed daze as if a bucket of cold water had been dumped on his head.

The American guards weren't here to keep him and his workers safe. They were here to keep him in line. The people of New Ashburn weren't hardworking entrepreneurs. They were vultures looking to make easy teeth at the Tuckers' expense. The conscripted laborers toiling at the factory weren't prisoners of war. They were slaves. And the factory wasn't his. It was Colonel Armstrong's. She'd stolen it right from under his nose. His birthright for a box of cigars.

Melissa Daly came up and watched the procession next to Bill. The master and the assistant watched the column of soldiers wend slowly on around the curve of a hill and into the forest. Melissa didn't say anything, but she didn't need to.∅

"I—I thought I was doing the right thing, 'Lissa. I was making so much, or about to, and I thought... how could it be a bad thing? But I'm not sure if I ever had a choice," Bill said, watching the procession march on and on. "I didn't have a choice. I didn't have a choice from the moment I walked into this damned junker town."

Melissa gave Bill a reassuring pat on the shoulder, but her words bit. "Sure you did. You just didn't want to go as far as the Americans did. When Armstrong stared you down, you blinked."

Bill's gaze dropped to the dry reeds of uncut broom sedge lining the road out of town. "I reckon so. I got into this looking to get something out of it, not give something up."

A footstep creaked on the wooden planks behind him, and he heard Omar speak up. "Never go into a deal without thinking about what you're willing to give up." There was a coldness in Omar's voice that went past his normal standoffishness. "I ain't givin' up Ella."

Bill kept on staring at the dead broom sedge. "I ain't willing to get my hands dirty."

"A powdermaker who ain't willing to get his hands dirty." Melissa shook her head. "Would you have your workers do it for you, if it came down to it, then?"

"No. I'm done having others do my work for me." Bill turned to climb down the ladder from the catwalk, then stopped. "I could use some help, though," he said to Melissa. "You worked with Ella. You know the workers. See if you can scare me up a few hands from among them. Able hands. Tell 'em it's for Ella."

"I've got a pistol and a couple chatterguns hid outside town. If you need 'em," Omar said.

As he slid down the ladder, Bill didn't look up or ask how Omar had come into possession of the guns. "If I do this, I ain't doing it the Americans' way. I'm doin' it my way."

Also by Ethan Warrener

For Home and Hearth
For the Loved and Lost

Sneak Peek at For the Loved and Lost

J ody Perkins woke to the sounds of men suffering the agonies of the damned. The sound of men burning stalked the edges of her mind, sounds which receded as she swam up from the somnolent depths of dreams which were not wholly dreams. Her hand went up to touch the burn on the side of her face. The marring she'd received from the leachate chemicals still tickled her sometimes, etching her face to the bone, sizzling her brain. She couldn't tell if it was from permanent nerve damage or the same mind-shackles that filled her ears with the sounds of burning slaves—prisoners.

She wondered if it weren't a mercy that Colonel Armstrong had ordered the injured slaves—prisoners, she reminded herself—hung. Or was it merely to save resources and keep Bill Puckett on track?

A wail carried through the cool night air outside her cramped quarters in Bill Puckett's new slap-dash office. The screams hadn't been mere dreams, nor memories. One casualty of the disaster in Bill's factory remained alive, and that casualty was a child. The cries belonged to little Earnest Taylor, and though slow healing had taken the edge off those first gut-wrenching shrieks, Jody knew she wouldn't sleep any more tonight even if the cries stopped immediately.

She got up and walked outside, then down the outdoor stairs running down the side of what was once some sort of garage and now served as Mr. Puckett's new office. Past the shuttered workshops stood New Ashburn's inner gate guarding the path up to the clan's citadel, once a weather station and now Colonel Armstrong's headquarters. It watched her, cold and imposing—her people's citadel, now an ever-watching tower. She shook her head at the bad dreams still clinging to her. She had no cause to fear Armstrong. She'd done nothing wrong. She'd been a valuable asset to the Americans. She *was* an American. Everyone here except the Sylvanian prisoners of war were citizens of the New American Federation, but... it looked more and more like two kinds of Americans peopled these parts, and only one kind was allowed into Armstrong's sanctum. The only exceptions had been Mister Ricky Brody and Miss Ella Holland, and they had gone in chains. These past few weeks had taxed Jody to the point of distraction, even without taking into account the disastrous fire at the factory. She touched a hand to the puckered skin on one side of her face and chewed her lip. She understood there was a war on, but she'd never seen any fighting. The front was more than a hundred miles away. Why did there have to be such strict military control? Couldn't Armstrong work something out with the powdermaker?

Jody turned to Mr. Puckett's new office. He would likely be sleeping down there, not even stretched out on the mattress the slaves—prisoners—had dragged in on the floor for him. No, he'd be in there with his head rested on the table, a pile of half-done notes and figures scattered in front of him, a whole mess Jody would try to organize in her vain struggle to standardize his mercurial approach to chemistry. He'd been driving himself as hard as his workers, trying to get the factory back up and running again, trying to appease Colonel Armstrong, trying to cobble together some semblance of a functioning formula after Miss Holland had destroyed or hidden Mr. Puckett's originals. Maybe he hoped he could get Miss Holland back, though after several weeks in the Americans' citadel, and considering what the Colonel had already done to those she'd deemed seditious, didn't hold out hope for it. Ricky Brody had emerged from American captivity, but he hadn't sabotaged Colonel Armstrong's nitrogel production, and even then, he'd come out... different.

Bill wasn't in his office, and the wails were coming from further off, in the direction of the western gate. Jody Perkins followed the sound of the cries down the lane, past empty workshops and smithies, until a group of figures resolved themselves down by the factory. A susurrus of hushed voices rose now to the level of hearing in between little Earnest's exhausted cries and whimpers. As she approached, she distinguished first the voices, then the forms, of Bill Puckett, Omar Walking, and Melissa Daly—the three Tuckers not taken up by Colonel Armstrong's disciplinary purge. The three of them had drawn closer together since Miss Ella and Mister Ricky had been detained, meeting often to commiserate, Jody supposed, or in this case to tend to Earnest's healing burns. The child's cries and whimpers obscured their words until Jody had drawn close.

"Can't hardly do anything with Captain Harlow breathing down my—" Mr. Puckett stopped at the sound of Jody's footsteps. "Who's that?"

"It's me. Earnest woke me up."

"We can't be giving him the ether no more. Doctor's worried it'll hurt him," Mr. Puckett said.

"We got him past the worst of it," Mrs. Daly said, perhaps to remind herself it wasn't as bad as it could be. "Now it's up to the willow tea and snuggles to do the trick."

"Can..." Jody stepped forward. "Can I hold him?"

Mrs. Daly sighed. "If he'll let you, I reckon you can."

Jody had worked with them long enough for Earnest to recognize her voice as "the paint lady." She lifted him up, close to her face, close to her own burns, and Earnest quieted as if he knew Jody understood his hurt. "I reckon he'll heal up nice."

"But he never shoulda been anywhere near the factory," Bill said of the thousandth time since the accident. "When I get this going again, 'Lissa, I'm a-gonna put you on kid duty all day. No more of this juggling three jobs at once."

"But she's your apprentice," Jody said. "The way Colonel Armstrong is right now, I don't reckon she'll allow for any unnecessary tasks. Maybe I could..." She shrugged, patting Earnest on the back.

"Watch him?" Bill said. "But you're working for me, too. I like your gumption, but—"

"Actually," Omar Walking, the steel-cut apprentice who rarely fraternized with even his own clansmen, spoke up for the first time. "That might not be a bad idea. Keep Earnest out of our hair while we get this mess at the factory cleaned up. Armstrong doesn't have to know about this, as long as she gets her nitrogel, right?"

Bill and Omar exchanged a look that went on longer than Jody expected. "Yeah, I guess that could work," the powdermaker said. "Thanks for the help, Miss Perkins. Just keep him cared for and out of trouble, well away from the factory, okay?"

Melissa Daly, Bill's half-breed apprentice, stepped forward to place a hand on the unbandaged side of Earnest's face in motherly affection. "I'll help you put him back to bed now that he's settled."

Jody went along without resistance, but she left with her mind more unsettled than when she first woke up. They were trying to get her out of the way. Of what, she did not know and had no desire to speculate.

Acknowledgements

Thank you to all the beta readers who worked their way through every draft of this steadily burgeoning work. For those of you with uncritical praise, thank you for the encouragement, for those of you who tore it to shreds, thank you for getting the iron hot enough to shape. For all of you, thank you for allowing me ample time to work my creative process out verbally. *Painfully* verbally. In particular, a huge thanks to my sister, Emily Beaver, without whom this novel likely would never have seen the light of day. Your continual feedback and advice has always been spot-on, and your patience inexhaustible.

Thank you to my editor, Oren Eades, for your feedback and encouragement. It's so gratifying for someone else to catch the same vision for your work. I knew I couldn't be the *only* one to see some potential in this...

A big thank you to my wife, who was at ground zero for most of the writing of this novel, who convinced me to split one story into two and then into three parts, and who refused to accept "okay" as a final draft. Thanks for bearing with me through my bouts of writer's block, my forgetfulness, and the whole tortured artist shtick.

Thanks to my creative writing teacher, Michael Czyzniejewski, who gave me the confidence to believe I just might pull this off.

This novel took thirteen years to write, and there likely wasn't a single friend or family member who wasn't roped into listening to my ramblings somehow. Even if you didn't think we were talking about this book, we were, and it helped.

About the author

Ethan Warrener grew up in Southwest Missouri, which resembles West Virginia if you *really* squint. If he's not writing or teaching, he's spending any extra free time with his wife and kids or playing too many video games. As you might expect from a Midwesterner, he's an occasional farmer, a regular churchgoer, and a huge metalhead. *The Tucker Clan Saga* took him about a third of his life to finish.

You can find out what he's up to and access exclusive content on his website: https://www.ethanwarrenerauthor.com/

www.ingramcontent.com/pod-product-compliance
Lightning Source LLC
Chambersburg PA
CBHW031332020726
47499CB00005B/1230